PENGUIN BOOKS

RING THE BELL BACKWARDS

Sybil Marshall was born and grew up in East Anglia. A villager all her life, she witnessed the breakdown of the old way of life in a rural community following the sudden growth of mechanized farming and the post-war attitude to sexual morality. Having been a village school-teacher, at the age of forty-seven she went to Cambridge University to read English. She became a Lecturer in Education at Sheffield University and subsequently Reader in Primary Education at the University of Sussex. In 1965 she devised Granada Television's popular programme *Picture Box*, and continued to act as adviser and to write the teachers' handbook until 1989.

As well as works on education, Sybil Marshall has written a number of non-fiction books recording life in her native fens in their pre-war isolation, including *Fenland Chronicle*, *The Silver New Nothing* and *A Pride of Tigers*. She won the Angel Prize for Literature for *Everyman's Book of English Folktales*. She has also written the Swithinford series of novels, which consists of the bestselling *A Nest of Magpies*, written when she was eighty years old, *Sharp through the Hawthorn*, *Strip the Willow*, *A Late Lark Singing* and, most recently, *Ring the Bell Backwards*. She has also published a collection of her short stories, entitled *The Chequer-board*. Most of her books are published in Penguin.

Dr Sybil Marshall lives in Ely, Cambridgeshire, with her husband, Ewart Oakeshott, FSA.

RING THE BELL
BACKWARDS

Sybil Marshall

PENGUIN BOOKS

PENGUIN BOOKS

Published by the Penguin Group
Penguin Books Ltd, 27 Wrights Lane, London W8 5TZ, England
Penguin Putnam Inc., 375 Hudson Street, New York, New York 10014, USA
Penguin Books Australia Ltd, Ringwood, Victoria, Australia
Penguin Books Canada Ltd, 10 Alcorn Avenue, Toronto, Ontario, Canada M4V 3B2
Penguin Books (NZ) Ltd, Private Bag 102902, NSMC, Auckland, New Zealand

Penguin Books Ltd, Registered Offices: Harmondsworth, Middlesex, England

First published by Michael Joseph 1999
Published in Penguin Books 2000
1

Set in Monotype Garamond
Printed in England by Clays Ltd, St Ives plc

Ave atque vale

With love enduring and timeless,
I salute the past, and the memory of
my only son, William Gregory,
stillborn 9 June, 1940:
and
with hope greet the future and the advent
of my first great-grandchild,
Evie,
born 15 December 1996

Benedict's
Dr William Burbage, Ph.D (Cantab.)
Mrs Frances Burbage, née Wagstaffe,
    formerly Catherwood

The Old Glebe
George Bridgefoot
Mrs Molly Bridgefoot

The Old Surgery
a) Nicholas Hadley-Gordon, sen. (Effendi)
b) Dr Terence Hardy

St Swithin's Church
Incumbent: Revd Nigel Delaprime
Churchwardens: George Bridgefoot
    and Kenneth Bean

The Old Rectory
Commander Elyot Franks RN (Retd)
Mrs Beth Franks, née Marriner
Emerald and Amethyst Petrie

Temperance Farm
Brian Bridgefoot
Mrs Rosemary Bridgefoot
Pansy Gifford, one of Marjorie Bridgefoot's
    twin daughters

Monastery Farm
a) Eric Choppen (private residence)
b) Marjorie Bridgefoot, widow of Vic Gifford
    Poppy Gifford, one of her twin daughters,
        engaged to 'young Nick' Hadley-Gordon

'Heartsease'
Restored for Dr Terence Hardy's occupation

Southside House
Gregory Taliaferro (pronounced Tolliver)
Mrs Jess Taliaferro, née Wagstaffe
'Jonce' Petrie (Jasper John Petrie Voss-Dering)

Danesum
Charles Bridgefoot
Mrs Charlotte Bridgefoot (Charlie), née Bellamy

Castle Hill Farm
Bob Bellamy
Mrs Jane Bellamy, née Hadley-Gordon
Jade and Agate Bellamy, formerly Petrie

Revels Cottage
Miss Anthea Pelham

Others
Sophie, housekeeper a
Hetty (Mrs Joe Noble)
Steven, Hetty and Joe's
Daniel Bates, widower o
   née Wainwright
Mrs Sarah Anne Potts (A

John Postlethwaite (Yorky,
Mrs Olive Hopkins
Ned Merriman, gardener and odd-job
   man at Benedict's
Mrs Tyrrell
Miss Amanda

In Cambridge

Roland Wagstaffe (formerly Catherwood),
   Fran Burbage's son
Monica Wagstaffe, his partner,
   Eric Choppen's daughter
William and Annette Wagstaffe,
   their twin children
Sapphire and Topaz Petrie

Nicholas Hadley-Gordon

In London

Dr Alex Marland
Mrs Lucy Marland
Georgina Marland, their daughter

Colin Brand

St Saviour's Church

Church Cottage, Spotted Cow Lane
The Revd Nigel Delaprime, DSO and bar,
   formerly of the Brigade of Guards

Dawn was just breaking when Bob Bellamy crept out of bed, careful not to let a footfall or a sudden movement disturb his wife, who lay on her back with one cat on her chest and another on her feet.

'Sh!' he whispered to Ali, who showed signs of rousing and uttering a Siamese good morning. 'Don't wake her! Let her sleep while she can.'

He stood looking down at them, with his back to the window, revelling in the sight. He had never been so happy in all his life as he was now. Somehow, Jane with a couple of cats encapsulated it all.

Then he turned to go, and glanced out of the window. The sun was just lifting itself above the horizon behind the little rise on which his farmhouse stood, together with a small, neglected but history-filled church a couple of hundred yards distant, now silhouetted against the late-September dawn sky. He moved towards the window and stood there gazing, the artist in him transfixed.

He watched the pale edge of the sky turn pink, with rays of light fanning from the east – the halo of a saucy little cherub peeping over the edge of the world before being chased away by the red face of a disgruntled sun who had a long and busy day's work ahead of him. As the top of the sun's head came into view, it set off a firework of colour, splitting the light's hidden spectrum so that its full range of colour leaked everywhere, as from a rainbow ripped open at its red end.

A range of gentle hillocks made of thin cloud lay parallel to the horizon and caught the first spilled colour, spreading it out sideways like a crumpled crimson scarf. The sun was still climbing, and the next range of fluffy high cloud was now turning to deep pink against duck-egg blue and lemon-yellow strips of sky. Higher and higher the colours crept, till Bob could no longer see from

1

that window the fancy frills of baby-pink edging still larger violet clouds above. He wanted to see how far westwards the flamboyant parasol extended. He knew how quickly the colours would fade, and to catch them he went to his daughter Charlie's old room and stood at the window which faced west.

The larger masses of cloud were breaking up as they fled from the blood-red east, and the colours chased them high into the sky, till those directly overhead were now deep pink roses in a heavenly dome-shaped garden. He stood breathless with awe and delight till the whole of the upturned bowl was full to its western brim with the dawn. Then he went downstairs and outside, to gaze at it till it faded.

From the top of Castle Hill, he could see a long way in the clear morning light. He knew where to look for landmarks. Just visible, the tower of Ely Cathedral; light was glinting on the Armada beacon on the tower of St Swithin's Church down in the village, where, apart from his household, all his nearest and dearest were. Charlie in bed at Danesum, Charles probably still beside her. It took a lot of will-power to get out of bed when you were as young as Charles, and you had a wife as beautiful and as full of life as Charlie was still cuddled up beside you. It was one of the prices farmers had to pay, but not too high a one when you owned the land you farmed, as he and Charles both did.

On second thoughts, though, it wouldn't be like Charlie to lie in late on such a morning, any more than Jane would, though for different reasons. Jane would have a guilty conscience if she wasn't up, had their two adopted foundlings washed and dressed and his breakfast ready before he had finished his 'yard work'. Charlie was much more likely to let Charles get his own breakfast and go without her own to saddle up Ginger and let him have his head for a riotous gallop. She wouldn't miss the chance of a morning ride this week, because next week the Michaelmas Term at Cambridge began, and she would be going up for the third and last year of her first degree course, on her way to full training as a veterinary surgeon.

The 'little bird' that carries speculations round places such as Old Swithinford had recently suggested that there might be an event to interrupt her training, and give Grandad Bridgefoot his longed-for wish. Well, Bob didn't care how soon she made him a grandfather, but common sense told him that the little bird was a bit previous with its message this time.

Just look at that sky! The colours were fading now, making the sky overhead even more beautiful; the east was still as lurid as he had ever seen it. His countryman's instinct told him that umbrellas were much more likely to be needed before the day was out than parasols of that flamboyant colour. Clouds in the west were banking up and turning purply-blue. The sun had disappeared and the sky had lost its blushes even as he stood by the front gate watching it. He wished he could paint like Greg Taliaferro; Bob would have bet his last sixpence that Greg wouldn't have missed that sky.

A cool wind was blowing up, as might have been expected after such a dawn. Bob fed his dog and the rest of his domestic pets before starting out to milk 'the house-cow'. He was only in his shirt sleeves and the chill met him as he turned the corner of the house: a deceitful little wind, pretending to be only an autumn breeze and part of the mellow, golden season; but its fingers were thin and penetrating, giving itself the lie, and hinting like the sky of the winter soon to come.

He felt the hair at the nape of his neck rise, sending what he called 'thrills' down his spine, while goose-pimples rose on his arms. What was it making his hackles rise like that? It wasn't the wind. It was the sixth sense he had inherited from his Celtic fenland forebears at work, warning him of trouble to come. It was a queer feeling that he was quite accustomed to, but couldn't ignore: a sort of emptiness inside him waiting to be filled by events that so far had not even cast a shadow before them. He turned this way and that, like a pointer trying to pick up a scent, in an attempt to pin down anything there might be for him to feel anxious about. He could think of nothing special. It was more a feeling of general unease that had not yet solidified. Could it be the fate of the little church? There was a possibility that it might be officially closed as unsafe, as well as redundant: the Rector, Nigel Delaprime, had too much on his plate at present with the urgent restoration of St Swithin's Church tower to give time to reading to empty pews at St Saviour's, even once a month. Bob loved the church just because it was there, but he loved it more because of the memories it contained for him. It was there he had picked up from the floor the proud, starving outcast whose son was lying in a coma not expected to live: Jane, who was now his wife. It was he who had filled the church to overflowing with wild-flowers for the wedding of Elyot and Beth Franks, securing them forever as two of his dearest friends. It was there that he had discovered William Burbage, the academic historian with whom he could share all his deepest feelings – the first academic he had ever met who did not scorn his queer sixth sense, and even sometimes trusted to it, in the same way that Bob trusted all William's factual knowledge of history.

That was the most treasured friendship of all because it also included William's wife, Fran. He and William had a lot of plans concerning the church before it was closed to them, or bulldozed down.

And lastly, there were the ghosts of the past that had welcomed him into their midst and could reach the spot inside him which nobody else could, not even Jane; that hurt him for no reason that he could think of, except that he recognized it as an echo of trouble somewhere along the path of history that led both ways, backwards into the past as well as forwards to the future. That's what William understood – that Bob was different from his fellow farmers who couldn't, as he constantly did, hear and listen to ancestral voices.

But his apprehension this morning wasn't coming from the direction of the little ruined church. It was when he looked down towards the village that he felt it most. That made him anxious, in case he had been too sanguine about Charlie.

He was soon disabused of that. There was nothing wrong with her, because she had just come into sight across the meadow in front of him, lying low on her horse's neck with her hair flying out behind her. Riding Ginger bareback in a mad, flat gallop. Well, she certainly had too much sense to do that if she were pregnant.

4

She slid off her panting steed and tied him to the gate, kissed her father and went to help him with his yard-work before going in with him to breakfast. He took her to task about the danger of being such a madcap. 'Doesn't Charles get worried about you?' he asked.

She really was the most beautiful girl in five parishes, he thought. She considered a moment before prettily and truthfully replying, 'I expect so. But *sacré bleu*, Dad! Who could resist the chance of a gallop on such a morning? Charles knows that Ginger is as sure-footed as a cat, and that I know how to handle him. I can't spare much time. I have to get down to work with my finals coming up in May. Besides, we have to set about making arrangements for the next step – dealing with all the regulations for turning Danesum's granary into a pet surgery, and finding me a fully qualified partner for my next stage of training in the field.

'I hope we can find a young and ambitious man who won't find Danesum too lonely, but he can have the firm's car while I ride round to make my calls – except emergencies – on horseback like vets used to do, especially down in the fens where cars couldn't go. Won't that be fun?'

'I shall have to speak to Charles,' he said, his eyes twinkling. 'I thought I was handing you over to somebody who would take as much care of you as I could myself.'

She became serious in an instant. 'You did,' she said. 'And I do worry him a bit, I know. Not this morning, though. He'd already gone. His mum had a slight car accident last night, and you know how distressed Grandad Bridgefoot gets if there's the slightest thing wrong with any of his family. So Charles went up as soon as it was light to see his mum at Temperance Farm first, and then on to the Old Glebe to see Grandad and find out if there was anything he could do to help anywhere. He phoned me from Glebe to say Gran was giving him breakfast.

'Dr Hardy says his mother's only suffering a bit of whiplash stiffness and shock, as far as he can see at present, but she has to take it easy for a few days, till he can be sure. Grandad had arranged to meet the Rector at the church to inspect the work before any men arrived, and went, luckily, while Charles was still there. The Rector had got there first, and was walking backwards, looking up at the tower, when he tripped over a footstone hidden by long grass, and couldn't get up. Grandad went back for Charles to help lift him. Sprained a thigh muscle, by the sound of it. Charles said he was "swearing like a trooper" as they tried to get him up. What did they expect? He was a trooper before he turned to the priesthood and became the padre instead. Charles said he was *nearly* as good at cursing in foreign languages as I am. A sort of back-handed compliment to one or other of us, but I'm not sure which.'

Bob laughed. She'd done him good. Maybe he'd simply picked up old George Bridgefoot's anxiety about his daughter-in-law and his friend the Rector: if there was 'trouble in the air', as folks say, it was general and not anything specifically concerning him.

*

Bob leaned on the gate to watch Charlie riding sedately down the hill towards the village. He knew he ought not to be standing there 'mozing', as his old fen friends would say, at such a busy time of the year, especially if he suspected bad weather ahead. He had two farms to manage now, but it was this, his 'high-land' farm, not the other in his native fenland, which was all below sea level, that he was giving his attention to.

He'd been very reluctant to have anything to do with a high-land farm in the first instance, but had given in mainly to please his university-educated son – and just look what that decision had brought him! True, there had been a bad start, but within the last seven years everything he had ever dreamed of had come true.

Bob had wanted nothing more than he had, except for his first wife and son to stop nagging him to get out of the fen and 'move with the times'. He had protested that he couldn't. He'd spent what he'd made on his children's education and his wife's increasing demands. He didn't grudge any of them a penny, because his own wants were so few; but there were limits to his tolerance. It went against his grain to be subjected to this sort of family blackmail.

His then wife hadn't wanted another child, and the old saw

6

that every baby brought its own love with it had been proved wrong in Charlie's case. Her mother had rejected her from the moment of her birth, so it had suited her in every way as well as adding a lot of cachet to the image of herself as a well-to-do farmer's wife with modern ideas for Charlie to be sent away to one of England's most expensive and renowned Ladies' Colleges. Yet when the girl had grown up as beautiful as she was clever, with social poise gained from her high-class school, her mother had seen in her only a dangerous rival. In vain did Bob plead for her to be allowed home more often, but his wife would not tolerate her 'stuck-up' daughter. She had begun to leave Bob behind to his pets and his dreams, while she took advantage of his growing bank-balance to indulge herself in longer and longer holidays abroad. The marriage had been a mistake, and began to founder. But it had brought him his children.

He hadn't wanted his family broken up, and though nothing would ever make him part with his tribal acres 'down the fen', to keep his family together he'd given in, and looked for a high-land farm to rent. His presence now at Castle Hill Farm was the result. It had been going at a cheap rent on a reasonably short lease because it needed a lot of hard work and experience to restore it to good heart. Bob took the chance it offered, but at first nothing had gone right.

Castle Hill was too far from Old Swithinford for its occupants to be part of the community, such as it was – a village dying of old age. The upheaval that had been the war had barely touched it except for its importance as an agricultural gold-mine of food for the nation and profit for the farmers. They were of the kind whose families had been there undisturbed (except for the pre-war 'bad times') for generation after generation and such permanence had made them inward-looking and self-sufficient. They didn't bother themselves much about strangers, especially such as Bob, who was 'only a tenant farmer' anyway, and a fen-tiger into the bargain. They made no particular effort to make the newcomers welcome. A less sensitive man might not have been aware of it, but Bob was. He had enough troubles without being given the cold shoulder by the only neighbours he now had.

His family did break up. His wife refused point-blank to stop in such a social desert, especially one so queer. It was too far out of the way, too lonely, and in any case too eerie. His son, having succeeded in uprooting him, decided to emigrate to Australia. His wife solved her problem by staying away for good, and Bob was condemned to live in solitary exclusion, except for the 'ghosts' and his many pets.

He had stuck it out because he had no other option, and in time began to meet some of the people from the village. In the end, it was that 'ol' fen feyness' of his that was ultimately responsible for his friendship with William and Fran. Then Charlie had come home to him, and he'd begun to love the place, and everything about it.

His first feelings of being a complete outsider had neither been his fault nor that of the old village. The great changes of the post-war period had taken a long time to reach Old Swithinford. The Swithinford Hall Estate, which had been owned by an aristocratic widow who was senile, had fallen into ruin. The farmers, before the war too poor and during the war too busy, had let their beautiful old houses and cottages fall into almost equally ruinous decay; mains water and electricity were laid on only to the centre of the village and to the larger houses, so that the rest remained as primitive as it had been pre-war. It seemed that the village had subsided into a state of elderly moribund complacency, like its old rector, who would rather muddle on till he died of old age than be bothered with improvements. After having survived the earthquake of the war, nobody anticipated the after-shocks that had to come.

One visible result of the war itself was a sad and regrettable reminder of what had once been. Benedict's, the house owned and lived in by the last genuine old country squire thereabouts, who had died in the second year of hostilities, had been requisitioned as a hostel for a Remand Home for boys from the East End of London during the second wave of evacuation. They had wrecked it – and it had stood derelict and dilapidated till the mid-sixties, when the first of a wave of changes began to reach out from the centre as far as such remote villages; a year or so before Bob had arrived.

But, as he now ruminated, that was all part of another story, one in which he'd played a part. The catalyst had been the arrival of the squire's grand-daughter, Fran, to buy Benedict's and restore it for her own occupation, soon to be accompanied by her step-cousin William, a history professor at the University of Cambridge. No insight was needed to appreciate how much they meant to each other now that they had met again, and their friendship had filled great empty spaces in Bob's romantic soul. Though of the modern world, they understood such a community, its traditions and customs, how it should work, and their influence soon began to be felt, in spite of the scandal that they had lived together under the same roof while William still had a legal wife somewhere else. Bob didn't care. He basked in their love for each other, and their willingly offered friendship.

Their influence was felt in another way. The glory of Benedict's restored gave other people ideas, but it took a disastrous fire to deliver the fate of the village into the hands of a stranger, Eric Choppen – a businessman who saw possibilities of making a good thing out of giving the entire village a face-lift. Then Jane had come into Bob's life, and changed everything for him. He had always believed in his dreams, and now had proof that dreams could come true.

The comatose village was alive again; consequently, it went on changing, as all live things do with the passage of time. There had been the advent of a second developer of a much more ruthless variety. Arnold Bailey had seized upon a chance to buy one of the old farms, knock down its ancient farmhouse and build a ticky-tacky new estate in its place. The ancient farm had been called Lane's End, and the new estate had kept the name. It had filled a gap between the old village and the next cluster of post-First War housing which all Old Swithinford dwellers knew as Hen Street; the gap till then only filled by a row of ugly council houses. Now Hen Street and the council houses had been absorbed into Lane's End and formed a unit, while the old, graciously restored houses and the renovated cottages formed another which, by common usage, had become 'Church End'.

In the spring of this year there had been the excitement of

two weddings in Church End, where all had shared in the rejoicings; that of William and Fran (at last), and the other of Charles Bridgefoot to Bob's daughter Charlie. A new Rector and a new doctor had settled in and become part of the community. The Old School had been sold to an anonymous buyer who had promptly given it back to the village to be converted to modern homes, 'almshouses' in all but their style, for the old who wanted to die where and as independently as they had lived.

There had been artistic success for Greg Taliaferro, and some degree of fame for the village in consequence; and there had been one death, which though perhaps of little note in itself, had made subtle but important changes to several lives.

Bob thought it all through as he stood watching Charlie till she had gone out of his sight. It had suddenly crossed his mind that the health and happiness of any place at any given moment was only as great as the sum of its parts. In this case, the parts were the people who lived there. So that rather tentative premonition he had felt this morning could mean that the period of settling down since Easter was now completed, and further disturbances might be brewing. Hadn't Charlie already reported two incidents?

His mind went rapidly round those for whom he cared most. Jane; the toddlers Jade and Agate, now legally adopted and no longer Petries but Bellamys; Jane's ex-diplomat father, Nicholas Hadley-Gordon, known to all his friends by her nickname for him, 'Effendi'; Commander Elyot Franks, RN (Retd) and his lovely wife Beth; the entire Bridgefoot family, into which Charlie had married; Greg Taliaferro and his wife Jess, Fran's cousin, who had helped Eric Choppen to blend his restored village with what was left of the old. And the two at Benedict's, now William and Fran Burbage. Though their house was not at the centre of the village, in some strange way they were, exerting a centripetal force that held the rest together. He had a sudden yearning to see William and Fran again, and was assured by the sun suddenly breaking through just then that it would not be long before he did.

*　　*　　*

Breakfast at Benedict's was always a leisurely affair nowadays; it still had something special about it. In the early days of Fran's return to Old Swithinford and the renewal of her old acquaintance-ship with William, a meal together had been a highlight. When William had become the tenant of part of the house – nothing more, though both had known they could not sit on the fence for ever – they had breakfasted together on Sundays, which had made Sunday a very special day.

Even after the die had been cast, and William had become Fran's husband in everything but legality, breakfast at leisure at the weekends had been something to look forward to, because on weekdays in term-time William had to leave early for work, and during vacations was more often away on lecture tours or doing business in the USA than at home. Morning domesticity while that state of affairs lasted had been only routine.

But it was two years now since William had started on a much overdue year of sabbatical leave, which for all sorts of reasons had extended itself into permanent retirement. They could, and did, breakfast together every day in relaxed compatibility. All the same, there was now a difference.

With the legalizing of their relationship and without the strain of his work, a lot of tension had gone out of their lives, and a lot of the drama. They had lost the sense of urgency, and were gently settling down to become an ordinary, middle-aged, middle-class married couple – except, of course, that they were by no means ordinary, either separately or as a couple.

Fran was aware of the change, and a bit regretful, though nobody in their right senses would expect life at such a high pitch of emotion as theirs had been to last long, let alone for ever. She was thinking so as they sat and ate in rather unwonted silence that particular morning.

They often sat over breakfast till their housekeeper Sophie

arrived, chatting to each other and sharing anything there was to share. Sophie had been their constant friend and playmate in childhood, when they had been left with their grandfather; and Sophie's mother, who was his housekeeper, had been the martinet who kept them, together with William's half-sister Jess, fed, clean, and well behaved.

With the war, all that had changed. They had gone their separate ways. Grandfather had died, and his large old house had been requisitioned. Not that Sophie had gone anywhere or done anything. She had been left at home, still unmarried, to care for her ageing and cantankerous mother; a fact taken by her two married sisters as having been arranged neatly and purely for their convenience by a merciful Providence. When her mother died, Sophie's life had become bleak indeed – till the sun broke through again for her with Fran's return to do up the old house, and needing her help once more.

As she waited for Sophie to arrive now, Fran was reflecting that it had seemed at the time to be a gift from the gods to both of them that they could set up a new version of their old relationship in the same dear old house. There was much more to that relationship than one woman working for another. To Sophie, those times when her poverty-stricken childhood had been lit up by the long spells of daily companionship at Benedict's with Fran, William and Jess represented the 'Golden Age'. She had never given up hope that one day a miracle would bring some semblance of it back – and the miracle had happened. As Sophie said, 'Thanks to 'Im Above.' Even when William had been made part of the equation, it had only cemented the friendship. Through Sophie and the rest of her family, they had reclaimed their place within the indigenous village community.

William laid down the letter he'd been reading, looked across at Fran, and caught her eye. He was immediately conscious of a discourteous neglect of her, and apologized, soothing away the silence between them with a contrite, charming smile.

'But I can tell you haven't been wasting your time. You never stop thinking and philosophizing do you? So tell me what thoughts have been engrossing you while I have been so rude as to give my attention to my mail instead of to you.'

'Only about our luck in getting Sophie back as part of our household,' she said. 'It's queer to realize exactly how much she's helped, when you really stop to think about it. Do you remember that when I was about sixteen, away at boarding-school, there was a lot of to-do as to whether or not I should stay where I was or go with my parents when Father was posted overseas? They'd actually got as far as taking me away from school when the international situation looked so black that they changed their minds, and decided I'd be safer based with Grandfather till things settled down a bit. So I was sent to the Grammar School here pro tem – and stayed. A co-ed school. I loved it – and it was certainly the best education I ever had, but that's beside the point.

'Thinking what finding Sophie again had meant reminded me of something that happened there. Our geography master – we called him Sappy – was absolutely decrepit, a poor old chap who was trying to hold out till the end of the year to retire, though he didn't make it. He was on his last legs, and his lessons were often no more than sort of mental arithmetic – oral tests of what we didn't know.

'One day, Sappy picked on a bright but cheeky individual called Davis, Arthur Davis, and shot a question at him. "Davis! What separates the mainland of Africa from the Arabian Peninsula?"

'"Nothing, sir," David said, without bothering to stand up.

'Poor old Sappy. He nearly went through the roof. He had a way of napping his eyes and barking when he was angry, which he was at such studied insolence. He just roared: "What do you, mean, boy? Stand up when you speak to me! How dare you loll there showing off your abysmal cheek and lack of any manners? Now answer me properly. What is it that separates Egypt from Arabia?"

'Arthur stood up, sagging like a rag doll, and added insult to injury. He just repeated, "Nothing, sir."

'We were all scared. I think we thought poor old Sappy might have a heart attack and die before our very eyes. He was coughing

13

and spluttering for what seemed like hours, but got over it at last and bellowed, "Explain yourself, Davis."

'I think Arthur was as scared as the rest of us by then. He straightened himself up, and said meekly, "I did answer the question, sir. You asked what separated those two countries, and I know you meant me to say 'the Red Sea' because that does lie between them. But, sir, it doesn't *separate* them, because they're joined underneath."

'That's what I meant about Sophie. We'd been parted from Benedict's and the village and all the things of our childhood for so long that we felt like strangers, but we weren't. Sophie hadn't forgotten us, and the years between hadn't really made much difference. Because of Sophie, we were still joined underneath.'

William regarded her with admiration. 'That puts it in a nutshell,' he said. 'I don't know how you do it, but you always manage to find a quotation or an aphorism or, like that story, a "modern instance" that leaves a lot to think about. And I've got plenty to think about as it is, so if I don't want to get caught like the Egyptians by the Red Sea sweeping down on me, I'd better get into my study before she comes.'

'Me, too. I don't want to get caught for a long chat this morning, because I must make a phone call before the lines get too busy. See you at coffee-time, then.'

*

An hour later, she was sitting alone with her elbows on her desk, gazing out on the garden, thinking. She had made her phone call, and hoped the order she had confirmed was sensible. It had only been to Eric Choppen, their friend who ran the Swithinford Hall Hotel and Sports Centre, and concerned nothing more than what she should give to William for his birthday. Eric had offered to advise and even act as her agent in the matter of a new electric typewriter of the very latest kind. He could not only get it at a discount, but at very short notice, too. This was Wednesday, and William's birthday was next Monday, but there had been a cogent reason for leaving it so late. It was all part of the larger problem of their gently changing relationship, and one instance of it that was really puzzling her.

She had heard Sophie arrive, but had not gone out to greet her, because the time had come when she simply had to think this problem through. She was so abstracted that it was only when Cat leapt from the floor and landed on her blotter, asking in a subdued throaty voice why the chief of her human slaves was not giving her enough attention, that Fran came back to reality. She welcomed any chance to put her thoughts into words, and Cat would do as well as anybody else as a sounding board, so she obliged Cat by rubbing her furry tummy as she turned upside down, cocked her beautiful seal-pointed head on one side, and listened.

'What's the matter with him, Cat? Why won't he begin? There must be a reason, or some mystery I haven't managed to fathom. And if I get within a mile of asking him directly, he just clams up. But why, Cat, why? It isn't as if I don't know all about Bob finding the old manuscript in the church up there, and William's delight in it. We've discussed it time and time again, especially after Beth Franks's too-holy-and-reverend father left us so suddenly without having disclosed the find to any church authority. William, I know, remained very concerned about his academic duty to report such a discovery – but Bob would have no truck with that. He'd found it, hadn't he, not William? And if he hadn't, it would never have been found, only thrown away with the rest of the rubble when, as now seems probable, the church itself is bulldozed down. He insisted that it remain in his keeping. As he said, nobody knew what it was, and until they did, there was nothing to declare. But by the time the Rector made his sudden, unannounced exit to Singapore, William had retired, and Bob had used the opportunity to pitch the parcel into William's lap. By which time his academic conscience wasn't pricking him so much about not declaring it, either – in view of what skulduggery he'd found some of his academic colleagues capable of.

'He was so excited about it when he first read it. An extraordinary piece of first-source evidence of seventeenth-century history during the Civil War that apparently no other historian had ever seen, is what he said. To make it more exciting, it had been written by a parson called Francis Wagstaffe, who could possibly have been one of my ancestors, considering that I was born Frances Wagstaffe.

'That's what I can't understand now, Cat. William hadn't felt free to do what he would like to do with it till then, but whatever academic integrity or law might decree, it seemed to Bob and me that we had more right to it than anybody else. I know William still has serious reservations about accepting it as history and, if it is, not declaring it; which would do his academic reputation harm. I guess he's still a bit worried on that score. But since he read the last, coded section of it, he's reluctant about letting anybody else see it. If I ask why, I get no answer.

'Are you listening, Cat? Because I don't know what I think till I hear what I say, any more than the child did who first gave rise to that wonderful bit of wisdom.

'When he declared that he wouldn't risk putting it out as factual history, documented though it was, we struck the idea of him writing the story not as direct translation, but as fiction. An historical novel. We even had fun inventing a pseudonym for him, and I thought he was all set to start on it.

'But something's preventing him. In its own right, that doesn't matter, but I'm afraid it might get between us, like this morning at breakfast-time. He's still reluctant. He pretends that he can't wait to start on it, but I'm beginning to wonder if he just says that to shut me up and stop me badgering him about it. Because the fact remains that he's no nearer to putting pen to paper than he was a year ago, and I'm absolutely stumped. Up a gum tree. He's my husband and I love him; I thought I knew him; but now I have to admit that I don't understand him. Can he have discovered something detrimental to the Wagstaffes, for example? As if I'd care three hundred and fifty years later! But what else can this eternal procrastination mean? That he doesn't want to share it with me? If that's the case, something's gone wrong somewhere. Sh! Listen.'

Sophie was singing. She could hardly be said to be musically gifted, and her repertoire was, to say the least, limited. It comprised Hymns Ancient and Modern, with a few scraps of folksongs learned at school thrown in. It wasn't often she raised her voice

16

solo, even when she had anything to sing about, but she was singing now.

> 'Praise him for his grace and favour
> To our fathers in distress;
> Praise him still the same as ever,
> Slow to chide, and swift to bless:
> Alleluia!
> Alleluia!
> Glorious in his faithfulness.'

Somewhat cynically, Fran wondered if the blessing Sophie had in mind was her freedom, at last, from the domination of her sister Thirzah, for a more domineering woman than Thirzah had never existed. A wave of contrition followed. Fran told herself that instead of criticizing in retrospect a woman who had never had the grace to thank anybody for anything, she should be following Sophie's example, and being grateful for all she had got, including William. She didn't want to find fault with him in any way – if she could help it. She wondered where he was, and what he was doing, because she simply had to get on with arrangements for this birthday, now so very imminent. She listened, and heard behind Sophie's singing a spirited rendering of the Mozart Horn Concerto. There was nothing wrong with William's musical ability, and his repertoire while whistling absent-mindedly was as abundant as Sophie's was meagre. She had long ago given up trying to judge his mood from it. All it told her now was that whatever else he was doing, it wasn't writing. She laughed to herself, recalling Michael Flanders's words, substituting some of her own making to fit the situation:

> *I once had a pen and I wanted to use it*
> *But now I can't find it amongst all this junk –*

She was startled to hear a decisive though discreet tap on her study window. Eric Choppen stood there, and by sign language was inviting her to join him. Amused but not puzzled by Eric's

17

antics, Fran signalled in dumb-show that she'd slip out to him at once. She guessed it must have something to do with her phone call. She crept out of her study into the hall, finding the huge front door ajar. Had it not been open, her feeble attempts to draw back the massive bolts would have alerted William. Eric put his finger to his lips and pulled her round the corner of the house, out of sight, where he bestowed on her a hearty kiss. It was all too much for Fran's too delicately balanced sense of humour, and she giggled.

'Sir, this is so sudden,' she said. 'And in broad daylight, too. How long have you been coveting thy neighbour's wife to bring you to this?'

'From the first moment I ever saw her, as you know perfectly well,' he replied with a grin nearly as mischievous as her own. 'But fear not, madam. I think we are safe from scandalous tongues, don't you? After all, if being co-grandparents of two-year-old twins can't make us respectable, what hope is there? I had to try to do the impossible and catch you for a minute without William, but for nothing more romantic than that typewriter. They happen to have just what you want in stock at Cambridge, and I'm on my way to fetch it now. But an electric typewriter has to be connected, and I thought I'd add a wall-mounted spotlight for him as my own birthday present. I gathered you wanted it to be a surprise, so I have to know when I can deliver it and bring my electrician to fix it. Can you get William out of the way for a while so that we can do it by Monday? With the weekend in between? It's going in his study, I presume, so it shouldn't take very long.'

She chuckled again. 'My dear Eric, have you ever seen the inside of William's study? It would take you till Monday to find a power-point! But you're quite right about me wanting it as a surprise for him – for Monday – so I shall have to employ a bit of guile myself to get him out of the way while Sophie makes room for you and the electrician to slide in sideways. I'll do my best. I'll suggest to him that we celebrate his birthday by going out for the whole day. Would that do?'

'You do your bit, and I'll do mine,' he said. 'So that's settled. And now I must go, because I've promised Marjorie I'd call at

Temperance on my way to see if there's anything she needs for Rosemary. Oh, I suppose you may not have heard that Rosemary had a bit of an accident last night? She was on her way to a meeting in Swithinford, and was stationary at the traffic lights when some young idiot in an old banger ran into the back of her. She's got a bit of whiplash injury, and can't move much, so of course Marjorie's on duty there, looking after her instead of looking after us – meaning me and Nigel. And he's gone and sprained a muscle in his thigh this morning as well, so I'm having to look after him, and I must be off quick. Not till I've closed this clandestine assignation with another kiss, though.'

He suited action to words, and she said as she drew away from him, 'What was that about the first time you met me? You were scared to death!'

'I know,' he said. 'Out of my depth. You danced with me, and saved me. So you can tell William why I covet his "trouble and strife".'

Fran waved him away, wondering yet again at the change in him since he had come to Old Swithinford as the big bad wolf huffing and puffing to blow their houses down – quite literally, in some cases. But as he had just admitted, he had been more of a fish out of water than a ravening wolf; he hadn't understood in the least the element he had leapt into, and had seen the decrepit village and its community only as a spot ripe for commercial exploitation. Nobody knew him, or anything about him, least of all that this venture was an attempt to shore up the ruin of his life after his adored wife had been killed in a plane crash. Details about him, such as his distinguished war service, and of his deep understanding of men, which had finally set him right with the villagers, had been slow to emerge. But they had all had to change their idea of him.

He had mellowed in every other way, but had not changed his mind about ever putting another woman in place of that adored wife. Luckily, it did not prevent him from enjoying the company of women like Fran on a social level, and he had always a special place in his heart for her who had welcomed him but neither patronized nor made eyes at him for his money. Then

19

George Bridgefoot's widowed daughter, Marjorie, who had her own reasons for deciding never to marry again, had taken him and Nigel, their bachelor Rector, under her wing. She had rented half of Monastery Farm and rumour and loose tongues had soon coupled him with Marjorie, but in truth there was nothing but a deep friendship and a mutual reliance on each other between them, which solved a lot of social problems for both.

As Fran turned back to go into the house, she thought of that first meeting with him at the Marlands' wedding. She remembered thinking then that he looked like a lost lamb rather than a prowling wolf, and having been more or less obliged to dance with him, had decided the best analogy for him was that of a stray dog in a church, expecting to be either kicked or led firmly out of a place he didn't belong in. How wrong they had all been!

She went into her own house by the big front door feeling that for the moment she had a better understanding of him than she had of William. Well, perhaps she would discover what the trouble with William was before long. Eric's quick appraisal of the birthday situation had lifted her spirits, and made it clear that the next move was hers. She had better go and make it straight away.

It was not yet coffee-time, so she went back to her study and sat down again to plan her immediate course of action. William was still whistling, so he was still in his study. It was one of their many blessings that they lived in a house large enough for them both to have a room to call their own, providing them with what Americans call 'psychological space'. There was, however, a great difference between his and hers.

Her study was always neat and orderly. She could lay her hand instantly on whatever she needed; her filing was always up to date, her correspondence answered promptly, and her accounts meticulously attended to. That was how she liked her psychological space in any case, wherever her workplace was. Sophie cleaned it, and Cat came and went, but otherwise it was hers.

William's was at the other extreme. It was always in a clutter. He threw letters down unopened, and was surprised and irritated when he couldn't find them a week later on a desk-top covered with piles of paper, each pile a miscellany in itself. Searching for anything in a drawer resembled a paper-chase, and it was a near impossibility to find a flat surface clear enough to set a cup down on. In consequence, it was a much more homely and welcoming place than hers was, which was no doubt why they often used it as a refuge; but it was hardly conducive to anything called 'work'.

Which in itself was strange, because William's mind was quite as ordered – perhaps even more so – than her own. He hated to see a picture awry, or a treasured *objet d'art* even a fraction out of its usual place. Yet *his* psychological space was always in confusion. Why?

Well, it was possible, she supposed, that this could be part of the trouble. Until his retirement from his University Chair, he'd had his own secretary. It was years since he had had to cope with the daily minutiae of his work himself. Could that possibly account, even in a microscopic way, for what appeared to be his obstinacy in not doing what she so much wanted him to do? It was so very uncharacteristic.

She called him 'Sir Galahad', because that's how she'd thought of him since he'd come back into her life, a peerless knight endued with all the chivalrous virtues of the medieval period he knew so much about. As strong and pliable and dependable as the tempered steel of a crusader's sword, with an intellect and wit as keen as its razor-sharp edge; and himself as dedicated as it was to upholding chivalric principles. He was always ready to put himself at the service of others – but as a sword in its scabbard of fine leather or rich velvet is kept safe and hidden till needed, he generally hid his rather out-dated values and principles under the cover of his enormous outward charm.

William was always courteous and gentle, and only those who knew him most intimately were aware of the core of hard steel that he also possessed. He was a man to be trusted and, above all, a man to love and be loved. Yet the steel was there, and occasionally made its presence felt, as in this present stubbornness in keeping from her whatever he had learned from the coded section of the manuscript.

*

Sophie met Fran as she went towards the kitchen. 'I were just a-coming to bring your coffee,' she said, 'when I 'eard you go out to that Mr Choppen. Why didn't 'e come to the door like a Christian?'

Fran saw the appropriate biblical quotation hovering. Sophie had never quite forgiven Eric for taking her for a country bumpkin, only for her to teach him a very salutary lesson; but Fran was in no mood to accept a lecture just now about their friendship with Eric. She got it in first.

'I know,' she said. '"*He that entereth not by the door into the sheepfold, but climbeth up some other way, the same is a thief and a robber.*" But it doesn't fit the case today. He called because I asked him, in a hurry because Marjorie needs his help with Rosemary after her accident. And he'd had to leave the Rector by himself, waiting for the doctor after his fall earlier today.' Wickedly watching Sophie's startled reaction to the news, she said innocently, 'Oh, hadn't you heard?' and put Sophie wise. It was not often she could tell Sophie anything she didn't know about village affairs.

'Well, whatever will 'appen next,' exclaimed Sophie, sitting down abruptly.

'That depends on William a bit, I think. Where is he and what's he doing?'

'In 'is study, but what 'e's up to I don't know. I took 'is coffee in there without asking, 'cos I wanted to speak to you by yourself. Tha's 'ow I come to see you out there with that – with Mr Choppen. There were piles o' paper everywhere an' 'e were a-whistling at the top of 'is voice, so I just set 'is coffee down and come out quick, do I should ha' been choked wi' muck and flue. 'E'll be sty-baked if I don't get the chance to clean that place of 'is'n up afore long.'

The state of William's study was a sore point with Sophie. Fran hastened to turn the conversation. 'What was it you wanted to say to me? As it happens, I wanted to get you by yourself.' Sophie was mollified.

'Ain't we heving no do at all for 'is birthday this year? I ain't 'eard nothing, but you ain't giving me much time, seeing it's only next Monday.'

'We had such a busy year till Easter, and with all that happened then and afterwards, we've decided to give it a miss this time round. We haven't actually discussed it, even between ourselves, but I think we might go out for the day, just the two of us.'

'Ah, well then,' said Sophie, looking pleased, 'let me know as soon as you're made up your mind, and I'll get Ned to 'elp me give 'is study a real good ol' foe out. Do you can persuade 'im to put out o' sight any o' them papers and things 'e wouldn't want us to see.'

They were interrupted by a crash, the sound of William's voice cursing and a bout of sneezing to which there seemed to be no end. Both listened, Fran ready to go if needed, when William appeared.

The front of his white shirt was soaked with coffee, and he held the broken cup in one hand, while the other clutched a large handkerchief, at the ready to deal with the next explosive sneeze. It was an inordinately loud one, blinding him as he strove to set the broken cup down. Sophie leaned over the table and took it from him.

'Bless you,' she said, following the centuries-old custom. He looked anything but grateful for the blessing, wrinkling his nose and sniffing in a futile attempt to ward off yet another even mightier sneeze. Sophie looked 'knowing' in a none-too-sympathetic way, and Fran's face was creased into a grin she simply couldn't prevent. She waited to hear if that king of sneezes was the last, and then inquired innocently if anything was wrong.

'No, of course there's nothing wrong!' snorted her husband, with as much dignity, under the circumstances, as he, Dr William Burbage, MA, Ph.D (Cantab.), Emeritus Professor of Medieval History of the University of Cambridge, and world-renowned historian, could muster. 'Why should anything be wrong? Don't I always take my coffee externally, and throw the cup into the fender? Am I not in the habit of hurling curses of medieval origin at the wastepaper basket I have just landed in, and then sneeze my head off? *A-A-A-tish-ooo*! If for no other reason than to amuse my womenfolk so that I may find them killing themselves with laughter they can't hide?'

He turned to Sophie, his face breaking into a genuine if rueful smile. 'I'm sorry, Sophie, but I'm afraid I've made the most infernal mess to clear up! I suppose it was bound to happen, because – believe it or not – I was actually trying to tidy my study. Honestly. I leaned across my desk to open the curtains, and the whole lot, fittings and all, came down on me.'

'There is them,' said Sophie placidly, 'as might say as it serves you right! I were just saying to Fran as I wondered we 'adn't found you choked with flue as I ain't been able to get at with an 'Oover no'ow. Some say such things 'appen according-lie to the plans of 'Im Above, but why 'E should concern 'Isself about you choking yourself wi' dust, or 'ow much flue there is under your desk, I can't answer. I do know as it'll take me a whull day to get that study like it should be. And I can't put them curtains back up by myself. Ned'll have to come in and give me a 'and with 'em. And we ought to take the carpet up while we're at it, and beat it over a clo'esline, like was all'us done in days gone by – and them 'eavy old velvet curtains as well. 'Oovers is all very well, but there's some still think the old wayses were as good if not better. We'll see to it come Monday.'

'That's my birthday,' William interposed.

'Well, what 'o that? We shan't be hexpecting you to 'elp beat no carpets. All you're got to do is to throw the clutter out, and then keep out of our way.'

'Let's go out for the day,' Fran said coaxingly, as if she'd only just thought of it.

'That sounds a good idea,' he said, one eye on Sophie. 'Shall we take a nostalgic trip to Hunstanton?'

'Goo where you like as long as you stop out all day, 'cos there's plenty o' work to keep me and Ned busy till bull's noon,' Sophie interposed.

She had given Fran time to think of an alternative. 'If I never stop philosophizing,' she said, 'neither do you. You told me the other day that you were having to adjust your ideas about the relationship of Time, as we understand it, to History. You know how fascinated I am, and have been always, about the nature of time – like a lot of others, judging by what they've written about it. Think of Ecclesiastes – Shakespeare – T. S. Eliot. Nobody understands it. When you said what you did, I read T. S. Eliot's *Four Quartets* again. Whatever else it may be, it's a wonderful and profound disquisition on the nature of time in relation to history. It's been running through my head ever since. "Little Gidding" is the poem I love best, and it made me want to go there again. It's so near to us here. Couldn't we spend Monday just tootling about, ending up at Little Gidding? We could have lunch somewhere on the way.'

William looked quite startled. 'Do you know that I've never been there? I should love to do that. I'll drive, and you can navigate. Let's pray for a nice day.'

'Eliot says it doesn't matter when you go or in what kind of weather. If you are the sort of person to feel its atmosphere, it has the same effect. And it does. I know.'

'Do you stop out long enough to let me and Ned get finished,' Sophie said. 'I'll leave your supper in the Aga, do you don't find no eating-'ouse on your way.'

It seemed that the plan satisfied everybody.

*   *   *

Monday was all they could have hoped for: a morning filled with amber autumn sunshine and the scent of harvest gathered in. Golden leaves danced to the music of their own rustling in the gentle breeze, just as William and Fran danced whenever chance offered. It was good to be out together on such a lovely day.

They wandered along wherever fancy took them, lunching at Brampton, taking side roads to out of the way places like Woolley, on and on through wide stretches of pastoral tranquillity, till they came to Little Gidding.

William admitted to vague knowledge of the Cambridge scholar Nicholas Ferrar, who in 1624 had bought the derelict Manor House at Little Gidding as a refuge for his family from the plague raging in London. Once settled, he had taken Holy

Orders and with his brother and sister and all their dependants had set up what amounted to a religious commune there. In time, it had become so well known both for its piety and the quality of the books, and the bookbinding, produced there, that King Charles had paid this little 'Community of Saints' three visits in all. But it had fallen under the displeasure of the Puritans, who put out a pamphlet accusing what they called 'The Armenian Nunnery' of Popish practices, and in 1646, by which time Nicholas Ferrar himself was dead, it was forced to disband, and its members to flee.

William was not as familiar with Eliot's poem about the place as Fran. He said that though he'd taken in the general drift of it, he'd found it difficult to understand, not being able to place the literary and philosophic references.

'I suspect that's only because you've got the factual history without all the legends – if that's all they are. Eliot obviously believed that when they had to leave in 1646, it wasn't just closed down, but sleighted. I think he must have heard the stories that remain about that, true or not. Local folklore says that by Cromwell's orders it was obliterated, so that no one in future times should ever be able to find even the foundations to prove where the house and all its appendages had ever been. A wall and a few other bits of the church were left, later made use of as a pigsty. The tale is that in one of his rages Cromwell ordered its destruction because he thought the commune had sheltered King Charles after he escaped from Oxford.'

William was silent, but Fran was well aware that he had heard every word. 'I'll read the poem more carefully, when I've seen the place,' he said. 'And get you to interpret the bits I don't understand.'

'Heavens! It isn't all that difficult for anybody with your intelligence – on the surface,' she said. 'It's only when you begin to follow him into the realm of philosophy that you have to work at it. And here we are – through that gateway. Oh! Somebody's changed it! "Restored" it, I suppose – but I do hope they won't build anything here again! It was the serenity that Nicholas Ferrar wanted, and that's still here whatever else has happened to it. It

26

still soaks right into your bones. Come on. Let's go and visit Nicholas's tomb.'

They stood by the altar-tomb, and the flat, dark, lichened stone of his brother's grave, looking across to where, in 1624, the household of forty souls had come, though there was nothing left to show where the Manor House had been. The field was still there, but the rest was gone. All gone – except for the serenity. Fran could see how moved William was.

'The peace is still here,' Fran said comfortingly, whispering, as if to herself:

'Annihilating all that's made,
To a green thought in a green shade.'

'I don't want to see any more,' William said suddenly. 'Not even the inside of the church. I want to keep this in my head.'

So they left, and turned homeward.

*

'It was a splendid idea,' he said as they arrived at Benedict's. 'A lovely birthday.'

Fran lingered outside the door of his study to let him go in alone. When he hadn't appeared again after several minutes, she crept away.

He was a bit overwhelmed. Nothing of any significance had been moved. It was still his own sanctum, though he could not but note the new typewriter, left with its cover off and a sheet of pristine white paper inserted, and the spotlight focused on the keyboard. Prepared for him to find. He stood taking it all in, then heaved a great, satisfied sigh. This was home, the place you started from, whatever the adventure. Here was peace and content, as well as inspiration – and Time.

He spoke aloud, thinking she was behind him. 'Thanks for everything, sweetheart,' he said. Then he went to find her.

Later that evening, sitting at her feet, he looked up at her and said, 'You've achieved your object, you know. You may be able to read me, but it still works both ways. I can read you, too. You thought I was another Achilles sulking in his tent, wanting to stand on his reputation for good deeds past. The trouble is that I didn't know quite what I was up against! Still don't, if I tell the truth. I needed to stand at Little Gidding, and breathe in the seventeenth century there, as your ancestor did.'

'Does Little Gidding come into the old book, then?' she asked, genuinely surprised.

'It does, my sweetheart. But that's all I'm going to tell you – till the book is finished.'

She breathed an enormous sigh compounded of relief and pleasure. 'Am I allowed to know anything more?' she asked.

'I can't tell you what I don't know, sweetheart,' he said. 'There is so much in that book of Bob's, and so many ways of looking at the task I so nonchalantly took on, sure I was capable of doing it. I'm not half so sure, now. That's why I'm stuck.'

'I was getting worried,' she confessed. 'The more you studied the period, the more I feared you were reverting to the academic historian: making sure any historical facts were authentic, and not prepared to give what Coleridge called "*the shaping spirit of your imagination*" a look-in. I'd begun to think Stuart obstinacy must be catching, you were showing so many signs of being like them.'

He looked quite startled, and then, regarding her very seriously, though with a quizzical smile, said, 'I seem to remember you telling me that Beth's father once called you a witch,' he said. 'I'm not at all sure he wasn't right!'

'Now what do you mean by that?' she asked.

He gave her a more Williamish grin than she had seen just lately. 'Wait and see, Mrs Burbage. As Sophie would say, "Them as lives longest'll see most."'

*   *   *

During that week, Bob's feelings of apprehension lessened, though they did not go away. Vague worries were dissipated even further when he went in to breakfast on the Tuesday after William's birthday, and heard the news Jane had for him. Her father was home, and all was well. He had been on a trip with Nick, her son, looking for a second-hand bookshop for sale.

Jane was radiant with pleasure. 'They've found the very place – in *Cambridge*!' she gloated. 'I never dreamed that would be possible! I only had a few words with Effendi, because he'll be up later today to tell us everything. But he did say that it's one of the oldest and best established second-hand bookshops in Cambridge, with a small flat above it. Exactly what they'd had in mind, so there was no point in shilly-shallying about the price. He made an offer for it on the spot, stock and all as it stood, and the widow of the man who used to run it till he died of old age accepted it without a quibble. Nick's apparently in a sort of seventh heaven, and is stopping in Cambridge tonight to go over the stock.

'But Effendi says it's left him a bit short of ready money after all the other expenses he's had recently, and to recoup he proposes to sell either the London flat or the Welsh cottage. He wants to know which we'd rather he parted with – as if it's anything to do with us, considering everything we owe to him. But I hope he'll keep the cottage where I was born. The London flat's too grand for the likes of me.

'Oh! And William rang, asking if you can meet him in the church at dockey-time today. I knew I needn't bother to ask you, so he'll be waiting in the church for you about eleven o'clock. Effendi's coming to lunch.'

*

In fact, Bob got there first, so William went in and sat down by him. So complete was their empathy that neither felt the need for greetings. They just sat in silence looking around them, till Bob said, 'How much time do you reckon we've got? Till we can't do this any more, I mean.'

William brought his gaze down from contemplation of the altar, and said, 'I suppose it will depend on what they decide to do with it. I hope the Rector's accident won't mean they'll act in a hurry, without giving it enough thought. He's got a very badly sprained thigh muscle, and it may be quite a time before he can get about again. But I can't see him and George Bridgefoot giving in without a fight if the Church Commissioners want to knock it down and sell the land. My guess is that it's more likely to end up in the hands of the Preservation of Ancient Churches people. Nobody knows nearly as much of its history as we do, because of what we've learned from the Reverend Francis's book. But there's a lot to find out yet. So we must make use of every minute that we still have to poke about here.'

'I reckoned so. What's next? Have you started writing your book yet?'

William shook his head. 'I want to, but I've got to get it right. It's all very well for Fran to say, "Turn it into a novel," but it isn't as easy as it sounds. You can't teach an old dog new tricks overnight, because he has to unlearn old ones first. I've been an academic historian too long. I find unlearning that sort of history much harder than learning to write a story. Perhaps it wasn't a very good idea – yet it's a challenge, and I want to try.'

'Tell me what you mean,' Bob said.

William hesitated. 'Bob ... I've told you most of what's in the old book, but not all. It is a most extraordinary story, and if it's true there's no doubt that I ought to have reported it as an archaeological find.'

'You didn't find it,' Bob said. 'I did. And we didn't know till we'd undone it what it was. I might well have just thrown it away.'

William ignored that. 'The trouble is that it's so good a story that I can't believe he – let's call him Francis – didn't make a lot of it up, and that's what I must find out before I tell anybody – even you and Fran, let alone reporting to the proper authorities. Don't let anybody else know anything about it, especially Fran. She's the one who mustn't get an inkling of it till either I find that it's true and decide to disclose it, or I write my own version of it. There are all sorts of snags in my way because I am an historian. I'm not always sure I understand exactly what Francis means. He *knew* of course – about the time, the place, and the people, which makes it so significant if it is genuine. It's a period of English history of enormous importance, and one that has been searched and researched nearly out of existence. The fact that other historians don't tell the same story as he does is what's causing my dilemma. If it's genuine there's no doubt I shall have to bring it to light in the end, but I may have to risk my reputation by doing what I want to with it first. I have an advantage over other researchers in that I know the district as well as Francis himself did. But I can't risk too much without verifying details somehow.'

Bob was looking puzzled and a bit incredulous. 'You mean that if he said it was raining cats and dogs one Wednesday morning and the droves were too sluddy for him to get where he wanted to go, you've somehow got to prove it did rain that particular Wednesday before you'll say so? If that's the sort of skerrick of truth that's going to hold you up, I reckon I can give up hope of ever reading it. I shall be the Methusalem-numbskull of all creation afore you get it done.'

William looked as surprised as he felt. 'As Aunt Sally said? How on earth do you come to be so familiar with *Huckleberry Finn* that it's ready on the end of your tongue like that? When did you read it?'

Bob brought into play his most impish twinkle and his broadest fen dialect. 'I dunno as I remember, mate. When I fust learnt to read for meself, I reckon. I know I were only a little ol' bor fust time round, but I'm read it at least twice a year ever since. Huck speaks my sort o' language. So y'see, I know as much about a few things as even a Cambridge scholar like you.'

William, delighted and duly chastened, apologized. One should never take Bob for granted. 'All right. You're Huck and I'm Tom. I have to have things done "reg'lar accordin' to the best authorities". But Huck got his own way, mostly, and I see your point. We don't have thirty-seven or -eight years to dig all the history up. We know, as Francis did, that this church goes back about five hundred years before his time, and we've already found the secret tunnel, for instance. I think there's more for us to find yet. That's all I meant. Too many other historians before me have had their say about the *period*, but I've got a new slant on it – and in any case they don't always agree with each other. Historiography sometimes gets in the way of history.

'What's that?'

'Historiography? The study of what different historians make of the same set of known facts. Writing history goes in fashions, like everything else. The more we research, the more we know, and the more we may disagree with each other.'

'Give me an example.'

'Oh dear . . . but I'll try. You've often said that you're "only a peasant". Now what do you mean by that?'

Bob thought. 'I reckon what I mean is as I'm a countryman from a family as has always worked on the land. Land as my family worked generation after generation till my old great-grandfather bought a field or two extra when the bit round Ugg Mere got drained enough to be worth buying. That field has growed into my farm. But Bellamys had farmed land round Ramsey forever afore that, as far as I can make out from tales as have come down from father to son.'

'Do they – did they *own* the land they farmed?'

Bob shook his head, not in denial, but indecision. 'I dunno, and that's the truth. They acted as if they did. Why, does it matter?'

'Well, it matters to me. The "peasantry" were by no means all the same then, and now to call anybody "a bloody peasant" is meant as an insult.'

Bob looked indignant. 'I call myself a peasant-farmer 'cos I work my own land, but that don't make me a country-bumpkin day-labourer going to work on a different farm every morning with a bottle o' cold tea and a thumb-bit in a flagon basket over my shoulder – though there's no disgrace in that. My old dad had to, till he come into the farm. Why, is it important to your book – or to what Francis wrote in his?'

'The word itself comes from the Norman-French – "came over with the conqueror" sort of thing. *Paysan* meaning "a countryman". But the conditions under which they farmed land depended on the arrangements by which they held it from the chap who did own it: as serfs who were little more than slaves, or as villeins who were "free-hold" tenants or "copyholders". In any case it was decided by custom and worked on the presumption that both parties to an agreement would keep the bargain they'd made.

'It's important because by the time of the Civil War things

had been changing for a couple of hundred years, and the old rules didn't always apply. It takes two to make – or break – a bargain, especially in a place like this that was liable to be dry one year and under water the next.'

Bob was intrigued, but he looked at his watch. 'I shall have to go,' he said, ''cos Effendi's coming to dinner and I promised Jane I wouldn't be late. But I want to know more, so come again as soon as you can. And till you do, is there anything I can be getting on with that'll help?'

'Yes. Two things. We know from raising it what's under that marble altar-table slab. I know now how and when it got there, but not why it was left there. Then there's that old tomb that we scraped and found the inscription on, the one that gave me the key to the code. I think there's more for us to find yet. Keep poking about while you can. Oh – and one other thing you'll be able to put me wise on better than any book.

'I've got to know what bits of fen drainage had been done by about 1640, especially round about Ugg Mere – where, in fact, your fen farm now is. Were the waterways then anything like they are now? Could you draw me a large-scale map of how they are now, and put on it any guesses you may have of where you think the courses may have been before?'

Bob grinned his pleased grin and put on his old pork-pie hat. 'There ain't no flies on you, William,' he said. 'If you want to know the time, ask a policeman. I reckon as I know every inch o' water down there as well as Mark Twain knowed the Mississippi, and for the same reason – he'd knowed it since he were kittled. Next week same time, if not afore?' He left William sitting and thinking hard.

*

George Bridgefoot stood leaning over the gate of the field in which his Jersey cows were happily grazing. Daisy was in calf again, and her first heifer calf, Dotty, was now allowed to join the others. Dora's calf was still in the yard.

Past the seventy mark, George was upright, hale and hearty (except for 'a touch of the screws' in his hip), and now that he had absorbed the worst of having to retire and hand over to his son before he was ready, as happy a man as could have been found anywhere.

He was, in fact (though he wouldn't have admitted it for the world), *enjoying* the retirement he had so feared. There was time now to take pleasure in the things he had always loved, but while he was the farmer, had felt he had to put into second place. Now he could take as much time as he liked to stand and admire those beautiful pedigree Jerseys, till they came up to him at the gate to be petted. They were Daniel Bates's choice of breed. But for Dan, George would have probably been influenced by his son Brian to go for a breed more in fashion. But Dan had been right.

Fran Burbage said Dan had chosen Jerseys because they were as unlike Thirzah, his domineering, fractious and bad-tempered late wife, as any breed she could think of. George smiled at the remembrance. Fran was very probably right, too, because the change in Dan since his wife had died was plain for all to see. On Sundays he was the Dan they had always known, in dark and sombre clothing suitable for church-going, and matched now by a mournful air befitting a man recently widowed; leading the singing as loudly and tunefully as he ever had, but managing to remind everybody that Thirzah had vacated her place beside him. His sorrowful mien was as obligatory as the black band round the upper arm for a year would have been in times not long gone by.

Week-a-day Dan was a very different man. His burden had rolled off his shoulders and lay buried in the churchyard. He was free as he had never been since he had married Sophie's sister on the rebound from the death of his first love. His life, his time, his cottage, his friends – especially George, with whom he had worked since they were young – were his own again. If there was a happier man than George, it was Dan.

He sang about the farm as heartily as he did in church, but he was no longer inhibited by fear that Thirzah would hear of it, and happily rendered folksongs his sweetheart Emily had sung to him and with him in the first flush of their courtship.

Thirzah had not thought them 'suitable' for a churchwarden to sing, besides never having got over her chagrin that she had only been his second choice. So very often these days, a sunny morning would find two elderly men leaning over the gate together, admiring their growing herd, with Dan raising his voice in freedom and joy just to be alive.

'How old are you, my sweet pretty maid,
How old are you, my honey?
She-ee answered me right cheerfully,
"I'm seventeen come Sunday"
With my doo-dum-day.
Fol-the-diddle-dol
Fol-the-dol, the diddle-dum-the-day.'

And George, recalling his own grandfather singing the same song, would add his deep voice to the 'diddle-dums', just as ably as it blended with Dan's if by any chance Dan's unconscious choice had been the grand old tune called 'Diadem' to his favourite hymn. When they reached the end of a verse, their two voices rose together in praise:

'Bring forth the roy-oy-al di-i-a-de-e-hem,
And crow-ow-ow-ow-ow – ow-ow-ow-ow-ow –
   ow-ow-ow-OWN Him,
Crown Him! [Dan, high]
Crown Him! [George, low]
And CROWN HIM LO-OR-HORD OF ALL.'
                                          [Both]

But Dan wasn't there, and George wasn't singing, this morning. He had other matters to think about. Mostly just niggles, though with one abiding sorrow that rarely left him altogether, which unexpected events like Rosemary's car bump brought back in full.

He had absolute faith in Dr Hardy, who said that his daughter-in-law was not seriously injured by the incident, but George had just seen the doctor's car go by again towards his son's farm. Why, if he wasn't quite sure? Then there was the Rector. A man whom service in the desert or very dangerous Commando raids hadn't ever managed to knock out, had been laid up by an ancient footstone in a churchyard; just at a time when he needed to be able to get about, especially in the matter of St Saviour's little church at Castle Hill. George had had the good news that young Nick Hadley-Gordon had got his heart's desire to run a second-hand bookshop in Cambridge, which meant that as soon as his grand-daughter Poppy had finished her teacher training, she and Nick could marry.

That was cause for rejoicing, but there was Pansy, Poppy's twin sister, to be considered. That was what was causing his heart to ache. Pansy had gone off the rails, got herself into real trouble, been very ill, had been nursed back to health by an elderly clergyman and his wife who were friends of the Rector's and to whom George felt a debt of gratitude that could never be properly repaid.

But Pansy refused adamantly to come home. Her mother, George's daughter Marjorie, said very little about it now, but George knew how much she grieved, and so did Molly, his wife.

George and Molly were fast approaching their Golden Wedding, and had it not been for Pansy, they would have been preparing a great party – but Molly had vetoed any mention of such a thing. Until very recently, she wouldn't even consider marking the occasion in any way at all, till out of the blue she had said that if he wanted to spend any money on it, what would please her most would be to get their four-hundred-year-old house, the Old Glebe, redecorated from top to bottom, and to have a few more modern gadgets fitted to make cleaning and cooking easier for her at her age. The only help she had, or had ever had, was what Marjorie voluntarily gave her. Well, if that's what she wanted, that's what she should have. Money was no object. He'd have a word with Eric Choppen as soon as he could, to recommend a good firm of decorators, but not till Rosemary was on her feet and well again. She and Marjorie would not want to be left out of it.

It was nearly mid-day. He turned away from the field, holding up his hand to William going by on his way home from seeing

Bob, as another car turned into the front gate. Only Marjorie, on her way home from staying the night with Rosy. She'd be able to give them the doctor's latest report.

Molly was fussing round her daughter by the time he went into the house. Marjorie was tall and handsome; she took after him, folks said. Molly was shorter, and more rounded now than she had once been, white-haired where once she had been a nut-brown maid, but essentially, her husband thought, the same girl as he'd married. Through thick and thin, they had found very little fault with each other, and her protective, caring but cheerful attitude towards Marjorie was just like her, George thought, though a bit surprising. He hadn't been aware that Marjorie needed any extra fuss.

'You do look tired, my pet,' Molly said. 'Sit down and let me get you a cup of tea while you tell us what the doctor said.'

Marjorie accepted, which in itself showed that Molly's perception was right. 'Much the same as last night. She's in pain if she tries to move, and there's no prospect of her being able to get up. Maybe not for a month. But the doctor did say that if she's no better tomorrow, he'd like another opinion. He'll get her an appointment for X-rays and such. Don't worry – it's a common enough occurrence these days. Brian's dealing with the insurance people, who say that there's no question of it being her fault. She was stationary; if another car runs into a stationary one, the driver of that is the culprit. But that won't cure serious injuries if Rosy has any. I know I ought to stop up at Temperance and look after her properly, but how can I now? The Rector's out of action, and a very bad patient according to Eric, who says he ought to know better. Eric's being wonderful, but you know him: his hands are always more than full with day-to-day business. He says that if we both take our eyes off Nigel at the same time, we shall find him on the floor, where he's tried to stand up and failed.

'I know men make a lot of fuss when they've got the finger-ache, but you'd expect an intelligent man like Nigel not to ask for trouble. Then there's Poppy ringing up every few minutes – or so it seems to me – full of plans for the future and excitement that I can't share. I know I ought to – but what about Pansy?'

And to their consternation, Marjorie laid her head down on the table in front of her, and cried.

'You're tired out,' Molly said, stroking her daughter's hair. 'You just sit there till the kettle's boiled and have a good strong cup of tea. A good cry won't hurt you.'

George sat down rather heavily in his own old Windsor chair and looked across at his daughter with more attention than he had given her lately. 'Are you sure you've told us the truth about Rosy?' he asked. 'If Hardy's told you anything you haven't told us, out with it now. She ain't your responsibility only, my duck. We shall have to get somebody else in to help if you can't manage. What with helping us here, and looking after your own house, and keeping house for Eric Choppen, seeing to the Rector, and now having to nurse him into the bargain, I don't wonder as you're knocked up! You can't go on long looking after four places and nursing two invalids, whoever they are.'

'Don't be silly, Dad! Rosy hasn't asked for help till this accident, nor the Rector – well, none of 'em have actually asked for it at all.'

'No,' said Molly, setting the cup of tea down in front of her. 'They just expect it. You're too good to all of them. It's none of my business, but I reckon you might as well learn your lesson now as go on till you wear yourself out and somebody else has to look after you. If you want to help other people, you've got to look after yourself first. Self-sacrifice is one o' them things as sound all right when parsons go on about it in church, but it don't make a lot o' sense in practice. I should ha' thought you'd ha' learnt that from that husband of yours. You never got much thanks for what you did for him – or Pansy, if it comes to that. So why are you killing yourself with tiredness for anybody? Me and your Dad, to start with? When I can't manage, we shall have to get somebody to do for us regular. And them two men you slave for could both well afford to get other help!'

'Because I love you and Dad, and Rosy – and Eric and Nigel, if it comes to that. And they both treat me like a lady, not a skivvy. As for Pansy, I'm her mother. Didn't you worry yourselves nearly to death about me? I'm all right, honestly. I don't sleep very well, mainly because of Pansy – and I had no sleep at all last night. I'm just dead beat this morning, that's all.'

'Go home and rest then, my gel,' George advised. 'I'll come up later on, to see if the Rector wants me to do anything while he can't.'

'Don't you go bladging to Eric,' she said, smiling at him through her tears. 'It isn't his fault.'

She went, and left them to chew the situation over between them.

'I will go and have a word with Eric, if I get the chance,' George said. 'But we can't interfere between him and Marge. They're fond of each other, if it is only as friends. It's been a blessing for all of us that it turned out like it has. And we're as helpless as Marge is to do anything about Pansy. We mustn't let on that we're worrying about any of 'em. For the time being, we'll pretend we don't notice. If we're going to have a lot o' decorating and such done here, that'll act as a blind. When I see Eric tonight, I'll find out about getting somebody to do what you want doing. It'll help to keep our own minds off things as we can't alter.'

She began to tell him all the ideas she had had – more to distract than to inform him. She knew quite well how most men hate having their familiar surroundings changed, and their usual 'muddle-along' routine disturbed.

So after supper, George went to Monastery Farm, which Eric Choppen shared with Marjorie, he living in one half and she as his tenant in the other. He found that during the day, Eric had insisted on his friend the Rector being moved from his own cottage into his side of the house, till such time as he could get about again. Marjorie, assured that Eric would look after the Rector till morning, had gone back to spend the night with her brother and his injured wife. That suited George; it meant a 'men only' meeting at Monastery Farm.

George hadn't been there for more than five minutes before Terence Hardy, the doctor, arrived. He was no stranger to Eric's sitting-room, but said he hadn't come to stop. He'd just looked in at Church Cottage, Nigel's house, on his way home, and, finding his patient fled, had guessed correctly where he'd be. In spite of all his protests, out came a bottle of brandy. A chance of a bit of all-male society never ought to be missed among such close friends as they, strange mixture though they were.

George asked Hardy outright what he made of Rosemary's injuries. The doctor answered as truthfully as he could: he couldn't tell for another day or two, but he didn't like the stiffness and the pain, and had no intention of letting any possible injury to her spine go for more than another twenty-four hours before having it investigated by every modern means possible. He was afraid that at the best she'd be in bed for what might amount to several weeks, and asked if he ought to arrange a private nurse for her.

'You'd better not suggest that to Marjorie,' Eric said, 'in spite of the fact that she's the one who's taking the brunt. But you know what she is – I daren't interfere.'

'No. Let her do as she likes,' George said. 'Mother and me have had a go at her, but you might as well whistle to the wind. It's always the same: a case of it making sense to whip the horse as will pull. As long as you keep one eye on her, I shan't interfere. But there's something else I want to ask you, Eric.' And he began to explain about the plans Molly had set her heart on up at the Old Glebe. 'I don't suppose you could help me out, could you? I know you've got a good decorator in your team.'

Eric frowned, and then slowly shook his head. 'I can't see how I can,' he answered, 'though you know I would if I could. I only keep one decorator permanently with my team, and he's got his work cut out for the next month or two. You see, I've promised Terry here faithfully to have his house ready for occupation by Christmas, and after all the restoration alterations, and fifty years of neglect, it's going to take him every minute till then. You've got no idea what a treasure Terry's got, because I don't suppose many folk remember that it's there at all, secreted as it has been behind that ramshackle lot of sheds and that awful new shop. We've decided to let it remain hidden from the road till we can pull the front down and reveal the transformation. I'd help if I could, but you wouldn't want me to let Terry down, I know.'

Terry was saying nothing, looking a bit anxious. It was Nigel, sitting in one of Eric's best armchairs with his bad leg supported on another, who caught his somewhat embarrassed expression, and deliberately lightened the tone of the discussion, thinking Terry might be feeling too much of a newcomer for his needs to be given such priority.

'Have you thought of a name for this desirable residence?' Nigel asked. 'Bean Pottage Cottage? It has been "full of Beans" for generations, I believe.'

'Or "Ye Old Gossip Shoppe"?' suggested Eric flippantly. 'As it was when Beryl Bean was there.'

George spoke soberly. 'You both ought to know better,' he said. 'Such things matter. We're all glad to have got rid of the eyesore, as well as the earsore – if there is such a thing – of Beryl's tongue. But I hope it'll be give a name as lets us forget what it was, and fit for what it will be, when it's a proper part of the old village again. A name as'll remind us as well how lucky we are to still have a doctor close to, specially one as belongs to us a'ready. A country name as suits a doctor – something like "Speedwell", or "Heartsease".'

Terry shot him a look of surprise and gratitude. 'I think I ought to consider that seriously,' he said. 'Thanks, Mr Bridgefoot. And while the others have been busy pulling my leg, I've been thinking about your problem. It's only a suggestion, mind you, but it might work. I've got a patient who lives in that last new block of flats where Lane's End joins Hen Street. A Yorkshireman with a problem or two of his own, nerves all to bits as a result of a marriage break-up. He's more or less over it now, but lives too much alone, and he's lonely out of his native territory. I keep an eye on him, because I like him and know what he's been through. He's set himself up as a painter and decorator and I've seen some of his work. The trouble is that he's a perfectionist, such as he don't suit sub-contractors for developers or councils who want jobs done quick and on the cheap. I get the impression that he can turn his hand to most things, and make a good job of whatever he takes on. I think if you asked him to tune the piano, he wouldn't turn a hair. He'd say, "Aye, Ah'll have a do at it. 'Twouldn't be t'first. Wheer beest a?" And when you led him to it he'd sit down

41

and play you a Haydn sonata or something of the kind. He's a Christmas stocking of a man: full of pleasant surprises.

'He'd be better at work, doing something he enjoys, than sitting alone and thinking too much. Besides, if he doesn't get work soon he'll never earn a reputation for being good at his job. He'd be in his element in your house. Would you consider him?'

'That I will,' said George, 'and welcome. Only don't let on to Molly what you've just told us about him. She'd be doing the painting between getting him cups of tea and making him put his feet up on the best settee. But if he's the sort of man he sounds, he might help to keep her mind off Rosy and Marge. And Pansy. Send him round.'

'I will,' promised Terry.

'Do you know what Effendi means to do with your end of his house when you leave it?' Eric asked Terry. 'The Beans' old twin-cottage is the very last in Church End big enough to be restored as a des. res. I seem to have been instrumental in turning Church End into an expensive, exclusive enclave for a well-off, middle-aged, smug, middle-class élite, like us. Not at all what I intended.'

'You be careful what you're saying,' protested George, 'if you're including me! I'm only a Bridgefoot as belongs here, and I ain't no stuck-up idle rich layabout yet, neither, old though I may be. Nor ain't Bob Bellamy. Such as us have got muck on our boots, and shall have till our dying day.'

'If it comes to that, I don't exactly sit on my behind twiddling my thumbs all day,' said Eric. 'If I had been that sort of a chap, you wouldn't be sitting here together now.'

'No. I'm the cuckoo in the nest,' Nigel said. 'Born with a silver spoon in my mouth that very nearly choked me. But I've learned. That little cottage down Spotted Cow Lane is the best real home I've ever had. It's people that matter. I'd say you restored the *village*, Eric, not just the houses, whatever you intended. You attracted the right sort of people, too. There's no denying that our little bunch is made up of folks who are fairly well-britched now, but they haven't always been; and we still have a lot of the other sort here. Peasantry, born to village life. All I'm trying to say is that this is still a village, whoever's come to live here.'

Eric was prepared to argue. 'I know that's the truth, but it's only the luck of the draw so far. As George says, his family's part of its foundations. His roots are here. So are Fran and William Burbage's.'

'And Elyot Franks's,' broke in George, 'even if he didn't know till he'd come into the legacy. But he needn't have stopped here, need he? He could have sold out to Eric, and cleared off. But he didn't. I reckon he felt the pull of his roots. Then there's Jane Bellamy. Her and Nick have been here ever since Nick was born. She'd forgot she'd ever been anything but a village woman when her rich father turned up – and he's one o' the right sort.'

'Yes, that's just what I'm saying. We can't expect our luck to last. The young folk who were born here in farm-labourers' cottages didn't want to stop in them a moment longer than they had to. They agreed to let their stud-and-mud homes be condemned as "uninhabitable" by a council who'd been responsible for setting up a "new town" and thought everybody must want to move into one of their new council houses. Before I ever set eyes on the place, that was. In most cases, the council judged correctly what the mood of the younger cottagers was. The few who didn't get moved then are saving up like mad now to buy a new house on Lane's End Estate. Keeping up with the Joneses. I'll bet if William was here, he'd give us a lecture about our new egalitarian society, and the general wish there was, as well as the need, to level everything out and start again after the war. But it's all happened too fast. I learned in the army, reinforced by what I found here, that the one thing bureaucracy can't do is to level people out. They find their own level, like water, and make up their social groups, wherever they are.'

' "Birds of a feather stick together", you mean?' asked George.

'That puts it better than I could. This used to be one village; one community. Now it might just as well be two, except for the administration that's still in the hands of those who built Swithinford New Town. Those of us left now in Church End tend to think alike about most things, but we're outnumbered by about two to one by the Lane's End-cum-Hen Streeters already.

Sooner or later, democracy will catch up with us. We've got to be prepared to work with those who'll want to run Lane's End, and before we know where we are we shall be outvoted about things that will matter to us, like where to stick the next lot of council houses up, and so on. I'm proud to say I think the hotel and sports facilities do something to keep our end up, and help the melding process of the two communities, and there are still a few in both lots who feel that the church is the focal point of any village. Terry living here, and his partners living in Lane's End is another happy chance. We've had good luck with newcomers so far. Let's just hope it may last.'

'Well! Hark who's talking!' said George. 'It ain't above five minutes since he was the newcomer we were all scared to death of – him and his big ideas! But you're right, Eric, all the same. Afore you come and stirred us up, we'd got sort of dozy, like a tired old dog as'll hardly open its eyes however hard you whistle. We owe you a lot, my boy. And we'll remember what you say – or, at least, I shall. And now I must be getting back to Molly, to cheer her up with the promise of Terry's painter.'

*   *   *

William was enjoying playing with his new toy, conscious of Fran's eye on him. He knew that before long she would ask if the new set-up in his study was getting him started on his novel, and though he appreciated her interest, it had the opposite effect on him. Instead of encouraging him she made him more aware of all the obstacles in his way. He had made up his mind on his way home from seeing Bob that he would forestall her by bringing up the subject himself.

However, he had been late for lunch, and Sophie had explained that she'd had to get lunch early because she had to go to see her Aunt Sar'anne; Fran was at work in her study because of a telephone call from London, so she'd give him his dinner and get off to see what Aunt Sar'anne wanted.

William, cynically suspecting a female plot to send him to his study, was irrationally irritated that just as he was about to show Fran that he was doing all he could to please her, she wasn't there to be talked to. But he told Sophie not to disturb her – he could look after himself, he said. So, while eating his lonely lunch, he rehearsed what he would tell Fran, which amounted to much the same as he had discussed with Bob. It had got him a bit further forward, insofar as to know your enemy was the first step in any battle. His enemy had turned out to be not Time, as he had been suspecting, because of the threat to his continued access to the church in which proof about a lot of the Reverend Francis's secrets lay hidden, but History and his own integrity as a historian. But he had to be careful even about that. If it came to a choice between sacrificing his integrity as an academic or retaining Bob's friendship, he'd choose Bob. When he'd finished his meal, he put his head into Fran's study to ascertain whether or not she really was 'at work'. She was. There was no doubt of it: hitting the keys of her typewriter with vicious precision and speed. It was clear that she was in no mood to be interrupted.

'Sorry, darling,' she said. 'Can you manage without me for an hour or two? They've found a snag in one of my scripts that they're actually ready to start filming – a silly little legal point that nobody's noticed till now, but which because they know it's based on a living person, might possibly be construed as libel against the television company. I don't suppose Aunt Sar'anne has ever heard the word, but they have to be careful. It'll take me the rest of this week to do it again, however hard I work. Drat – I do hate to be rushed! I get into a tizzy and can't type for toffee.'

He was instantly contrite, and blew her a kiss from the door as he made for his own study. For once she really did look harassed, which was very unlike her. What he had to say to her could wait. He'd go and sit at his desk and try to see his way through some of his own confusion.

Bob had put his finger on the trouble. He couldn't go on vacillating. He had to make up his mind what line he was going to take, and then stick to it. There wasn't time to verify it all as historical research had to be verified, nor any need. Readers of history read history; readers of fiction want a story. He'd simply have to learn how to get information over to his readers without giving them constant lectures on history. If he didn't there'd be no book, and therefore no readers. No publisher would put out a half-breed in the first place, because they knew their readers wouldn't struggle with long passages of historical exposition if it held the story up and let the action get cold. Why on earth hadn't he cottoned on to it before now?

He sat back in his chair, his irritation with Fran turning gradually into admiration. She'd been able to turn mundane details of an old woman's life into televised popular entertainment without dwelling on the history of the late Victorian or Edwardian period; she had made them obvious from the action and drama of the story.

He put a clean sheet of paper into his typewriter. It would perhaps clear his mind to write down some of the most obvious difficulties. He was becoming interested in his problems for their own sake.

(a) How to cope with a story that hapened in the course of a few months three-hundred and more ago, which dependED on some knowledge of that period--and s of the previous fiveb hundred or so years.before.

(b) Time *is* a fourth dimension Everything takes place in time. Can't be Ignored. Concept of history as opposed to that of Time.

(c) Ask Fran whatshemeant about T/S. E. dealing with just that question in Lit. Gidd.

(d) Details Look up macauley on historian v. novelist. Essay on Hallum's Histoy of England ? Walter Scott ? Hazlitt on Land Tenure ?

He paused to think. He mustn't be as long-winded as Scott! Nor so casual about historical facts . . .

(e) Other HIStorical novelists ? Examplees.? Dumas? Covan Doyle ?

He glanced at his watch. Where had the time gone? It was certainly time he made Fran a cup of tea. He took the paper out of the typewriter, folded it, and put it in his pocket as he went kitchenwards.

*   *   *

Nicholas Hadley-Gordon, ex-diplomat, known to all his intimates as 'Effendi', was another happy man as he walked up the hill to have lunch with his daughter and her family at Castle Hill Farm.

Like Tennyson's Ulysses, much had he seen and known:

> cities of men
> And manners, climates, councils, governments . . .

The resemblance went still further for, like Ulysses, Effendi could truly say that he had been a part of all that he had met; yet until recently experience had remained for him still 'an arch where-through Gleams that untravelled world'. But years had kept passing, and he had been only too aware that there would soon be an end to his travels, and that 'Death closes all'.

In material terms, life had treated him well; but as he had neared retirement he had almost been afraid to face a future in which change would no longer keep him occupied, and make him likely to look back on his life with more regret than content. He faced old age and death alone. He had neither family nor friends he cared for enough to make the last voyage a happy one.

Then, just as he was philosophically reaching the point of resigned acceptance, a miracle had occurred. He had found his long-lost daughter – and her son – in this remote East Anglian village of Old Swithinford. It was not 'too late to seek a newer world'. For him Old Swithinford had turned out to be 'the Happy Isles'.

Once lunch was over, Jane dispatched her two adopted toddlers for an afternoon outing with her daily help. She cleared the table and washed up while Bob and her father smoked their pipes and chatted till the coffee was ready, when the discussion Effendi had come for was broached.

'All I want from you is your preference: which should I put

47

on the market to recoup a bit after buying Nick his bookshop? Do please understand that I haven't beggared myself by putting my fingers into so many pies lately. It's been to me the equivalent of another "diplomatic posting", engineered by me for my own benefit and pleasure. A voyage of discovery that's yielding huge profits. My pension is enough to secure me whatever I want for the rest of my life, so we are not talking income or indebtedness. Just practical common sense. The Old Surgery is my home for good, but I now have a family to consider. Is any of them likely to want or need a very opulent London service flat? Or a cottage in mid Wales? Would you, or any of the rest of them, prefer to have ready money available should the need for backing any further venture arise, rather than a foothold in London or a holiday home? That's what it boils down to.'

Jane answered, knowing that Bob would never dream of letting his wishes sway any such decision. Effendi had been the Genie of the Lamp for him already. She didn't hesitate. 'I don't know why you're asking,' she said. 'Nick's got his heart's desire, and Charlie's made her plans. She could hardly make veterinary calls on horseback from Eaton Square. We shan't have to consider Jade and Aggie for at least another twelve years or so. So as I see it, the point at issue is what you propose to do with your own time. Won't you want to keep in touch with London, and all your old colleagues? Won't you be bored here all the time?'

'No,' he said. 'That's what I really wanted to tell you. But I'd rather you told me your preference first. Jane. Which shall I keep?'

'The house where I was born – the cottage in Wales,' she said promptly. 'No comparison. Now tell us what you've got up your sleeve.'

'I can always use a hotel if I want to go to London,' he answered. 'But I don't want to be bothered. I have other things to do – a project of my own that I've had in mind for quite a while. I want to write my memoirs.'

'What a marvellous idea!' Jane exclaimed, but with just a shade of anxiety in her tone. 'But, memoirs, Effendi? All your memories?'

'My dear girl, the first lesson every diplomat must learn is discretion! And you shall be editor-in-chief.'

'So what's happening now to make you want to begin on it?'

'Terry Hardy moving out of his end of my house at Christmas or thereabouts,' he answered. 'I'm no typist. If I can find a retired secretary who'd like a part-time job, I can offer her, or him, accommodation on the spot. I don't want a full-time secretary – I've suffered too much from them in the past. I know what they are, and I don't want to be "managed". I want a typist, that's all.'

'Wouldn't it make more sense to advertise for a housekeeper who can also type?' Jane asked. 'If you're going to be busy writing morn and noon and night, wouldn't a live-in-more-or-less housekeeper be useful?'

Effendi smiled his charming smile and got a mischievous twinkle back from Bob. 'As I said, I don't want any female – other than you – to "manage" me,' he said. 'Besides, I should upset my very happy relationship with your Mrs What's-her-name. But the fact that I can offer accommodation might get me the right sort of typing help. So if you are sure you want me to hang on to Cregrina rather than Eaton Square, I'll set the ball rolling.'

Bob stood up, ready to go and leave the other two alone. 'And as my old mother used to say – though how she came to know anything about such things beats me – "You never know your luck till the ball stops rolling".'

His wife and his father-in-law watched him go off towards the church, his unloaded gun in the crook of his arm, and his head tilted towards the afternoon sky. 'I hope,' said Effendi, rather soberly, 'that that last remark wasn't one of his prophetic utterances. It's quite a responsibility, bringing another stranger into this tight little corner of old England.'

*   *   *

Sophie, knowing that Fran was tied to her typewriter, called in to Benedict's again on her way home in the evening, and prepared their supper. Fran was very grateful to her, because she'd had an exhausting day, and wanted nothing but to sit down and hear what William had been doing. She wasn't too tired, though, to wonder what Sophie had been doing as well, to make her so late home. She asked.

'Well, as you know, I do all I can for Dan, keeping 'is 'ouse clean and tidy, like, and leaving 'im a few bits o' cake and such. Thirz' were never one to let a man be – allus a-shaking up 'is cushions when 'e'd got 'em 'ow 'e liked 'em, and grumbling if he dropped a crumb or 'ung is cap on the back of 'is chair. So I don't pester 'im no more than I can 'elp by being there when 'e is, but I like to do little things as 'e'd never ask for. One thing I will say for Thirz' is that she were a good cook, and never grudged victuals. I reckon 'e must miss that. So I keep 'is cake tin filled with buns and 'is biscuit tin wi' biscuits, and now and then, like today, I put 'im a meal in the oven and leave 'im a note to say as it's there when 'e comes 'ome.

'Then I just dropped in at Aunt Sar'anne's, like I do most morning and nights, to make sure she's all right, 'cos be she as spry as she may, she's still very near ninety-three. And 'appy as she is down Mary Budd Cluss, she misses the company she 'ad while she were 'ere. But she ain't 'erself at all today. She says it's only a bit of a cold, but I shall goo early tomorrow morning to make sure, afore I come. So if you don't want nothing else done now, I'll get off 'ome meself. I get tired a lot quicker now than I used to, once.'

'So do I,' said Fran. 'We're none of us so young as we used to be.'

The early October evenings were turning chilly now, and when they went into the sitting-room after supper, it was to find that Ned, their gardener-handyman, had lit the first fire of the winter. It was cosy and warm and relaxing. So they sat and chatted.

'I didn't realize that Sophie had taken on Dan and Aunt Sar'anne as regular pensioners requiring her free services,' Fran said. 'I don't wonder she's tired! Doing for us is more than a full-time job anyway – nobody else would do half what she does for what we pay her. But I daren't offend her by suggesting extra help or advising her not to make herself too indispensable to Dan and Aunt Sar'anne. We should be up the pole if she failed us to look after them!'

'It "don't bear thinking about",' said William, quoting Sophie herself. 'Are you too tired to talk to me?'

'Depends what about,' she replied. 'I'm not likely to be very quick on the uptake tonight. But try me.'

He told her of his visit to Bob, editing it carefully. 'I suppose it's his complete lack of what one might call "sophistication" that helps,' William said. 'He doesn't have need to achieve wisdom, as Ecclesiastes put it. It's built into him. He goes straight to the point and usually solves the problem by a kind of instinct.'

He went on to tell her of Bob's unexpected reference to *Huckleberry Finn*, and its aptness to the point at issue: like Tom Sawyer, in his case doing a lot of 'reg'lar' historical research that wasn't absolutely necessary, considering the time it would take.

'He made me see it in a flash,' William said. 'And he cleared my mind to some extent about the historiographical situation: not to take too much notice of what other historians have written about that period. It's been one of the best researched periods of our history, and will go on being so. But each researcher is inclined to have his own ideas. They are mainly writing for other academics, not for a general readership. It furthers our knowledge, but I'm not sure if we do much to further any real understanding of the past. As C. V. Wedgwood said: "Specialization is essential to knowledge, but it can be fatal to understanding."

'I remember hearing her give the Leslie Stephens Lecture in Cambridge twenty years or so ago. She called it "A Sense of the Past". She made no bones about the fact that a good historical novelist – she quoted Dumas – often had a better sense of the past than even historians such as Gibbon. My feet are stuck in the mud of historical facts and I'm afraid to let my imagination try its wings. Possibly because I have a reputation to lose. That's why I can't get started. I'm scared.'

Fran laughed, taken by surprise. 'My Sir Galahad, *scared*? I don't believe it!'

'My dear girl,' he said, 'it's true. Heroes such as you insist on making of me aren't those who don't feel fear. Real heroes are those who are scared to death but won't show it; they hide their fear and get on with the job. Ask Eric. Ask Elyot. Ask Nigel.

They know, as well as I do, what fear is. When you get into the heat of action, the instinct for self-preservation takes over, you forget to be frightened and experience a sort of desperate excitement. The Vikings used to work themselves up deliberately into that state before a fight, tearing their clothes till they were "bare-sark", and chewing the rim of their shields. "Going berserk", as people say, with no notion at all of what it means. But I may be getting somewhere – with Bob's and Dame Veronica's help. And yours, my darling, when you have time to read and explicate T. S. Eliot with me. I've been trying by myself, but I get bogged down.'

'Not tonight, please. I'm not up to it. You have to be alert to the fact that he's a poet as well as a philosopher, and pick up all the undertones and overtones of the words he uses, as well as the significance of all the quotations from others that he makes use of, from many other cultures besides our own. Every word's a challenge, and the way he uses it's subtle hint to make you think more for yourself.'

'Give me an example – till you feel up to giving me a proper lesson.'

'Well, in *The Four Quartets* he's exploring the concept of Time in its relation to History and both in the wider context of Eternity. So there are constant references to the way we measure different sorts of time. *We*, nowadays, "measure" passing time by our watches and clocks and the pips on the radio. But time was when there was no measure but the sun – till the medieval age of bells. So when he says "the bell" has helped Time to bury another day, you don't just accept that he uses "bell" because it's a nice euphonious word with romantic associations. He means you to imagine how bells once marked out your life-span for you. Then he drops a hint that to consider History as part of Time is not to ring the bell backwards, because history is still going on. Incidentally, he borrowed that from Charles Lamb! You have to dig for all his meanings. Like doing a bit of historical research.'

'So I mustn't be content merely to ring the bell backwards. I have to remember what Leslie Stephens said about Walter Scott: that he made his readers realize that their ancestors were "as alive as they are". Pity. It would make a wonderful title for my book. *Ring the Bell Backwards*. Except that every campanologist in the country would write scathingly to me explaining that it is not possible to ring a bell backwards – at least without dire consequences.'

'Let 'em,' she said, sitting up suddenly to give her reaction the emphasis she felt it warranted. 'It's a marvellous title. Stick to it. If for no other reason than to please me.'

He raised one eyebrow at her. 'That's the main reason for putting myself through all this in the first – and the last – case,' he said. 'I'm still afraid I shall find ringing the bell backwards beyond my power to do.'

'Don't give up, Sir Galahad. Get your teeth into it, and it'll get easier.'

'Into my shield, like the Vikings? I wonder if that can possibly be the origin of that saying?'

They were off on a new tack. That's what made them so compatible. There was still so much time for them to go on talking – and so far they had never run out of topics.

When he went, as was usual, to make their last drink of the day, he put his hand in his pocket and discovered his page of typed notes there. He handed it to her. 'See,' he said. 'I wasn't wasting my time while you were so busy this afternoon. I was doing a lot of thinking.'

She handed it back to him when he returned with two steaming cups of hot chocolate. 'I do see,' she said. 'And I see another reason why you'll be the Methusalem of all creation by the time you get it finished if you don't have the help of a trained typist.' They went to bed still laughing at his ineptitude with a bit of new technology, erudite as he might be.

*　　*　　*

Fran managed to catch the last post on Friday with her rewritten script, and then confessed how bored she'd been having to do it a second time. 'I've had enough of Aunt Sar'anne now to last me a lifetime,' she said. 'In fact, I think I need a break. I haven't any more commissions pending, or any new ideas. I seem to have run out of them – but that's happened before. All I really need is a bit of a holiday from my typewriter. Time for gossip with Beth and Jane, and even Jess, though she's like a blue-bottle, always buzzing about with something important to do. You have to catch her before you can talk to her. I want to be an ordinary housewife for a week or two, and wait for inspiration.'

William looked at her a bit quizzically. 'Am I hearing aright?' he asked. 'Because if you had asked me, instead of telling me, I should have said it was high time, too. You look tired out. Do that. Put your feet up. I've got plenty to do just now without worrying about "my novel". Proofs of my last bit of research arrived on Friday, so I shall have to lay off everything else till I get them back to the publishers.'

'Well, proofs are always a chore, but a change is sometimes as good as a rest. Leave them alone till Monday, and let's both spend the weekend idling.' He agreed, though reminding her that he had another date with Bob on Tuesday.

However, pleasant as a weekend just idling proved to be, things not so pleasant were waiting in the wings for Monday. When Sophie arrived, a bit late, she didn't look well – as Fran remarked.

'I don't feel myself, rightly,' Sophie admitted. 'Aunt Sar'anne's 'ad a touch o' the flu, and I reckon I must hev got it from 'er. I come to tell you –'cos I shall hev to goo and see as she's all right tonight – but I ache all over and don't want nothing to eat. So if it's all right with you I reckon I ought to goo back 'ome to bed till I hev to get up and goo to see to Aunt Sar'anne again. There's no sense in me stopping 'ere and giving it to you. There's several of 'em down Miss Budd's Cluss sickening for it. I shan't be able to do for 'em all, much as I'd be willing, if I ain't well myself. But I can't be in two places at once, even if I ain't a-bed myself. You'll hev to manage without me for a little while, somehow.'

'Get off home while you can,' William more or less ordered her. 'And go straight to bed. I'll ring the doctor and ask him to see to Aunt Sar'anne and the others.'

It was proof of how ill she felt that she didn't argue. She just went, as Fran said afterwards, like Adam and Eve out of Eden:

'with wandering steps and slow', not in the least like her usual sturdy self. It was the first time they had ever known her to succumb to illness.

*

Dr Hardy thought it a bit early in the season for a bad epidemic of flu, but he was more than busy with those who had given each other very bad colds, especially the old who were gathered together in Mary Budd Close. It appeared that Sophie had been doing whatever she could for any who were 'laid up', as well as all her other duties, and it didn't take the doctor long to see that a good deal of her trouble was that she was worn out. He forbade her to go back to work anywhere for at least a month, and then she must take it easy, and when she protested that 'them up Benedict's' couldn't get on without her, he said he'd tell them that they had to. Did she know of anybody who might stand in for her and help them out till she was fit again?

'Well,' she had said grudgingly, 'I know as Olive 'Opkins is been give the sack from Beryl Bean's shop in Hen Street, 'cos 'er and Beryl couldn't agree no longer, and Olive told me 'erself as she found walking to and from Hen Street night and morning too much for 'er anyway. But she ain't the sort they'd want at Benedict's, even as a stop-gap. Fran'll come to see me as soon as you tell 'er it's safe for 'er to come without catching flu, and I'll tell 'er myself about Olive 'Opkins.'

The doctor was pleased enough to leave it like that. He had a lot on his hands, and on his mind, some of which none but himself and perhaps one other had any notion of. He was a bit worried by the Rector's injury; the swelling in his thigh was not going down as quickly as it should have done. He guessed that to be Nigel's own fault – he wouldn't obey orders to keep his leg up and not put his considerable weight on it any oftener than he could possibly help. Nigel received his orders with a charming smile, then did as he had always done, which was to please himself according to what his common sense and his devotion to duty required of him. He was still staying at Monastery Farm with Eric, and because Eric was busy, and Marjorie otherwise engaged looking after her sister-in-law, Nigel felt it his duty to do a good deal of what Marjorie would have done, as well as trying to keep his arm over all church affairs.

Terence's personal affairs needed attention, too. He was planning to move into 'Heartsease' as soon as ever possible. The T-part at the back, which had once separated as well as joined the two original cottages, had been made into two rooms: a surgery for him and a waiting-room for his receptionist. He couldn't leave his present accommodation till that was ready, and when he left, his part of Effendi's house would need some alteration and touching up. He consulted Effendi, who told him there was no hurry, but he intended to do it up himself to offer as bait to the right sort of person to provide him with some clerical help in the future. Terry recommended his 'Yorky' patient – when George Bridgefoot had finished with him – which reminded Terry that Yorky hadn't even been introduced to George yet. It was the next thing he must see to when he had time from his medical duties.

It was on Tuesday, while William went to keep his appointment with Bob, that Fran went to visit Sophie in her own little cottage, and Dr Hardy collected John Postlethwaite and escorted him to the Old Glebe, where they were expected, with the kettle ready on the hob.

Molly had formed a mental picture of their visitor that certainly did not fit the man who now stood before her. After George's brief report that he was one of Terry's patients who still needed the doctor's eye on him, she had expected him to be small, thin and frail, looking too old for his years. She took in the reality with some surprise. What she saw was as good a specimen of manhood as the doctor himself, though, if anything, slightly the younger. He was handsome, with a ready smile and twinkling eyes, and there was nothing in the least 'poor working-class' about him, either in his neat casual dress or his manner.

Molly found herself a bit nonplussed. She fussed with the kettle and a tea-pot while George bade both welcome, and asked them to sit down. Terry declined, saying he was going straight on to Temperance Farm to see Rosemary, and would call for John on his way back – if it was all right with them. So the newcomer sat down, and Molly turned towards him. 'Will you have a cup of tea, Mr Postlethwaite, or would you rather have coffee?' she asked.

'There's nowt better'n a cup o' tea,' he said. 'If it's all t'same t'thee. But don't call me Mr Postlethwaite. That's a name as I wouldn't saddle a stray dog wi' meself, but then I couldn't help it being my name, seein' as it were my father's. But tha's no need to remind me o' that old – o' him. Most folk round here call me "Yorky".'

George looked pleased. He was countryman enough to know the social value of nicknames when it came to people working together. Molly missed the top of the tea-pot in looking and listening to him, and sent a dollop of hot water hissing and spurting on to the hot stove.

Yorky was on his feet in a flash, and had taken the boiling kettle from her. 'Nay, let me do that, Gran,' he said, and proceeded to pour out three cups of tea expertly, sugaring George's exactly to his liking, and waiting to help an astounded Molly to sit down again before handing her hers. From that moment, he became 'Yorky', Molly became 'Gran', and George, 't'Boss'. Yorky was taken on a tour of the house, keeping very silent as he looked about him at the ancient walls and odd corners, the uneven floors and the polished old oak of the furniture.

'There's a lot to be done,' George said. 'More'n I thought. I can see as Mother's right.'

'Ah could do a lot more if thee'd gimme t'job and let me do it my way,' said Yorky. 'Ah just loove everything as tha's got here. Ah'd very near do it for nowt, just for t'pleasure. Tek your time to make your mind oop about givin' me t'job.'

'I don't need to,' George said. 'You just come and do whatever Mother wants done.'

'Aye. Me and Gran'll do fine together. Here's doctor back. Shall Ah mek another coop o' tea fo' tha, Gran, afore I goo?'

Molly accepted. George chuckled to himself as he remembered warning Terry not to let her know how 'poorly' his patient was. It looked very much as if the shoe was going to be on the other foot. Molly was going to get the share of attention she deserved.

Terry came back in, followed by Marjorie; the tea was made, handed round, and a subtle change came over Yorky, though only the doctor noted it in particular. The Yorkshire dialect and the broad Yorkshire brogue were replaced by perfect English with a Yorkshire accent. Terence had encountered it before, on his visits to John in his own house. He summed his patient up as an educated man who would never let anyone despise his working-class roots. It was his test of new acquaintances. If they showed any signs of 'side' he had no use for them; if they accepted him for what he was, he would give them service of the kind not always easy to come by these days. Terry was well satisfied with his little experiment. He was not so satisfied with his patient. Rosemary was not doing as well as she ought to be.

*

Fran had only ever been into Sophie's little home once before. She had wondered why she had never been invited again, but had worked out the reason for herself. She had paid Sophie that one uninvited visit at the very blackest moment of Sophie's bleak life. After years of spinsterhood, her childhood sweetheart, who had waited unmarried for her all through the years of her martyrdom to her old mother, had come into money of an amount undreamed of in such circles as theirs by winning a large premium bond prize. Emboldened by it he had gone secretly to ask Sophie to marry him. She had accepted, but had asked that he waited just a little longer before letting it be known. 'Just till she got used to it' is what she had said, but what she had meant, and what he had known she meant, was until she made sure it was right in the sight of 'Im Above, and in that of her sister Thirzah, the other powerful overseer of her life. And while James Bean (better known as 'Jelly') waited, he indulged himself in his other great love, which was for cars. On the spur of the moment he bought himself a hot-rod sports model, and broke his neck by running into a bridge before ever getting it home.

By chance, Fran had happened to be the only one in Jelly's confidence; but she had been away when the tragedy occurred. When William rang to tell her of it, she had rushed back to be at Sophie's side, going immediately to the tiny cottage which had once been a medieval dovecote.

Her visit was one of the most painful and ineradicable memories of her life. She hoped she would never again have to endure at first hand such terrible suffering, or such proud, stoic courage – let alone both at once.

Then Eric Choppen had arrived in the village, his eye on all such quaint bits of property as the Dovecote; but Sophie, by this time a wealthy woman by the standards of her peers, having inherited a third of her sweetheart's assets, had outbid Eric, and put him in his place. Then she herself had carried out such modernization as Eric had proposed 'when the Dovecote was his'. It was her proud challenge to Fate that she should keep the little home she had so very nearly shared with Jelly.

Fran had concluded that seeing her on that occasion was too painful a memory for Sophie to endure, and too vivid a reminder of what might have been. Time had gradually done its healing, and Fran had received an invitation, via the doctor, to go to see her old playmate. So she went.

Sophie was up and about, though still looking tired and listless. 'I should ha' been back to work a-Monday morning, do the doctor would ha' let me,' she said. ''E says as this flu as is about now takes a long while to get over properly – and why I'm 'ad it so bad is that I'm been doing too much for a long while. 'E asked me if I'd been suffering from what 'e called "stress". I said as I didn't rightly know what 'e meant and 'e said the same sort o' thing as what William 'ad in the spring. But when it all come out, 'e meant as I'd never really got over Jelly being took from me like that, and Thirz' being as she was afore she died. It 'ad all been too much for me. So if I don't want to go same way as Thirz', 'e says, I'm got to stop working so much and enj'y meself more. So I told 'im as I couldn't do better than do as I 'ave since you come back, and that I couldn't and wouldn't stop doing for you and 'im, not for nobody. I telled 'im straight out that if I couldn't come up and be with you, and do my duty to Aunt Sar'anne and Dan, I might just as well die out o' the way, and go to be with my Jelly in 'Eaven. 'E couldn't and didn't answer that, so I reckon as 'e'll soon let me back to work again now.'

'My dear Sophie, we hate being without you as much as you hate not coming; but you must take Dr Hardy's advice and not wear yourself out with work quite so much. Benedict's is too big a house for you to run and keep clean as well as doing all the cooking for us, you know. How would it be if we tried to get somebody else to come in as well, to do all the rough work, under your supervision? Didn't I hear you say something about Olive 'Opkins being out of work? I don't know much about her, but I do remember her working for Miss Budd and I'm sure anybody good enough for her would be good enough for us – and you.'

Sophie sniffed – always a sign of her disapproval – but she was being torn both ways. In the metaphorical parlance always ready on the end of country tongues, 'half a loaf is better than no bread at all'.

'Miss put up with Olive partly 'cos nobody else could do with 'er, and partly 'cos she was so sorry for 'er after Job, as is 'er 'usband, got catched poaching and 'ad to go to court. 'Is lawyer told 'im as 'e'd go to prison if 'e said too much in court – and come the day, 'e never opened 'is mouth except to tell 'em 'is name. And from that time on, 'e's been like Zacharias in the Bible, struck dumb most o' the time. So by that, she's the one who's done the talking; but she never was quite all there, somehow – a farthing or so short in the shilling, like. She don't mean no 'arm, like Beryl Bean does, but she can't carry nothing as is said to 'er properly in 'er ead, if you know what I mean. I will say for 'er as she's a good worker, as long as you don't let 'er running on about nothing all the while aggravate you. I'm used to 'er. I were at Miss's school with 'er, and I'm knowed 'er all our lives. If she were to come for two hours three times a week to do the kitchen floors and such, it'd be a 'elp, and she wouldn't worrit me. I could get on with what I was doing, and not listen no more than I wanted to. D'you think the doctor'd let me back if you was to ask 'im – under them conditions?'

'It's worth a try,' Fran said, and went home looking forward to repeating Sophie to William. She remembered Olive vaguely as a fairly tall woman with big bones showing beneath too little flesh and flat planes in face and figure. Mary Budd was always kind to her and about her, but Mary had a waspish tongue on occasion, and a gift for terse comment. Fran recalled one or two of her exasperated quips at Olive's expense: that her face appeared to have been cut out with a shovel, and that she must have been out in a gale when the wind changed, because her face had never changed its expression since. The voice of her dear old friend rang in Fran's ears on the way home, making her chuckle. Clicking her tongue, Mary had once declared in exasperation, *vis-à-vis* her char, 'She's like one of George Eliot's characters said about somebody: "Some folks go on talking like some clocks go on striking, not to tell you the time, but because there's something wrong with their insides." That's Olive to a T.'

Fran understood that there were likely to be snags; it would be wise to warn Olive that the arrangement might only be a temporary measure. Olive wouldn't worry William much if she was there only two hours three times a week, and she would get a lot of pleasure listening to Sophie and Olive. Before Fran left, the idea had been approved, after prayers from Sophie both to 'Im Above and the spirit of Jelly, who had never left her absolutely alone to cope with anything.

The doctor, thanking his lucky stars that some folks still used common sense, gave the arrangement his blessing. Olive would start next Monday, when Sophie, if well enough, would come in her new role as 'housekeeper' to enjoy the overlordship of her erstwhile schoolmate.

It was proving to be an eventful day. Knowing that William would be out most of the morning, Fran decided to drop in on Beth Franks at the Old Rectory for a chat. She was let in very prettily by the oldest of the two girls Beth and Elyot had given a home to, temporarily in the first place when Fran and William had been left to care for seven abandoned children. Emerald Petrie was now nearly nineteen and exquisitely beautiful, as was her sister Amethyst, only thirteen months younger; both were now fixtures in the household of 'the Commander' and his wife, much loved and very useful into the bargain, as grown-up daughters should be.

Emerald had a struggling toddler round her waist, and told Fran she was about to put Wyn – Beth and Elyot's baby son – down for his nap. Buffy – Mrs Franks she corrected herself – was in the sitting-room, putting her feet up for half-an-hour at Dr Hardy's suggestion.

'Heavens!' exclaimed Fran. 'Is everybody in this village ill?'

Emerald smiled a brilliant, rather mischievous smile. 'Not exactly ill,' she said, 'but obeying the Commander's orders. She knows it's the easiest way in the long run, and Dr Hardy did say it might be a good idea.'

It wasn't at all like Beth to be idling in the middle of the morning, and Fran expressed her surprise. 'What's the matter, Beth, to put Elyot in such a stew? Anything serious?'

Beth's face lit up with a smile that would have melted a gargoyle, but with enough mischief in it to have caused even the gargoyle to wink back. 'Now, really, Fran, I give you three guesses. I'm pregnant again, and Elyot sounded off action stations the moment the MO assured him I'd got the signal correct. It'll be Elyot he'll have to keep an eye on, not me, so it's a good thing we see so much of him.'

Fran, leaning over to kiss her, said, 'What marvellous news, Beth. I'm so glad!'

Beth returned the kiss as warmly as it was given. 'I wanted you to be the first to know,' she said, 'so I gave orders that nobody else should be told till I'd seen you. But we've only been sure for about a week.'

'A girl, of course, this time,' Fran said. 'What did we decide she'd be called if Wyn had turned out to be female? Wasn't it Arethusa Bellona Calliope?'

'Yes, it was,' said Elyot from the door he had just entered. 'Let's have a drink to her.' He poured out two gin and tonics for the ladies, and made himself a 'horse's neck'.

'To my daughter, Arethusa,' he said, raising his glass.

*

William had found Bob waiting for him, as arranged, in the church.

'Any news yet?' Bob asked, a bit anxiously.

William shook his head. 'I think we may be in luck, though. They'll probably have to postpone any decision till Nigel's back in action. Have you had time to do any scouting round?'

'Not much. I'm too busy. My two farms are just too far apart to make looking after both of 'em easy at this time of the year. Effendi says we ought to get a farm manager, but I can't see myself as a gentleman farmer, somehow, so I ain't rushing into that afore it's necessary. But Effendi does know how many beans make five, so I'll consider it next spring. Effendi's going to be busy this winter, anyway, writing his memories – no, that ain't the right word – his memoirs. He can't be looking for a typist made to measure for himself and a farm manager made to measure for me at the same time. He wants a typist ready to start straight after Christmas, as soon as the doctor leaves the other end of his house vacant.'

'If he thinks he'll get one of the modern little fluffy-headed typists to live in a place like Old Swithinford, he's got another think coming,' William said dryly. 'It might be more sensible for him to look for a mature ex-secretary, already retired but bored by not having enough to do and willing to earn some extra pin-money. But women who've been full-blooded secretaries are usually real old bossy-boots, and I can't see Effendi being bossed by anybody, however suave he always is. Does he want his typist full time?'

'No, I think he just wants one on tap. A couple of days some weeks and three – or none – the next.'

'Well, good luck to him!' William said, and meant it. He wanted exactly the same sort of help himself. It would be almost too good to be true if he and Effendi could share the services of a suitable, efficient typist. He turned his thoughts back to what he needed one for: the book. 'So you haven't much to report?'

'No. I drawed you the map you asked for, though I can't do more than guess what it might have been from one year to the next three hundred year ago. Y'see, every winter, if the floods come up, or the river banks overflowed, they quite likely wouldn't go down again along the same course. The water would take the easiest way. Besides, land on high places as was used for grazing in summer got flooded in the winter, and if any chap had the chance, he'd give nature a bit of a helping hand to drain the water off his land on to somebody else's. But I dare say the main rivers didn't change course very much. Anyway, I've done my best till

I know exactly what it is you're after. And I did come down and poke about here one day for a little while, like you asked me to. I spent most of my time looking at that slab down there as we found were put where it is to cover up the church end o' the secret tunnel. You said it had been the top o' the altar, as had been throwed down by a gang o' Puritans. I reckon so as well, 'cos from what I can see the hole it sits in were cut to match the slab, not the other way round. So my guess is as they tried to carry it outside to smash it, and when they found out how heavy it was, they just dropped it. And then when that man with more money than sense a hundred year or so ago had the church and my house done up, they throwed the broken bits o' the old cover away, and made the hole bigger to fit this one. I had a good look at the top of the altar as it is now, and it's nothing but a nice bit o' mahogany made to fit the pedestal part. It's fixed, so I couldn't shift it by myself.'

'Thanks, Bob. That's enough for the time being. Any chance of seeing you again next week, same place, same time?'

'Unless anything very urgent crops up,' Bob answered. 'I'll make time, somehow. I look forward to it all the week.'

So they parted, and William went home to hear from Fran all about Olive 'Opkins, and Beth's surprising news; and in exchange to tell her of the slight chance of Effendi getting a typist that he might share. Things were certainly looking up a bit.

They had a scratch lunch of mushroom omelettes and rice pudding. 'It'll be nice to have Sophie's square meals again,' he said. 'Even if we have to pay for them by listening to the Hopkins woman.'

''Opkins,' Fran corrected. 'She won't be the same if you insist on aspirating her.'

'I'm more likely to want to asphyxiate her, I think,' he said, 'from what I've heard.'

He told her of his visit to Bob as they sat after lunch, especially about the difficulties of getting rid of water in the undrained parts of the fen before the Civil War period.

'That's the sort of difficulty I'm up against,' he said. 'All sorts of people have had their say about "the drainage of the fens", meaning, of course, the main overall scheme of cutting off the big loop of the Ouse by taking a tangent across it – the so-called "Bedford" cuts. But there were little bits of drainage going on all the time, from natural causes, such as water finding its own level again after a flood, and bits of private enterprise to redirect the flow by digging a ditch or two that had nothing to do with the Duke of Bedford's scheme. The fens aren't easy to understand. I've read other historians who make broad statements such as: "Oliver Cromwell was born in the little fenland town of Huntingdon". Huntingdon isn't "in the fens", and never was. Nor is St Ives, where it is claimed that Cromwell "farmed", though all he did as far as I can understand was to rent land there. Some of the fields he ran cattle on, according to Bob, were water-meadows by the river, which still flood sometimes in winter, and suggest "fens" to the uninitiated. But then, I've heard university dons letting students believe Cambridge to be "in the fens".

'It may not matter to the general reader that "the King of the Fens" was never more than a tenant farmer after he sold his little inheritance at Huntingdon, but it did matter at the time, because it must have had an effect on Cromwell's character.'

'Wait a minute,' Fran said. 'Didn't his uncle at Ely leave him a lot of property? A house and some land?'

'He certainly left him a house, and perhaps the copyhold lease of the cathedral's glebe lands. I can't trace Cromwell himself buying, or even owning, land in his own right while he lived in Ely. From what I can make out – though as yet I haven't really been far enough into the question of land tenure before the Civil War – it was very much still in the process of change. Till then, people who farmed glebe lands may have had some proprietary rights over the lease, but they still had to pay the Church rent for it in some way. So they were, in effect, only tenants. In the society of the time, that would have lowered his social degree – his standing in the local hierarchy. Bob has a more practical slant on it. He asks, How could he have gone on farming if he was in London as a law-student? He wasn't a big enough landowner to have employed an expensive steward; but he must have occupied some sort of mezzanine degree to have been eligible either as

Governor of Ely or Member for Cambridge. Historical novels, I find, demand a lot of complementary research about matters that are not exactly part of the story. The more I think about it, the more I realize how important such things are in understanding the characters involved. Cromwell claimed to have been "born gentle". It obviously mattered to him. Perhaps that's why even the very best of historical novelists succumb to the temptation of showing off all they know, whether or not it's germane to their tale. Then what the reader gets is eighty per cent history and twenty per cent story instead of the other way round. I've read somewhere that Conan Doyle said that, and he certainly knew how to write a good tale. But he didn't pretend to be a historian, and his details weren't all that accurate by more up-to-date research.

'Hell! Who can that be?' He went to answer the shrilling telephone.

'Eric,' he announced. 'With an invitation to us to join Greg and Jess at Monastery Farm for tonight's meal. Nigel will be there as well – he's still living there. It's ad hoc, so Eric will order whatever we choose to be brought up from the hotel. I gather the meeting has a purpose. Eric said he'd been right in his forecast that democracy would soon catch up with us – as if I knew what he meant. I said we'd go about six-thirty. Leave the washing-up. I want to go and check on tenure of glebe lands, while I remember – that's if I can find any reference to it.'

'I'll do the washing-up,' she said. 'I'm rather enjoying being a housewife. I'd even cook if you'd let me without leaving what you are supposed to be doing to come and help me. And a thought has just struck me, but there's no time now to get you interested in it. Another time.'

*

Fran and William were surprised to find Bob and Jane at Monastery Farm as well as Greg and Jess. Over their welcoming drinks, Eric explained why they were there, apart from the chance of a pleasant get-together. Jess and Greg had a problem which might have far-reaching effects for the future well-being of their community. The problem had begun with Joe and Hetty Noble, but he had thought it wiser not to ask them tonight. Hetty Noble was Sophie's youngest sister, and when her only daughter had produced an illegitimate child, she and her husband Joe had been more or less forced to bring the child up; his mother had abandoned him to their care when fate and fortune took her to live in America.

When William and Fran had been left with the totally abandoned family of John Petrie on their hands, friends and neighbours had rallied round, taking in and succouring temporarily (as was at first supposed) seven of the eight waifs. To all intents and purposes, John Petrie was a dropout hippie, though in fact he was anything but that. A highly educated man, his real name was John Petrie Voss-Dering. For Greg and Jess, William's half-sister and her husband, the chance to help his children had been almost a miracle, providing the one thing they had lacked to make their new-found relationship with each other complete. They had taken in three-year-old Jasper, the only one of the children actually fathered by the man they had all called 'Daddy'. Now they had been legally allowed to keep him, though only as foster parents; they had renamed him 'Jonce', by which his father had been known as a child.

Jonce was now almost five, and of school age. This brought William into the picture as well, because he had given the dying John Petrie a solemn promise that he would always oversee and, if necessary, provide for his son's education, and under John's will, had been named as the child's legal guardian should the child's mother die or abandon him. She had since done both.

At the time of John Petrie's death, nobody could have foreseen how well it would all turn out for the other children. Seven out of the family of eight, who had never before been separated however difficult the conditions under which they lived, had had to be split overnight among four households, with one lost sheep, Basher, still 'somewhere in Wales'. He remained on William's conscience, but to all the rest his absence was more of a blessing than a loss. Jonce and Hetty's little grandson Stevie were very close in age, and as Hetty was already 'doing domestic' for Jess, she had undertaken the care of little Jonce while Jess and Greg were at work. So the two little boys, both with traumatic starts, had begun a new life more or less as twins.

'As it's really your problem in the first place, Greg,' Eric said, 'I suggest that you explain to the others what this is all about. Bob and Jane are here because before long they'll face the same problem – and, as I said, there may be much more behind it than appears on the surface.'

Greg Taliaferro was an artist to his fingertips, and like many another artist immersed in his work, was not the most efficient sort of man when it came to dealing with the more mundane practical aspects of life. Not that it mattered much in their case, because Jess was efficient enough for both. But they were both now up against something that they had never previously had cause to consider.

'We really ought to have had Joe and Hetty here,' Greg began, 'because all this started with them. But they're only over the road at our house if we need them. A day or two ago Joe was visited by some sort of official – a welfare officer, or some such – wanting to know why young Stevie wasn't attending school. His fifth birthday is just coming up, and it appears that children are expected to start school at the beginning of the term in which their fifth birthday falls. Joe wanted to know what we intended to do about Jonce, because Stevie's only a few weeks the elder. We didn't know. We'd been meaning to talk to William, but we just kept putting it off – you know how time flies. But Jonce will have to start school after Christmas, and now we're forced to think about it, it's a much bigger problem than we'd expected.'

Jess intervened. 'Joe'll be in trouble if Stevie doesn't start attending now, at once. Which means one of two things. He'll either have to go by himself, on a bus, to the primary school at Swithinford, or we send Jonce with him.'

Greg's mobile face often gave his feelings away, as it did now. 'Be gone all day from about half-past eight in the morning till four o'clock! Among absolute strangers, at their age!' he said. 'There's neither sense nor reason in it! And Joe says there's no others in Church End technically "infants" – not a single one that Jonce and Stevie have played with. Children up to the age of nine use the same transport, which goes round seven other villages picking them up. That's our first personal problem. Jonce is a terrible traveller! He starts being travel-sick at the thought of any journey unless he's doped with pills and given somebody's complete attention in a front seat. He reacts before he even gets into a car. We can only suppose it to be the traumatic effect of that terrible trek home from Wales when his father died on the way. But what alternative have we?'

'And just think!' Jess said. 'If we make special arrangements for Jonce, what will poor little Stevie do? They've been inseparable for the last eighteen months. It would be nothing short of cruel to part them. I can't and won't subject Jonce to that! Nor to him having hysterics and starting to be sick every morning as the bus comes in sight! It would scar him psychologically for the rest of his life.'

'I suppose this is what we call "progress",' Fran said. 'Oh, for Mary Budd and her little village school!'

'I suppose we could cut out the bus journey,' Greg said. 'Joe's his own master, and has a van. If we foot the expense, including Joe's time, he could take them and fetch them back. It would cut the length of the journey.'

'But, Greg,' said Fran. 'Isn't Joe and a van the very thing to bring back to Jonce the memory of that journey home from Wales? Jonce must associate Joe with those two days of hell.'

The ensuing silence was broken by Bob's voice, raised rather apologetically. In such a gathering, his slow, shy delivery and slight embarrassment were emphasized by a stronger use of fenland vernacular than he used in the ordinary way. But what he said was usually the very epitome of common sense, and the rest turned to him in relief.

'I reckon that'd be asking for trouble,' he said. 'How's a chap like Joe going to keep his hand over his work if he's tied to the clock at both ends of every day? If they can't go on the bus with the other kids, you'll have to lay on a taxi, or one of you take 'em yourself. But Hetty don't drive, and Jess has a job same as Joe does. Besides, there's other things to be took into consideration, I reckon. There'd be nothing as'd put other kids against 'em, and get 'em off to a bad start, worse than being seen to be "different". If they don't travel with 'em, they'll still have to mix with the other kids when they get to school. They'd be labelled as too stuck-up to go with the rest, or else dubbed straight away as spoilt little namby-pambies, the sort the tough kids pick on to tease and bully. There's a lot o' that sort in Hen Street and Lane's End, as have come from town schools – not like village schools used to be.'

'Bob's right,' said Jane. 'If I can help it, Jade and Aggie shall never have to put up with what Nick did just because he was "different" too – in his case because he didn't have a father in evidence. Children can be so cruel to each other.'

'Gosh,' exclaimed Jess. 'It's worse than I thought. None of us has the least idea what sort of reputation the allocated school in Swithinford has, or what sort of education it offers. We ought to have found such things out before now.'

'Especially,' added William, 'because of the controversy raging at present between the advocates for old-fashioned Victorian methods, especially in primary schools, and the so-called "child-centred" methods advocated very recently by the Plowden Report.'

'We shall have to bring ourselves up to date on primary education,' said Jess. 'So where and how do we start?'

'Not here and now,' said Eric firmly. 'I called you together because this is only the first rumblings of what may be a political storm brewing. And if you're wondering what on earth it has to do with me, I'll tell you. Whatever else I may have become, I'm still potentially a developer with a lot of business contacts. I keep my ears open. I gather that the primary, or 'first school' or whatever they call it, that now takes children from Old Swithinford is bursting at the seams because of the influx of children from all the unplanned estates that are springing up all round, like Lane's End. Nobody can be blamed for not anticipating such rapid development as there has been, but as far as I know, there are no plans on the horizon for extra infant or nursery places.'

'Why on earth did they close village schools before they knew?' Fran asked. 'From what one hears, now it's too late, many of them were islands of educational excellence. Like Mary Budd's was here.'

'Careful, darling,' said William. 'Don't generalize from the one or two examples you happen to have heard about. They weren't by any means all like Mary's, or all in the charge of people of her calibre – especially the one-teacher schools. I heard a Chief Education Officer say that many such schools in his patch were nothing but sinecures for lazy women, or heaven-sent cheap accommodation for graduates with research-student husbands. Nobody learns from history! After any upheaval such as a war, or even a landslide election as in 1945, political leaders tend to act first and think afterwards. Then they spend years trying to undo their mistakes, hoping nobody will notice. But, to be fair to the planners, communities such as Old Swithinford asked in some measure for what they got. Farmers with more money than sense followed each other like sheep to send their children to tin-pot private boarding-schools, just to keep up with the Joneses, lest their little Maisie or Daphne might have to sit next to one of their own farm-labourer's children.

'Now people like us want the kind of school we used to have on our doorstep. Are we being fair? *We* can be sure that our children receive a lot of their education at home, but you can't take that for granted in a place like Hen Street. Oh dear, why do you let me get on my soap-box? None of this is going to solve anything for Greg and Jess, or for Jonce and Stevie.'

He subsided apologetically. Greg gave him an admiring beam of a smile. 'You did suggest an alternative, though: the possibility of private education. Isn't there still a prep school in Swithinford? Children five to thirteen; day pupils as well as boarders? We'd pay Stevie's fees.' The horrified silence told Greg what a bloomer he had made.

'Same distance away; same difficulty about travel sickness and transport. Doesn't solve anything,' said Jess cuttingly. 'Unless you're suggesting that we let them become boarders.'

'Only over my dead body!' said William. 'No boarding for Jonce. I remember too well what it was like to be sent away from home at seven, never mind five.'

'Over my dead body too,' exclaimed Jess. 'I'll give up work and take them anywhere, sick or not sick, before I'll let Jonce be a *boarder*!'

'And don't be an idiot, Greg,' put in Fran. 'It would kill Hetty and Joe to be "beholden" to you for Stevie's fees. But there's more to it than that!'

Eric said dryly, 'It's you, Jess, being idiotic, not Greg. It would be like cutting your head off to cure toothache! And I'd want a say in you giving up your job as my Executive Officer –' But the hubbub of everybody wanting to speak stopped him, and above all the noise rose Fran's voice, pitched high and sounding almost hysterical.

'No! Please not,' she cried, on the verge of tears. 'How can you even suggest such a thing after what happened before? Oh! Of course! You weren't here then, Greg, so you wouldn't remember. In fact, none of you know the worst about that school except William. It was just as he said. The stuck-up wife of a rich farmer sent her child by another man to that very school and caused the most awful tragedy. The child was so unhappy – he was socially maladjusted anyway – and nobody, but nobody, not even I, would listen to Mary Budd's warnings. She guessed – she knew that he was a pyromaniac. The fire he started burned the old de ffranksbridge Hall down, and five people died as a result. You can't blame the school, though they didn't understand just how maladjusted the boy was. The people to blame are those who sent him there for their own benefit when all he needed was love and attention *at home*. As all children do. I can't bear to think about it. I watched the fire from our landing window knowing who had set it going, and who was likely to die in it. And there was nothing we could do but stand there and let it happen – too late.'

She collapsed, sobbing helplessly, into the arms of William who had risen from his own chair, pulled her up from hers, and sat down again with her on his knee, soothing her as if she had been the child in question.

'And I was there with you, my sweetheart,' he said, deliberately oblivious to the rest of them. 'It was the first time you'd ever really let me be of any practical use to you – and was a great landmark for us, whatever the other awful facts were. You mustn't get it out of proportion. It was a most unusual case. I grant you that Melvyn was a very disturbed little boy, and that Jonce and

Steven are both vulnerable because of what has already happened to them, but Melvyn wasn't blessed with anybody who cared about him. We are all proving we do care for Jonce and Stevie. Perhaps poor Melvyn was destined to be a social catalyst. Ssh! Darling, ssh! It's all in the past, now, and we can't alter it. Look at the other side of it. Because of that fire, Eric came, then Elyot, who caused Beth to stop among us. Where would John Petrie's children be now but for them? We should never have heard of Nigel but for Eric, and perhaps, without that traumatic evening of the fire, even I might not be here. As Sophie would say "God moves in a mysterious way His wonders to perform." Old Swithinford has reason to be grateful to young Melvyn Thackeray.'

They settled down to eat. The conversation returned to the finding of a school for Jonce and Stevie.

'But there are some little country schools left,' Bob said, shyly. 'They'd soon get used to a bit of a journey, if it was somebody they knowed taking them, and they enjoyed themselves when they got there. Start looking for one, only look in the other direction. Till a few year ago all this part was Huntingdonshire. It might be the second smallest county, and a bit behindhand in a lot o' things, but not about schools. Before Cambridgeshire got its village colleges, Hunts had had the sense to move their grammar schools into places full of history, like Ramsey Abbey and Kimbolton Castle and then Hinchinbrooke House. And they didn't rush to close the little village schools, either, 'cos distances across fens and empty spaces of farmland were too far for littl'uns to go. A lot o' them schools are *still open*. There's some our side o' the river, between here and St Ives. No farther away than Swithinford, and a lot easier to get to.'

It was Jane who broke the rather astounded silence. 'I've heard from our daily help about one in particular, at Fenley; only a two-teacher school but with a great reputation for "child-centred" education. Why don't we find out about that, and see if there's room there for two more? Surely we can manage transport if enough of us are willing to take turns?'

There was a general air of relaxation, as if the main problem was already solved. So with the coffee and liqueurs, Eric called

73

them to attention again, saying that if that was settled, he'd like to begin on the second item of his agenda, which was very much linked to the first, and perhaps of even greater consequence in the long run.

'We've just proved how necessary it is to keep one eye on the future – and the unexpected,' he said. 'Little Jonce and Stevie have led us indirectly to another problem. I found this village ready for commercial exploitation – I won't apologize, because you all know the story. It was then a more or less self-contained entity, a sleepy backwater turned in on itself. It used to be the "big village", and Hen Street was an unwanted hanger-on. Now, possibly because of the catastrophe Fran mentioned, it has changed. It's got cut into two, with Church End now the hanger-on to a much larger, more up-to-date and still-growing community that everybody calls Lane's End. Officially, administratively, it's all still Old Swithinford, but we are watching this part of it becoming the unimportant elderly relative. With every week that passes now, our numbers get smaller, and the Lane's End community gets bigger. Which means that in any future planning, we shall be outvoted just by numbers alone. We need to be on the *qui vive* to keep a bit of the say in the future. You may not have heard yet, but our County Councillor, who was also a member of our District Council, has just announced his retirement, so next spring there will be local elections – the thin end of the wedge for Lane's End to take us over.

'What if they do? Think again. If all the power is at Lane's End, where will a new school be, say, in five years' time? Lanes' End-cum-Hen Street is already jampacked with new houses, all the gaps filled. The land beyond is too low to be suitable for building. It would need to be placed as centrally as possible between the two parts of what was once Old Swithinford. But in such cases, might is right, even to the extent of compulsory purchase for such a project as a school. A primary school would require five unoccupied acres. Wouldn't we want a say in that? OK, you may be thinking that this is the "Not in my backyard" syndrome, which as reasonable people we ought not to subscribe to; but what if, instead of a good new school, the land was wanted

74

for a huge block of ugly council houses, or a supermarket – say in the Front Cluss of Benedict's? Quite possible, if we don't make plans not to let ourselves be ridden over roughshod.'

They were all looking aghast at him. They read about such things every day in the newspapers; but they had never considered how it might ever be them fighting for *their* own environment, *their* privileged positions, the value of *their* properties. They turned towards Eric like sheep towards their shepherd.

'Well, go on!' said Jess. 'What do you want us to do?'

'Put up a candidate from this end to counteract the one Lane's End has in mind.'

William, first to recover, asked if Eric knew, or had even heard a rumour, of Lane's End having a candidate ready and waiting.

Yes. He had it on unimpeachable authority. One Mr Greenslade, a native of Swithinford before it was a 'new' town. Seized his chance to set up its first fish and chip shop, making himself a small fortune. But fish and chip shops by law have to close at midnight; take-aways can stay open all night to serve the needs of shift-workers. So he set up a string of take-aways, Chinese and Indian, and got into big business. It paid him handsomely to give some of his time to local politics. This was his big chance.

'You suggest that we oppose him with a candidate who has rural rather than urban interests?' said William. 'Can we find one – and if we did, would he stand a chance?'

'We've got to,' said Eric bluntly. 'Or take the consequences.'

'Are you offering yourself as the candidate?' asked Jane.

Eric actually spluttered. 'Good God, no!' he said. 'That would be the pot calling the kettle black. I'm the very last person to be thought of.'

'William, then?' said Greg, as if it were a foregone conclusion.

Stunned, William sought for strong enough words to express his horror at the thought. 'Use your loaf, Greg!' he exploded, when his breath came back. 'You do know me better than that! Do you really think I went through all that heart-burning about leaving my academic career last year in order to get involved in *local politics*? I hate politics – of any kind. And if I remain in my right mind, I'll never willingly attend another committee meeting.

In any case, I'm writing another book. Sorry, but if you're relying on me, we might as well make up our minds now to go *en bloc* to vote for Mr Greenslade. Why not you?'

Jess and Fran caught each other's eyes, and burst out laughing. The image of Councillor Greg Taliaferro was too much for either of them.

'George Bridgefoot's too old, and Charles too young. Brian is in the right position, but . . . I think not the right man,' said Eric, seriously and a bit tentatively. 'George and Charles both have their scale of values firmly set. George's are perhaps outdated, but sound: there's still a lot of England to be kept rural. Charles wants to "get on" and go with the times, but not at the expense of losing all his rural inheritance. Brian got hold of the wrong end of the stick a little while back, and has never wholly recovered. He could still be led astray to chase money, which is sad because it applies to us all, and in any case he's no fool. But – if I may say so in confidence – I don't think he carries the same prestige as his father or his son.' He was looking towards Bob, who got the message, and nodded. He agreed absolutely with what Eric said, but would rather not voice an opinion of his daughter's father-in-law.

'So who's left?' asked Greg. 'What Eric's getting at is that our candidate should be somebody who can not only hold his own against a go-getter like Mr Greenslade, but command a bit of that old-fashioned quality called "respect" for his know-how, his knowledge of people, his presence – for himself, as it were. Somebody with his roots in rural England – best of all in Old Swithinford. That cuts out Eric, me and Bob. William's out on other grounds. Effendi? He'd know all the ropes.'

'He's a furriner, like me,' said Bob. 'Will be for the next seven year or so.'

Nigel spoke from his couch for the first time. 'Hasn't Greg just picked our candidate?' he asked. 'Somebody who commands respect and *knows the ropes*? Who better than Elyot? Sum him up: the right age; a man of the world; used to dealing with men; a commanding personality who is already a magistrate; and, back to the school issue, a man who has a young child –'

'Two,' interrupted Fran.

'Er – two what?' asked Nigel, wondering if Fran's distress earlier had temporarily thrown her off-balance. She chuckled.

'Two children,' she said. 'Beth's pregnant again.' That stopped the meeting in its tracks; but soon Nigel took up his thread again.

'All right, a man with *two* children to be educated – in their native village. *Their* village. He may call himself Franks but we know that his real name is "de ffranksbridge". His roots go back almost to the Conquest. He's our man, without a shadow of doubt.'

There was such implicit agreement that silence reigned for a minute or two, until William said, one eyebrow lifted in enquiry, 'And "who is going to bell the cat?"'

Fran, slowly and with conviction, said, 'Beth, of course. This is women's work. Leave it to us. Jess, Jane, me – and Beth.'

*   *   *

By the end of October, as days began to shorten perceptibly and blue shadows lengthened under every hedge, the unaccountable feeling of encircling gloom began to lift. The first week of November, as so often, was sunny and bright; banner-like leaves still clung to branches, cheerily waving farewell to autumn, and waiting for the first frost to bring them fluttering down. Fran, going out to look at the sky and feeling a somewhat blustery west wind blowing none too gently on her, quoted to herself:

O, Wind,
If Winter comes, can Spring be far behind?

Not for an optimistic poet, she thought; but too far for them to let winter catch them out before they addressed themselves to some important matters. If Elyot was to be persuaded to stand as their candidate, the subject had to be broached to Beth first, and as soon as possible. There was also the question of selecting a suitable school for Jonce and Stevie. Fran liked the sound of

77

the school in Fenley which Jane had heard recommended as being a bit out of the ordinary, but that was Jess and Greg's business before anybody else's, even William's. So she rang Jess, who agreed that they should waste no time, and as she could be free by about three o'clock that very afternoon, they decided on the spot to invite Jane and Beth to Benedict's for a 'chaffinching' session (their euphemism for a female-only gathering, as hen-chaffinches flock together in winter gardens).

The three already in the know put their suggestion about Elyot boldly to Beth, rather prepared for her to take the attitude of the female of the species and be deadlier than her husband in repudiating any such idea. They got a welcome surprise.

For one thing, Beth, who had once been close to giving up all hope of ever marrying and having children, was by nature one of those women who bloom during pregnancy. As far as she was concerned, life just now was as perfect as she had ever dreamed it could be, and if she had any fault to find with it at all, it was that Elyot was too much like an old hen clucking after its chickens. She had reached a point of wishing privately that he had more to think about than her condition, and more to do than fuss round her. If normal election precedents were followed, those in question would take place in May, when she would be just about at full term. She said she couldn't have wished for better; she considered having babies to be women's work – well, once the baby had been conceived – and though she was appreciating and even lapping up Elyot's care of her, when it came to actually producing the child, she'd rather be left to get on with it by herself. Hadn't she contrived to do just that when her son Ailwyn was born?

Besides, she said, Elyot was showing signs of boredom again, as he had done once before, when the novelty of ceasing to be an unmarried retired naval officer and becoming a very wealthy country gentleman (with a wife and a child he had never even expected he might want, let alone come by) had worn off. When it had begun to show itself the first time, he'd been rescued by finding their new medical man a very compatible companion, with a similarly lapsed passion for ship-modelling.

'If it hadn't been for Terry Hardy, I guess he'd have gone

back before now to having too many little pick-me-ups in private,' she said. 'I don't miss the evidence that he mixes himself a horse's neck oftener than he lets me see him do it now. Not that it worries me. He's in no danger of becoming an alcoholic. He has too much respect for himself as a man for that.

'Terry was an absolute blessing to us all, but especially to Elyot, because of the ship-modelling. It satisfied Elyot in all sorts of ways: soothed his nostalgia for his ship, and gave his memory something else other than the torpedo disaster it suffered to work on, besides providing him with male companionship and soaking up a lot of spare time when his other male friends were at work.

'But Terry has too much on his plate at present to give Elyot and the model as much time as he used to. What with supervising the growing practice and the conversion of Casablanca into the new Health Centre, keeping one eye on the restoration of the old cottage behind the DIY shop for his own eventual occupation – he's up to his neck in work as much as Bob or Eric. We three happen to be in the secret about his relationship with Anthea, but if it isn't already common knowledge in the village, there's something going wrong with the grapevine!

'He and Anthea no longer have to pretend to meet each other by accident in our house, but I'm sure everybody who sees his car outside her cottage so often must be putting two and two together. And we are so afraid of spoiling any romance that we lean over backwards to be discreet and not ask questions. But whatever the reason, Terry's defection has left Elyot with time on his hands. I should be very glad for him to have something new to think about, especially if it would satisfy his niggling conscience towards anything that could even vaguely be regarded as "duty". So I give the idea my unqualified blessing, and will do all I can to persuade him. But I can't promise anything – he's used to having his own way, and giving rather than taking orders. I guess they all still think of themselves as superior beings, when it comes to the crunch.'

'Men!' said Jess, and all four burst out laughing. They ranged in age from Fran and Jess, both past the fifty mark, through Jane, not quite forty, to Beth who was thirty-seven; but four better advertisements for marriage as an institution could hardly have been found, though a more heterogeneous sample of men than their husbands comprised could hardly have been found either: one academic historian, one up-and-coming portrait artist, one fen-tiger farmer and one career naval officer (retd).

But they had no intention of letting men override their good ideas. Having settled Elyot's future, they turned serious attention to the question of finding Jonce and Stevie a school they could feel happy about. As Fran said, they weren't really very well qualified to pronounce on state primary schools. Only Beth had ever attended such a school as a pupil – in London – just post-war, and that was nothing to go by. Jane knew most about country schools from her experience as a mother, because her son Nick had attended a primary school at Swithinford – Mary Budd's little school in Old Swithinford having been closed. But even Jane's knowledge was out-dated. At that period, Swithinford was not a new town.

'In any case, I'm no judge,' Jane said. 'Nick wasn't the product of a normal home. As Bob hinted the other night, he was "different". Put bluntly, he was an outcast – the bastard son of a girl from nowhere. If it hadn't been for Charles Bridgefoot and Robert Fairey protecting him, I just daren't think what might have happened, even among children mainly from a rural background. I had no option but to send him there, so I had to trust to luck and the intelligence I knew he'd got. I hoped that somehow he'd find his own level, and of course that's just what he's done. Bob says he doesn't know why I worried so much. Don't I know that cream will always rise to the top?'

She paused a moment before going on, thinking hers the odd man out among their four husbands. 'Bob's a sort of natural philosopher, with his fenland sixth sense to help him,' she said, 'but I notice all the same that one of his favourite country sayings is that "experience makes fools wise". Perhaps I did worry too much. So I won't presume to judge. Then there's Charlie. In spite of what Bob says, his daughter had an expensive private education just to please her mother. But can any of us find fault with Charlie? Going on my own experience with Nick, I say that in the early years it's the home and parents that matter most, and it's silly to spend good money on private education if you can get better education for nothing on your doorstep. Which brings us back to Jonce and Stevie.'

'That's exactly what William says,' Fran said, 'though he feels an obligation to do his best for Jonce. He'll leave the actual decision to Jess and Greg, of course. The trouble with William is that he looks at education today, as he does everything else, through a spy-glass of history. What he says is interesting, but not much practical help. What it shows me is a glaring example of how things planned in theory on paper aren't by any means guaranteed to work out in practice.

'As we walked home the other evening he went on talking about education. There was a movement towards a lot of social levelling, but it takes more time to achieve that than to knock down bombed slums and build new estates. They had to build new schools, but they couldn't build new children. And in any case, so many children were scarred for life by the war, the blitz, exile from home and family as evacuees, or both. Such damaged children had to be treated as individuals, like it or not, because of what they had individually endured. I can see that aspect of it. People are people. All different. So I can't help feeling that "child-centred" education had to be right then, for war-damaged children.'

Beth took that up. 'I was intending to be a teacher, before my mother died,' she said. 'I had knowledge of the newer methods: one of its leaders called it "the Creative Revolution" because it relied a lot on the arts to heal spiritual damage, as well as recognizing the arts as an instinctive and natural way of communication which often works where speech fails. As my speciality was music, it seemed ideal to me for all early education, even if the powers that were insisted on more formal methods for the secondary schools. I was absolutely delighted when the Plowden Report in 1967 so heartily endorsed it. But it's much harder work for the teachers, and there were – still are – many problems, like controversy and violent opposition from the die-hards, most of whom took the line that it was easier to "discipline" children if you had them in classes of thirty or more. Which is nonsense – philosophically and morally stupid. Discipline can't be laid on from the outside, by any method known to humanity. It has to be self-discipline first.'

'I saw the situation at first hand,' put in Jane. 'I don't see how anybody could have expected the London overspill to mix happily with children whose rural culture was so different.'

'Yes, I can see that,' said Jess. 'It's all very well to state in principle that all children are equal in the sight of God, but that doesn't make them all alike. Any educational policy that relies on treating all children as if they were so many green peas ready for a canning factory begins on the wrong premise. Besides, I think Bob's right. Experience does matter – even if you are only five.'

'The new method's still encountering a lot of opposition,' said Beth. 'But I *know* that where it's applied by teachers who understand the philosophy of it and accept that it's harder work than standing in front of a class cane in hand and shooting facts at them like hard peas from a pea-shooter, it works like a dream. But hide-bound teachers won't give it a chance. However, it does sound as if that school Jane had heard about must be run on "child-centred" lines. We ought to find out, soon.'

'You, then?' asked Jess persuasively. 'You're the only one of us who knows anything about it. How do we start? We've got to find a school for Jonce and Stevie pronto. This week, in fact.'

'I think,' said Beth, 'that either Nigel or I might manage to set up a visit, because ten to one it's still a C. of E. school, so either or both of us could pull that string. If you want me to, I'll try.' And on that hopeful note, the chaffinching party broke up.

*

It was only a matter of days before Elyot had succumbed to Beth's blandishments and was beginning to interest himself in local government. Meanwhile, a call from Nigel to the headteacher of the school Bob had identified secured an invitation for both himself and Beth to pay them a visit. As Nigel was still an invalid, Beth had to be both chauffeur and carer, and in that secondary role was able to take in a lot of the signs she knew how to read, while a well-briefed Nigel posed relevant questions.

Reporting to Eric later that same evening, and describing all he had seen and heard, Nigel remarked somewhat wistfully, 'I didn't have half the chances those children have. I only went to Eton.'

*

The problem solved and driving arrangements made, next Monday was the day on which the two little boys were to attend school for the first time. Jess asked Beth to go with her to take them, and make the necessary introductions. Stevie arrived with Hetty, dressed 'to the nines' as Sophie would have said, in new clothes sent over from America, because the one thing his mother did for her offspring was to load him with unsuitable garments he didn't need. Hetty, of course, had done what she felt to be right, but Jess thought that if anything could have picked the poor child out as being "different", his grandmother had achieved it. Stevie himself looked sulky and down in the mouth. Jess guessed that he'd been severely admonished to behave himself, and warned of dire punishments if he didn't. Jonce was a mixture of apprehension and excitement. He asked Jess over and over again if she was quite sure that 'Tollybear' (his name for Greg) would still be there when he got home again. Though nearing five, he'd changed little in appearance from the cherub Fran had found wandering lost and naked under a hedgerow on the Swithinford road a couple of years previously, except that he was taller and had lost his rotundity of belly. His face below the halo of copper-coloured curls this morning wore the puzzled little frown that had so enchanted Fran at that first meeting.

Stevie was as dark as Jonce was fair, his straight hair neatly cropped round a little bullet head. They stood silently taking comfort from each other as they waited for Beth and her car.

Greg was not in evidence. It was too much for him. As Bob's antennae were tuned to the wavelength of ancestral voices, and Fran's sharpened so that she missed no detail of any special occasion, so Greg's artistic temperament made him extra sensitive to all nuances of emotion. He'd got up that morning feeling this day to be a landmark, because Jonce was taking his first step on the journey that would eventually take him away from them.

It was all very well for him to tell himself that he was being silly, and that all parents had to face the day when they must let go of their children, and count themselves lucky that they had not been snatched away by Fate till then. He argued with his heart, as he put on his smock and set a canvas up on his easel, telling himself that he would be far unhappier today if Jonce were taking this first flutter from the nest unloved and unloving, instead of being adoring and adored. But reason stood no chance this morning. At the last minute, he crept out of his studio and looked at the little tableau as the boys were being helped into the car – and found he just couldn't take it. He rushed back into his sanctum with tears trickling down his sensitive, mobile face.

Jess had administered a travel sickness pill to Jonce, which had calmed him so that he appeared to be the happier of the two children. Greg heard the car start and drive away. Hetty was busy in the kitchen – he could hear the clattering of crockery – but there was no sound of children's voices, as there had been till now. No sound of Jonce at the piano, practising the last piece Greg had taught him to play; no demands at his door for paint and paper; no giggling and puppy fighting; no voices raised in singing the rhymes he'd taught them. He drew a huge sigh of longing to be able to peep into the school, to satisfy himself that they were not missing him as much as he was missing them.

He pricked up his ears at the sound of a car stopping at the front door and, glad of any distraction, went to open it – but Jess was inside before he got there. Panic seized him. Had Jonce reacted badly after all, and started to vomit as soon as the car moved?

Jess had come in alone and was hurriedly looking around for him. 'Ah, there you are!' she said. 'We had to turn back, because we'd forgotten something. I've got all Stevie's details from Hetty, and of course I know all about Jonce – except what name to register him by. We ought to have consulted William. What do you think?'

It was rather a poser. None of the eight children of which Jonce was one had been born in wedlock and consequently had been registered in their mother's name. But the man who had brought them up had called himself 'John Petrie', and by his name they had all been known. When he had died, the four oldest, all girls, had refused to be anything else. The next, who was a boy, had been taken by his mother, and was presumably still using her surname of Garnett. Jonce had been the oldest of her next batch, and the only one John Petrie had fathered; when dying he had requested William to see that his son's name be changed in due course to the family name he had a right to – Voss-Dering. Jess and Greg had been too old to be allowed to adopt Jonce legally, so they had never raised the issue of his taking their name. They were only his foster-parents, by William's happy consent. Jonce would have told anybody that his name was Jasper Petrie. But by what name was he now to be registered at school?

'Ring William,' Jess said.

Greg did, only to find that it was something William hadn't given a thought to either. 'Ask Jess to come round on your way back to school,' William said. 'I'll talk to Fran and I think you ought to come as well.'

'Hurry up,' Jess commanded. 'We shall be late as it is, and it won't do to get them off on the wrong foot by being *too* late.' So Greg climbed into the car just as he was, and took Jonce on to his knee. The cherubic face lost its tension and its frown as if by magic, and Greg's heart was wrung afresh. He knew by instinct that the child had been remembering another eventful journey when his daddy had been there as they set out, but not when they got back. The chance that Greg had appeared in his sight again had reassured the child. Greg made up his mind that he would go on to school with him, and leave him happy, promising to help to fetch him back at the end of the day.

William was very apologetic. He had intended to get Jonce's name legally changed by deed-poll, but thought it hadn't mattered yet. So was Jonce to go through his early years of education as Garnett, Petrie, Taliaferro, or – Voss-Dering?

Fran decided. 'What his father asked for,' she said. 'The name of his family, which Jonce has a moral right to.'

'I agree,' declared William. 'Register him as John Jasper Petrie Voss-Dering – and tell them to call him "Jonce Petrie".'

So in the event it was Greg, still wearing his clean artist's smock, who gave a hand to each little boy as they climbed out of the car outside the ugly school building. It was of Victorian design: one large room and one smaller one, with windows too high to see into – or the children to see out of. But the windows were open, and a hubbub of sound was escaping through them. Beth grinned a happy smile. 'I hear a joyful noise unto the Lord,' she said. 'I think we're in luck.'

None of them had ever seen a classroom so full of happy activity. Christmas was only a few weeks away, and Mrs Tyrrell had announced that very morning that they could now begin to think and plan for it. There was paint and paper everywhere, mostly being used on the floor. At one end of the room, a group of the oldest children was busy stringing marionettes. Greg's interest was caught by a long painted frieze that went all round the room, depicting the procession of joyous animals being released two by two from the confines of the Ark. He found loquacious children around him, all wanting to show him which pair was their contribution to the whole.

He didn't dare ask what he wanted to know: who had had the bright idea of showing the animals coming out, instead of going in; and why was there a pair of geese heading doggedly back up the gang-plank instead of going down to freedom? He caught the eye of a bright little girl of nine or so, pointed to the erring geese and raised his eloquent eyebrows in interrogation. She giggled.

'Well,' she said, 'we drew lots for the animals, and me and my friend got the geese. So we thought about it, like Mrs Tyrrell told us to.'

By this time her friend had sidled up to join in the conversation. 'And we said we kept hearing all the time how they went into the Ark, like the song says, two-by-two, but Mrs Tyrrell said she wanted us to think about what they'd feel like coming out, and how Noah would have to organize it carefully when he let them loose.'

The first little girl chimed in again. 'We said we'd been told often that geese are silly birds, so we made them look as if they were just being silly.'

Greg looked round for Mrs Tyrrell, but there was no teacher in sight, nor any sign of Jess, Beth, Jonce and Stevie. Yet all activities were going on just the same.

'Which song?' he asked the two little girls, as he sat down on the piano-stool, which was too close for him to ignore its invitation. 'This one?' And he began to play, and sing, 'The animals went in two by two, hurrah! Hurrah!'

He was found a few minutes later by Jess, Beth and the teacher, surrounded by singing children. He stopped, rose and apologized profusely to the smiling teacher. Jess had no fears – she knew his ability to charm the robin off a box of starch without even trying.

Mrs Tyrrell gave back smile for smile, and thanked him. Then, turning to the children, she said, 'And don't any of you ever again let me hear you grumbling at having to put your smocks on before you start to paint.'

It was only then that Greg remembered that he was still wearing his smock, and registered that the children who had previously been painting on the floor were all wearing cut-down old shirts, converted thereby into smocks.

Of Jonce or Stevie, no more was seen or heard. All was well. They were already entranced in a story 'Miss Amanda' was reading. Greg heard it all repeated by two excited little boys looking forward to the next day, as, true to his promise, he went with Fran to fetch them home in the afternoon. All was well on that front.

*　　*　　*

Sophie was out and about again, taking walks which included visits to Dan, Aunt Sar'anne at Mary Budd Close, and Benedict's. She managed to be at Benedict's so that she could get Fran and William their morning coffee, and, of course, partake of it with them, daintily holding her cup like a Victorian lady out to afternoon tea. Fran picked up that this was a delicate hint of her changed status in the Burbage household: she was no less 'their' Sophie, but she was preparing to be rather more than their domestic help when Olive 'Opkins should also be there 'to do the rough' under her supervision.

William was quick to recognize the remnants of the hierarchy of degrees, which both Sophie and Olive understood. Sophie had been notched up a step, and was practising for Olive's entrance on the scene, planned for next week.

Fran, with William's help, had that particular morning done the necessary chores that Sophie's absence left undone, and had subsided at the kitchen table waiting for William to make coffee, long before Sophie arrived.

'What was it that you were going to tell me the other evening when we had to leave to go to Monastery Farm?' he asked Fran. 'We were talking about Cromwell.'

Fran searched her memory. There were so many things that it could have been, but she had been trying hard to keep her resolution not to badger him. As long as Bob found time for him, she tried not to interfere till asked. But her slight irritation with him was still there, partly because she had no work with which to occupy herself.

As far as she could recall, all that had been produced so far was William's typed list of matters still to be researched. She knew, from long experience, that the best cure for any sort of block in the creative process was just to begin, ready or not; in the words of the cliché: 'to take the plunge'. It might not be a very happy experience, but then neither was standing dithering on the brink. Yet that's what William was still doing. Nobody so far had succeeded in making him jump in. But if and when he did ask her anything, she did her best to act as his sounding board without pushing him further. He had been saying that he must research the whole question of land tenure. He'd probably been doing that – inside out, upside down, and back to front, while as far as she in her impatience could make out, all he really needed to know was under what conditions Cromwell had farmed at Ely.

There were times when she wished she didn't love him so much. This morning was one of them. The desire to lash him into action with her tongue was strong, but it died as he looked up at her and read her thoughts. So close were they in spirit that they had always been able to do that, and neither passing years, nor having achieved, at last, legal marital status, nor even the fact William was now at home, all day and every day, 'under her feet' in the house, had had any effect on their togetherness at all.

'Don't say it,' he said, giving her a smile so warm and loving that she almost felt it melting her irritation as it went down to reach her heart, as linctus soothes the bronchial tubes. He reached both hands out across the table to her, and she laid hers into them. Then he got up and went round the table to her, pulling her up out of her chair so that he could put his arms round her. She tucked hers under his jacket, as she had always done, and laid her head on his chest.

Suddenly she remembered. 'I know!' she said triumphantly. 'But it's really only another question, something allied to what you'd said. We'd just agreed that one of your stumbling-blocks is that all the history you know gets in the way. That is unusual – I've been reading historical novels since my schooldays, but for the life of me I can't remember one written by someone who'd been an academic historian first. Can you?'

He sat down again, and they rummaged through their accumulated memories of historical novels. They knew of archaeologists who wrote detective novels; classical scholars who wrote whodunnits set in classical times; modern amateurs who wrote good fiction set in other periods, stories lit by their love of history and illuminated by their imagination. The result was good reading, but not always true to history. Sir Walter Scott, who had set the fashion, was a prime example.

'I think you may have hit the bull's-eye,' William said, ruefully. 'We've set our hearts on me performing what appears to be an impossible task. Perhaps I've known that subconsciously all the time. Would it be wise to admit defeat, and give up? Only fools attempt the impossible.'

Her face crumpled with disappointment. She had tried urging, persuading, flattering, railing at him. Nothing had worked. Yet she also knew that disappointed as she was, he was more so. He felt that he had been selected by Calliope herself as the one to do justice to that precious old manuscript, but above all else he wanted to write the story for her sake. He had said so – but only he yet knew the special reason why.

She was fighting back tears, but to agree with him would be defeat indeed. She reached her hands across the table to him, and made him look at her.

'Darling,' she said. 'No. Not yet. As Browning said, *"a man's reach should exceed his grasp, Or what's a heaven for?"'*

She saw the shaft go home, and he squeezed her hands as he straightened up. 'You win,' he said. 'Let's go back to Cromwell for a moment. His character puzzles me, yet on his personality one of the most important events in all our history hung. Voltaire said of him that he ruled England with a Bible in one hand and a sword in the other, and that he combined all the crimes of a usurper with all the qualities of a great king.

'But Voltaire said so *after he was dead*, when he'd been Lord Protector of England and had somehow managed to put England back on the map. After he had reached the very acme of power. What puzzles me is how he ever achieved such power. A man given by nature to violent swings of mood to the very end of his life. A man who, though born into the gentry, had to climb to those dizzy heights from a lower place on the social scale. I go round and round that point, wondering what chance, what conditions of time and place, what his personality and what his powerful relatives had to do with it. John Hampden was a relative, and so were several others who first defied the king. Incidentally, your reverend ancestor knew him personally when both were young, though Cromwell was eleven years the elder. Ask yourself what would have happened to the man Jonce will one day be, but for the chance of you finding him? Or Stevie if he'd been left only to his pop-star mother's tender mercy? I promise you, sweetheart, that sooner or later I'll stretch my reach to grasp my pen. Or at least my glorious new typewriter.'

She went to him again to kiss and be kissed, and so Sophie found them. Over Fran's shoulder, William caught the slight grimace of disapproval on Sophie's face.

'Hello, Sophie,' he said, deliberately not letting go of Fran. 'What's the matter?'

She turned to put the kettle on again. 'I were only just a-thinking as it's all right for me to see you be'aving like a couple o' them film-stars as we 'ear so much about on telly, 'cos I'm used to it b'now, though I do hev to say that I ain't caught you at it quite so much just lately. But what Olive'll make of it do you be'ave like that in front of 'er, I don't care to think. I'm said it afore and I'll say it again – she don't mean no 'arm by it, but it's as if 'er 'ead is so empty she's got to fill it up, like, with the sound of 'er own voice. And what she says often don't make no sense – though it's got worse as she's got older. I'm just warning you, like, not to put things into 'er 'ead as she can spluther out to other folks to make what they like of. She don't set out to make mischief, do Miss wouldn't ha' put up with 'er as 'er daily 'elp as long as she did.

'When we was children, Miss used to make us write out a proverb every morning to practise our 'andwriting, like, and she'd explain 'em to us so we didn't forget 'em. "Empty vessels make the most sound." That's Olive all over, if you see what I mean, and if Miss was alive to 'ear me say it, she'd agree. But what I mean is that such as Olive ain't used to seeing married men over fifty a-kissing their wives in public.'

She sat down with the coffee William had poured for her, his eye on Fran lest she reacted in any way. She was, as he had guessed she would be, struggling not to laugh.

'We'll do our best, and try to behave,' William assured Sophie solemnly. 'Tell us what else is new.'

It was the suggestion Sophie had been hoping for, because she did have a bit of news in her budget. Her self-imposed rule about not repeating gossip, the details of which she wasn't sure of, forbade her to bring the subject up, but if anybody asked her direct, it allowed her to answer.

'I'm been to see Dan'el,' she said. 'And 'e ain't 'appy about them at the Old Glebe. As you know, there ain't much as George don't tell Dan'el, but this last lot Dan can't make out. Y'see, 'e knows about it being George and Molly's Golden Wedding at the start o' December. It ain't like them not to want a do for it. Me and Dan talked it over, to see if we could think why not. Dan said 'e reckoned it must be 'cos Rosemary ain't got over that accident, and Marge is wearing 'erself to skin and bone going from place to place looking after the Rector and Rosemary as well as 'er Mam and Dad. But some'ow it don't make no sense to me and Dan. Lucy and 'er 'usband could ha' set it up for 'em, or young Charles and 'is wife – she comes 'ome every weekend. Do, they could hev it like they did for George's birthday, at the 'otel. But then we wondered if it was all to do with them twins o' Marge's – Poppy being away at college and not thinking about nothing nor nobody, only marrying young Nick 'Adley soon as ever she can, and Pansy as 'as never been 'ome since she went off with that young Bailey. They don't even know where she is, and nobody's seen 'ide nor 'air of 'er since last Easter. Dan's as sure as sure can be that it's her at the bottom of it all. What do you reckon?'

'That you're probably right,' said William.

'And I'm glad you've mentioned it,' added Fran. 'We must remember to send cards and flowers for Molly, on the day.'

Sophie had done her duty, and was satisfied. But there was more to be said. 'Dan says George let on that Molly told 'im she'd rather 'e spent money on heving the old 'ouse done up than a party as all their children couldn't be at, and Dr Hardy 'as got one o' his patients as is a decorator to goo and do it for 'em. A chap as none of us knows as comes from Yorkshire. Dan says 'e's a nice fellow – can't do no wrong for Molly, seems. He calls 'er "Gran" to 'er face and George just agrees that whatever he suggests and Molly wants, that's what'll be done. I only 'ope 'e's as honest as Dan says 'e looks and seems to be. But it don't seem right for an old couple like that to put such faith in a furriner. Still, Dan'll be there to keep 'is eye on 'im.'

'And so, I suppose, will Marjorie,' said William.

There was something about the way Sophie set her lips and didn't answer that irritated Fran. She decided that it was time she broke up this nearly-gossip session, and as it was a fine morning, take a walk herself as far as the Old Glebe.

William said that he wanted to see Effendi, so what about lunch? Fran said it might be a good idea for him to take the car, pick her up at the Old Glebe, and for them to go on to the hotel for a snack lunch. He agreed, so she set out on foot.

*

Fran met George outside the door of the Old Glebe, in his shirt sleeves, trying to look busy. He was as fond of her as she of him, and their relationship now had a definite aura of 'family belonging' about it. He greeted her with delight, and flung back the huge heavy oak door for her.

'Come in, my gel, come in,' he said, giving her a bear-hug and a spanking kiss. Then he raised his voice to send it round twists and turns to wherever in the ancient house Molly might be. 'Mother! Mother! Where are you? Here's Fran.

'We're in a bit of a mess,' he apologized. 'As you'll see, we're having a lot of alterations and spring-cleaning done, even if it ain't spring.'

Fran looked at him with mock severity. 'I hope that doesn't mean that "Father's papering the parlour",' she said. 'Or Molly, either. Neither of you ought to be going up and down ladders, however much you enjoy it.'

She stood a moment looking round, taking in at a glance how much the large farmhouse kitchen had been updated without losing its character. All had been redesigned to make life easier and more comfortable for an ageing couple.

George was still holding the door but had let it swing backwards on its hinges, obscuring the wall behind it. It was from there that Molly's raised voice answered him.

'Ask her in, then, and shut the door, you great numbskull. You've got me and Yorky trapped.'

George shut the door, and revealed Molly holding the great old longcase clock steady against the wall, while Yorky, standing on a stool, was pinned tight against the clock's brass works, the head of the clock having been lifted off to stand on the floor. He had in one hand a large-sized hammer, and in the other a wooden peg.

'I can't leave go, Fran my duck,' said Molly, ''cos Yorky had

93

just got the old clock level when Father flung the door open. Sit down while we get the job finished. George, put the kettle on.'

'Don't do nowt o't'sort, Boss. It'll mebbe tek me all o' two minutes t'finish job, if Gran can hold on till then. Ah'm tea-mekker in this house while I'm 'ere – or coffee, if it's coffee tha wants.'

Fran looked up into the stranger's face, and was given a wide smile in return for her own. 'What *are* you doing?' she asked.

'Well, see tha, Gran told me as never since day as they moved here as t'clock ever told 'em right time. No wonder – there's nowhere on t'floor it can stand level! Clocks like this were never expected to stand level on floors, 'cos there was no way they could. That's why they've got hole in t'back – so as they could hang on't wall to keep 'em level. But t'peg had broke, and I were joost about to put a new 'un through t'hole in't clock and hammer it in't wall by t'one as I'd drilled when Boss opened door to you and caught us.'

He banged expertly for a couple of minutes, and then said, 'All right, Gran. Tha can let go now. That peg as t'Boss found me were just perfect.'

Molly came out happily and greeted Fran. The clock's head was carefully adjusted, the long ropes manipulated, and the huge, misshapen lead weight brought up as high as it would go. Then Yorky set the brass pendulum swinging, and adjusted the bell to strike the right hour next time. The bottom of the clock's case appeared to be standing, and was indeed taking some of the weight, but the rest hung from the peg like a plumbline. The pendulum swung with slow, majestic deliberation as they stood round and listened to the balance of its tick and its tock. Yorky stood back, beaming on Molly, and said, 'There you go, Gran.'

'Will that spalt-peg be strong enough to hold it?' George asked. 'It's all I could find in a hurry.'

'Might ha' been made for t'job, though Ah'm never 'eard o' whatever you called it afore.'

'It don't matter what it's called, as far as I know,' George answered, gazing at the old clock with satisfaction, 'so long as it's done its job. When I stand here afore going to bed every night I all'us think of all them other Bridgefoots as have done exactly what I've been doing. I'm the eighth generation, father to son, Brian'll be nine, and Charles ten, and there may even be another in view before I have to hand the job over. So there you are. That old clock knows more about Bridgefoot history than I do. And as to that spalt-peg: there won't be many left in another ten year as could tell you what it is. Spalt-pegs is what we used for thatching the tops o' corn-stacks to keep the rain out till it was our turn to have the steam threshing tackle afore such things as combine-harvesters was ever thought of.'

Fran's ears were wide open, storing it up for William. As George had said, it was another bit of history. Besides, she never missed picking up an East-Anglian dialect or outdated term if she could help it.

She looked at the Yorkshireman whom she found returning her scrutiny appraisingly and approvingly. She put out her hand, taking the initiative, and was given another warm, twinkling smile as well as his hand in return. 'I've heard about you from our doctor,' she said. 'But I'm afraid I don't remember your name.'

'John Postlethwaite,' he said. 'But everybody calls me "Yorky", and that suits me fine.'

George remembered his manners. 'This is Mrs Burbage from Benedict's House,' he said.

'Aye, I could ha' told thee that,' Yorky replied. 'So now, pet,' he said, turning back to her, 'if tha'll tell me whether tha wants tea or coffee, I'll go and mek it for thee.'

He went into the large pantry that opened directly off the kitchen, and Molly whispered to Fran what a treasure he was. 'He's the sort of workman you don't often find nowadays – takes his time and makes a wonderful job of whatever he does. However, I hope you didn't mind him calling you pet – I think it means he's took to you. He calls Marge "pet" all the time.' She raised her voice and sent it into the pantry. 'Yorky! Make another cup of coffee, please. Here's William, Fran's husband coming.'

The tea and the coffee came in with a plate of Molly's home-made biscuits, and when he had been introduced to William, Yorky sat down next to him; before five minutes had passed they were deep in conversation. Yorky showed no sign of wanting to disturb the gathering so he could get on. Time passed in pleasurable comfort, and Marge arrived to join them.

William rose by habit as she entered, but Yorky beat him to it in finding her a chair. 'Sit down, pet,' he said. 'Tha looks ready to drop.'

They could see he was right; Marge was very pale and drooping with weariness. George looked hard at her, but asked no questions.

'Don't fuss, Dad,' she said, smiling wanly. 'I didn't get much sleep last night, that's all.'

'Have a good strong cup of coffee, pet,' said Yorky, going to fetch one for her.

'And give her a drop of brandy, Father,' ordered Molly.

'We'll get out of your way,' said William. 'We're going to the hotel for a snack.'

'Stop here and have a bite with us, do,' said Molly. 'Marge will, won't you, my duck? You don't have to get anybody else's lunch, do you? It'll only mean me doing a few more potatoes.' She paused, disconcerted. 'Only . . . I don't know whether what I've got for our dockey's fit for visitors! I spoke without thinking.' Molly actually blushed, at which William, quick on the uptake of her use of 'dockey', accepted her offer on the spot.

'I haven't had a real dockey since Sophie's mother gave us what she'd cooked for herself and her children when Grandfather had visitors at his table and we had to have ours in the kitchen with Kezia,' he said. 'We liked it a lot better than what they were having in the dining-room. So tell us what it is and please let us share it – if you're sure there'll be enough to go round.'

Molly was, as Sophie would have said, 'in a real puggatery'. William and Fran had eaten at the Old Glebe many times before, but only as guests who were expected and specially catered for.

'Come on, Mam, you asked 'em to stop. What's cooking that you're ashamed of?' There was a touch of asperity in Marjorie's voice that surprised Fran.

'One of your dad's favourites – just an old-fashioned onion dumpling with a suet crust. It's simmering on top of the Rayburn as we've had put in to what used to be the scullery,' she explained to Fran and William.

'Sounds lovely,' said William. 'Kezia used to make them for us. My mouth's watering already.'

'But I haven't got anything for pudding,' Molly said. 'You don't want a lot after a suet crust, but there's still time for me to throw a bread-and-butter pudding together. You see, Yorky was working in the scullery, doing the ceiling, but while Father was out o' the way he come down to see to the clock. It was so good to see you two, I forgot what sort of a muddle we were in.'

She still looked ready to cry with vexation. Fran indicated to William with her eyebrows that perhaps after all it would be wise for them to remember an imaginary appointment somewhere else. But Yorky, looking on with concern at the droop of Marjorie's head, and the worry in George's face, intercepted the look, and as good as told them to stay where they were.

'Now, Gran,' he said soothingly, 'ceiling can wait, but it looks t'me as if a good meal's just what Marge wants. How long is it since tha had a proper meal, pet? Sit tha down, all o' thee. A few more spuds and carrots? I niver 'eard such a to-do about a bit o' coooking since Adam left Doombarton! And as for dessert – what about apple amber and ice-cream wi' butterscotch sauce? Ah weren't prize-winning chef in Yorkshire once for nowt. Coom wi' me, Gran, and show me where things are, and then leave it t'me. I'll let tha know when tha canst set table.'

He shepherded Molly into the back regions, and left the others silent with surprise, till Fran began to laugh.

'Well, I'll be sugared!' exclaimed George, looking as astounded as he felt. Marge joined Fran in her laughter, her face lighting up.

'He really is what Mam calls him: a treasure,' she said. 'I'm beginning to wonder what we ever did without him. Has he had any of the panic attacks Dr Hardy warned us about yet?'

George sobered. 'Yes. Once or twice he's had to knock off work and go home, and sometimes hasn't turned up when he has promised. I asked him why, 'cos we were expecting him. He said there's no telling when or where the fits o' panic will hit him – he was on his way but when he got to the end o' the road he just couldn't come no further. Went round and round the village till at last he turned tail and went home to bed.'

'Poor chap!' Marge said. 'It's funny, because he has just the opposite effect on me. Cheers me up, and stops me from worrying.'

Her father looked keenly at her across the table. 'So while your mother's out of the way, why don't you tell us what's the matter now? Is it Rosy again?'

She nodded, holding back tears. 'I had to get Dr Hardy back to her last night,' she said. 'She was in such terrible pain, and there was nothing Brian or I could do to help. He gave her an injection, but it didn't work. I had to let Brian get a bit of sleep as he'd got to work this morning, but I didn't get any. We got the doctor back as soon as he could leave the surgery, and he's given her a stronger dose now, so she is asleep, and Bri says he'll stop with her till I get back. But the doctor says he must insist on her going into hospital for more X-rays and tests. He's fixing it up as soon as he can.'

At this precise moment, Daniel Bates appeared at the door and asked if George could go to help him with one of the cows that had torn her bag on a bit of barbed wire. George put on his cap and went, telling them he'd be back in ten minutes.

'Good!' said Marjorie. 'Now I can tell you. The doctor's worried about Rosy but she won't listen to him. That's because there's less than ten days to Mam and Dad's Golden Wedding day, and none of us want it to go by without a family get-together. As things are, there's no chance of a party.'

Her face twisted, but she went on calmly and firmly. 'Eric would have arranged a family dinner at the hotel, or even have sent a meal ready-cooked down here, but we all knew what Mam and Dad would want if they couldn't have a real 'do': just all of us here, together. Rosy says she'll be here if we have to bring her on a stretcher. When we thought she'd be better by then, we'd arranged that she and I would come and cook a family meal for all the rest in Mam's new kitchen. Lucy and Alex and Georgina will stay at the hotel. If we can keep the secret, I'll still come and do all the meal, or do it at home and bring it up here to finish off. But even so, we shan't all be here – even if Rosy can come.'

She put her head in her hands, and covered her face. 'O dear!' she said. 'If only I wasn't so tired. I can't think properly. I don't mind sitting up with Rosy – in fact, it's better to be doing something than lying in bed worrying. Dad and Mam haven't mentioned their Golden Wedding for my sake. We shall all be here, except Pansy. But I don't even know where she is.'

'Ssh!' warned William. 'Here's your dad, and I think we're going to be told that dockey's ready at any minute. Couldn't you go home for an hour or two's rest this afternoon if we stand in? Fran could go to Temperance and be with Rosemary, if it's really necessary, while I hold the fort looking after Nigel if Eric's at work. I could help Nigel as well as Eric could, or you. Come on, be a good girl and be sensible.'

Marjorie dried her eyes, hastily powdered her nose and said, 'Thanks, Dr Burbage, but I shall manage,' and she got up to set the kitchen table for their meal. Fran helped her, uneasy at something in her manner. She couldn't pin her own unease down, and decided that she was letting the whole unhappy situation of the Bridgefoots get under her skin. Fond as she was of them, there was no sense in that.

Marjorie did her best to eat the delicious meal Yorky served up. George and Molly accepted her explanation that she was too tired to eat much, but Yorky was not deceived.

'Go home to bed, pet,' he said, 'as William suggested. I shan't start decorating again today. Leave it all to me. I'll clear up and wash up, and see that Gran puts her feet up. And I'll come early in't morning, in case I'm wanted,' he added. 'Just take tha mind off things here, pet. I'll look after 'em for thee.'

He said goodbye to them, saw Marjorie to her car, and watched both cars out of the gate. William and Fran drove behind Marjorie to Monastery Farm, where Fran went in with her to make sure she went to lie down, promising she should be roused in time to be back at Temperance within two hours.

William went to the other part of the house, to wait, or do what he could for Nigel. He was glad to be able to talk to Nigel unhampered. He told him that it was plain Dr Hardy had grave doubts about Rosemary, and suspected that he was withholding the whole truth of his fears even from Marjorie. He asked if Eric and Nigel had been told anything more in confidence. Eric especially, as he was so close to Marjorie.

Nigel said he doubted it. Eric was exceedingly busy with plans for the hotel's Christmas season, but neither of them had seen Marjorie to talk to for the last two weeks. She came and went in the middle of the day to do what she could for them when Eric was at work, and by the time he got home she'd gone back to Temperance. Eric was, in any case, giving a lot of time just now to Elyot.

Fran came in and reported that Marjorie had 'gone out like a light', and was fast asleep. She'd confessed that it was the first time for ages she'd felt able to sleep – she felt safe leaving her mother and father in Yorky's care. And she'd added, Fran reported, a bit dubiously, ' "*I* feel safe when he's about, too." '

Nigel looked surprised, but William said she was probably so worn out she hardly knew what she was saying.

'She's under some sort of stress we don't know of, I think,' said Fran. 'She's not acting like the Marjorie we know.'

'I noticed a difference in her,' William said, 'but I put it down to tiredness. It was as if Yorky being there had some sort of strange influence on her. As if she'd teamed up with him against the rest of us. She seemed to want to distance herself from us in front of him. She called me "Professor" instead of "William", and even addressed you as "Mrs Burbage". She never alluded to Terry as anything but "Dr Hardy" either, yet she's been on Christian name terms with us for ages. It seemed today as if she was intent on making a "them and us" sort of distinction.'

'What absolute nonsense,' Fran exploded. 'I guess all she was doing was trying to keep a rather ebullient Yorkshireman in his place.'

'If so, she's not as bright as I give her credit for,' William said. 'He doesn't claim any sort of "place". Like water, he finds his own level according to where he is and who happens to be there. I thought Marjorie was laying claim to him as her ally, one that she's conscious of needing just at present. If I dare use historical terms, I should say she was making it clear to us that, Bridgefoot by birth, she's nearer to his "degree" in the social hierarchy than ours. She wanted him, not us, to understand that.'

'Well, perhaps, but if she's downgrading herself to suit him, it isn't because of any shortcoming in herself. She's as proud as every other Bridgefoot! I'm afraid she may be feeling bad about Pansy not being in evidence to take her rightful place beside Charles and Charlie and young Georgina. Feeling guilty that she's letting the side down. She didn't want any reference made to Pansy in front of Yorky – I noticed that. But why on earth should it matter to her what he thinks? Is Eric neglecting her just when she needs him most?'

Nigel looked pained, and intervened, for him rather stiffly and with a hint of reproof in his tone. 'My dear Fran, have you any idea what you are suggesting? It's quite unthinkable. The relationship between Marjorie and Eric is what it has always been, ideal for both. She has no use for any man other than as a friend, which he is, and vice versa. They have made that absolutely clear to each other. Don't start creating dramas about your friends. They're not fictional characters for you to manipulate. Once you let loose your creative urge on us, I shall find myself married off to the first widow it's my duty to pay a consolation visit to. Truly, Fran dear, I mean it. It could be dangerous.'

Fran looked affronted, and William, with an apologetic smile at his wife, did his best to restore amity. 'She can't help it, you know,' he said. 'She's an incurable romantic at heart, and loves match-making.'

'Well, look who's talking,' Fran rejoined indignantly. 'Beth and Elyot, Bob and Jane, Roland and Monica – to say nothing of a certain Mrs Frances Catherwood and Dr William Burbage. Come on, Professor, let me take you home and put your nose down to some work. I think it's your mind that needs occupation.'

'Sorry, Mrs Burbage, but I'm on duty here. Didn't you hear me promise Marjorie I'd hold the fort and see that she got back to Temperance and Rosemary on time?'

'No need,' said Nigel. 'Terry gave me leave to start walking on my leg again this morning. I'll take over. Off you go home.'

So William and Fran went back home – thankfully. They had a lot to talk about.

*

The afternoon was drawing in, and the sight of the fire Ned had lit blazing cheerily in their sitting-room welcomed them. So after a leisurely cup of tea, they began to review the day.

Fran asked William what news there was on the Effendi front. He'd gone to see Effendi with a purpose in mind: to suggest that a typist work for both of them part-time, thereby making it as near to a full-time job as possible. Effendi was all for it. It could mean securing the services of a more efficient typist-cum-secretary.

'The snag is that we can't begin to look for one till Effendi knows what Terry's plans are. He won't offer the surgery end of his house as a bait to a secretary if there's any chance of Terry wanting to keep it. Not that another month or two will make any difference to me at this point. I'm nowhere near to wanting a typist yet. And it's no use you looking at me like that, my darling. I simply can't start writing till I know what I'm doing – and so far I'm not sure. There's plenty of time.'

Fran controlled her niggling irritation with him as well as she could. So he had found yet another plank to cling to before he had to strike out and begin to swim! Her silence told him what she was feeling, but he decided not to pursue it.

'I needed to see Bob, but when I rang Jane said he was really too busy to give me any time this week – he's afraid the weather will break before he gets the fen farm drilled. But he left a message for me, suggesting a practical and pleasurable outing. He thinks that if, as he put it, "the water does come up", I ought to go and see it, and experience "the feel of the fen" in water-logged conditions. By which he means as near as I can ever get to knowing what it would have been like before the Duke of Bedford's scheme for draining the fens was completed. He suggested we should walk some of the main watercourses, while he explained how they were used up until 1934. I should love to do that, even if there were no ulterior motive.'

Fran agreed that it was a splendid idea. William mused a while before going on.

'It's part of what's causing my shilly-shallying,' he said. 'Any novelist worth his salt can get himself *au fait* with what he needs for the plot, but the *dramatis personae* have to become real in his imagination before he can see why they act or react as they do. He has to be able to get right into the minds of his characters, get under their skins, see what they see, hear what they hear, feel what they feel, almost know them well enough to think like them. And that's an even bigger task for an historical novelist than for his contemporary counterpart. I haven't quite got there yet.'

'Why do you say "he"? All good novelists aren't male. Writing novels was considered a woman's craft before it ever became a man's, I believe,' was Fran's reply.

He grinned. 'Sorry,' he said. 'It's habit. In our day we were taught grammar, and didn't get away with solecisms on the grounds that they are what is now called "common usage". The rule we were taught at school was that "the male embraces the female". I rather like the idea of sticking to that.'

'Go on,' she said. 'Don't sidetrack yourself.'

'Well, all I was really saying was that I have to find exactly the right historical voice, especially because . . .'

'Because of what?'

'It's really the last great hurdle, darling, a decision I must soon make. I'm not quite ready to tell you yet, but I will as soon as ever I'm sure what I'm doing. The fellow who wrote that manuscript was like you, writing just came naturally to him. I'm fascinated by his story, and want to do him justice, but that's what I can't trust myself to do – yet. Be patient with me just a little longer.'

So she changed the subject, and told him instead about the incident of the grandfather clock. 'When George said how he stood in front of it every night to wind it up, and thought of the seven generations of Bridgefoots before him who had done exactly the same thing, he sent shivers down my spine. He went on to say how satisfying it was for him to know that there was first Brian and then Charles to do it after him. And that if he was very lucky, he might even live to see another generation – the eleventh – to carry it on. And then he added, "That's history".

'I wish you'd been there, because you'd have felt as I did. I could see what it meant to George, who in his way was making the same point as T. S. Eliot about his feelings for Burnt Norton and East Coker and Little Gidding. Every little detail of the time and place adds up to what history is. As Eliot said, "now" is part of history.'

She let it sink in, and knew that William had been moved by her story. When he spoke again, he had made a leap of association with it.

'That's perhaps the underlying cause of Marjorie's distress, although she may not know it. The history of Old Swithinford's made up of the past experience of families like the Bridgefoots, within the larger scope of regional or national events. In their particular instance, an old clock is keeping it safe, like cremation urns have preserved old bones from time immemorial. Even Elyot Franks hasn't got such a solid, tangible container full of his family's long history as that old clock is of the Bridgefoots'. Everything he might have had of that kind was either burnt in the fire that destroyed his ancestral home, or lost in fusty old lawyers' boxes. But you do have a kind of "family chest", in Bob's old manuscript. If only I'm capable of digging what's in it out for you! Then it can be passed to Roland, and young William, and goodness knows how many generations after that. Holding Wagstaffe history together as long as the line lasts. That's the danger! Suppose Marjorie had been George's only child! The line – the direct thread of Bridgefoot history – would have been near to breaking-point now. It would have been up to Pansy or Poppy to keep it going, and Pansy wouldn't have been a very safe custodian. Poppy might have been better, but her duty now is to keep the Hadley-Gordon line going. There's no one else but Nick who can. I'll bet George has always seen Brian as a weak link in the chain, because Brian hasn't inherited much feeling for his family. But he has had the luck to marry Rosemary, and she's taken it over, caring for it more than he does, so that it has come to Charles still strong. What if *he* fails, as he once so nearly did when all he wanted was to die because he thought he'd lost Charlie for ever? I hope she'll prove herself a good custodian by producing a whole raft of young

Bridgefoots – heirs and spares. That's continuity, and that's history – the intertwining of past, present and future.'

'You're almost quoting T. S. Eliot, if not exactly in his words. But as far as I know, it had no personal application to him. I don't think he had any sons to follow him.'

'I'm in the same boat. My line stops with me. I can't really look backwards because I don't know much at first hand, nor forward – except through you. But sharing everything else with you gives me a half-share in the future. Greg has a tiny share-holding too, because of Jonce. I like the thought that both Greg and I will contribute something to Old Swithinford's future.'

He got up to fetch them a drink and to break the tension before it became too emotional and too personal. 'By the way,' he said, as he came back, 'did you know that the difficulty of chauffeuring Jonce and Stevie to school has been neatly solved? Greg has appointed himself chauffeur-in-chief, as well as pianist and scene-painter and producer of the school's Christmas concert. Up to his neck in it, and loving every minute. That's a turn-up for the books nobody could have foreseen.'

*   *   *

It was nothing unusual for Fran to wake before it was light, and simply lie contentedly thinking till William roused and went to get her a cup of tea. She never minded these musing sessions – in fact, she did most of her best creative work in them. She arranged plots, and listened to her fictional characters giving voice (it never failed to surprise her how valuable to any writer a 'mind's ear' is, as well as a 'mind's eye'). Quite often, by the time she got up and dressed, she had constructed in her mind what would, by tea-time, be set down in typescript. But – by chance as well as her own decision to take a bit of a break – she had no work on hand, and consequently nothing much on that front to engage her interest this morning.

It was a strange and none-too-comfortable prospect for her. She'd said she was content to be a housewife for a while. What on earth could she have been thinking of? She'd never tried it before. In fact, when it came to the crunch, she had to admit that she wasn't at all fond of housework, especially when it depended on her to do it. She'd begun to miss Sophie and her devotion to everything pertaining to the smooth running of Benedict's more than she cared to admit. She'd become accustomed to leaving everything to Sophie, including catering and cooking. All that was required of her in the normal course of events was to agree – or not – to Sophie's suggestions, and perform small housewifely 'duties' such as making the occasional drinks and washing up afterwards when Sophie wasn't present.

The truth was that she wasn't, and never had been, primarily a housewife, though she loved her particular, special house. It was so much more than a house; it was a home. 'Home' was concerned with people, and 'house' with the care of rooms and chattels. The house and chattels of Benedict's were very dear to her, and she appreciated the care Sophie lavished on them, but her own first interest, as well as her first concern, was for the people whose home it was.

Yes, she had missed Sophie more than she had thought she would, and by no means all because of what Sophie did to keep Benedict's running on oiled wheels. She'd had to cope now for almost a month without her, and didn't deny herself the pleasure of anticipating the return of her stalwart help, plus the unknown quantity of Olive, next Monday morning. Olive might prove a mixed blessing, but the prospect of getting to know her was, to Fran, rather titillating.

But she would have time on her hands. Something she had not had for . . . she truly couldn't remember the last time! So what was she going to do with it? She scanned the future horizon. Well, there were still her friends, and always William.

No, that wasn't so. It was true that for the past two years or so he had been at liberty to follow her every whim and desire, but it wouldn't necessarily be so in the future. She began on a nostalgic train of thought that ended in a slightly dangerous mood of melancholy, which she attempted to shake off by applying a good dash of common sense.

William. He'd changed her life, and she'd changed his, but she had too much sense not to see that both had to go on adjusting to more changes, not only because time and circumstance had shaken them down into a different sort of relationship, but also because nobody with a grain of sense could suppose that the rest of their lives was going to be one long perpetual honeymoon. Sophie's slight breakdown had perhaps heralded an inevitable break in the previous pattern of their daily life.

To please herself, she had decided that she'd had enough of being tied to her typewriter with deadlines rushing up on her. She'd wanted to feel free for a while, but at the very same time it was she who had made up her mind that William shouldn't be! He was now the one who was going to be tied to his study – if he ever started – so that he wouldn't be at her every beck and call as he had been.

She couldn't in all honesty go on nagging him to get on with his novel, as she had done lately, and still expect him to provide her with constant companionship and an escort whenever it suited her. And if that applied to William, was she also taking too much for granted with regard to her friends? There was no certainty that just because she had time on her hands, her friends would be equally free of obligations.

Jess had more than a full-time job, especially while the hotel was gearing up for Christmas; Greg was busy, even without his new interest in Fenley School's Christmas activities; Beth was having another baby. That was something she could share, because she would always be welcome at the Old Rectory, but with Elyot about to enter local politics, Beth might find her time otherwise committed.

Jane? Of course, there was always calm, dependable Jane. But even there Fran met a small demur, because she knew that there were things afoot with Effendi and Nick that were absorbing a lot of the small amount of time Jane could call her own after making a home out of that large and extraordinary house, and giving so much out of herself to Jade and Aggie. In contrast to herself, Jane seemed to delight in being a housewife. Fran looked backwards across their very different earlier lives, and couldn't wonder any more about Jane than she could about Beth. She must be careful not to intrude too much on either of them, both now so happy to be wives and mothers when for very different reasons each had given up the hope or expectation most other young women have.

She turned over on to her back, put her hands behind her head and stared at the ceiling, scanning briefly the years behind her. Never a very sensible thing to do, to look back on a past you couldn't alter, and certainly not when you were already feeling a bit blue. Yet she felt compelled, this morning, to follow that path.

She'd gone straight from university into marriage and work. That was in 1935, when from Whitehall war-clouds were already to be seen on the horizon, and only too visible wherever you looked in East Anglia's flat fields, so suitable for the building of aerodromes, as they were then called.

She'd got engaged to a fellow graduate heading for the Civil Service, while she had accepted a job with a publisher in London. Her fiancé's parents lived in Leeds, where his father, none too robust in health, was heading for retirement. It made sense for them to marry at once, go north and share his parents' large house, so that his obligations to both wife and parents were together under the same roof. Besides saving money, it meant he wouldn't have to share his free time between them, and could save travelling time.

Fran's own parents, abroad, had not been consulted, and – she was filled with anguished regret at the thought now – Grandfather had never asked nor expected to be. He'd done everything he could to set them out on their own feet, and was content that they should do so. So she had married Brian Catherwood with no fuss in a register office, secured another job in Leeds, and before she'd had time to think, or so it seemed now as she looked back on it, she'd had two babies. Just about as quick as it was respectably possible. By which time it was 1938 – Munich time.

Brian warned her then in no uncertain terms that war was inevitable. It was lucky, they thought, that she had moved out of

London to the comparative safety of Leeds. She'd given up work when she'd found herself pregnant, but had soon realized that it didn't need both her and her mother-in-law to run the house, especially when her father-in-law retired. He was reasonably active, and delighted to take his share of caring for his grandchildren. Brian visited them as often as he could; but when her previous publisher offered her a job in Leeds she grabbed at it. Brian had been transferred to a hush-hush unit 'somewhere in the north'; women in wartime were required to pull their weight, whether they wanted to or not. She had been pleased to have something at once pleasant and useful to engage her.

How hard it was now to make herself believe that she was the same woman as she had been then! She'd enjoyed being a mother, but that hadn't stopped her being truly involved in the work she did for two apparently innocuous 'family' or 'professional' magazines, which in actual fact blatantly carried in their so innocent pages vital information for the Government's Intelligence Service. So had begun her career in journalism, and from that time on she had never been 'just' a housewife.

The news of Brian's death had come as a bolt from the blue. It almost killed his parents; it changed her life. She and her children were the old couple's only emotional prop, and in return their care became her personal responsibility. How glad she had been then of her work, though she'd had no need of the money it brought her. Her babies grew into the children whose education was looked after by the Civil Service's pension fund. Brian's parents had no use for their savings, except to provide legacies for their grandchildren, and to keep their house in good repair – a 'home' for them all till in the course of nature she should inherit it. The older and weaker her parents-in-law grew, the less they could cope with their loss and sorrow, and the more they clung to anything that had been their son's – including his wife. It had been a difficult period for her, one she could hardly have sustained but for her interest in work. With the end of the war her job with the magazines ceased, so she took to other kinds of writing, with such success that she had never thereafter wanted for ideas to occupy her pen or her creative instinct.

Till now. Still in nostalgic mood, she wondered what she would do with the day – no, the many days ahead of her. She had never, even in that time alone in Leeds, had to confess to herself that she was in danger of being bored. She wouldn't admit to that possibility now. She set her chin firm, and told herself that if nothing else turned up for her to give her attention to, she'd find something else to write, though she hadn't at present a single idea in her head.

William reappeared at her bedside with her morning tea, bright, spruce and eager. Obviously full of plans. She would *not* confess to him that she wasn't. In the past, between batches of scripts or commissions for plays, there had always been plenty of things and people to interest her in the village. William teased her that she would run to meet trouble – other people's trouble, that is. He joked that it wasn't all gas and gaiters being the partner of an 'agony aunt'. She'd had to admit that he was right. Sometimes she'd felt so much like a sponge whose purpose in life was to soak up other people's miseries that she'd been glad of a bit of his loving asperity to squeeze her dry again.

She'd begun to worry about the Bridgefoot family. Going over what William had said last night, she thought she'd never realized what a rock Rosemary had been to the others; Rosemary, who'd had such a hard childhood after her mother had died and left her to the mercy of an embittered, loveless aunt. When rescued by Brian, and thereafter finding herself part of a family brimming over with love and consideration for each other, her gratitude to them was boundless, and she'd poured it out in reciprocal devotion to all of them, never able to do enough for any of them. It must be hurting her so much that she was likely to be the one to spoil the Golden Wedding for George and Molly, though through no fault of her own. From the moment she'd become a Bridgefoot, she and Marjorie had become friends as well as 'sisters'. When Marjorie had been in trouble, it was to Rosemary she'd turned first. Now, when Rosemary longed to return a scrap of the boundless love she'd received by helping Marjorie, she was out of action. Fran wondered if she dared offer herself as a substitute for Rosemary, but decided against it. She'd been offered no chance or the slightest hint of an invitation to interfere. Indeed, she'd been warned off any such notion last night by the Rector.

She wished she knew why Rosemary's 'slight whiplash injury' should be having such long after-effects. There was only one person who could enlighten her on that, and he certainly wouldn't. Professional etiquette forbade Terry Hardy to give her a clue if she dared to ask, which she didn't.

She got up and went down to breakfast still feeling slightly miserable at the idea of being at such a loose end. William's mood didn't match. He was whistling merrily as he prepared coffee and toast for her, and then sat down to tell her his plans.

'Do you mind if I'm away all day?' he asked. 'Bob's too busy to see me this week, so I propose to spend my day – or days – in libraries. I've scoured the History Faculty Library and the University Library, but neither has yielded much that I didn't know already. What I need is a lucky strike – something directly focused on Cromwell and his family that I don't already know. Just a hint or two of something not quite so generally known and written about him. There's been such a mound of research done about him by Ph.D. students and modern historians that I doubt if the County Archives have another single item about him left undiscovered. But tiny things of no importance to historians or researchers following their own thesis may get overlooked. I've never bothered till now to read Wise and Noble's little book on Ramsey Abbey, though Grandfather had it when I was a boy. I suppose I despised it – a couple of Victorian clergymen's digest 'for the vulgar'. What has caught my attention now is that they were familiar with medieval Latin, and some of what they have distilled it from is the Librum Ramsiensis in the British Museum Library, which I've never seen. Some of the details they've included from the registers of Ramsey Church give fascinating little insights into Cromwell's immediate large family. So I propose to follow them up a bit on my own account. I shan't be late today because I shall only be in Cambridge, and wherever I go, I can never get back here to you fast enough. You don't mind, do you?'

Of course she didn't mind, and said so, though privately she thought he might have remembered that in this particular week there would be nobody else here – not even Sophie; and that she had no work on hand to keep her occupied. After all his endless procrastination, he might at least have left it just one more week!

'I can't help wishing there was something I could do to help out at the Old Glebe,' she said. 'I still think Marjorie's got more on her plate than she can manage.'

'Well, sweetheart, I'd wait to find out before barging in. You're not endowed with Bob's sixth sense to know what's afoot before it happens. It goes without saying that we shall both do all we can if or when we're needed. Now, though, I'm going to get off quick, before I lose my urge to do something really positive at last.'

She saw him off, and went back to clear up the breakfast table and wash up, talking intermittently to Cat, simply to break the silence. It was no use sitting still and expecting Sophie to walk in – or Ned even, because he had asked specifically to be allowed to go and help Bill Edgeley this morning. She felt cut off from everybody, including their special group of friends. She leaned on her elbows over a fresh cup of coffee, and thought about that. What had Eric called them? A coterie made up of middle-aged, well-to-do, middle-class people. That was undoubtedly true, but never intended. It was the result of Eric's initiative and flair. But she mustn't be unfair to Eric. He had, after a bad start, also restored a lot of what had been very down-at-heel cottages, which had had the effect of keeping some of the former farm-labouring families among them. Their contribution to a truly rural community was much in evidence now as it had always been, especially with regard to safe-guarding old-fashioned values such as 'proper pride' and independence. Sophie and her family, for example.

Sophie was the one most likely to be in the know about what was happening at the Old Glebe because of Daniel's closeness to George. But Sophie was not at hand to be asked. It was going to be a very long and frustrating day, she thought.

She went into the sitting-room. It was so beautiful a room that just to set foot in it was usually enough to lift her spirits, but not now. The first thing her eyes lit on was the 'chimney-piece' picture, 'The Burbages at Home', restored to its rightful place by

Greg when the Summer Exhibition had come to an end. It was a replica of what both William and she vaguely remembered hanging there in their childhood, and which Bob had dreamed about so often that he had been able to describe it in detail to Greg. They had all realized that the original must have been a Gainsborough chimney-piece.

Fran stood looking at the replacement, loving it for its own sake, and because it had been a joint wedding present to them by their band of friends, who had commissioned it from Greg, and who, in turn, had excelled himself. Best of all, perhaps, was the way he had caught, in the posed figures wearing eighteenth-century dress, incredible likenesses of herself and William.

If she had felt guilty once before this morning when remembering Grandfather, whose inherited treasure the genuine Gainsborough must have been, guilt on different grounds flooded over her now. Where had that valuable, original Gainsborough gone – and why? Nobody, as far as she knew, had ever been told, because they had never asked. She could guess.

She knew that Grandfather had fallen on bad times during the first war; he must have been very short of ready money, to part with his last treasured asset. For what reason, except to raise money for his family herself, Jess and William included?

No wonder this room always felt so overflowing with love – real love, which as St Paul wrote, '*suffereth long, and is kind . . . never faileth*'. Grandfather's ghost, still exuding love and understanding, was still there, and had been since he had died. And it was there now, close to her, soothing her. Other ghosts too. The room was full of them, memories so vivid that they were almost palpable, of events as well as of people.

Dear old Mary Budd, the last village schoolteacher, revered and beloved for ever by those who, like Sophie, had sat in rows before her: the first friend Fran had made on her return to Old Swithinford. It had been she who, having realized that 'somebody had to play God', had brought about the long-delayed consummation of love between Fran and William.

Happy events to conjure back again, as well as sad ones: those wonderful parties when they'd rolled up the carpets and danced, as they had on her fiftieth birthday. What an event that had been! A turning-point for a lot of lives.

Her memories of it were like vignettes, small, vivid, but merging into each other; Sophie's embarrassed whisper to her in the shadowy hall that she had locked 'the bailiff's man' in Fran's study, fearing the worst when a stranger had appeared in the midst of the rejoicings to say he was not expected but had come to stop. He was, in fact, Fran's son, Roland, into whose ready arms Eric's daughter Monica had promptly fainted at her first sight of him. As a result of that reunion, Fran and Eric now shared twin grandchildren, living only as far away as Cambridge.

Then she caught her breath on the memory of that moment when she had returned to the room, leaving Roland and Monica healing 'cut love' in her study, to find a set standing ready, at George Bridgefoot's request, to perform the old country-dance called 'Haste to the Wedding'.

Beth was standing up with William as her partner when Fran entered, but had insisted on relinquishing William to Fran. She was preparing to sit down beside Bob on the piano stool, when the stiff shy, ex-naval commander was on his feet requesting the pleasure of Beth as his partner. Never in her life would Fran forget the memory of the girl whom they had only previously known as the sad, repressed, spinster daughter of the then Rector sinking into the most stately, débutante-like curtsey, and turning up to him such a rosy, merry, glowing face that he had succumbed to her there and then. What a happy outcome to the visit of Sophie's imaginary 'bailiff's man'!

Except that it had left Eric sitting alone, the odd man out, which, though so much water had flowed under the bridge since then, Fran sometimes felt he still was.

And Thirzah had been there, very didactic, insistent that they finish their 'caperings' before midnight ushered in 'the Lord's Day'. Thirzah, now for ever only a memory, but who had taken with her to her grave so much of the spirit of the past.

Yet there were a lot of friends and neighbours left, and wherever there were people, there was drama, especially in a small closed community where everybody knew everybody else and their secrets as well. She didn't doubt that there was more drama ahead. Some sad – such as the strong possibility of her daughter Kate and two grandchildren going to live overseas if her son-in-law Jeremy got the promotion he was hoping for. That was something all parents had to accept. Hadn't she, Jess and William deserted Grandfather to go their own way?

There was much to look forward to, as well: her approaching birthday, which happened to fall on the very same day as George and Molly's Golden Wedding. She hadn't heard of any plans being made for either event, but she was sure William wouldn't forget her birthday, though this year it might be spent, as William's had been, in a low key way, *à deux* – because at present their gang of close friends was separated into its component parts. Perhaps that's why, in her solitude, she felt so melancholy. Yet if that were the case, she ought to be doing something about it. Somebody had to set the social ball rolling again. What was preventing her from being that person?

Was it her suspicion that the rest of them had some reason for holding back? Who or what were they waiting for, that none of them had made any move towards their normal, happy gregariousness? Could Dr Hardy's proposed move to Heartsease, as soon as Eric should declare it habitable, have anything to do with it?

House – or home? Ah . . . was that the pea under their usual comfortable mattress of friendship? Terry was certainly playing his cards very close to his chest.

They who counted him a friend had been delightedly hoping and even expecting a romantic turning point to what they knew of his previously none-too-happy life. There was no doubt that from the moment he had met her, he had been very interested in their other newcomer, Anthea Pelham. A strikingly beautiful, but very cool and aloof young woman, who had gone out of her way to make it clear to all of them that she had no romantic notions whatsoever about men, however handsome and charming and otherwise eligible, and certainly not for a doctor who at forty-odd had made a mess of three previous marriages.

Yet things *had* been different between them since last Easter

Monday, when – in his role as the nearest doctor – he had attended her after a car accident. As Beth had said the other day, however circumspect everybody in the know had been about that dramatic day, nobody could but wonder if there was something between them.

That accident had truly been the stuff of high drama. Anthea had been rescued, unconscious, by Jane's son Nick and Charlie Bridgefoot. Charlie had stayed while Nick had run to fetch Dr Hardy. When he arrived she had helped to undress Anthea – revealing the terrible secret she had been hiding. The body to which that beautiful face and those wonderful legs belonged was a mutilated mass of terrible burn scars and skin-grafting from shoulder to waist, where her left breast should have been.

The shock to the doctor was almost worse than Anthea's knowledge that he now knew this about her. His first thoughts had been wholly for her – not physically, but emotionally. His heart went out to her. She must have been steeling herself against any revelation all the time, to him most of all. It explained so much of her strange, off-putting behaviour towards him. With that hidden but cruelly disfigured body, what could her feelings be towards any man who showed any interest in her?

He had been blind, professionally as well as personally, too obsessed with his own hurt feelings to look for any other cause but that his marital reputation had gone before him. Now he realized that in fact she had been as drawn towards him as he towards her, and that of the two of them, she must have suffered far the worse.

What he had felt for her at that moment was greater and deeper than anything he had ever felt before towards any woman. He dared not stop, there and then, to explore his feelings, but he did know that he must not be the first thing she saw when she came round from her swoon. That would be turning the knife in the wound she had so bravely sought to conceal. Hurriedly and apologetically he had assured young Charlie Bridgefoot that Anthea was not seriously hurt and would soon come round. And then he had run away.

But Fate had been playing ducks and drakes with a lot of the human pieces on his chequer board that day. Charlie was needed for another emergency. She could not leave her post, so Charles, who had been sent to fetch her home, on his own initiative went straight to Benedict's, to ask Fran to take over from Charlie.

Which was how she was in the know. Once she had seen Anthea's awful disfigurement she understood how such a tangle of ravelled emotions should have hardened themselves into a knot. There had to be some way of undoing it. She listened without comment to Anthea's flat recital of her story, till the girl wore out her stoicism, and lay quiet, supinely grieving.

Then Fran had crept out, and surreptitiously summoned the doctor back. So she'd been there, peeping through a half-closed door nearby, when he had fallen on his knees by Anthea's couch and laid his face against the place where her left, amputated breast should have matched the perfect one still there on her right side.

By common consent, those who had been involved had kept their knowledge strictly to themselves. Charlie told Charles; Fran told William; and Terry told Beth and Elyot. They, and they only, had any details, or any inkling of how the matter might resolve itself. Anthea had recovered and gone back to her part-time job as Eric's linguist/translator at the hotel; Terry's personal life had had to come second to the many professional calls on his time – but still Fran and Beth had allowed themselves to hope. When Terry and Anthea were together, Love was in the air, and Fran and Beth both had good reasons for being sensitive to its every nuance.

But recently, something had gone awry. Fran's delicately attuned antennae had been raised and she was uneasy. It was nearing mid-day, but there was still an afternoon of solitude to be endured.

She took herself into William's study. He didn't seem so far away from her there, but the ghosts were still about. The photograph of William's father looked down at her, as it always did, with the half-sideways smile that made her feel they had known each other intimately, though she'd been only a baby when he'd been killed. She knew it had to be a trick of the light, but when she looked at him, he always appeared to wink at her. This morning it reduced her to tears, because she felt he was trying to uplift her, letting her know how much he appreciated the love she had given to his son: the sort of Love that wiped out sorrow, disappointment and loss. She winked back at Burbage senior, and squared her shoulders to find herself some occupation. It was having nothing to do that was getting at her.

Her heart leapt at the sound of car wheels on the gravel – but it was not William home early. It was Nigel, alone.

*

She was at the door, and had pulled it open for him before he had climbed gingerly out of his car and limped towards her.

'Driving yourself?' she asked as he greeted her. 'Is that wise?'

'I got my discharge from Terry yesterday, as you know, and I must say I'm relieved,' he answered. 'I wouldn't have believed what a huge spanner such a silly little accident could throw into the works. It couldn't have happened at a worse time – but then no time's ever the right time. With the church tower in the unsafe state it is and Christmas approaching, I had more than enough to do even on two good legs. I jib at clambering up and down ladders to see that the job is being done well, but can't leave it to my churchwardens. One's too old, like me, and the other's in another of his huffs. It is, of course, strictly the business of the rural dean to see that the work's being carried out well, but such officials are very good at delegating authority when it suits them. Then I – we have to make a decision about St Saviour's soon, but till I catch up with my schedule, that will have to wait. Is William about?'

'Sorry, but no. He's going to be away most of the day.'

'Good! Better luck than I expected or deserved.'

She laughed. 'I can't imagine what that can possibly mean, but I have to confess I'm glad to see you, too. I was having a fit of the blues. Come in and let me get you a drink. Alcoholic or otherwise?'

'Both, please. No, I won't sit down till – till you join me, and we can drink together.' He was still standing in the sitting-room when she returned.

'Do sit down,' she said, motioning him towards William's chair.

118

'Not till I have apologized to you for my discourtesy to you yesterday afternoon,' he said. 'More or less telling you to mind your own business. It just shows you how tetchy I'm getting, and you happened to touch a rather sore spot. I may be worried about my responsibility for a couple of ancient churches, but to tell you the truth, I'm much more anxious about some of my friends. Perhaps I've had too long to sit and think. There's a sort of virus of unease going about, and we all keep infecting each other with it. Unfortunately, our doctor's got it badly, so it isn't much good consulting him. I came up to apologize, and consult you instead.'

'I've got it, too,' she said, 'but it's nothing whatever to do with what you said yesterday. So sit down, drink up, and tell me what's worrying you.'

He went straight to the point. 'You seemed to suspect that all was not well between Eric and Marjorie. Was that intuition, or do you know more than I do? They are avoiding each other.'

'*Are they?* Are you sure? And why on earth should I know, if you don't?'

'Because you're connected with the village grapevine. People are careful what they tell me unless they need me as a confessor. But you hear both sides of any story because of your closeness to Sophie. She knows what's going on at the Old Glebe because there's nothing George doesn't tell Daniel, and he gives Sophie edited versions which eventually reach you. Marjorie is a Bridgefoot. George is her father. If Marjorie's in distress, as I think she is, then Dan would know, and I hoped you might have gleaned some idea why. I haven't been able to pick up even a hint from Eric. It isn't like him to hold out on me, but he's a past master at putting on the carapace of a hard-headed businessman when he wants to cover any personal feelings.'

She shook her head. 'Sorry, but the grapevine's out of order at the moment. Sophie's been "laid up", too, as you must know. She's been allowed out this last week for little walks, and has visited Dan, calling here on her way back home. But if she's heard anything, she's kept it to herself. She's coming back to work soon, with Mrs Hopkins to help till she's fully recovered. So all I know is only what my own observations at the Glebe yesterday told me, which was that Marjorie had more troubles than simple physical tiredness would account for.'

'Go on. Because of my leg, I'm a bit out of touch. What made you say what you did about Eric neglecting Marjorie?'

'Silly reaction to the strange remark she murmured to herself when half asleep and didn't expect me to hear – that she felt safe when Yorky, the man who is doing up the Glebe, is about. I had noticed that they do get on extremely well together, and he's a very attractive man as well as a fascinating character. But Marjorie isn't likely to fall for any stranger, Prince Charming though he may act. I got the impression that she was turning to him because for some reason she needs extra moral support just now, and she isn't getting it from Eric. She may not think of him in any way as "hers", but nobody can deny how close they've been for a long time. It's an absolutely instinctive reaction for any woman who has cause to think she's being spurned or neglected to show the man concerned that he isn't the only pebble on the beach.'

'And vice-versa,' he said. 'But if we make two and two equal four, there must be a reason. Does your intuition give you any clues as to what Marjorie may be needing extra support for?'

'We've wondered. I think it may centre on George and Molly's Golden Wedding. None of the Bridgefoots are running true to form, and while Rosemary's accident may be the obvious reason for it, I think there's more to it than that. If there's any internal Bridgefoot matter that Marjorie is obliged to keep dark even from Eric, that could quite easily be the root of any coolness between them. If, as I suspect, he has rushed in where angels fear to tread to offer his help, and she has rejected it, he'd be the one to feel spurned, put on his businessman's persona, and withdraw.'

'I'd agree entirely if it were a case of a lovers' tiff, but we know it isn't that. So what is it?'

'I've been asking myself that. A Golden Wedding's an event that nobody ever celebrates more than once. I expect it's been on the Bridgefoot agenda for at least a couple of years, and plans made, Bridgefoot fashion, for one last great gathering of the clans at a party in the barn, as in past time-honoured tradition. The very last such party they could ever hope to have. George and

Molly, seeing how impossible it was once Rosemary was put out of action to help Marjorie organize it, swallowed their disappointment, and settled for a lunch at the Old Glebe – family only I have heard.

'But Rosemary isn't getting better. Brian's not the man to take any disruption of his plans equably, and I wouldn't wonder if he's putting himself out, possibly with Terry. He doesn't trust doctors unless he personally picks them on reputation, and pays huge fees for their attention. We've had experience of that before. But Marjorie adores her brother, who can't do wrong for her. I wouldn't wonder if she's doing his share as well as her own to see to anything – like organizing the family lunch. My guess is that Eric leapt to her aid by suggesting either that it was held at the hotel, or that he'd look after everything wherever it was held. But he doesn't yet quite understand folks like the Bridgefoots, or not enough to appreciate the finer points. If Marjorie knew his suggestions wouldn't satisfy her parents, and refused, naturally he'd be hurt. You know as well as anybody what a darling old softie he is under that businessman's skin. But up pops Yorky, a former prize-winning chef, and offers his help, which she accepts – and which, naturally, puts Eric's back up. So he withdraws, and Yorky becomes her secret ally. I imagine that by now Marjorie, with Yorky's help, has it all set up. Her near collapse yesterday could be the effect of physical tiredness, but I can't help feeling there's more to it than that. What do you think?'

'I think you're very probably right, and it reminds me that even a tough old bachelor like me should never be above seeking help from a woman's intuition. Something more? Yes. We don't know this new Marjorie. The other one is tough physically, and morally as steady as a rock. She'd neither have her head turned by a stranger she's known only five minutes, however handsome, charming, willing and skilful, nor let anything like having to agree to a second-best Golden Wedding lunch for her parents faze her to the state she was in last night. So what else can it be?'

'I wonder. Two possibilities occur to me. One is that as it's a family-only party, and all the others will be there, the black sheep of the family, *her daughter*, will be conspicuous by her absence.

121

Rubbing it in that she, Marjorie, let the side down by marrying Vic Gifford. Perhaps that's what she can't take! It could be why she's turning away from Eric. He's one of "us", and perhaps Yorky has made her see us again as Vic saw us: smug, middle-class snobs with too much money who cling to old-fashioned values like courtesy and kindness – the sort of things Vic despised because he didn't have them by nature, and money couldn't buy them for him.

'That in the end Marjorie detested him only makes her memories worse. Perhaps she thinks her association with him damns her from ever making the grade, especially because of Pansy. If Eric is being a bit "cool" to her, she's turned instinctively towards a man whom she guesses, if she doesn't already know, has good reason to understand her point of view. And, as you said yourself yesterday, she may have begun to realize that there must be more wrong with Rosemary than anybody has been told.'

Nigel got up and hobbled up and down the room. He turned a troubled face towards her. 'It all adds up. Very silly, but perfectly feasible,' he said. 'Firstly, if Hardy knows or even suspects something worse than whiplash injury he's in the usual doctor's dilemma – only worse. He's dealing with friends, and knows what it would do to them if he told them anything at this juncture. But he must do something. He has a professional duty to himself and to his patient to inform someone – who should be her husband – of his fears. But Brian lacks the moral guts that the rest of the family possess. He'd fly into a rage against Terry and demand a whole raft of "second opinions", or let the cat out of the bag to everybody, including Rosemary herself, which is the last thing Terry may want. My guess is that if Terry needed to compromise, while waiting for the result of yet another batch of tests, for example, it would be Marjorie he'd choose to trust, if only to warn that the proposed Golden Wedding lunch may have to be cancelled or postponed.'

It made all too much sense to Fran. 'You said "firstly". What's under "secondly"?'

'I told you our doctor has got the bug himself. I've seen a lot of him lately, and I think he's been as glad to sit down and talk to me for a few minutes as I have been to listen to him. His plans have all gone wrong, and he's unhappy on personal grounds. We can only suppose that to be a case of *cherchez la femme*. She doesn't take a lot of identifying, does she? It's none of our business, so we can't ask either of the principals outright. So how do we begin to find the needle in that haystack?'

Fran's widow's cruse of sympathy was overflowing, but her natural reaction when friends or neighbours were in trouble was not to stand off grieving and wishing she could do something about it, but to tackle it head on, as William teased her, 'like a bull at a gate'. She thought rapidly and then said, 'The mutual link in all this has to be the Old Rectory – Beth and Elyot. Elyot is Terry's closest male friend, and Beth's always been in his confidence. If anything has gone wrong between Terry and Anthea, they'll know. About the Bridgefoots: short of asking Marjorie herself, I think I'm about the one person George would tell – if he knows. Would you like me to nose about and try to pick up a scent for us to follow at both places?'

'That's just what I was hoping you'd say, and one reason I was glad William wouldn't be here. I was afraid it would go against his grain, and caution, to encourage you to "interfere". I see no other way – time's against us. And as it happens I may have to go away myself for two or three days, now that I'm allowed to use my leg again. Tell William from me that at any rate my absence will hold up any decision about St Saviour's. I know how he feels about that.'

'But not why he feels so strongly. We'll tell you all as soon as we can, but it will please William more than you could ever guess if it were never to be closed at all. Do put your thinking cap on to devise some way of saving it.'

'I'll promise you at least that much. But I must go, so can we go back to your bloodhound expedition? I think it's truly very urgent, especially if I do have to set out sooner than I expected. Could you possibly go sniffing around this very afternoon?'

'As soon as ever I've fed Cat,' she said. 'Must you go? Can't you stop and share a sandwich or something?'

'Not without offending Eric,' he said. 'We're all touchy.'

*   *   *

Fran was out of luck at the Old Glebe. George was out, having had his dockey early so that he and Dan could visit a dairy herd, with some idea of investing in a young Jersey bull. Daisy and Dora's calves had both been heifers, and they were in calf again; but if they wanted to build the herd up, they had to decide soon whether to invest in a bull, or rely on artificial insemination. Both men were satisfied with the results of artificial insemination, but instinctively held to the opinion that 'nature's way's best'.

Besides, Dan said, he supposed you could trust vets as far as breeds went, but how did they know what sort of temper the bulls had? He'd been a cowman all his working life, and he knowed what he was talking about. He'd dealt with bulls 'as had been the devil's own'. He'd had others as had been sweeter-natured and better-tempered than any cow. As far as he could see, there was no sense in asking for trouble. So they'd just gone to have a look before they made their minds up.

Fran learned all this from Molly, whom she had found sitting comfortably in her chair for an after-lunch siesta.

Fran said she didn't want to disturb her. Molly laughed, and said that she was pleased to see anybody. She never had been one for 'wanting to sit about' in the daytime, though she did very often fall asleep nowadays in her chair in the evening; but since what had been the kitchen had turned into what Marge called 'the living-room', and what had been the scullery was made into the kitchen, Marge had insisted on her mother having a nap in her chair after dinner, whether she wanted to or not.

Molly sounded slightly aggrieved. 'I did agree with Father that as we couldn't have the party we'd planned for our Golden Wedding, we'd have some alterations made – but I never intended anything like this,' she said. 'I liked it as it was. All I wanted was a more up-to-date cooking range, and a bit of a general clean-up and a lick of fresh paint. But between Marge's ideas and Yorky's being able to turn his hand to anything, I haven't had much say in it – and I wouldn't let Father know for the world as I'd ever so much rather it had been left as it was. As long as he thinks it suits me, it'll suit him.

'Marge calls this "the living-room", though me and Father can't get our tongues round that. We call it "the house-place", like it would have been when we were young at home – the place where the family met for meals and talk. But I wouldn't upset Marge neither. She's doing what she thinks is right, bless her, and makes me sit here while she flies round to wash up and such before going up to Monastery Farm to do a bit for herself and keep Eric Choppen's place tidy. She's doing too much, and we all know it – but nothing'll stop her. Yorky sort of keeps an eye on her, and leaves off whatever he's doing to help her when he's here. He's in the new kitchen helping her now – though whatever's taking 'em so long I can't think.'

Fran listened, but Molly's disclosures didn't make her feel any happier. She was picking up a scent she didn't like much. Molly chattered on, having gone back to why George was away, and why they'd had their dockey so early.

'Brian don't go along with his dad at all about having a bull,' she said. 'Not that it's anything to do with him, now; he don't go in for mixed farming anyway. But Charles goes along with his grandad, because of him and Charlie having plans for breeding horses up at Danesum when Charlie's a qualified vet. Charles is like a bit fell off his grandfather, so they usually agree about most things. I don't bother my head about it, though I do like to see animals about a farm. Tractors and combine harvesters and such are all very well, but however much they cost, you can't breed from 'em.'

'Bob Bellamy would be on your side,' Fran said. 'Now that he and Effendi are in it together and he can do more or less what he likes, he says his farm in the fen is the place to grow crops, and Castle Hill the place for animals of all sorts. I heard him talking to Charlie about it.'

'Yes,' said Molly. 'She told Grandad so, when her and Charles were here talking about this bull with Father. Charlie said it's supposed not to be a good thing to breed too long without a bit o' new blood in the stock. Her dad said it depended on the stock, as anybody who had enough sense to look at people might know – specially in places like the fens.'

'I know,' said Fran. 'There was a programme on the telly not long ago, one evening when we were at Castle Hill, about there being so many cases of "mental deficiency" to be cared for in the fens. A psychologist had got hold of the tale about the fens "being a hotbed of incest" and said that after a few generations the result was likely to be a good many people needing psychiatric help. It rubbed Bob up the wrong way.

'For one thing, as he pointed out, the shrink, when challenged, admitted that most of his patients weren't fen-folk at all. They were people from towns who'd moved into the fen because they thought it was cheaper, but who'd had no idea what they'd let themselves in for. They couldn't stand the conditions.

'But what put Bob's hackles up was this man taking it for granted that the myth of incest in the fens was true, and saying so on the telly, because nowadays folk think what's said on telly must be gospel truth. Bob really got on his high horse about it. He said there's no more proof of cases of incest in the fens than there is anywhere else. It depends what you mean by incest. If you only mean in-breeding, that's a different thing. In isolated places, like in the fens when they were first drained, there was no choice except to marry into what other few families were there. But that didn't make them a race of half-sharp idiots, though he didn't deny that now and then a baby's born that will always be a penny or two short of a shilling. That can happen anywhere.

'Then William chipped in to say that upper-middle-class Victorian families did just the same – married their own cousins – though for a different reason. In their case it was to keep the money they'd made in the family. Like the Forsytes, in Galsworthy's *Forsyte Saga*.

'Anyway, living conditions in the fens up to the end of the first war – and after it, in a lot of places – were so bad, and doctors so scarce and expensive, that only the strongest and healthiest children lived to grow up and have children themselves. So real genuine fen-folk weren't weaklings or idiots. They were, in fact, examples of Darwin's theory about the survival of the fittest.'

Marjorie came in from the new kitchen at this point, dressed ready to leave, with Yorky hovering behind her. She had not heard Fran arrive, and looked both confused and startled at the sight of her. It was all too plain to see that she'd been crying. She greeted Fran shortly, told her mother brusquely to stay with her feet up, and leave anything there was still to do to Yorky. Then she left, a very solicitous Yorky seeing her to her car and standing looking after her till it had gone out of sight.

Fran took the opportunity of excusing herself, and turned her car towards the Old Rectory, where she found an almost identical situation existing: an unwilling Beth, looking the very picture of health, sitting with her feet up, under orders from her husband not to get up or do anything till he should return. The sight of this second specimen of healthy womanhood made victim of unnecessary and unwanted protection caught Fran's funny-bone, and she began to laugh, Beth joining in. There's no medicine like laughter for chasing away the blues, so Fran sat down by Beth and launched at once into a clear and concise reason for her visit.

As Beth listened with care – a habit not only bred in her, but also acquired from long practice – Fran got the impression that she wasn't telling Beth anything she didn't already know or suspect, but which was for the time being *sub rosa*.

'I'm breaking confidences,' Beth said. 'But if everybody's keeping secrets from everybody else, I don't wonder we're creating a mare's nest – or do I mean a hornet's? There must be a real cause for anxiety somewhere amongst this confusion. Let's clear it up if we can. I'll tell you what I know, if you'll return the compliment. Let's consider Eric first.

'We've seen quite a lot of him lately and put it down to the fact that he's doing all he can to persuade Elyot to be our candidate; but we think there are other reasons for him spending so much time with us. We know that one of his cherished plans has gone wrong, and we share his disappointment; but what we can't make out is why he doesn't want to go home, even though Nigel, his friend, his hero, and his role model – if a man like Eric can be said to need such a thing – is there, at his invitation. It sometimes looks as if he's actually trying to avoid Nigel, and would rather be doing anything and go anywhere but home. It doesn't make sense to me. What do you make of it?'

Fran shook her head, wondering if it was wise to voice her thoughts even to Beth. But she had to. 'Are you sure it's Nigel he's trying to avoid?' she asked.

'Who else could it be?'

'I think your premise that he's avoiding anybody may be wrong. I personally think it's more likely that he's *missing* somebody that Nigel's presence can't make up for. Marjorie.'

Beth looked considerably startled. 'Marjorie? He knows as well as we that she's up to her neck in other things. Besides, we all know what their relationship is. He's as adamant about that as ever. You must be barking up the wrong tree there, Fran.'

'For once, I don't agree with you. I'm not saying anything but that he's a man used to having things done his way, and though she's still looking after his house and his creature comforts as well as she can – she isn't there when he goes home. It may be nothing but a case of him having "*grown accustomed to her face*". Or it may remind him too much of the time when the face that was missing when he went home was his wife's. But it isn't healthy. I'm afraid he may think she's avoiding him, and if so, whatever he feels, he'll stop out of her way.

'Why should she be avoiding him?'

'Because she could have something else – even somebody else – on her mind.'

'That,' said Beth, 'to me, is so unthinkable that I suggest we don't waste any more time on it till we have more evidence.'

'OK. So what's this plan of Eric's that's gone wrong?'

'If I let on to you, you must promise not to know a word about it. It started with Terry Hardy's house. It's more or less finished now, and Eric's delighted with what they've managed to do, especially because it is the very last of any size he can restore in Church End.

'So he'd had the idea of making the "unveiling" of it a bit of a ceremony, asking all Terry's friends to be there when the bulldozers knock down the shop-front and the two old sheds that hide it from the road, so that we get first view of it in all its new beauty.

'Then – well, you know how these ideas grow, once they take root – we would all go off and have lunch together to celebrate. Somebody remembered that it was your birthday – being kept quiet, we guessed, so as not to clash with the Bridgefoot Golden Wedding. But none of us wanted your birthday to go unmarked, and said so. Then Effendi said he thought it was about time he hosted a lunch in his own house, and with Eric's help it could be arranged in every way so as not to interfere or clash with whatever the Bridgefoots did or didn't do. But we had to acknowledge the Golden Wedding, and agreed that it would make more sense if we all subscribed to a present worth having instead of smothering the old couple with an *embarras de bibelots*. It all looked so inviting – till it was knocked on the head.'

Fran's spirits went down again. It had been such a lovely idea: a tribute to the bonds of friendship that had seemed endangered, as well as the *caritas* she believed in. She was conscious of deep disappointment, and not only on her own behalf.

'Who's knocked it on the head? And why?'

'Terry. Anthea's run back.'

Fran was stunned. 'That's bloody ridiculous,' she said. 'We can't let it happen.'

Beth had never heard Fran swear before, and her first instinct was to laugh. But she agreed with its vehemence. 'No,' she countered. 'We can't, and we won't.'

'Then tell me all you know. Let's go over it and see where we start from.'

'The first we knew of it was from Effendi. He precipitated it by asking Terry whether or not he wanted to keep his end of the Old Surgery, when the time came for him to take over his new home. According to Jane, Terry replied that his plans weren't fixed firmly enough yet for him to give an answer. Effendi didn't press him, though he said he'd like an answer soon because if Terry didn't want to keep it he hoped to use it as a bait to get himself – and William – a reliable typist.

'So, now that the restoration of the old cottage is more or less completed, Effendi asked him again to let him know as soon as possible. He was surprised, and then devastated, by Terry's curt reply, which was to the effect that he was actually on his way to see Eric to ask him to put the restored cottage on the market. He himself would be leaving as soon as he was assured that the strength of the multiple practice now installed at Casablanca Health Centre could cope adequately with both parts of the village.

'Jane said her father felt guilty, as if it were all his fault. That's how this bug is spreading. I couldn't and didn't believe it – so when Terry called last week to visit me professionally, I took my courage in both hands and asked him if it was true.

'I don't want to go through that again. He tried to be calm and businesslike, but I knew he couldn't hold out, and he didn't. He sat down and put his face in his hands, and cried – with the tears dripping through his fingers on to the carpet – and told me.

'He'd been making a lot of dream-come-true plans. Hired a young locum for a month, to give him time to get the cottage furnished and so on, and booked himself off altogether for two weeks over Christmas, planning to whip Anthea away to marry him *en route* to a honeymoon in a friend's villa in Portugal. It meant asking Eric if he could spare Anthea at Christmas – and that's how and why Eric had been so full of plans for all of us, though he was sworn to secrecy.

'But the next I knew, it was Eric in distress. He'd had to ask Terry to finalize his plans so that he could get a replacement for Anthea if at all possible at such short notice, which of course in effect forced Terry to propose to Anthea. To ask her, formally, like the gentleman he is, to marry him, and tell her his plans.'

Beth paused, tears falling. 'She turned him down. Point blank. Said he was taking far too much for granted. She thought she'd made it quite clear to him that no such thing was possible, or ever would be. She'd thought that when he'd discovered her reason for keeping her distance, she could presume that he would be gentleman enough not to ask anything more of her than the relationship they'd had since. Oh, Fran, it was awful! He's just flattened – and terribly humiliated yet again.'

'It's unbelievable,' Fran exclaimed. 'More than just daft. It's mad – and cruel. And it can't all be Anthea's fault, can it? Look, *we* know what they mean to each other. Don't *they* know? Not just that they happen to love each other – which I'd swear my life away that they do – but that they are each other's salvation? If they can't rescue themselves from whatever evil spirit it is singling both of them out for endless misery, we're all done for. All our defences are down. Doesn't love matter any more to anybody? What can we do?'

'You usually say, "Leave it to the gods",' Beth said. 'That's more or less what I've been doing till now. Hoping it would come right.'

'I still say so. But the gods did their bit for them when Anthea had her accident – as they did when they arranged for William to come so unexpectedly back into my life. But it seems to me the gods often need a bit of help from people on the spot. In our case, they got it from dear old Mary Budd and, of all unlikely people, Sophie. I guess you'll say that your God never needs human help, but I think that's what He's always hoping for! Now it looks to me that He – or whatever we mean by "the gods" – needs you and me. Are you with me?'

'Do you dare ask?'

Fran stood up, leaned over Beth, and kissed her. 'All right then. Into battle we go. We've either got to bring those two idiots to their senses, or play some trick on them like Mary and Sophie did on us. Shall we try reason first? Which of them would you rather tackle?'

'Terry. He'll listen to me even if he rejects my advice. I think the same about you and Anthea. But we may need a trick or two up our sleeves as well. We'll think of something, once we're over the first big hurdle. I'd be happier if Elyot knew what I was about, though. Do you mind if I tell him?'

'Don't be daft. Do you think I'd manage it without William? And we can, I think, leave any necessary bamboozling to Eric – if at the same time we can solve his problem. He adores acting the part of fairy godmother, old softie that he is.'

'I think I have obeyed my husband's dictat long enough,' Beth said, getting up. 'I'll go and tell Emerald we're ready for a nice cup of tea.'

Fran looked at her watch. It was much later than she thought.

'I don't think I dare stop, much as I would like to,' she said. 'I have no idea what time to expect William home, but if he gets there first and I'm missing, without leaving him a note, I shan't have a husband when I do get home. He'll have died of fright and guilt. Besides, I think it would be best if I went to see Anthea after dark, when she's home from work. Nigel rather impressed on me that we mustn't let any grass grow under our feet.'

So, in spite of Beth's entreaties, she left for home at once.

*

Approaching the turning to Benedict's, Fran saw a car behind her flashing its lights at her. She must have beaten William home by a short head. She took no more notice of it till she had driven on to the gravel, and stopped, glancing into her mirror. It was not William. It was Yorky.

The house was in darkness, though she could see the glow of the fire Ned had lit in the sitting-room. William was not back yet – and a thick November fog was rising with the gathering dusk. She didn't know where he was, but in this fog he could be a long time.

What was Yorky up to, following her home? He'd got out of his car and was coming after her towards the door. She was not a woman scared by her own shadow, and had never been afraid of the dark, or suspicious of strange men. All the same she hesitated before opening the door. Benedict's was very isolated, and she was quite alone. But when he spoke, she knew at once she had nothing to fear.

'Sorry, pet,' he said. 'Have I put wind up tha? I never thowt about that. When I saw tha in front o' me, it coom to me in't flash that t'best I could do was to tell you. I left t'Glebe in a fit o' panic as has been cooming on all day. I was afraid I might not get home – especially if fog coom up. But Ah'm wooried. I couldn't ha' been luckier than to meet thee. Sommat's oop at Glebe.'

If anything could have put her completely at ease, it was his use of broad Yorkshire dialect. He used it most, just as Sophie used her vernacular, when he was in distress. She turned the key, and ushered him into her kitchen.

'Sit down,' she said. 'I'll get you a drink. You look all in.'

'No thanks, pet. I never touch stoof, only on Saturday nights in't pub, and then I only tek a few Yorkshire bitters. I don't tek wines and spirits much, specially when I'm in one o' these panics.'

'Then let's have a cup of tea,' she said. 'I'm nearly dying for one.' He let her put the kettle on and she looked at him closely. He was very pale, and sweating profusely.

'Are you all right?' she asked anxiously.

'Not feeling meself,' he said. 'So I'd better tell tha quick what I know, and then get off home while I can still drive.'

He was ill. She had no doubt this was genuine. 'Tell me what's wrong at the Glebe, and if necessary I'll take you home.' He pulled himself together with an effort.

'Well, pet, see tha – I'd bin working oop to this all day, only I couldn't go home 'cos I'd promised Marge to be there when she coom. We were going to hev a bit of a confab, 'cos though it's a secret yet, Gran and t'Boss is going to get t'fam'ly meal as Marge and Rosemary had set their hearts on for t'old un's Golden Wedding. Ah'm going to help Marge, and do all t'coooking and waiting on. So Marge and me has been setting it all quiet like, together. O God, aye.

'But time kept going and she didn't coom, and I started to woory 'cos t'fog was coming up, and when Ah'm bad I can't see t'drive. So I went out and set in't car on't road outside t'gates, so's I were ready to drive off soon as she did coom. She pulled up behind me, but didn't get out, so I did, and went to see what were t'matter.'

He paused. 'She were just sitting there sloomped over t'wheel and sobbing fit to brek her heart. I got in aside of her, and asked what t'matter was. She said she couldn't face her mam and dad today. I put my arms round her, and let her cry it out, but I wasn't feeling too good myself, and in t'end we both drove off separate ways. But I hope she lets Gran and t'Boss know why she didn't call. They'll be wooried t'death! I niver thowt o' that till now, neither.'

Fran understood that she was being asked to find an excuse to ring the Old Glebe and say that Marjorie had had to go straight home. She told him she'd do that.

'Did she tell you what was making her so upset?' she asked, her mind flying to Pansy.

'Aye – well, Ah picked it up as well as I could. She said I hadn't to let on to nobody, but Ah've got to tell thee, 'cos I might have to let her down when she needs me most, poor pet. It's something she's more than just wooried about up at Temperance. Ah think it must be about her they call Rosemary. Then I had to leave her, and Ah'd better leave thee while I can, but Ah'd feel better, if tha'd do what tha can to help Marge and t'others. Tell 'em not to woory about me – I shall be back to work as soon as I dare coom out again.'

She spoke sharply. 'Don't be silly,' she said. 'How can I help if I don't know what it's about? Whatever it is, George and Molly will try to find out. They'll all have to know soon, anyway. Was it something Dr Hardy had told Marjorie?'

'Aye, must be, I think. My head was so queer that I niver took it in properly. But it must be soom'at real bad, the way Marge was carrying on.'

He got up to go, thanked her and went, staggering a little as he walked. She watched him go with trepidation, and extracted from him a promise to ring her as soon as he was safely back in his flat.

It was quite dark by now, and the fog was getting thicker. She sat down and tried to work out what she ought to do. Wait till Yorky was safe home – in the fog it would take him about ten minutes. What then? Ring the Glebe with some cock and bull story of why Marjorie hadn't called as usual? Ring Marjorie? Go to see her, and tell her what she knew, and how she knew? Wait for William?

She had promised Beth to see Anthea tonight. Where was William, when she needed him? And why was he so late? She'd have to go soon, and leave him a note. She stood up suddenly, and felt giddy, so she sat down again. She knew why she felt so queer. She'd had nothing at all to eat since a very meagre early breakfast, and she had been 'giving out of herself' all day. Food, that's all she needed. She went rather dazedly into the pantry and found a tin of soup. Back in the kitchen again she reached up to take a saucepan from a high shelf, and as she looked up the feeling of dizziness returned. She couldn't be going to faint, could she? She'd never fainted in her whole life before. She mustn't do it now. But she felt herself falling, clutched at the table, and found William was there to catch her. Contact with him brought her round at once, and before he'd got his coat off he'd got her into her chair, and taken charge.

'Food?' He said he'd had enough during the day to last him a week, so he'd feed her before he listened to her story. He made her an omelette with mushrooms, cut thin bread and butter for her, laced her coffee with rum and when she'd eaten it – which she did to please him, hunger having vanished at the welcome sight of him – he came and sat down with hands stretched across the table to hold hers.

'And now, my precious, tell me why you haven't eaten since I left you all those hours ago, and what you've been doing all day? My doings can wait. What's happened to get you into this state?'

She told him, adding that there was still a great deal more for her to do before she could relax at home, fog or no fog. 'Where ought I to go first, do you think?'

'You mean "we", don't you, darling? Wherever you go, I'm coming too. But sit still where you are while I go and ring the Glebe,' he said. 'They won't be nearly so likely to question me as closely as they would you. I'll just say I met Yorky, who'd forgotten to tell them that Marge had had to go straight on home. I shall probably find she's already done it herself.'

'Depends on what Terry had to say to Marge. I think that settles it. Let's go to Monastery Farm first, with the hope of seeing Nigel as well as Marge while there. He didn't say he'd moved back to his own house yet. We'd better get off at once, though, or Marjorie will have gone back to Rosemary at Temperance before we can catch her.'

*

Marjorie was, in fact, all ready to set out when they arrived. She'd made valiant efforts to disguise with careful make-up any visible signs of her afternoon's distress. As Nigel had said, she was a woman of exceedingly strong character, especially on behalf of those she loved.

She told them she had very little time to give them because she must get back to Temperance early, and asked outright what had prompted their visit. Fran saw no reason why she shouldn't be equally as blunt. Yorky, in spite of Marjorie's prohibition, had been forced to tell her that Marge was in distress, and was worried about her. He had asked Fran to make sure she was all right.

Marjorie sat down again, gathering courage. She longed to share her secret with someone other than the doctor; to unburden herself just a little to Fran would help her keep her chin up.

William, sitting silent, rather anxiously observing the two women, thought sardonically how it always happened that the sponge was at hand when anybody else needed it. *He* had wanted Fran's attention that evening, though not as a sponge, and had been looking forward to it. But once again, he had no choice but to follow her lead. When other people needed her, she needed him.

Marjorie had herself under control, and said what she had to say without further tears. It was mainly that the pain that Rosemary had been enduring came from a misplaced vertebra, which lying flat in bed should soon put right; but Terry was worried about a deterioration in her general health, even after allowing for the shock of her accident. He was insisting on getting a second opinion – without telling Brian, because Brian was liable to throw a temper if Hardy even tried to talk to him.

'He can't help it you know,' Marjorie said in defence of the brother she adored. 'He's always the same. I'm sure it's only because he's so worried about Rosy. You've only got to look at him to see he's making himself ill. But Dr Hardy said he had no choice – he was afraid it might be the early stages of something really serious.

'You see what that could mean?' Marjorie went on in a low,

tense voice. 'It may be something like multiple sclerosis, so she'd never be strong enough again to do all that's asked of a farmer's wife. She may deteriorate so slowly that people think it's all put on – Brian for one, especially if he thought Terry wasn't capable of dealing properly with her. He's impatient with her for not letting him get a posh private doctor from London. Remember how he was when Charles was so ill? We know how he is about doctors. Worry makes him angry, and he thrashes about like a fish on a hook and upsets everybody. Dr Hardy doesn't know him so well as we do, but he's shrewd and says there's no point in worrying Bri if we can manage without him knowing. He says Bri might make a scene and rob Rosy of her will-power to get better. She'd suffer like a herring on a grid-iron rather than let her illness spoil even an hour of his happiness. What he doesn't know, he can't tell anybody.'

'So he's told you instead, and left you to carry the worry! That isn't fair. You shouldn't be asked to take everything on your shoulders,' said William. 'After all, Brian's her husband. He should be warned, at least.'

'No!' said Marjorie vehemently. 'He's my brother, and I know him best.' She squared her handsome shoulders. 'I'm not alone, in any case,' she said. 'Dr Hardy understands, and will do all he can. Yorky half knows and I'm glad he chose you to share it with. But please keep all I've said to yourselves.'

She stood up, ready to leave. 'I think I was picked out to be one to suffer and keep the pain to myself. I'm used to it, so I shall manage. But thank you. I'm glad you know. Now I must go. Thanks for setting Mam and Dad's mind at rest, William. I rang them just after you did, and I'm going to call there for ten minutes now, on my way to Temperance.'

She left, and they went through to the other side of the house to give Nigel what encouragement they could without telling him the truth. As it happened, he was on the telephone in another room, so he called to them to sit down and help themselves, till he could be with them in five minutes. They were glad of the chance to think over what Marjorie had revealed.

'She's taking on more than she should,' Fran said. 'It was her attitude to Brian that surprised me. She adores him – but she made it clear that she agrees with Terry about him. It was as if she was protecting *him*, not Rosemary, though she knows who'll have to be Rosemary's chief support. She'll give up everything and everybody else to do what she thinks is her duty, so that her beloved Brian doesn't have to.'

'Yes, but the Bridgefoots are almost tribal in their closeness. They'll all pull together. But she did say she felt better for us knowing. What did she mean by that?'

'I think she means physically, especially in the immediate future, with special regard to Yorky if he fails her about the Golden Wedding party. I guess that's all "the future" means to her, till it's over.

'Her anxiety may be more general in spite of her strength of character. She put up such a fight when her husband was killed, and felt she had landed in a bed of roses afterwards. The barometer was set fair for her to be reasonably happy ever after – except for her everlasting worry about Pansy.'

'It won't be so sunny for any of us if Terry goes and Elyot spends his life at Council meetings,' William said. 'I agree with you that just now it's a case of first things first. There's just over a week to go to that family gathering at Glebe, and she can't face up to having either to cancel it, or take it on without Rosemary or Yorky to help. She wasn't looking forward to it very much in her own right anyway because Pansy wouldn't be there; but she wasn't prepared to let her own feelings spoil anything for the others. There's nothing we can do, my darling, but give her what moral support we can. She'll cope. If there's anything we can do, we won't let her down.'

They stopped abruptly as Nigel came back into the room, but he had heard what William was saying. 'Neither would Eric, if he could help it. But as I said, they're avoiding each other. Heaven only knows why. I don't suppose it's any of our business, but what I just heard William saying *is*, besides being the reason for me being glad to see Fran again tonight.

'You see, *I know where Pansy is, and what she's doing!* And that's where I'm going, first thing tomorrow morning. Would it help if

I could persuade her to come home in time to be here for the Golden Wedding?'

Fran's voice was awed when at last she found it. 'Is it really possible?' she asked.

'Fran, my dear, you have yet to learn that with God nothing is impossible. It's the human factor that so often fails.'

'I'll believe you,' she said. 'Please tell us all you can.'

'I've just been consulting Eric, and warning him that I must get back to my own place at once. Then – for your ears only – I shall be called away on urgent business. Only you two will know why, and I shan't tell even you where I'm going.

'Eric's plans await the result of your other bloodhound sniffing, Fran. Can you tell me anything yet?'

'Only that I'm going straight from here up to see Anthea. Beth will tackle Terry by calling him in to see her tonight, and then asking him outright – as I shall Anthea. May William stop with you while I go? If I need you, William, I'll ring you here – if Nigel doesn't mind.'

'I shall be pleased,' Nigel answered. 'Eric should be home soon, as well.'

William stood up, determined. 'I shall take you up to Anthea,' he said. 'I'm taking no risks. Call me here when you're ready, and I'll fetch you. There's too much danger in the air everywhere at present for my liking.'

*

William waited until the door of Anthea's cottage opened and Fran was let inside. Anthea was alone, and though she welcomed Fran politely, there was an air of defensiveness about her that put Fran on her guard. She had not been in that room since Easter Monday, when she had seen Terry on his knees beside Anthea's couch as she watched through the crack of the hall door. The divan was no longer in the middle of the room, but Fran knew that both she and Anthea were remembering that day. Anthea invited her to sit down, and then rather ostentatiously drew the curtains and straightened cushions, signs of embarrassment that Fran recognized only too well.

'How pretty you've made this room,' she said.

139

'Yes. I shall be sad to leave it. I expect you've heard that I'm giving it up from the end of December.'

Fran was disconcerted by her cool, precise speech. This was the pre-accident, stand-offish Anthea she thought they'd seen the last of. While she hesitated how to answer, Anthea came and stood stiffly in front of her.

'I've a lot of other things to do tonight, Fran, so please say what you came to say, and then leave me alone. I don't know who Terence has been bleating to, but it's as clear as a pikestaff that the news is going the rounds, and I suppose you've been deputed to confirm it. I had thought that only Eric would be told.'

Fran, whose deep well of sympathetic understanding had been dipped into so many times already that day found suddenly, and a bit to her dismay, that it had run dry. She was affronted, and suddenly the well of *caritas* that she'd set out with was filled with anger as flammable and explosive as high-aviation gas. It burst into flame as she got to her feet, and tried to control her voice.

'I came to ask if there was any way we could help save a situation that – whether you recognize it or not – affects us all. If it comes to having to choose between the two of you, we would rather lose a fool of a woman who doesn't know when she's lucky than a splendid doctor, whom she has wounded beyond recovery. Since you ask, I know what I know because he "bleated", as you so elegantly phrased it, to Beth Franks. He's absolutely heart-broken, and utterly defeated. If what you're doing is taking out on him the feelings of revenge you harbour against whatever man it was caused you to come here in the first place, Terence is well rid of you, as indeed we shall all be. We have no room among us for an embittered she-devil, however beautiful, or a tempest-raising fool who believes herself to be the only unlucky victim of circumstance. There are, sadly, a lot of others who've suffered, and in worse case than you need be if you had any sense. If in future you're lonely, it will serve you right. Opportunity for happiness such as you're throwing away seldom knocks twice. I wish you goodnight, and goodbye.'

She stood up and stalked towards the door, an enraged earth-mother goddess longing to spank a wilful, ungrateful child. Her eyes were shooting sparks of anger, and her tightened mouth was trying to hold back a further torrent of scalding words.

Anthea, her proud defiance of cruel Fate cowed and frightened by this all too human but hardly recognizable Fran, crumpled on to the divan, and whimpered, 'Don't Fran! Please don't . . . Come back and let me explain.'

An explosion of gas empties its container in one vivid eruption. Though feeling very weak at the knees and suddenly very feeble, Fran turned back. Anthea got up and stumbled towards her. Fran led her back to the divan, and waited till the tempest of tears was past.

'So?' she asked, her voice still cold. 'What happened? Let me warn you that I don't propose to sit here and listen to a tirade of complaints about a man with a heart of gold actually daring to try to lay it at your elegant feet. He'd built himself a castle of dreams made out of the ruins of three other marriages. You slighted it. Why? Because he dared to love you enough to want to marry you? Because it insulted your image of yourself to have to admit you would be wife number four? You, the ice-queen of airline tickets to romantic places, to come down to be a village doctor's wife?

'You have no conception of what Love is any more than he had, till that day all the physical attraction you'd had for him from the minute he set eyes on you vanished like dew against the sun of the other sort of Love: the kind that comes from the heart before it gets to the loins. Most people in your sort of society nowadays don't know there is a difference between Love and "lerve", but you've had a second chance to learn, and scorned it. You didn't love him enough to risk it, so you turned him down – and broke him. He won't be able to stand against it this time. He'll be finished as a doctor and as a man. He can't live now without either the Love he thought he'd found, or the self-esteem he thought he'd recovered. He's giving up, too, as soon as he can find someone he can hand his patients over to, so that at least he won't have to despise himself professionally as well as in every other way.'

141

She stood up again, and looked down at the moaning woman on the divan. 'I hope you're satisfied, that's all.'

'Oh Fran – don't, don't. You've got it all wrong. Let me tell you.'

Struck with sudden fear, and shame at being so rude and hasty in her judgement, Fran hesitated. Whatever the reason, there was no doubt that Anthea was suffering already. She had no right to be executioner as well as judge and jury. She had lost her temper, which she didn't often do. The only way to make amends was to sit down again and listen to the defence.

'You've got it all wrong, Fran, honestly. The truth's quite the opposite to what you think. I hadn't expected him to marry me – you know why. I had told myself hundreds of times that I must make the most of what I had while I had it, before some other woman as whole and beautiful as I used to be came over his horizon and took him from me. I'd steeled myself against that.

'Then one day, when his house was nearly finished, he just rushed at me with a proposal that he should marry me and share it with him. Not a word of warning, and it was hardly a romantic proposal. I can only think that he hadn't prepared himself to make it any more than I had to consider it. I wondered who had been getting at him to "do the right thing" by me. Somebody like your Sophie, or George Bridgefoot – or even Beth. It took my breath away, and he demanded an answer there and then. I couldn't believe he really meant it; I thought there must be some hidden reason for it. I knew what I had to do.'

Her head came up proudly as she looked Fran straight in the eye. 'I love him far too much to let him sacrifice himself on only half a woman he has been kind to. You speak as if you are the only authority on Love, but others besides you have had some experience, you know. I happen to know as well as Beth does what the Bible says about Love – that it never puts itself first – and my training as an air-hostess endorsed that in very practical terms. Why is it always the captain who is the last to leave a sinking ship? An air-hostess's duty is to get the passengers out before escaping herself. I had to save him, whatever happened to me. But oh, Fran, I had no idea how hard it would be! I love him so much! I love him! I love him! And if I've hurt him as much as you say, he'll never forgive me now. What good can you and Beth do? What can I, or anybody else do, now? Nothing! Nothing! Nothing!'

Fran gathered the despairing girl up into her arms, and stroked the curly head, her own tears dropping silently to mingle with Anthea's. She found her handkerchief, and wiped both faces till the beautiful, stricken one was lifted to look beseechingly into hers, even attempting a brave smile of gratitude.

The gods did need help. As she thought what Nigel had said, hope came flooding back. Fran's empty cruse was filling fast again.

'Anthea,' she said. 'I apologize. Forgive me now – but we mustn't waste any more time just grieving. We're not too late. I didn't mean to interfere, honestly. How could we – Beth and I – stand by and let two people we love as much as we do you and Terry ruin both your lives without making some sort of effort to save you? My part in our plan was to find out your real reason for turning Terry down. You've told me. Beth has undertaken to get him to her side while I'm with you, to beg him at least not to give up his livelihood here till we know if there is any hope. It seemed possible to us that you hadn't meant quite what you said. We simply had to try. *And we're not too late.* I'm terribly sorry I lost my temper, but thank whatever gods there be that it means we have time to put things right.'

'But it's all round the village by now,' said Anthea. 'That I've turned him down, I mean, and that he's leaving, and why. I don't see how meekly giving in can restore his prestige with his patients, or his self-esteem can be restored to him just by asking me again.'

'Thousands of men have had to, I think; women being the idiots they often are. But I'm afraid I've got another muddle to sort out tonight. In any case, I still have a husband who's had no supper and who, if I don't ring him to fetch me at once, will begin to think I've run off with Terry under your very nose.'

Anthea smiled a weak smile at Fran's feeble joke.

Fran went to ring William, and when she returned Anthea

143

was sitting thoughtfully. 'Fran, just one more thing. Tell me what to do now.'

Fran went back to kiss her again. 'Swear to me to act just as you have been doing since Easter. Terry will be given the same advice. Be hopeful – and ready for anything.'

'I swear,' said Anthea solemnly. She didn't know whether to laugh or cry as Fran slammed the door behind herself.

*

The fog had thickened. Fran stood at the gate waiting for William. He cautiously negotiated a three-point turn in the narrow lane. She wished she needn't keep him out longer, but hoped he would understand once she was able to tell him what a tangled web had been spun around her since he had left her this morning. It wasn't a web of deceit – in fact, far from it. It had only become tangled because the two main threads had got crossed, and time was short to put them right separately. Nobody was deceiving anybody else deliberately; secrets were only being kept in order to help. She hadn't had time to explain the complexity to William properly before dropping him into the middle of it.

'Back to Monastery Farm, and Nigel, next, I suppose,' she said, as she got into the car beside him.

His reply was curt, but decisive. So he wasn't in a very good mood. Oh dear, she did so much need his usual empathy with her tonight, but she could see she was going to have to tread warily.

'No. Not tonight. You've had enough for one day, and so have I.'

'But I promised!' she said.

'Too bad. I didn't. I wasn't consulted. I gather that we are all lost in a maze of secrets as thick as this damned fog is, and I'm not properly briefed about any of them. I've had a most uncomfortable evening avoiding pitfalls I didn't know were there. You'd told me just enough to make me careful. Nigel isn't at Monastery Farm now, anyway. I helped him get back to his own quarters in Spotted Cow Lane before Eric came back, because Nigel was afraid he would resent him leaving, and prevent him if he could. He said I was to tell you that he would ring you first thing tomorrow morning.

144

'I had to go back there to wait for you to ring me, and Eric did come in, saying that when he left the Old Rectory, Beth was still expecting you. He had no more idea what it was all about than I have, except that he knew Terry had visited Beth earlier. I took it upon myself to ring Beth and say the fog was too thick for me – figuratively as well as actually, since I had no real idea what was going on and had spent the whole evening like a cat on hot bricks. So I insist on taking you straight home. Beth asked me to tell you to ring her early tomorrow.

'Perhaps I can stop playing Blind Man's Buff now. The only thing I'm at all clear about is what Nigel and I decided we couldn't be clear about. So for the moment, Fran, for God's sake stop being agony Aunt Jemima, and give some attention to me. This village is becoming a bloody madhouse.'

He'd reached the end of the lane where it met the road; another car creeping through the dense fog on the wrong side of the road was far too close to him. He braked violently, and swore under his breath. He really was in a bad mood. She knew it wasn't exactly her fault, but she could see what a difficult position she had put him in. It wasn't like him not to offer her his loving support when he knew she was in distress – and she had been, and was again now. Not only because she was feeling the effect of all the long day, but because she had given promises that he, without consulting her, had made her break. He was right in one thing though, she'd had enough. It was touch and go whether his present attitude would make her angry again, or dissolve her into tears.

She clenched her fists till her nails dug into her palms and made up her mind that whatever he said, or did, would not provoke a quarrel between them. Though he was in a bad mood, he was still 'her' William: poor Sir Galahad lost in a fog and with one of his spurs caught in the fringe of his horse's trappings, so that however much he wanted to, he couldn't get off his high horse. The thought amused her, and she felt better. They were very nearly home now. They crept down the avenue of trees towards the house, but try as he might, William's mind was not on his driving. He misjudged the distance, and turned too soon.

There was a scraping sound as he grazed the offside mudguard of his car on the stout gatepost, and stopped abruptly.

'Beelzebub and the pit,' he hissed. 'Damnation seize the whole bloody boiling of 'em!' He was trying to back off the gatepost without more damage to his car. 'That's what you get for trying to be civilized,' he said. 'Bloody mayhem!'

He was so right! It was all too silly for words, but she was afraid that if she tried to speak to soothe him she would burst into tears. She was fishing for her already damp handkerchief when he silently – and, it seemed to her, contemptuously – handed her his unopened clean one. She took it and pressed it to her mouth – and at that moment the tangled spur freed itself too suddenly, and they left the gatepost backwards at high speed. Then the engine shuddered, and stopped.

He put the lights out, and was silent. She laid her cheek against his coat – and, fog or no fog, however exasperated, he could not resist the nearness of her. He let go of the wheel to put his arms round her, and she felt rather than heard him heave a great sigh.

As they sat like that at the very gates of their Shangri-la, their battered morale began to raise its head again.

'I'm sorry, my darling,' she said. 'But I truly couldn't help it. Don't be cross with me.'

'I'm not cross with you,' he said, tightening his arms. 'Only with myself. I ought to have more sense. If you will marry a madwoman, you should expect to live in a madhouse. But, sweetheart, I wouldn't live anywhere else than here or with any other woman but you for . . .' He had switched on the lights again, and was now edging the car safely between the wide gateposts, his concentration restored.

'. . . all the tea in China!' she finished for him, as the car engine fell into silence.

'Let China keep its tea,' he said. 'It's not good enough for me. No, for all the stars in the Milky Way and every daisy in spring.'

Tears were pricking under her eyelids now, as she leaned towards him. 'What a lovely thing to say,' she said.

'Well, my darling, that's just how much I love you. You can't see the stars now for the fog, and it isn't spring. But the stars are still in our sky, and the daisies alive under our feet. If we lose sight of them like we did a few minutes ago, just remember they're still there. And will be, always. For ever and a day.'

*　　*　　*

The fog had lifted by the next morning, but as William said, after yesterday nothing would have pleased him better than to stay in bed with Fran's head on his shoulder. He wanted to tell her all about his activities the day before. He'd come home bursting to get her advice on his last great decision – truly – before he could start to write.

But he had found her – and therefore himself – embroiled in such a tangle of other people's troubles that he had known he would have to wait his turn for her attention; and as it had been his interference that had postponed her obligations till this morning, he'd resigned himself to wait. But if she didn't mind, while she dealt with Nigel and Beth, he'd go up to see Bob. There was something they had to do urgently, before anybody else went poking about round the little church.

Fran breathed a sigh of relief. She knew he'd had a lot of justification for being fed-up, and for becoming so touchy and bossy last night. The very last thing she wanted at this troubled time was to get 'off hooks', as Sophie would say, with him. So she welcomed his decision to occupy both his time and his mind with something other than a feeling of obligation to help her.

William's mention of Nigel reminded her of something he'd said last night: that the only thing he'd been at all clear about was what he and Nigel had decided they couldn't be clear about. Perhaps she'd better find out what that was before she plunged back into the troubled waters. She asked him to tell her.

'We talked mostly, as I told you, about the general malaise that appears to be affecting everybody, without actually asking each other any questions or giving anything away to each other.

We stalked each other like a couple of strange tomcats, both of us afraid of letting any other cat out of any other bag. The safest subject was one that you and I had witnessed: Marjorie's outburst. We agreed that she had not told us the truth – well, not the whole truth.'

There was certainly more to her worry than she had told them. Neither Fran nor William could conjecture what the new element was.

'She's not normally the sort of woman to give up, sit down and cry. She may indeed be very upset at Terry's fear of complications, but nothing is yet confirmed,' William said. 'She isn't a Jess, always ready to play the tragedy queen at the drop of a hat! She's more likely to be fighting-angry than tragically rushing forward to what might be. Something's obviously distressing her – but I've got no idea what.'

'She sounds like Mariana in the moated grange,' said Fran, for once rather sceptical. 'Behaving more like an adolescent girl suffering from a bout of love-sickness than a middle-aged woman finding herself with a bit of an overload, and wailing:

> '"*I am aweary, aweary,*
> *I would that I were dead!*"

'But Marjorie? It can't be anything of that kind with her, so we're probably doing her a great injustice. And yet it seems to involve Yorky. Why? Just because she thinks she may have to cope without him at a family lunch-party? That doesn't make much sense!

'Do you suppose it possible that she's fallen for him? A long delayed reaction to her determination never to have any sort of sexual relationship with any man again, once she was free of her disgusting husband? Or could it be that because she sees in Yorky something different, it's roused her enough to make her mad with Eric for sticking to their reciprocal resolve never to be more than friends? That doesn't make sense, either. It isn't as if they're a couple of silly mooning teenagers. So what is the molehill she's building into a mountain? Or is there really a mountain that we

148

can't see, and she can't climb alone? I'll keep my ears open for clues.'

During breakfast, William remarked on Sophie's long absence. 'I think we haven't realized how lucky we've been till now, always being able to rely on her to supply our every want, and lighten our darkness every morning as well. I miss her.'

Fran laughed delightedly. It pleased her enormously that he should admit so spontaneously to feelings she'd had herself, but had thought wise not to give voice to. 'Keep your crest up, Galahad. You've only got to go it alone a few days longer, till the rest of your lance catches up with you. By Monday, you'll have your sergeant at your side again, and your varlet, Olive 'Opkins.'

'Honestly? What a prospect! Sophie the Faithful, and Olive the Unknown Quantity. Well, that *is* something to look forward to. Till then, I imagine we have to do what we can to rout the forces ranged against us. Whatever I said last night, my darling, you know I'm with you every step of the way. It's just that I'm afraid of saying or doing the wrong thing because I'm not yet fully briefed. If you need me today, try ringing here first, and if you get no answer, try Jane to see if I'm with Bob. I think you ought to get off. Nigel will be champing at the bit, and Beth straining at the leash. Oh dear. Whatever should we do without such clichés?'

'God only knows,' she said and, catching his eye, they both chuckled. A good start to the day.

Nigel was ready to set off when she reached Spotted Cow Lane. He asked her indoors, and she told him briefly what he wanted to know. Yes, she had seen Anthea, and there was hope that with care and Eric's assistance, things could be put right. She had not yet been able to see Beth, but she fully believed that Terry was as much in love as he'd ever been, and that if everybody trod warily, he might be persuaded to think hard before bolting yet again. That was as much as she dared promise.

The Marjorie problem was more difficult. She could only tell him of her conviction that whatever was the cause of Marjorie's distress, to get Pansy back into the fold could do nothing but good. She urged him to do his best to see that the girl came home in time.

He promised, but said time was short, especially as the two issues, on the surface nothing whatsoever to do with each other, had somehow now become interlocked.

'I hate to ask you,' he said, 'but I think the next thing, after you've found out what Beth made of Terry, is for somebody to see Eric – and as soon as possible. Will you do it? Go and bring him up to date – as far as you and I understand the situation – and ask his advice and help. He won't refuse. I couldn't broach it to him myself last night because I had no idea what Anthea's feelings were. If I get off now, I shall pray for there to have been some sort of resolution when I return. You see, I'm beginning to worry about Eric, too, and I feel that by going away just now I'm letting him down. But I do think Pansy must come first. Even friendship has its drawbacks.' He left, and she went straight on to see Beth.

'Difficult,' said Beth, as soon as they were alone, 'but I think not hopeless. Terry's been confiding in me ever since he became our friend as well as our doctor, and I've known all along how damaged he is by what he says were all his own mistakes and failures. Not, in my judgement, by any means all his fault. So all the way along I've stuck to the old adage that it's never too late to mend. In some ways, I was right.

'But, Fran, I'm afraid I'm not a very good psychologist. What I'd missed was that in this small closed community, he was too much aware of the eyes focused on him, knowing he had to live down three failed marriages and defend himself in a moot-court before a jury made up of people such as Beryl Bean and Thirzah Bates. People who hated change being forced on them, and full of resentment against him because he was young compared with "Old Henderson". Not the same as the doctor they had lost. Then they heard of his marital disasters, and suspected him of being a "snake-in-the-grass". I didn't realize either how very sensitive he is. It must have taken a lot of guts and will-power to stay here and stick it out.'

Fran nodded. 'He seemed to be winning, too. It didn't take

him long to find out how to fill Dr Henderson's shoes. I think that restored his professional pride, and believing Anthea cared for him gave him back his lost self-esteem as a man. All for nothing.'

Beth was near tears. 'She smashed his dreams to smithereens. Scorned him. Put him back where he was, only worse. He won't lower his pride ever to ask her again. He said so, flat. And his self-esteem is too low for him to go on battling against what he now feels is inimical Fate. He wants to bolt – yet again. He won't listen to any whisper of hope. Look.'

She took from a tiny drawer in an occasional table by her side a jeweller's ring-box, and sprung the lid open. Inside on a bed of velvet was a Victorian gold band set with a half-hoop of large diamonds between two other rows of smaller rose-diamonds. It was exquisite, and Fran held it lovingly and admiringly as she looked up at Beth for explanation.

'His mother's,' Beth said. 'Treasured beyond measure by him for her sake – so much so that when he was contemplating marriage for the first time, he couldn't bring himself to give it to a girl he knew was not worthy to wear it. Then came Marcia, and the boot was on the other foot. It wasn't good enough for her – by *her* reckoning. She had a much grander one of her own grandmother's which she insisted on lending him to give back to her, pretending it was one of his family's heirlooms.

'He didn't even think of giving it to number three. I think I told you how by that time he was utterly cynical about any connection between love and marriage. As far as he was concerned, marriage was a good cover for a great deal of promiscuous sex, and served only to maintain his professional reputation, because that wife was the daughter of one of his partners. I blame Marcia for most of it.

'As he told me, his genuine love for Anthea was something new to him, and this ring became his amulet. He had it in his pocket to give her when he asked her to marry him. As he handed it to me he said that it's probably been a bringer of ill-luck all the time and the sooner he got rid of it, and any hopes of what it had stood for, the better.

151

'I gave it back to him and after one more look at it he pitched it in the fire! I yelled at him not to be such a flaming idiot, and that if he didn't want it, he needn't destroy it. I scrambled to rescue it out of the flames and gave it back to him. Then I let into him – I couldn't help it, Fran. I asked him if he had a shred of conscience, because if not his pretence of being a doctor who cared for suffering humanity had no credence at all! Its worth, I said, could save the lives of hundreds of starving children, and if he didn't consider that, his professionalism as a caring medical man was as false as his protestations as a lover had ever proved him to be!

'He was stung and hurt, I could see, and tossed it into my lap, saying that if that's what I thought of him, I could have the damned thing to do as I liked with. And then he stalked out. I'm sorry, Fran. I haven't been at all successful. I've only made him worse. What shall I do with this?'

'Keep it, for the time being. The matter isn't over and done with. It may yet be a good-luck charm. Let's believe in it till we know. We've still got to go on trying. What a pair of fools he and Anthea are, and what a ridiculous unholy mess they've got themselves into!'

Fran launched into a brief but accurate account of her trip to Anthea's cottage last evening. 'So,' she said, 'it seems to be up to us. Nigel has asked me to go to see Eric, to enlist his help, if we can. He says we must persuade him to delay Terry's instructions to put the restored cottage on the market – any excuse will do. But the wheel has come full circle. It all started because Effendi hustled Terry before he wasn't quite ready, by asking whether or not he wanted to keep his present accommodation at the Old Surgery after Christmas. So we need to see Effendi as well – he won't mind things being held up, when he knows the reason why. William isn't ready for a typist yet, and I doubt if Effendi is. But he must be told what's happening. And in any case Eric's first plans had depended to some extent on him.

'Nigel says Eric's the key, and I think I agree with him. I believe that Eric is the *deus ex machina* the gods keep ready to come to their aid when they don't know what to do next. Come with me to see him – and bring the amulet. We'll call on Effendi on our way home.'

They were told at the hotel that Mr Choppen had been there that morning, but had gone home again. He often did that, just lately. Deflated, they turned back to Monastery Farm, and there they found him, sitting alone behind a newspaper over a drink in an otherwise empty and silent house. He was rather embarrassed to see them there, seeming to feel a need to explain to them why he was.

'I'm redundant everywhere at this time of day,' he said. 'The hotel's got to the point where it runs on oiled wheels and doesn't need me. The Estate Manager's the best we've ever had, and in any case I know nothing about farming. There are no more old cottages or houses to restore, and if I ever did intend to be a developer, in the modern sense of the word, I've lost my taste for it. I'm at a loose end. I've been glad to have Nigel to come home to, and hoped to keep him for a bit longer, but he's got too much on his plate already and, as I'm sure you know, William helped him to escape last night. I hate the house as empty as this. You caught me contemplating either moving back into the hotel, or selling out and looking for fresh territory to conquer.'

No mention of Marjorie. Fran felt a cold hollow in the pit of her stomach.

'Nigel sent me to see you. We want your help. Please don't pretend you don't know what it's all about: the end of Anthea's little romance with Terry. I understand from Anthea, whom I went to see last night, that she has asked you to release her at once from her job, and her lease of the cottage. Beth says Terry has asked you to put his cottage on the market.

'Nigel, who incidentally sends you his apologies, said he would beg of you not to be in too much of a hurry to oblige either of them. Just in case things can still be put right. Anthea doesn't mean what she said to Terry at all. I know because she told me so. And from what Terry told Beth, his present attitude boils down to piqued pride and his predilection to bolt at the first hint of any "woman trouble". They're both in love far more than either of them realized till all this happened. It's nothing but a silly misunderstanding, but it'll prove a tragic one if we can't stop it from getting worse.'

Eric sat up, and put aside his newspaper. He was looking interested as well as grave. 'Go on,' he said.

'Well, first, you must forgive Beth for letting the cat out of the bag about the plans you had to unveil the cottage on my birthday followed by a celebration lunch. William and I haven't arranged anything, partly because we're still without Sophie's help, and partly because we'd decided to lie low until George and Molly's Golden Wedding day was over. But couldn't we still have our birthday lunch, while the Bridgefoots are having their family gathering at the Old Glebe at the same time? Beth and I want to play a little game.'

'We'll still celebrate your birthday if you'd like to, but I don't see how I can do anything about Terry and Anthea. They appear to be washed up and I'm left with the business end of it on my hands. One expensive desirable residence to be disposed of, a cottage to be let, and a new member of staff to find before Christmas. Business shouldn't ever be mixed with pleasure, and friendship only curdles both. I should be out of my depth trying to play fairy godmother to a couple of seasoned warriors in the love stakes like those two are, anyway.

'And to tell the truth, I'm in none too good a mood myself to want to have anything to do with anybody's affairs of the heart – and, honestly, I'd advise you not to try. I can't see even a gleam of hope if the two of them won't play; it could be a most awful fiasco to try to involve them. I know well enough how far you'd both be willing to stick your necks out, but I'm afraid I think it would be better for you to stay right out of it. Don't risk it. You don't have a magic wand.'

'No,' said Fran stubbornly. 'But we do have a lucky charm. Tell us exactly why you're so pessimistic. It isn't like you.'

Eric's dubious expression was replaced by a grave one. He spoke slowly, as one with bad news to impart. 'There's much more to it than disappointment over spoiled plans,' he said, 'sad though a middle-aged romance on the rocks may be in its own right. It's really the same sort of crisis as William's fight for

154

tradition against Bailey and his modern ideas – when we won. It's a running battle between the old and the new. The old won that battle, but not the war. Though Bailey is out of it, another try at taking us over has been looming, and I've watched it growing, though I must say, I didn't expect it to be brought to a head over a lover's quarrel. When I first came here the old village was in ruins, and I saw the possibility of developing it with new housing estates – that was, until I arrived. Then the sentimental streak in me rebelled against helping to destroy anything so typically English. It occurred to me that it might be just as successful to restore the old instead of bulldozing it down and building new. It worked – and the real miracle was that it was in time to preserve the old community spirit as well. But in a way, we've been too successful. Church End has become a community by itself, broken away from the new, larger village of Old Swithinford, just as that broke away from Swithinford town in the first place. I drew your attention to the potential danger of us being outnumbered by the rest as voters within our local government democracy. Unless we keep our own end up, we shall simply be swamped, and this bit of English countryside I've had such a hand in restoring will be lost for ever. It depends on us. But what happens? Just when we need to stick firmly together, our centre falls apart, the break-up sparked off by a lovers' quarrel. Only a pointer – what it really means is that we're all too busy with our own concerns to see how much we're giving away of what we'd already gained.

'Nigel's got two old churches to save on his plate; William and Effendi are both preoccupied with books they want to write; Bob's got two farms to look after; and Greg's fame as an artist's brought him too many commissions. We still had – perhaps still have, I can't be sure – two assets other than Elyot as our prospective candidate on local councils. One, the Bridgefoots, the very essence of rural English countryside; and two, what we had hardly hoped for, a new doctor prepared to walk in his predecessor's footsteps, as a sort of keystone to the arch. As likely to be needed by one side as the other; by well-to-do and poor, by young and old, by male and female. Willing to learn the inside as well as the outside of us as a community. Just what we needed. But he turns out to be only half the man we thought him. He runs away – from a woman! And there's something amiss with the Bridgefoots, as well. I don't know what, but it's eating into their roots. Is the time right for anybody to be playing with ideas of magic wands and happy romantic endings?

'I can't help. No, I won't help. I'll do anything in my power to help you two to do what you've set your heart on; but not put my oar in as a businessman. As it is, you place me in a dilemma. I can't go ahead with what I'd sentimentally planned for unveiling Terry's house with bit of fun and ceremony, obviously. But I will set up the lunch party for your birthday, Fran – that has nothing to do with business. If you insist on enlarging that to fit your plans, it's nothing to do with me, or my business links with Hardy or with Anthea.

'Keep me posted. And now if you'll excuse me I must get back to the hotel to see what mischance has happened there in my absence.'

*

'Well, that's better than nothing, I suppose,' Beth said as they drove away towards Effendi's house. 'A base to start from is useful. I wasn't at all surprised by Eric's little sermon: he's been preaching it a lot lately to Elyot. I'm afraid it isn't doing much good. If anything, it's putting Elyot off. But he's right about one thing: we're all getting far too turned in on ourselves as individuals. We've got to find a way of snapping out of it.'

Effendi was his usual welcoming, courteous self, and both women breathed a sigh of relief at his easy acceptance of going along with whatever Eric suggested for the birthday party, including sending out invitations for as many as his dining table would accommodate. He said they would have to provide him with a list of guests.

'And there,' said Fran to Beth as they went back to the Old Rectory for a snack lunch, 'is where we are left holding the baby. Do we invite Terence, or Anthea, or both – or neither?'

'Both, of course,' said Beth stoutly. 'They can't have lost all their social marbles. They can but accept or refuse, but this amulet in my pocket tells me to hope that they will both be there. We shall simply invite them, and . . .'

'And what? Leave it to the gods, I suppose. I must say, Beth, that there are times when you almost take my breath away. You, orthodox cradle Christian as you are, being prepared to put your trust in a bit of folk-magic, and a gang of unknown "gods"!'

Beth answered her more seriously than Fran had expected. 'None of us can do without a bit of magic,' she said. 'And all religions depend upon the Unknown. "The gods" as a whole include my own particular one, anyway.' Fran felt duly chastened.

*

William was late coming in, looking relaxed and cheerful. They sat long over their supper, which Fran had enjoyed cooking, her mind now on the future instead of the past, and just chatted.

Later, in the sitting-room, she gave William a guarded résumé of her day's doings. She didn't want to bore him with too much more of the same that had caused his burst of impatience last night. He listened, and at the end of her tale remarked that if it had concerned anybody but herself and Beth, he'd have begun to doubt the state of their minds, so hopeless was the cause they were espousing. Ought they really to be contemplating trying to turn the course of other people's private lives?

But as it was them – well, only fools and saints attempted the impossible, and only saints succeeded. He'd go along with them as far as he could be any good, and give their magic a chance.

'One can't know Bob as well as we do,' he said, 'and dismiss magic altogether. I've been with him all day today, or I should probably be a lot more sceptical. I want to talk about what he and I did today, but let's leave it till the morning. It's time you gave me a bit of your attention, and I need your advice. But then, is there ever a time when I don't need you in some way or another?'

'You shall have every moment of my time and attention tomorrow, if you want it,' she said. 'Let the gods look after the destiny of Terry and Anthea by themselves till after the weekend.'

He smiled the smile that still turned her heart over. 'They managed things all right for us,' he said. 'If anybody ought to be willing to trust them, we should.'

* * *

It was over the next morning's leisurely breakfast that William began to tell her of his trip out with Bob yesterday. He'd gone straight up to Castle Hill, and was just in time to catch Bob setting out for his fen farm. A good chance for William to see the fen at its least attractive, Bob said, on a cold and slightly misty November morning. Neither of them had anything of any great importance to do, why not take advantage of it?

'I guessed he had a plan in mind. He must know that I haven't lived the greater part of my life in and around Cambridge without knowing the geography of the area, but as to "knowing the fens", that's a different question. I've driven across there to get to the A1 times without number, usually either talking to a passenger, or preoccupied with other matters, or feeling sorry for myself. Unless you actually set out on a sight-seeing expedition, a car's about the very worst place from which to observe anything properly, especially for the driver. And if you're alone, the car's just a tin box on wheels inside which you're trapped with your own immediate concerns.

'Like researching history: you tend to take notice most of what you're looking for, and therefore latch on to what you know already, and skip details that might be relevant if you gave them enough attention. The day we went to Little Gidding was a sort of revelation to me. Why did that affect me so much?

'I've stood on many battlefields before, and visited all sorts of famous historical places, without any shivers going up and down my spine like I had that day. I expect I'd got blasé about it, but I think I understand now that I was so loaded with factual history that the aura of the places themselves didn't get through to me as it did, for instance, to T. S. Eliot when he visited spots he knew to be soaked through and through with Time. It's so easy to see what you already know, and miss the feelings that transform them into something new and other. I didn't know the fens till Bob showed me yesterday, and I saw, and I felt them. For the first time.'

'As Alexander Pope said,' she put in, '"*Man sees only what he knows*". But go on, tell me. Everything.' So William took up his tale again.

They had simply 'tootled along' together, each filling gaps in the other's knowledge. Bob was always fascinated by history, because, as William said, he had a true sense of the past, as if he belonged to it as well as to the present. But he only knew what facts of history he had picked up for himself by reading, and by listening avidly to William in the last year or two.

On the other hand, he had specialist knowledge of things that were, of course, important scraps of history to which William had barely given a thought. Bob knew a great deal about what the fens must have been before drainage, because of his deep knowledge of their strange characteristics, which few people other than indigenous fen-folk had. He explained in detail how the drainage system worked now, what it had been like before 1934, and pointed examples out as they went.

Happy just to be together, they ambled their way via Somersham to Chatteris and from there by a very narrow by-road to meet Vermuyden's Drain, which Bob referred to as 'the Forty Foot'. Along its bleak bank, they overlooked wide fens on either side as far as Ramsey Hollow, passed the site of the medieval abbey, and entered Ramsey town. They went down 'the Great Whyte' and left Ramsey towards St Mary's (named after its church) and St Mary's Bridge. A mile or so out of town, the road ran by the side of 'Ramsey River' – a name newly coined, Bob commented contemptuously, by know-all newcomers for what was, in fact, the old course of the River Nene. At St Mary's Bridge, Bob told William that his farm lay to their left, in the area of what had once been Ugg Mere, and said he would take him there later; but he thought they'd go first to have another look at 'the Holme Post'.

'It's one thing to think you know all about peat,' Bob said, 'like how fertile it is, and how lucky farmers are who own a few fields of it. Folks who don't know think it's all peat land round here, and though there is a lot of it, not all fields are peaty by a

159

long way. And dealing with them that are ain't all sunshine, specially nowadays. Folks bred and born here still know more about peat than archaeologists from Cambridge who make studies of it and write books about it.'

Bob had looked sideways at his enthralled listener with a mischievous twinkle in his eye. 'And you know what a fenman'd say about that, I reckon?'

'No,' said William. 'Tell me.'

Bob laughed. 'Why, that "knowing beats thinking's arse off". But the scholars are got to come while there's any peat left. At this rate it'll all be gone in another hundred year. It's shrinking, year by year, drained too well since the new pumps at St Germans were put in. When peat's wet, it swells, and when it's dried out, it shrivels to black dust as'll blow away. So the more they pump to keep it from flooding, the lower it gets, so they have to pump still harder – and there we go round the mulberry bush. In a fen blow, you lose your topsoil and your seedling crops with it. Still, there's plenty of peat left in some places. That's what I want to show you.'

William, of course, had read about this, and even heard of the Holme Post. But he hadn't till that moment realized its significance. They went along the Herne Road till they came to a left turning towards Holme. The landscape through which they were now travelling, Holme Fen, was familiar to him only because of the many old maps he had pored over while reading 'Bob's manuscript'. He could hardly believe his eyes when he caught sight of a very small and worn-out finger post pointing uncertainly to a 'Daintree Farm'. So even that small detail from the manuscript was still accurately identifiable!

He began to feel lost in time as well as space. The day was dark and inclined to be misty, the fog spreading out to a veiled horizon under the dome of grey sky, which trapped a vista of nothing but fields of jet-black earth, chequered by dykes filled with black-brown water, only relieved here and there by clumps of last year's reed and sedge where dykes had not been 'roded'.

A savage place, and yet, somehow, a peaceful one; its great expanse dwarfed puny men into submission to its wild, cold, bleak majesty. Here and there were signs of occupation – a bridge over a wide drain, with what had once been a riverside pub still lived in if no longer a public house; very infrequently the sound of a tractor at work, so far away that it melted into the mysterious horizon. And then, suddenly, the scene began to change.

Trees. Silver birch. At first only a lone one here and there, then clumps of several, then a whole wood. It was enchantingly strange and beautiful in the pallid light, the silver trunks holding up the delicate tracery of bare branches, hardly moving in the windless calm. 'Holme Wood,' Bob informed him, but said nothing more. Bob was now communing with nature as William was with the past.

'How long have there been trees round here?' he asked Bob just as they turned into a small side road among the trees, and Bob answered by pointing out to him an enormous heap of huge, rugged, greyish-black logs lying close to the verge.

'About ready for burning,' Bob remarked, 'soon as it's dry enough. We usually wait till there's forty or fifty ton to be got rid of – even more, sometimes. It's the fen farmer's bane and always has been, though I must say we hadn't ought to grumble about it now, with tractors and things to help us haul 'em out and get 'em to bits. We call 'em "black oaks", and chaps from Cambridge and such say "bog oaks", though they ain't all oak. There's a lot of pine and a few others like walnut and yew and hornbeam among 'em. That stuff's what's left of the "buried forests". So the answer to your question, as far as I understand folks as study such things have estimated, is "about four thousand year".

'But these silver birch ain't got nothing to do with them buried forests, except as I reckon it shows how quick the highest bits of the fens would go back to woodland if we let it. It seems as if they expected to be able to farm this land round here once Whittlesey Mere had been drained, but it were no good for agriculture straight off – too wet and soggy. So they set it with trees: pine and birch and a few other sorts, as growed up quick and beautiful in these conditions. Then when two wars come, one so quick after the other, and wood was wanted so bad, they very nearly cleared it. The birch self-sowed itself again.'

William was remembering. Of course he had heard of the buried forests but admitted to himself with shame that he'd never before been interested enough to look for the evidence of them that lay about here everywhere in full view. He tucked the subject away in his mind to ask Bob at a later date, because just at that moment Bob had drawn the car to the side of a small stream where a narrow little foot-bridge crossed it.

They got out, and Bob led the way over the bridge and a few yards into the now very thick wood. And there it stood: the Holme Post.

'I know very vaguely what it is and why it's here,' William said. 'But start right at the beginning, and explain it as you go.'

'Well, as you can see, it's only an old iron stanchion as is got a royal crown on top. That's 'cos it was one that they were going to throw away when they took some of the Crystal Palace down after the Great Exhibition in Queen Victoria's time. I don't know who it was, but somebody as knowed about peat shrinking got it and put it here – in 1852, it says on it – just drove it down through the peat till it rested on the blue clay underneath. More than twenty-two feet down.

'Since then it's acted as a sort of gauge to show how fast the peat's shrinking. Between 1852 and 1932 it had shrunk at the rate of about a foot every ten year. I reckon the rate of shrinkage must be a lot faster now. But there it is. Go and have a good look at it while you've got the chance.'

William did as he was bid, wondering slightly why Bob didn't accompany him. As he walked away into a little clearing on one side of the post, he was watching, and turned just in time to see Bob leap high into the air, on purpose, then come down heavily, while William experienced a very strange sensation. The earth beneath his feet bounced like a jelly till it shudderingly stopped. Bob jumped again, his face crumpled into his mischievous grin.

They walked back to the car. 'I reckon there must be about twelve foot of peat still left there,' he said. 'And there's places it wouldn't be safe to stand still on for long in case you sunk into it. There's quite a few dykes and drains as we say "ain't got no bottom". In spite of all their pumping it's just soft, black, oozy

162

mud. We'll go back now to Holme village, and then have a quick look where Holme Wood House used to be, the home of Admiral Wells in Nelson's time. We can get a snack at The Admiral, as is named after him. Then we'll go and have a quick look at my farm. We mustn't be too long, in case it might get foggy again, and then we shouldn't half catch it from our missuses.'

Fran was a good listener. She had heard much more than the words William had used to tell his story: there was the excitement in his tone, which had to be due to more than his interest in the nature of peat; and she'd followed a separate thread of understanding in her own mind of his statement that you couldn't spend a day in Bob's company and not feel the vibrations of something 'magical' about him.

William had fallen silent and she could almost hear the wheels going round in his mind. She had more sense than to speak, move, or do anything at all that could interrupt his train of thought. It seemed for that silent minute or two as if time had stopped; but when he looked up and at her, it was with a rather startled look of enormous excitement.

He stood up and went to her, reached for her hands and held her eyes with his. She could feel him trembling as he pulled her to him and almost clung to her for support as he said, breathlessly, 'Darling, I know now why I was so moved at Little Gidding, and again in Holme Wood yesterday. I've deliberately been very sparing of what I've told you of the contents of Bob's book – on purpose, because before I let you into a secret I think it holds, I must be sure that that bit is true, and can be proved. But I've told you enough for you to know that what your old relative had to tell constitutes a very important part of English history, which I'll admit now has to do with both Holme Fen and Little Gidding.

'But what I have only just realized is that *I am the only man in the whole world who knows what happened at either of those places, when it did, and why it did*. It's incredible. Too much for me to take!'

He hid his face in the nook between her neck and her shoulder, clinging to her until the shock of his discovery gradually wore off, and then went to fetch a bottle of champagne.

*

It was not until after lunch that Fran thought William's euphoria had subsided enough for her to remind him that he'd said he wanted to consult her (yet again!) about 'the final problem'.

'Yes,' he said. 'I still do, but we didn't have time to do the church as well as the fens, so I'm not quite as far forward as I'd hoped. I think I've been silly not to tell you more, but I have my reasons, honestly, sweetheart. There are bits of Bob's book I don't want to divulge to anybody yet. You know only the bare outline: that it was written by the incumbent of the church at Castle Hill during the Civil War period, a Francis Wagstaffe, who may have been your ancestor.

'I don't think you've ever really appreciated the sort of Catch 22 situation I've been in. If the manuscript is genuine, I ought to have declared it; I haven't yet lost the chance. But, when I'd solved the code and read to the end, I couldn't believe it *could* be genuine. Too good to be true. That's where so many fakers of "antique" artefacts make mistakes. They queer their own pitch. Experts usually tend to err on the side of caution. Their reputation depends on them never being proved wrong – which they are, occasionally, when something of absolutely indubitable provenance turns up almost literally as good as new. It doesn't harm the experts that way round; but to have declared as genuine what turns out to be a fake is death to them. Some fakers have been so good at their trade that they've foxed the greatest experts. Lately, it's become a minefield for historians and archaeologists and museum curators, especially as there's a growing market for such fakes, though analytical science is more or less keeping up with the fakers' expertise now. Anyway, I have had to bear caution in mind, and not let my desire for it to be genuine blind me to the fact that it could just be a clever fake.

'If I had the least doubt, I couldn't deal with it either as history or "faction", under my own name. But in my judgement it rings true. Too much for me to doubt that it's a product of the seventeenth century. Yet even that's contradictory.

'It has too authentic a "feel" about it to be a modern fake intended for sale one day at Sotheby's. On the other hand, the style's so "modern" in tone that it's difficult to accept it as an *unadulterated* work of seventeenth-century origin. So did somebody else find something like it, improve on it, fake the appearance of it, and then hide it till the time was ripe? Faking antique artefacts had a good run in the 1890s, and there are still unscrupulous dealers benefiting from their efforts. There could have been such a dealer about when the church was restored in the nineteenth century, somebody who found the original, souped it up, hid it and intended one day to "find" it again. Perhaps just as the last war broke out, so he may never have lived to retrieve it and make use of it. Only a possibility, but one I simply had to consider, though it didn't make much sense. The ledger, the paper, the faded ink and the way it was packaged – all perfectly possible by a good faker – wouldn't have been a good enough bet financially, unless he'd had a customer waiting. Nobody would go to all that trouble just on chance. He'd have damned it as a fake if he had let on that he knew anything of what was in the sealed packet. As good a faker as that wouldn't have done it simply in the hope that when it was found he could prove any right to it. So what other explanatory options are there? That it was genuinely seventeenth century, but fiction – or faction – written by somebody who had nothing else to do to occupy his time? As Bunyan did, for example, when in prison?

'Possible, but the snag sticks out a mile. If it was *ever* intended for publication, why put the most important section of it into a code that nobody could read and not leave the key to the code? I've been struggling with all these problems from the first. Problems that I couldn't expect Bob to understand. I couldn't *prove* that what I believed to be new and invaluable "documentary evidence" was genuine.

'Documentary evidence is what modern historians make their touchstone, but it is as open to doubt as any other artefact unless it can be substantiated by some other parallel proof. I told you that I daren't simply translate it and publish it under my own name. That would have risked discrediting my personal integrity, and my reputation.

'Your instant response was that if it was a good story, why not accept it as that? Translate it, write it up as fiction, and use a pseudonym. It was an intriguing idea, and I nearly fell for it. We even invented a title and a pen-name for me to hide behind.

'But at that point, *I hadn't read all of it*. When I'd decoded the last part, I was convinced that it was absolutely genuine, and very important *as history*. But without a bit more proof than I had, it would still have been dangerous to me and my reputation. I ought not to have done anything with it without sanction.

'Your alternative, to publish it only as a rattling good tale by a wholly fictitious author – who in any case hadn't the faintest notion of how to tackle the job – lost a lot of its attraction. Somebody "out there" would soon have put two and two together and identified me as the author! So I compromised for the time – thank goodness you went along with me – and decided that if published at all, as history or as fiction, I'd let it stand under my own name. Sink or swim.

'Darling, I know what a hopeless, procrastinating old ditherer I've appeared to be, but my compromise was a necessary delaying tactic. There's a lot in it that you don't yet know, and that I can't – no, *I won't* disclose to you till I've done everything in my power to prove it "right" or just another fake. Go on believing in me!

'Then the end bit of it has personal bearing on the Wagstaffes of the time and on this house, Benedict's. Have you never wondered why it was named "Benedict's", when first built in the eighteenth century? Has it never occurred to you what a coincidence it is that what we know as the church of St Saviour is in fact the Church of St Saviour *and St Benedict*? Built in the middle ages by the *Benedictine* monks of Ramsey Abbey?

'The penny began to drop for me when I asked myself why the end – the most important bit – was written in such haste, and in code to which only hints of a key were left. There could be only one explanation. *The author was running scared, in peril of his life.* From whom if not from his neighbour, Oliver Cromwell? From the beginning it is made clear that the writer knew Cromwell personally, and their families had been personally acquainted for generations. But Oliver, apparently, had always been a threat to this branch of the Wagstaffes.

166

'The more I think about it, the more convinced I am that what he set down is true. So I'm going to write it as fiction, under my own name; a compromise that will satisfy my conscience, because if it is ever published I'll give my explanations and excuses as a historian, and then, with your permission, I'll hand the original over to sow the seeds of more academic research by future historians.'

She interrupted him. 'Why will you want my permission?'

'Too long to go into it now, but I imagine there might have to be a coroner's inquest as to whose it is. Bob's, because he found it? The Church Commissioners', because it was found in a church? Or yours, if Francis is proved to be your *direct* ancestor? And the book itself gives hints that something else may still be hidden in the church which would provide the proof I need. There's still more. I know what I'm looking for, but Bob has no idea. He says that whatever it is, he "feels" it's still there and we've missed it. While the church still stands and we can go on searching, we shall. But please, darling, will you promise not to quiz me too much about it? It's my great secret, and it's for you, personally – I think possibly my greatest ever love-gift to you, if ever I get it done and can lay it at your feet. But you mustn't be impatient. I can and will start on it soon.

'Which brings me to the immediate problem, on which I do need your advice. Let's accept for the moment that the Reverend Francis Wagstaffe was your ancestor, or at least a member of the Wagstaffe family. He had, like you, a gift for writing. Once his pen was down on the paper, words just flowed. I've still got to find out whether I can emulate him. I've never had any trouble writing history, but that was from the outside, so to speak.

'Most novelists choose the "omniscient narrator" style, because it gives them scope to play god with their characters. But this is one man's personal story, and written, naturally, in the first person. I know I should try to do the same, but from my perspective of the twentieth century that limits me. He was writing of his times, and took for granted that he would be understood. I can't take it for granted that my readers now will understand, if I don't somehow make it clear. Ordinary language, for example: if he

167

mentions his mother's "portion" he could take it for granted that most people would know he was talking about the size of her dowry; my readers would expect it to refer to the size of the piece of cake on her plate.

'The third person style allows the author to explain in his own voice, but it distances him from the story. And that is – truly, sweetheart – my last great problem. First person narrative, or third? What do you think?'

She was quiet for what seemed a long time, filled with such satisfaction and pleasure that she hardly dared answer. In the end, she said, rather tentatively, 'That must be your own decision. I can't even advise, because I have no idea how the original reads; but surely if you choose first person, it must at least reflect his style – even to the use of archaisms that make it sound genuine. I can't help more than that, because I don't know.'

He got up, went to his study, and came back with a sheaf of typed sheets of paper.

'Then listen to a page or two I've translated directly from him. It doesn't solve the problem, because it happens that in this extract he's looking backwards into history, but it does show how he can tackle telling a story. Sit still, and I'll read it to you.'

Taking her delighted silence for consent, he began.

The Wagstaffes were in these parts before the Cromwells, though as to which were 'gentled' first, there is doubt. The Cromwells claim that their origins are noble, and some say can be traced back to some obscure ancestor in Wales; but there was a Lord Cromwell at the time of the war in France. Whether or not he has anything to do with the present family, I don't know. The family I know has direct connections with Thomas Cromwell, who, though he became the Earl of Essex, reputedly started life as a brewer from Putney. I think it very possible that the first Wagstaffe was knighted before any of Oliver's relations received the accolade.

The story of how that happened was enough to set any boy's blood on fire, and I never got tired of hearing it, perhaps because the hero of it was my namesake, another Francis Wagstaffe.

Like me, he was a youngest son. When his father died and his brother had inherited their little estate in the Soke of Somersham, he took himself off to the wars to seek his fortune as a mercenary soldier, owning nothing but his horse, and expecting nothing but what his sword could win for him. He fought for whomever would pay most for his services, and there was no lack of takers, because the powerful French were determined to recapture parts of Italy that had once been theirs, particularly Naples. The struggle went on for years, and good soldiers did well for themselves by swapping sides, and sharing in the loot when they won.

As the years went by, it happened that the throne of France fell to a young, handsome man only a little over twenty years old, King Francis the First. (Yet another chivalrous soldier who shared a name with me!) He was very tall, and a good leader. His head was full of the romances of chivalry and the deeds of noble knights of the past, as well as those who were still fighting for or against him. He was as keen to wage war against his Italian foes as any of those who had been King of France before him, so he gathered together a huge army of men and set out to win Naples back, marching them over the mountains and down towards Milan.

It was the details of the tale that had been handed down to us from father to son that excited me so much. That other Francis Wagstaffe had been there!

He wanted to fight for King Francis and, as he had, like all Wagstaffes before and since, a great love of horses, when the chance came he joined a famous cavalry regiment of French *gens d'armes*. So it was that in September 1515, he was with King Francis's army at a village called Marignano, about twelve miles distant from Milan.

Now it happened that King Francis had just had made for him, by the famous armourers of Augsburg, a new and most beautiful armour, beautifully shaped to fit him exactly, and most wonderfully decorated. He was, so the story goes, just trying it on for the first time in his tent when one of his knights rushed in to tell him that the Swiss army was attacking.

Grabbing his sword, King Francis rushed out, and soon a furious battle was in progress. He was wearing his fine armour, and it inspired him to great deeds of valour, so that the fact that it had been much battered at the end of the day was a source of great pride to him. It signified that he was more than a mere king. He had proved himself to be as gallant a knight as any on the field as well. Now there was with him the famous knight of the time, one 'Picquet', by which nickname Pierre de Terrail, Seigneur de Bayard, (*Le Chevalier Sans Peur et Sans Reproche*) was known from coast to coast for his peerless chivalry and deeds of valour.

During the heat of the battle, King Francis had several times been in danger, and on one occasion would have come off worst in a bout against a strong and skilled German knight, but for the intervention of a nameless combatant who took on the German, unhorsed him, stood on him and, offering the point of his sword to the eyeslits of the fallen warrior's visor, demanded surrender – which he promptly got.

In his tent after the battle was over, King Francis sent for 'Picquet', went down on one knee before him, and begged the famous warrior to knight him, there and then, on the field of battle, in his battered new harness. Bayard obeyed, and performed the ceremony of knighting his King, in complete reversal of the usual ceremony of the king knighting a few who had fought honourably for him in the field. By custom, a man thus newly knighted then had the privilege of knighting another of his own choice. So King Francis, now a knight of valour himself, followed the custom, and called for the unknown warrior who had saved his life.

The man had great difficulty in kneeling before the King, because during the bout with the German knight, he had taken a great blow across the top of his knee from the

German's sword, which had separated and bent the metal lames at the top of his poleyn, and forced them into his leg between poleyn and cuish. It was a bad wound, and his armour could not be taken off while steel was still embedded in flesh above the knee. However, somehow or other the unknown man did kneel, and was duly knighted. He was, of course, from that moment, *Sir* Francis Wagstaffe.

By the laws of chivalry, he claimed the splendid armour of his prisoner, and better still, his destrier, the sort of warhorse every knight longed to own. Then there was a large ransom to be negotiated for sparing his prisoner's life, which, added to the considerable loot Sir Francis had already amassed from several years of war as a mercenary soldier, made him rich indeed in every way but one. The sword cut above his knee was such that he would never be able to fight again. He sold the splendid armour back to its previous owner, but the horse he could not bring himself to part with. Instead, he turned homewards towards England, and one day a year or so later, rode stiff-legged into Somersham on his rouncy, with a squire leading the destrier at his side. It was a full stallion of great strength and beauty with a touch of Arab in it, a deep chestnut with a white blaze on its forehead.

Sir Francis renamed it Bayard, after the famous French knight, 'Picquet'.

William stopped reading and looked up at Fran. Her expression told him most of what he wanted to know. Her voice, when she spoke, had a distinct quaver in it, inspired by a kind of awe. 'Is it all like that?' she asked.

He tried to be as pragmatic as he could, under the circumstances. 'No,' he said. 'In that passage, he was enjoying the remembrance of himself being young and still not disillusioned by experience. But for much of his narrative, he's a man with a great load of worry on his shoulders, and, as I suggested, in great fear for himself and all he loves. He writes as he feels – up and down – but you can judge his easy style from what I've read out. So what's it to be? First person or third?'

171

'There's no question,' she said. 'First. I promise I won't badger you as I have been doing. I truly didn't understand. Now I do. I've been hindering you, not helping at all. I'm sorry, darling. Take your time. Begin when it suits you. I'll try to keep out of your hair.'

'And what will you do, if I immerse myself in it and neglect you?'

'That'll be the day,' she said, and had the pleasure of seeing him agree with her. 'I shall find plenty to do, don't you worry! Just at present, I've got too much on my plate with what's happening to our friends.'

'So what's new about that?' he said, getting up and walking up and down in thought – but without either the impatience or the tension he'd been showing lately. 'I can begin to write as soon as I like, now. However, having waited so long, it can wait a bit longer. Eric may be right that this is rather a crucial time for us at Church End. It's too much of a risk for any of us to withdraw our share of responsibility, at least for this coming week till your proposed birthday lunch is over, and the Bridgefoot family gathering. Maybe Bob and I could spend some time in the church over the coming weekend.'

'Nigel said he thought there was no hurry to close the church,' she said. 'But you can't trust anybody, and Nigel won't have the final say. I think you'd be wise to go while it's still there. Forget about me, and all the rest.'

'That isn't possible. But I can't see any way I can help you, especially as I don't know what it is you and Beth propose to do.'

'Neither do we. We haven't a clue. But as Thirzah would have said, doubtless the Lord will provide. Eric seems unduly worried about everything. He's getting himself into a real state. He must have his reasons. Beth and I will have to stumble about in the dark waiting to pick up a magic wand – at least till Nigel comes back, and we hear a bit more from Eric of what he has decided to do about Terry's cottage. I think Beth and I may have to beard him in his den again.'

*　　*　　*

Fran had kept in touch with Anthea by telephone, finding her subdued but resolute. She'd keep her promise to Fran to do whatever was asked of her. Fran was slightly worried that William had demanded such a lot of her time that day, but it had been worth it. She couldn't and didn't regret it. But time was rushing towards her birthday. She must go to see Beth as to their next move tomorrow morning. She asked William what his plans were.

He said he hoped Bob might have time to go exploring with him, but till he had heard from Bob, he didn't know. If she didn't find him at home when she got back, she'd know where he was. So she was up bright and early next day, to get as much in as was possible. There was only a week left.

She sensed something amiss at the Old Rectory as soon as she got there. Nothing to report, Beth said, in a half-hearted sort of way. She hadn't seen either Eric or Terry. Then, in a rush of embarrassment, she said, 'I'm afraid Elyot isn't very pleased about it. He says it's none of our business. The matter between Terry and Eric *is* business, and no concern of ours whatsoever. The trouble between Terry and Anthea is personal, and concerns only the two of them. He has very little sympathy for Anthea – acting like a silly sixteen-year-old, he says, instead of the mature woman we know her to be. He's browned off with Terry as well; says he's overdoing his show of righteous indignation and disappointment, using it as good cover for his relief at getting out of a situation he never meant to get into. Scornful of Terry pretending it's his pride preventing him from making any further attempt to put it right, and once more intending to cut and run. Oh, I know you'll say Elyot's a fine one to talk! That he wouldn't have stopped to face the music at all himself if William hadn't made him! But – it's making life very difficult for me, just at present.

'He thinks us, you and I, the two biggest fools in Christendom for meddling, and says so. In fact, he's come as near to giving me orders to have nothing more to do with it as he ever has. As for the Bridgefoots, he says if there are any in Old Swithinford who can steer their own course without interference, they can. He can't tell you what to do, but I am to mind my own business.

'He's no more like himself, just at present, than anybody else is. I know he's been used to giving orders, and expecting them to be obeyed, but he's never before tried it on me! I thought I'd got out of that situation when I married him, but . . .'

She was very cast down, and looked appealingly at Fran, who was trying to keep her own sea legs in the face of this sudden squall. She had to comfort Beth before they could get anywhere, but *she* wasn't going to take Elyot's lordly orders.

'If William said what I think he probably feels, I'm pretty sure he'd agree to some extent with Elyot,' Fran said. 'But he hasn't said so. He's leaving it to me to do as I think fit, and whatever I do, he'll back me. So of course you must do as you think best; but I disagree with Elyot. It isn't true that the Terry–Anthea affair is none of our business. It was you, even more than I, who from the beginning had Terry's confidences, and together we tried to engineer a cure for his guilt and enough warmth and love to melt the ice-maiden Anthea was pretending to be. Elyot not only stood by and watched us do it, he actually played an important part at our Shrove Tuesday Love Feast – the first time our machinations showed any signs of being effective. And it was Eric whose romantic notions set up the present urgent situation. We've already involved Nigel and Effendi. Can we run back altogether, even if we would? I can't. It's my birthday they wanted to take notice of in the first instance, before any of this other silly business cropped up.

'Do you want to withdraw? If you do, please say so now and I'll either cancel everything on some pretext or other, or go it alone. For heaven's sake, don't quarrel with Elyot about it! I still think Eric may be right, that it's only a lovers' tiff got out of control. The danger is that it could grow, like the old nursery rhyme warning that it was *"For the want of a nail"* in the first instance that the war was lost. It's obvious that it's already affecting all of us in our happy little circle here in Church End. Next it could be all Old Swithinford, then Swithinford District Council and the County Council – old Uncle Tom Cobbleigh and all.

'Don't cry, Beth, it isn't good for you. Just go along with Elyot for the time being, and let him think he's won – as long as you make sure he accepts the invitation to my birthday lunch, if there is one.'

Beth was tearful. She was not one to give in easily; but as Fran knew, in Beth's hagiography, Elyot ranked only a little below the Holy Ghost.

'But what will *you* do?' Beth said. 'I'm so ashamed of letting you down, Fran.'

Fran stood up to go. 'Echo answers, "What?"' she said. 'God only knows. You declared that we could rely on Him to help.'

Beth sobbed aloud. 'Oh Fran, don't be angry with me. I don't like letting my friends down any more than you do, but I think I must go along with Elyot in this. He's so much more a man of the world than William is. All those years in the Navy have given him a core made of iron that I don't usually see or feel. William's different. You get round him to do whatever you want. So do I with Elyot, generally, but these circumstances aren't normal. According to Elyot, only incredibly stupid.'

'One shouldn't take either Elyot or William at face value,' Fran said. 'If Elyot's a man of iron, William's a man of steel, which is even tougher, I believe, in the long run, but more flexible. Steel bends, and iron doesn't, but they both have their uses. If necessary, I'll bend to William's persuasion, but he's never tried giving me orders. To answer your question of what I propose to do next, the answer is, I think, to go and see Eric again. I'll let you know.'

She left hurriedly. She had no intention of falling out with Beth, but once in her car she discovered how upset and angry she was. She tried to think, but cursed instead, surprised to find how many good medieval curses she had picked up from William. That Beth, of all people, should run back, and leave her to cope alone! She wanted to get away before she encountered Elyot, so she switched on her engine, let in her clutch, and roared out of the gates.

Once clear of the house, however, she pulled up again till she could see to drive more carefully, and tried to review the situation she was now in rationally. She wasn't going home with her tail between her legs yet! She was going into battle, which meant into Eric's room at the hotel. As always, words rushed in to fill the void of the few seconds ahead of her before she could decide where she stood.

> *'Shall we fight or shall we fly?*
> *Good Sir Richard, tell us now,*
> *For to fight is but to die!'*

Well, so it might be, but she wasn't used to turning her back on trouble any more than old Sir Richard Grenville on an unexpected enemy force. So she said to herself, like him, *'Fight on! Fight on!'*

Eric was sitting rather glumly at his desk, but as he rose to welcome her showed pleasure in discovering who his unexpected visitor was. She'd been a bit afraid that she might find he had reverted to the man who had first come among them, businesslike before all else; but she knew at once that however difficult her battle with him might be, she would leave him with their mutual affection and respect unharmed.

Looking closely at him, though, she was aware of stress in him that was unusual nowadays. No, not stress, *distress*. If she needed help, he needed comfort. Why, or how, she didn't yet know. He always declared himself to be 'a hard man', but the one they had found inside this self-created image had turned out to be anything but that: 'as soft as cart-grease', as Bob would say. So what had happened now to make him don his protective armour again? Would that be of any use? Isn't there a chink in every armour?

He was getting her a drink, bless him. She needed it. She looked affectionately at his back, and words floated unbidden into her head.

> *Dipped in the River Styx,*
> *One part alone stayed dry.*

Of course she knew what his Achilles' heel was! Remembrance of great love lost. He was taking his time to get the drink, composing himself before facing her again. What was it William's father had written in that heart-breaking little poem called 'Lost Love'?

Why should a man's heart know
A winter after June?
And after sunshine, snow?

What random arrow had found the chink in Eric's armour? Being reminded of his own lost love by what was happening to Terry and Anthea?

He set the drink before her. 'So, Fran my dear, why are you in such a state? And what can I do for you?' (*Or I for you?* said her heart.)

She sipped her drink, and told him her tale. She must do something to restore the status quo ante. She wasn't asking him to change his mind about anything he'd decided, but it would be a help if he'd let her know what it was, and if there had been any developments since she had seen him last.

'I'm in the same boat as you,' he said. 'Not knowing my friends from my enemies, except that, as Bob Bellamy said, I'm a "furriner" and you're not. All the same, it was I who created the village we've got now, and I'm reluctant to let all that time and effort go down the drain. It seems to me that all the rest of you are so damn satisfied with it just as it is that you don't give a tinker's cuss for the future. I do. William must understand, but even he's got more immediate things on his mind to bother much about it. It's up his street, though: a question of social history affecting us all.

'I'm no historian, and certainly no modern sociologist. But I am a practical man whose livelihood and personal happiness is influenced by what's going on, and I observe it and meditate about it.

'In the past, working people went in droves from their impoverished conditions in the countryside towards the new industrial towns. In the course of time, they created a new class of industrial factory workers, who tried hard to cling to their country culture, and failed. A new, urban culture emerged, half rural, half urban, then wholly urban.

'After the last war, the tide turned and flowed the other way. I was well aware of it because it gave me the opportunity to use my own expertise as a developer. Folks wanted to get out of the bomb-battered industrial towns and back into the country, bringing their new urban working-class culture with them. *That's* what's happening here now, under our very noses: they're swamping what's left of rural England by the sheer weight of their numbers. Rural ways of life are having to give way to theirs because in any democracy it's only numbers that count.

'I think it's gone far enough. We've lost sight of the larger picture. In already developed areas – 'new towns' particularly – the urban values count most. But there's still an enormous amount of English countryside left with a lot of its stable values untouched. If we don't want all of it to disappear completely, we've got to make a stand somewhere and bring the facts to notice, before it's too late.

'I thought we knew which we preferred here, and would make a stand together. I was wrong. Forgive me for thinking in military terms. I thought our bridgehead was unassailable: the Bridgefoot family – and no pun intended. Theirs was the castle round which the rest of the community has established itself. I'd have bet my bottom dollar it would have stood any siege. Wrong again.

'It's only a sand castle. They've lost their self-esteem, and the tide will wash them away, and us with them. They think I'm stirring up trouble, wanting us to get involved in local politics, and they don't want to be associated with me. I'm being given the cold shoulder. But whether they like it or not, this latest spot of trouble started in their bailiwick, with Terry Hardy in it somehow up to his professional chin, and prepared to renege on the rest of us. I can't make sense of it. Can you?'

'Only that there's something out of the ordinary going on, and they seem to be burying their heads in the sand. From what I gathered, Marjorie's involved most. Perhaps a bit of the past's rising up to hit her just when she's too worried to take it. That's only a wild guess.'

'My guess, too, as it happens, but why is she turning away from those of us who could and would have helped her?'

'A matter of pride? Is Pansy at the bottom of it? Because she thinks all the trouble with Pansy is her fault for marrying beneath her in the first place?'

'She's not so damned silly as that,' he said, forcefully. 'But I can't push my nose in where I'm not wanted, can I? Especially as I understand she has somebody else's shoulder to cry on. Not that she has ever for a single moment tried crying on mine,' he said, giving her a wry smile. 'Jess is the only one who's done that – on occasion. But that's beside the point. I just wish I knew what's wrong. I have no explanation.'

'None of us has,' she said. 'That's why I'm here. Nigel thinks there's still hope that it's all a storm in a tea-cup down at the Glebe, which can be put right if he's lucky. I think that's where you come in. Have you agreed to act on his advice to go slow with regard to Terry's cottage? And with not letting Anthea off the hook too soon?'

'That was easy. Both are matters subject to business contracts. I've simply indicated to both Anthea and Terence that I shall expect them to keep their side of the bargain with me. I've said that I shan't take the cottage off Terry's hands. He must settle with me and then dispose of it himself. I can't insist that Anthea stays and lives in the cottage she hired on a long lease, but there's no sub-letting clause, so if she leaves, she'll still have it on her hands till the lease runs out. That's as much as I can do to help delay the departure of either of them, which was what I gathered you and Beth and Nigel were all asking me to do. A sort of stay of execution.'

'Thank you, Eric,' she said. And there was such relief in her voice that he looked very keenly at her.

'I don't suppose you would care to tell me what it is you've got up your sleeve?' he asked.

'There isn't anything up there yet except hope. Can you tell me whether or not the birthday lunch for me is still on?'

He nodded. 'In Effendi's hands.'

'And yours? Then somehow or other, I've got to work a miracle – all by myself. And I damned well will! Just you wait and see!'

'I'd back you against anybody,' he said, 'when it comes to wheedling the gods round to your side. They may even have a smile or two to spare yet for the Bridgefoots. I guess all that's wrong with me is that I've taken umbrage because they won't let me help. We don't breed folk like them any more, and we can't afford to lose a single one, specially such as George and Molly. The very salt of the earth.'

She rose to go, and he put out both hands to her. She laid hers in them, and leaned forward to kiss him. She felt better. Although no nearer to solving her own problem, she felt nearer to understanding his. No time for that just now, though.

How could she get a peep behind the scenes at the Old Glebe? By going to see Bob, of course. His daughter had married into the Bridgefoot clan and she had inherited a lot of her father's feyness. Fran could but ask. It was still early, so she headed the car towards Castle Hill.

She was lucky enough to come upon Bob driving some bullocks into the field by the church, a hundred yards or so from the house. He let the last one go through the gate, shut it carefully, and came to her. His face showed his anxiety.

'No,' she said, opening the passenger door for him. 'Nothing's wrong with William. It's me who wants a private word with you.'

He got in the car with her, and waited. She went straight to the point, and he listened, gravely.

'We haven't seen Charlie since term began,' he said. She's working hard and a lot depends on her doing well. But I can't say that I'm comfortable in my mind. I haven't been since one morning in September when the sunrise was just a bit too full of colour. I couldn't *place* the reason for my feeling as I did that morning that things weren't right. It was too spread out, same as the too-red dawn was, all over the sky, east and west alike. But in this last week, the feeling's been getting clearer to me, circling round and round like a bird of prey hovering over Glebe, ready to swoop.

'Don't ask me to explain more than that, 'cos I can't, and wouldn't want to if I could. I shouldn't have said as much as I have done to anybody else but you. Besides, I ain't sure about it myself – it comes and goes. I tell myself that that must mean there's good as well as bad to come. I try not to take too much notice of it. But between you and me and the gatepost, I should say that something's wrong up at the Glebe as won't come to light for a longish while yet. Don't say nothing to anybody else, will you? I can be wrong.'

'Bob!' she said. 'You know me better than that, surely.'

'Yes,' he said. 'If I hadn't done, I shouldn't have been fool enough to give you a hint. And mind, it is only a hint. I've got no more idea than you have what it might be about. Not Charlie, anyway. So don't go worriting yourself before there's any need to on that count.' She promised, and he got out of the car.

'Give Jane my love, and say I'm sorry I haven't time to come in and see her today. William, I believe, has a date with you later on.'

'I'm waiting for him now,' he said. He raised his old pork-pie hat to her as she drove away, smiling broadly.

*

She really had no idea what to do next, except to trust in the gods and keep her powder dry ... No, drat it, the last person she wanted any advice from was Oliver Cromwell! She never had liked the sound of him much.

She had to go back and report to Beth. Whatever happened, she mustn't let anything upset that friendship.

She drove into the gates of the Old Rectory, where Elyot's car was standing. She had no wish to meet him, but refused to retreat. At any rate, Beth was not forced to play the invalid now against her will. Instead she was playing her piano, as Fran could hear. A straw in the wind?

She was greeted warmly by Elyot as well as Beth, though he was on his way out and excused himself at once. 'Good,' said Beth. 'I'm so glad you've come back. You were quite right about us having already put our oar in with regard to Terry and Anthea. I was prepared earlier to go along with Elyot altogether, but I want you to know that I'm really on your side. I mustn't let him think he's always in the right. I won't go on willingly putting my feet up every afternoon because I happen to be in a condition that females have been in ever since mankind was created. How on earth could the human race have survived if all men took Elyot's view? But I am in a cleft stick, Fran, because Elyot's worried and the last thing I want to do is to add to it! I know that he's genuinely anxious about me and the child – not because of my advanced age, but of his! He's coming up to sixty, and it might as well be ninety, to hear him go on about it. He's forever seeing his solicitors about making wills and setting up trusts and all the rest: "putting his affairs in order". When I protest, he simply says he's doing his duty and "running a tight ship". Guaranteed, of course, to make me feel a lot happier! But I try to say nothing, and let him have his own way as much as I can.

'Only I know him well enough to understand that none of this is what's causing his present mood, and I do know what is. First, Terry's defection. Of all his cronies here, the one whom he'll miss most is Terry. I believe Elyot's seeing it as a sort of mutiny on Terry's part – a trusted member of the crew letting his captain down – so he's angry, and blaming Terry instead of sympathizing and trying to help him.

'And Eric's no substitute for Terry. If anything, he's another irritant. He seems to be thinking of nothing but preventing Church End from becoming a suburb of Swithinford new town based on supermarkets and take-away chains and bingo halls and all other such modern "amenities". The more he lectures Elyot about it, the more Elyot's back goes up! Eric seems to be obsessed by it.'

'I know,' said Fran. 'I've just had the lecture myself.'

'I've still got such a lot to learn, Fran. I didn't understand Elyot well enough. He's worried about having got involved in local politics. He says there's no difference between local politics and national politics or world politics. It's all corrupt "from truck to kelson", whatever that means. Apparently, the Senior Service took their orders from politicians, but had a sort of gentleman's agreement not to become involved in the politics. Now he's committed himself, he's not happy, but says he's obliged to stick to his guns and would have to have a very good reason for "striking his flag". The last straw was when he discovered last week that the elections would probably fall just when Arethusa is due – as we already guessed. So do you see, Fran, why, though I'm absolutely with you in spirit, I can't go against Elyot? We came as near as we've ever been to having a real row after you left this morning. If it means me being a meek little wife for a month or two, well, I'll do it for love. After all, it's nothing to the state of subservience he rescued me from, is it?' Beth reached out and took Fran's hand. 'If you were in my place, Fran, you'd do it for William, and I'm pretty sure that in the end, it'll come right. You will go on without me, won't you?'

Fran bent and kissed her. Of course she would, but how it was to be done still remained as much of a blank wall in front of her as ever. As she rose to go, she said, 'By the way, Beth, what have you done with Terry's ring?'

Beth looked so startled that for a moment Fran panicked, feeling as if all her resolution were draining away through holes in her shoe-soles. Beth couldn't have disposed of it yet! There hadn't been time. But she, Fran, had got to have that talisman with her if she had to go it alone.

'I'd forgotten all about it,' Beth said, blushing guiltily. 'I shoved it into my workbox when you left before Elyot should see it and tell me what to do with it. Honestly, I'd forgotten it. I hope it's still there – but Wyn's been playing with my workbox . . . Please look for it, Fran. I daren't.'

Of course it was still there. The little box might have intrigued the toddler, but if he had tried to open it, the catch had beaten him. Fran sprung the box open and there the ring lay, glowing and sparkling in a sudden beam of light. Fran put it into Beth's hands.

'A ray of hope,' Beth said. 'What will you do with it?'

And Fran knew the answer. 'Give it back to Terry,' she said, 'as soon as possible. Nobody has any claim to it but the person he eventually gives it to for the right reason. To him it's as sacred a symbol of endless love as any wedding ring, which is why he couldn't even offer it to any of the three women he supposedly "married". As sacred to him – and whoever gets it – as the ring you wore round your neck between your two weddings to Elyot; or this that William put on my finger on Hunstanton Pier, when it seemed that it would have to remain for ever nothing more than a symbol of what might have been. Even if that had been so, I couldn't have let anybody throw it into the sea – as William threw my first one. Gosh, Beth, it fills me with hope. If you can't do anything else to help me, just pray that somehow Terry and I will cross each other's paths today. If I meet him unexpectedly, I shall know that the gods are on our side.'

*　　*　　*

Fran went straight home.

In the ordinary way, she'd have been disappointed that William wasn't there to tell of her morning's doings, but for once she didn't care. She needed time to think, because whatever advice she got from anybody, even William, the fact remained that it was she who had to act, and there was no more time to spare for dithering about and wondering what to do next.

Besides, as she had told Beth, she wasn't at all certain that if he told the truth William might not have a lot of sympathy with Elyot's point of view. He'd often let it faze him that she took on other people's troubles, but whatever he thought or said now could make no difference. She wouldn't worry him if she could help it, or distract him from his own thoughts.

As she prepared herself a quick snack, she reviewed her morning's encounters with Beth, Eric, Bob, then Beth again. Whatever it was that was disturbing the tenor of their lives, 'the domino effect' was accelerating. She sighed. What could be causing such a general all-round drop in morale? She didn't know and she couldn't guess; but if she was going to be able to do anything to prevent it getting worse, she had to find out how, where and with whom it had all begun.

Reflection led her to the conclusion that it centred on Terence

184

Hardy, the 'new' doctor whom they had welcomed into their midst, and who was now counted among their friends. He was, as doctors worthy of their salt in rural communities had always been, the tried-and-trusted link between all sorts and conditions of people, yet he was now, apparently, prepared to let them all down. Showing the white flag again and running away, instead of making any show of courage or stamina in the face of trouble. And by doing so, he was about to ruin two lives, one of them his own, and leave all the rest of them bickering among themselves, miserable and soggily dispirited.

If it had been anyone but he, she thought, she would not have shrunk from a bold confrontation and asked what it was all about; but because he was a medical man, he held all the aces. He would hide behind his Hippocratic oath, and put her off coldly with the assertion that he could not be expected to divulge any professional secrets. Even to tell her of his own might mean disclosing those of other patients. This was an unfair advantage when the moral well-being and happiness of so many of them depended on him as much as it would have done in an epidemic of measles or scarlet-fever in years gone by.

He might as well have gone round injecting them all with a serum to produce apathetic melancholy. Yet she was convinced that they had not been wrong in their judgement of him, or in putting their faith in him.

She was surprised to discover how much it was affecting Eric. She felt sure that her diagnosis of it – that this unhappy contretemps had rubbed a sore place in him, the memory of lost love – was correct in principle; but it didn't account for him taking such umbrage at the Bridgefoots. She recalled his unguarded remark about Marjorie having somebody else's shoulder to cry on, immediately regretted, as she had been quick to notice, and speedily covered up by reference to Jess's tantrums, and neutralized by unstinted praise of George and Molly. But he was not acting in character, and somehow making himself the odd man out where generally they could have relied on him to put things right – with regard to practical matters, anyway.

Elyot's way of dealing with the unease was almost as

unexpected. Beth had given her chapter and verse for his reasons for being irritable and short-tempered, and so unlike the charming, lovable, courteous man he usually was. A cold, frightening reason for his behaviour flashed through her mind. Why should he be so mad with *Terry*? Could it be that he was reacting as Roman Emperors had been wont to do, turning savagely on a messenger who was the bearer of bad news? Had Terry had to tell him that all was not well with Beth's second pregnancy? Cold shivers ran down Fran's spine, and she sought wildly for something to contradict that thought. Wouldn't Bob have sensed it? He'd said his uneasiness was circling round the Old Glebe, not the Old Rectory! She was letting it frustrate her that she was unable to pin the origin of the trouble down, because it meant that she had no idea where to begin to smooth it out. Damn her bloody birthday! She hadn't asked anybody to do anything about it, but now it loomed over them like a battle they knew had got to be fought before this silly war amongst themselves would be over. And however much she felt like taking Terry's line and not being there when the day came, she couldn't; it might save her embarrassment and distress, but it would only make the general situation worse.

She was sinking into a mood of helpless inertia and apathy when a bang on the huge old lion-headed knocker on the front door startled her into action.

It must be Nigel, back from his trip! Who else could it be? At least whoever her visitor was had roused her from her lethargy, and she was glad. It was just plain silly to be sitting there 'maunch-gutting' and wasting precious time.

She ran to the door and pulled it open, calling, 'Come in! Come in!' Whoever the visitor was, he was welcome.

It was not Nigel. It was Terence Hardy, clutching in his hand a large white envelope. The gasp she gave at the sight of him was like an invigorating draught of oxygen into her lungs. *The gods were on* her *side!*

But her first reaction of jubilation was immediately counteracted as she looked more closely at him. He had aged so much since she had last seen him that she hardly recognized him. His cheeks were sunken, and his eyes were deep-shadowed hollows with pupils like dull stone pebbles. She could have sworn that those silvery hairs at his temples had not been there when she had last set eyes on him only a few days ago. Whatever censure she had previously been storing up against him melted at this visible proof of his suffering, and in its place came a rush of warm, loving sympathy for him.

'Terry!' she exclaimed, holding out both hands to him. 'How good to see you. Go and make yourself comfortable in the sitting-room while I put the kettle on.'

She needed to escape long enough to compose herself, and make up her mind how to deal with this chance the gods were offering her. She pushed her hand deep into her skirt pocket and her questing fingers came upon a small hard object, and closed round it. She had the amulet.

He was standing by the window, looking down the garden, letter in hand. He turned at her entrance – and without attempting to speak, handed her the envelope. She raised her eyebrows in interrogation, but he had turned his back on her again.

'Am I supposed to open this?' she asked. He nodded. She pulled from the envelope a white gilt-edged card, hand-written.

The Reverend Nigel Delaprime and Nicholas Hadley-Gordon
invite you to lunch at the Old Surgery
at 1.30 p.m. on Saturday 6 December,
to help them celebrate the birthday of their dear friend (and yours),
Frances Burbage.

RSVP (a.s.a.p.)

He turned at last. 'What am I supposed to do about that?' he asked. 'I can't possibly accept. Why was I invited?'

'Because you were wanted, I suppose. Why else?'

He grimaced as if with a pang of toothache. 'Wanted? By whom? Maybe out of courtesy by Effendi and Nigel, but not, I think, by anybody else likely to be there. I've blotted my copybook. Would you care to tell me who else has been invited?'

'I don't know. The invitation isn't from me – as you can see. In view of the Bridgefoot Golden Wedding, William and I had agreed to let my birthday pass unnoticed this year, but our friends had different ideas – some of which I gather have had to be abandoned. So I think this is a compromise; just a gesture of friendship. In which case, the guest-list must have more or less written itself and naturally it included you. I shall be disappointed if you're not there, anyway.'

He didn't answer, and her patience with him suddenly ran out. 'Oh, for heaven's sake, man, do sit down!' she said.

He did, though somewhat unwillingly, replying stiffly, 'Then I'm afraid you'll have to be disappointed. Nobody else will be. I'm *persona non grata* with all the others. I should be a fish out of water. An outcast.'

'What on earth are you talking about? Yes, I dare say Anthea has been invited. So what? You're a middle-aged professional man, and she's not exactly a simple village maiden. Have both of you lost your wits as well as your *savoir faire*? Why make your personal antagonism public by openly snubbing all your friends? Especially Effendi, even if it was he who upset your apple cart in the first instance. He had no intention of interfering with your personal affairs, he just wanted to know whether or not he could start advertising for a typist-cum-secretary. How did he know you would jump the gun as you did?'

She was suddenly angry with him again, and he was quite aware of it. He almost cringed, looking so hurt and helpless that sympathy made her hastily change tack again. She waited until he had pulled himself together and then said, in a softer tone of voice, 'So what else is wrong, Terry? What's stopping you from accepting that first rebuff from Anthea like a man, and trying again? Showing her what she's missing? And why involve all the rest of us? As far as I can see, it's nothing to do with anybody but you and Anthea. Besides, you have a duty to us all as a professional man on whom we have come to rely. What have we, your friends, done to set you so much against us?'

'I thought it was the other way round. Eric's turned nasty on me, at any rate. Won't release me by taking the cottage off my hands. I had no idea he could be as hard a customer as that. Then there's Elyot, too, acting as if I was a *matelot* who'd dropped his broom overboard at a naval revue. I appear to be beneath the contempt of the Lord High Admiral Franks now . . .' He suddenly stood up, and faced her. 'Don't tell me, I know. It's all my own fault. I don't blame Anthea for turning me down. How could I expect anything different? I wasn't worthy of her friendship, let alone her love and trust. Or that of any of you. It is I, myself, who's wrecked everything again, as I have done all my adult life. Messed up every bloody chance I ever had. The damage was done before any of you ever set eyes on me. I arrived here a cynical doctor looking for a promising practice, to keep me in the lifestyle I'd got used to. I wasn't happy, and never expected to be again.'

He paused, his face softening a little at the remembrance. 'It was very different from what I had expected. Like dropping into a warm bath after battling your way through one snowdrift after another, until I began to think my luck had turned at last. In that state of mind, I made the worst mistake a doctor can make. I got involved with my patients. One especially.'

He was silent again, castigating himself for failures past and present. She was suffering with him, and knew that what he needed most was a sympathetic ear and perhaps a lap to pour his congealed unhappiness into, so as to be able to examine it more objectively. As a doctor, not as the suffering patient. Resignedly, she accepted what seemed to be her rôle. She wanted to help him, and if that was the way to do it, it wasn't really asking much.

'Sit down again Terry, please,' she said, soothingly. 'Tell me what went wrong in the first place, and why you blame yourself for whatever it was. I can't believe it's all justified. Circumstances alter cases. What got you off on the wrong foot? Was that truly all your own fault? If not, whose was it?'

He made a wry face, and said, 'My mother's, I suppose, for dying just at the wrong time. That's why I have such a strong feeling now for John Postlethwaite. He's in the same boat for the same reason. One of several patients I'm about to let down.'

'Let down? How?'

'By running away again. I don't know any other way out.'

'Tell me,' she said. This time it was almost a command.

To her enormous relief, he sat down suddenly, as if the starch of anger had gone out of him and left him limp. He'd be easier to deal with like that, she thought, than the stiff, bitter, hurt and isolated man he had been till now. She fetched him a stiff brandy; then she waited silently while he took a sip or two, set down his glass by his side, and looked up at her with the first hint of a smile she had seen so far.

'Do you really want to hear?' he asked. 'It's not a very happy story.'

'I don't know till I hear it,' she said composedly. 'So start at the beginning.'

He toyed with his glass, looking down at it to make up his mind; but her composure had calmed him, and in the end he began to tell her.

He was now forty-four, an only child who had been eight when the war broke out. His father had been a 'boss' engineer in a big shipyard on the Tyne, his mother a teacher. It had been an almost ideal domestic background for an intelligent child who also loved to use his hands. His father was forever designing ships and making up models of them. It was while he had been helping with the fine details of such a model that he had been told by the shipyard's medical man that he had surgeon's hands, and the fire of ambition had been lit in him. His mother had supported him with all her heart; his father had only said that he didn't care what his son did for a living so long as he was happy doing it.

'Such a lovely man,' Terry said wistfully. 'Always was, and still is – in spite of everything.'

'Still alive?' Fran had determined not to break into his story, but surprise jerked this out of her. Again, she saw that bitter look of helpless defeat flit across his face.

'After a fashion. Looked after by my aunt – his widowed sister. The yard was bombed, and he was dug out from the rubble brain-damaged. It would probably have been better for us all if he had been killed outright. He was in and out of a neurological hospital and a home for the rest of the war and for some time afterwards. Mum went back to teaching, and I headed for a university, to read medicine. Then a miracle happened, or so we

190

thought. Dad suddenly got better, and was allowed home again.'

He got up, and strode around the room, fighting for self-control. He stopped in front of her, looking down at her. 'Do you believe in God, Fran? Beth's sort of god, or Nigel's? Nigel says his God is a just god, and Beth claims hers to be a god full of love. Mum and I believed Him to be both when we got my dad back.

'He turned out to be neither. *God?* He was only cruelty personified. He let us look again into the paradise of our happy home, and then drove us out and closed the gates. Mum developed an inoperable cancer, probably because of all the stress she'd endured, and died. Dad went to pieces. He just couldn't function without her. He still lives at home, and has spells of lucidity, when he enjoys pottering about in his greenhouse and his "workshop". When he's well enough he still builds model ships; but there are long periods of amnesia when he doesn't recognize anybody, even me. But you see, when I found myself here among all of you, who knew about Love, it felt as if I was at home again. And now I have to lose it all over again.'

There was a long pause, in which Fran was struggling to hold her tears back, and he gazed sadly back into the past.

'We'd always been such good friends, Dad and I. I was in my first year of surgical training when Mum died, so I got leave to go home to be with him, till he'd got over the shock. He talked about Mum all the time, as if remembering tiny incidents in their lives together brought her closer to him again.

'It was having to listen, and see her through his eyes, and all the glimpses of them together that hurt me then almost more than I could bear. Like the evening when he told me how they met and the distress he'd been in because he couldn't afford a proper engagement ring for her. He was a good storyteller, and savoured all the little details, so I heard how his father, my grandfather, had asked him what he was moping about, and he'd confessed the truth. Grandad, he said, just went upstairs and fetched a ring, telling Dad he might as well have it now when he needed it, as wait till Grandad was dead. He'd have got it one day in any case. It was the ring that his father – my great-grandfather

191

– had given to his bride in much palmier Victorian days, and a family treasure.

'My dad put his hand in his pocket, and fished it out. I'd seen my mother wearing it hundreds of times, of course, but had never thought to ask her anything about it. Dad went on to tell how when he'd been sitting with her on the night that she died, and the hospital had taken off all her jewellery except her wedding ring, she'd asked him to put her engagement ring back on her finger so that she could die wearing it. But she'd given him instructions to take it off again once she was dead, and keep it safe until he was ready to pass it on to me with her love, to give to *my* love when that time should come.

'Dad just sat there looking at it lying in the palm of his hand, with tears running down his cheeks, till he kissed it, and held it out for me to take. I was standing up to take it from him when he just crumpled up at my feet. The sorrow and the stress had been too much for him, and that poignant memory was the last straw. He's never been himself again since.

'So I lost both of them, and everything I loved, more or less at once. I went back to my hospital a different person, mad with grief and loneliness, and got too involved with the first girl who made a dead set at me. I look back on that episode now as if it belongs to another lifetime, regretting my stupidity but glad – *glad* – that lonely as I was, and guilty as I felt for letting such a girl seduce me into thinking I was obliged to marry her, I never even considered giving her that ring. I knew that she wasn't, and never would be, the "love" my mother had meant her precious ring for. She and Dad had shown me what they'd meant by love. I hadn't forgotten.

'Marcia? I offered it, but she rejected it as "not classy enough". So I put it away. When my daughter was born I thought that one day I might give it to her to wear as a dress-ring.'

He had some difficulty in going on, and had recourse to the brandy glass again before saying rather huskily, 'She doesn't even acknowledge me when we meet in the street.

'Never mind the rest. You know it, anyway. When I came here, hard-boiled and cynical as I was, I found myself back amongst people who all seemed to understand relationships in terms other than money and sex. Then came Anthea, as hard and disparaging of me as I had been of myself. Her apparent contempt for me as a man shook me. She seemed to have the same modern, cynical outlook on anything called love as I had myself by then. It was a sort of game we were playing, trying to call each other's bluff.

'But I found out that it was not bluff at all. When I knew her real reason for keeping me at arm's length, and realized what she'd been through in body, mind and spirit, the attraction she'd always held for me turned into the genuine thing. Love, as I now understood it; the same sort as my mum and dad had known. I didn't push my luck, but I was pretty sure she returned it. So I had the ring ready to give to her when I thought the time ripe. I can't say she rejected the ring, because she never saw it. She certainly rejected me! That was when despair finally boiled over inside me. I should never have any use for that ring now! It occurred to me that I was not worthy of it, and it had never been meant I should use it. It should have been buried with Mum. For me it had only ever been associated with loss of love and bad luck. How did it come then that I had it? Because my mother died before her time and took my father with her. What memories could it ever have for me but those of loneliness and despair?

'I'd got it in my pocket, hating it and wondering how to get rid of it, when I went to see Beth professionally last week. *Everything* had gone wrong for me by then and suddenly my anger rose in me like bile – and I pitched the ring into the fire – in front of Beth's eyes.

'She was horrified, and screamed at me, all sorts of accusations that afterwards I had to admit were true. Asking me what sort of a doctor I was to destroy such a valuable thing when its worth would have saved the lives of hundreds of children dying of starvation in Ethiopia. She rescued it from the fire for me but I threw it back into her lap and walked out on her.

'It was all very silly and childish, and I regretted it the moment I was out of the house: partly for the ring's associations with the only time I was ever really happy, and partly because I felt that with it I had thrown away the last remnants of any personal integrity I'd ever had. But Beth had pointed out to me, without meaning to, what I needed most. A respectable escape route, and somewhere to run to. Perhaps what's left of me as a doctor may yet do a bit of good in Ethiopia.

'So that's it, Fran. As soon as I can free myself of my obligations here, that's where I shall head for. As it happens, I can't "bolt", as you once put it, as easily as I have done before, because this time there are a few patients I can't bring myself to walk out on – and, of course, I must stay long enough to realize enough money to pay Eric for the restoration of the cottage. But you must see why it would be impossible for me to come to your birthday lunch! An unprincipled outsider that nobody has any further use for! Why pretend otherwise?'

He sat with his head in his hands, a man defeated. She clasped the ring in her pocket and wished she had Bob's instinct of knowing how to deal with people in Terry's state of emotional crisis. Bob would know how to soothe the wounds without pretending that they didn't exist. But Bob wasn't there, and she was. It was she who had to deal with the distraught doctor, and at once, while sadness and regret had softened him a little, and robbed him for the moment of his rigid, unyielding and inflexible anger against himself. Not too much womanly sympathy, said the voice of her common sense. She took a deep breath, and began, coolly, to sum up.

'Thank you for telling me, Terry,' she said. 'But I think you're making a very big mistake. As far as I can judge, you have suffered from time and circumstance, as much a victim of the war as your father was. Only people who have lived through wars know that they don't stop when an armistice is signed. Their effects linger on and on and on, and affect the lives of all sorts of people who were never anywhere near a battlefield or in a blitz. It's made worse for them if they insist on blaming themselves for what happened. It only adds remorse to regret, because they're really trying to punish themselves for sins that were not their fault, which makes nonsense of what everybody else suffered. Take William, if you need an example. He survived the Battle of Britain, which should speak for itself; but because he had married the wrong woman in the middle of it, as so many others did, he concluded that what he had to endure as a result was all his fault. He condemned himself to a lifetime of loneliness and worry, jealous of his friend Mac who had not survived. He wasted twenty years, with nothing except work and what he considered to be his duty to fill his time, because the past had gone and there didn't seem to be any future. Well, you know him now. Time brought him consolation and compensation. Or consider Elyot. He had a dreadful wartime experience that *almost* robbed him of Beth – but again, it was only "almost". Terry, I know I'm an incurable optimist, but it does seem to me that those who stick it out *and forgive themselves* – for what Fate did to them or caused them to do for the wrong reasons – those people give Love a chance to forgive them, and come to their help.

'So now there's you. You've just said that when you first came here, you hadn't much self-esteem left. *We didn't know that.* We judged you as we found you, for ourselves. You soon had plenty of esteem in the eyes of the village, if not in your own. You won it by showing that you cared, even for people like Thirzah Bates, though you had so little to live for. But if you give in to your instinct to cut and run again, you'll lose all that you've gained, and despise yourself more than ever. What for? Because of what Fate did to *you*? What did it do to Anthea? Was what happened to her her fault? Not as far as I can see.

'She followed the trend of the time, and fell for the wrong sort of man. Then that awful accident happened, in which she got all the hurt, in every way. He ran away. What must that have done to her self-esteem? Now you are running away from her. Have you ever tried putting yourself in her place?

'Will you deserting now do anything to put back her trust in anybody? Or make her life in future any happier, wherever she goes to try to start again? Both of you are chickening out. Giving up before there's any need to. Doesn't being loved and looked up to in the village mean anything to you? Or that you carry with you the honour and mystique that men of your profession have always had in rural communities like this?

'If you had a patient who wouldn't fight for his own life *in extremis*, would you give up and run away from him? You know you wouldn't – you'd fight for him and with him to the last ditch. Yet you won't even consider fighting for yourself! You've made a niche for yourself here, and we rely on you. Are you going to punish us because you haven't yet achieved all this and heaven too?

'Be a man, Terry. Stay and fight for our sakes, and try your luck with Anthea at least once more. Give yourself another chance – or perhaps what I really mean is, give Love another chance. If you can find the courage to face Anthea again – in public, supported by friends – you'll be shaking your fist in the face of the bad luck you believe is still dogging you. Wise men have thought and said that fortune – the gods under a different name – favours the brave, and all the world loves a lover. If you let them, the gods will be on your side. And if you won't make the effort for yourself, or for patients who have put their trust in you, or your friends who love you and don't want to lose you, do it for your parents. They understood Love. Don't let them down!'

She had risen without knowing it, carried away by the passionate feeling inside her that this was a battle she simply had to win. It wasn't any longer just Terry's war, it was her own and everybody else's. It was part of their struggle against the brash new culture of post-war selfishness, geared only to money and what money will buy, not to the older values of love and friendship and reliance on each other. That was the core of the struggle they were now engaged in between the old-fashioned culture of the countryside and the new sort based on the urban economy, which was threatening to overwhelm them. What Eric, in his own way, was urging them to stand up and fight for.

'Don't, Fran! Don't!' Terry cried. 'You're only making me even more ashamed of myself than ever. Will you be satisfied if I promise to accept this invitation and try to keep my promise, even if at the last minute I chicken out again? I can't be sure of myself.'

'No,' she said. 'I won't be satisfied. I want a solemn promise that you will not only be there, but show everybody what sort of a man you are. Anthea especially. Don't try to avoid her. Remember that, if nothing else, she's still one of your patients. I know I'm asking a lot of you, but it isn't just for your own sake. It's for Anthea's, too, and Beth's and, indeed, for the whole lot of us. Whether you know it or not, the spirit of our old rural community is in the same danger of breaking up as you are, and, in my opinion, you're the king-pin. Don't let us down, or yourself or, most of all, your mother.'

'Leave her out of it,' he said curtly. 'She must have given up on me years ago – and I've already let her down anyway. I threw away the token she left of her belief in me. That's gone for good, and the remnants of my self-esteem and integrity went with it. All I can promise you is to try, for your sake.'

It was the lead she had been waiting for. She fumbled inside her pocket, and managed to free the ring from its case. Then she held her closed fist out towards him.

'Open your hand,' she said. 'If you'll only trust the gods, they may work miracles.' Mesmerized by her intensity, he looked up at her, and obeyed, like a child before a magician.

She dropped the ring into his open palm, heard his gasp – and fled from the room.

*   *   *

'I wish,' said Bob, 'as I knowed what we were looking for, and why. I reckon as it might help a bit.'

William laughed. He always felt happy in Bob's company, especially when they sat, as now, side by side in St Saviour's Church. He was terribly tempted to give a proper answer, and rely on Bob's keen nose, like a pointer's, to lead them towards a sensible place to start looking; but if he told him anything, he would have to tell him all. That wouldn't be fair to Fran, whom he had no intention of telling anything till he could tell her everything. There was too much chance that it would only lead to disappointment for him to dare to give her even a hint of what was so incredibly possible, but not by any stretch of imagination

197

probable. He would have to let Bob follow him blindly for a bit longer, looking for something that so far existed only as a figment of William's imagination. Bob was about the only man he could expect to go on doing that – but he, William, couldn't have it both ways.

If he was asking Bob to look for a concrete object, which he was, it wasn't fair to leave him quite so much in the dark. Bob's curiosity was insatiable, his belief in William unshakable, and the depth of his imagination unplumbable. He had that rare and extraordinary gift of knowing how to 'be still' when alone. When leaning with his back to the churchyard wall, watching the rooks flying home to their new rookery; or with his face turned upwards on a breezy summer afternoon to watch the ever-changing shapes of white cumulus against the blue sky, he slipped into a trance-like state that put him in touch with things beyond the scope of most ordinary men's comprehension. Those who knew him well could never doubt the extent of Bob's understanding of the mystical elements in life.

William's appreciation of his friend's 'otherness' in this respect added to his reticence with regard to the manuscript, and therefore to his dilemma. He could not bring himself to let Bob know that he had even the slightest doubt about the manuscript's authenticity, because Bob believed in it with all his heart. From the moment he had found it, he had told William of his conviction that it had been 'meant' that he should find it, and that William, and only he, should be the one to discover what was in it. He had never once wavered about that.

Knowing what a special place Bob had in Fran's heart, William had not confessed to her that one of his main reasons for almost giving up on the project altogether had been his fear of hurting Bob. He could not contemplate either damaging Bob's belief in his own sixth sense by hinting of any academic uncertainty on his part; nor, if publication of it made it a bone of contention in the field of academic history, the hurt Bob would suffer if it caused William to be held in contempt by other so-called experts.

William recalled that since he had seen Bob he had firmly decided on compromise. That being so, if he and Bob were to go on searching for the vital bit of evidence he needed while yet they had time, he should perhaps put Bob a little more into the picture.

'It's for Fran's sake, mostly, that I want to find the bit of evidence I'm looking for,' William said, 'as well as my own, and yours. The story itself is another version of what anybody could read in a school text-book, but as told in the manuscript it's much more real and exciting. Especially when you live where it actually happened, and can identify the places mentioned. You know as much about the history of the church up to the time that old manuscript was written as I do. But what *is* history?

'Academic historians argue all the time as to whether the characters of any period make the events, or the events throw up the characters. In this case, I'm more interested in the people than the events. I've told you that the Cromwells are involved, Oliver in particular – the one to be found in every history text-book.

'But to the writer of that manuscript he was a real live man, and a queer customer in several ways. Not that I need tell you that, because you've grown up knowing all the local tales of him. Historians still take sides about him. People who actually knew him had more chance of judging his queer, moody personality. Our Reverend Francis had known him since childhood.

'So I'll tell you a snippet of the story according to him. By the early summer of 1646, Parliament had the King on the run. The Royalist forces had been scattered, but the best of them were still doing everything they could to save King Charles's skin, as well as their own. If the Parliamentarians, led by Cromwell, won outright, their skins would be about all they still had to lose, anyway.

'Around this time, according to the Reverend Francis, he had a couple of visitors. One was his youngest brother, and the other an unknown Cavalier. They knew what danger they courted by coming into Cromwell country here, but the unknown one had a very personal reason for coming.'

'A woman, ten to one,' said Bob.

'You're too quick on the uptake. Keep what I'm telling you to yourself. I don't want Fran to know I've told you anything I haven't told her.

'The stranger was a Royalist officer, one of the many aristocrats who had staked everything they had for the King. They'd come here from Oxford, scorning any disguise. However, as it happened, the one hope of saving anything for the King at this point depended on this man and Francis's brother getting safely to where Charles was. He was therefore travelling under a false name. Francis didn't know then who he was.

'He'd got only a few short hours, in any case. Francis put two and two together, and offered advice and the bit of help he was able to provide. During the afternoon of that day, while waiting for the dusk to fall, he and the lady concerned walked together from your house to the church. When they returned, Francis saw that his advice had been taken, and something that could have identified the Cavalier, had he been captured, had been left behind – here in the church.

'He rode away soon after, and Francis never saw him again; but things were too hot for Francis himself just then for him to spend time searching, even if he had dared to be seen doing so. He kept quiet, and went on with his writing till, as we know, something happened that made him leave it almost in mid-sentence. And when he eventually did come back to it, he felt obliged to invent a code to set the rest down in.

'Then, probably without much hope of saving his own skin anyway, and certainly not if what he had written should be found and read, he wrapped the book up and hid it, though not necessarily where you found it.

'That's what's defeating me. So much has happened to the church since that day. But I do need to know more about that visitor. I know what it was he might have left hidden, but considering what the Puritans did to churches in the next few years, to say nothing of how folks ever since have helped themselves to things left in churches, we have about as much chance of finding anything now as the proverbial needle in the haystack. I do have one idea where we might look though, from a tiny bit of the book.'

'I see,' said Bob. 'Getting at it from the other end. Like the police have to in a murder case, or tracing a missing person they think may have been done in. Taking hundreds of statements and discarding ninety-nine point nine per cent of them. So it ain't no good me telling you as I keep dreaming about seeing a black man with two fingers missing and his hair tied up in witch-locks leaving his earring stuck under a pew with chewing gum?'

William favoured him with a broad grin. 'No,' he said, 'I should have to discard that as evidence if for no other reason but that there were no pews then – or chewing-gum, as far as I know. "Your evidence will be duly noted, and filed, sir. Thank you." You've got the idea, Bob.'

'What sort of thing might it have been?'

'Well . . . a signet ring, for example, a ring with the family crest incised, intended to be used as a seal. Or anything with the family arms on it.'

'A hand-gun, with the arms on the stock?'

'Possibly, but in his situation, I doubt if he would have wanted to part with his pistol. He'd have left that in his saddle-bag, primed and ready for use on himself if it proved necessary, and if he were in danger of being caught. Before they tortured any secrets out of him.'

'An axe, then? If he was running away, he might have had to cut his way through brushwood or carr, especially round here.'

'Something around that size, I think,' William said seriously. He hated deceiving Bob like this, because he knew perfectly well what it was that had been left behind. But one never knew what help Bob's imagination could throw up.

'A few weeks before this visit, the church had been ransacked by a gang of Puritans. Francis describes how they'd smashed a couple of windows, torn up the altar rail and reduced it to kindling, dug up some of the floor and then tried to carry the marble altar table away to smash it. But they'd found it heavier than they'd expected, and just dropped it.

'And there it lay, I suppose, till at some later date, after the fire, it was used to cover up the church end of the secret tunnel from your cellar – as you know, because you helped me to raise it just far enough to satisfy our curiosity. So there was no top to the altar till Francis's men covered it with a big oak door. When the church was restored in the middle of the last century, they put a new mahogany top on the altar, which is there now. If our Cavalier and his friend had heaved and strained, they could just about have levered up that old door enough to drop a long thin object in. It's just possible that the Victorian restorer had enough respect for the altar to clean it up but leave what they found in it where it was. I think you and I together wouldn't have much difficulty in raising it enough to look. Shall we try?'

It gave them very little trouble, in fact, but the stone box which supported the altar itself had been emptied, swept and cleaned out. They replaced the altar top and its cloth in silent disappointment.

'Well,' said William. 'If we didn't find the murder weapon, at least we didn't find the corpse instead. I believe in medieval times it was not unusual for bodies that were either sainted or in need of disposal on the quiet to be secreted inside such altars. I shall have to go on thinking and hoping, that's all.'

Bob said, in rather embarrassed tones, that he hoped William wouldn't want much of his help during the next week because Jane had promised to act as her father's hostess for Fran's birthday lunch at Effendi's house next Saturday.

'And none of us'll have any time for anything else that day,' he said.

William had more or less forgotten about the arrangement, and felt guilty. He said so. Bob gave him an understanding grin in return.

'Now if Fran was like most women, you wouldn't half catch it. But you and me are lucky that way, I reckon. Take your mind off what it is you're still looking for, and give it to what you've got.'

Good advice, thought William. He said goodbye to Bob quickly, and hurried home.

*

Fran had slipped into the breakfast room when she left Terry, alert in case she had to return. After five minutes or so of anxious waiting, she heard his step in the hall, and the big front door slam behind him. It was only then that she began to feel the strain of the morning. She sat down where she was until her heart steadied a little, and the slight nausea she had been feeling while waiting began to recede.

She looked at her watch. *Still only half-past two?* Incredulous, she shook it, thinking it must have stopped; it seemed like a week of wet Sundays since she had left Benedict's that morning. There was only about another hour and a half of daylight, so it wouldn't be long before William was home. She not only wanted him, she needed him. The strain on her had been too great, and she knew the symptoms.

She mustn't give in now! If she allowed the tumult of emotion inside her to get the better of her, the result would be one of her tempestuous moods of rage and despair, as her morale plummeted to the bottomless pit of misery. They usually only caught her out when other matters of little account in their own right piled up on her till she had to get rid of the weight of them somehow – usually by having a violent quarrel with a totally unprepared and innocent William.

She always felt great while the rage lasted. She was an angry Athena well supplied by Zeus with thunderbolts to hurl, a regal, ruthless goddess filled with indignation, spitting out words like flaming arrows and dowsing the victim next minute with the icy scorn of her contempt. As William had once said, when one such tempest was safely over, as deadly a mixture of fire and ice as one could ever encounter except perhaps while witnessing, as he had once done, the eruption of a volcano from beneath an Icelandic sea. But then would come the awful reaction, when the sea was empty and wide, and the earth nothing but bare black rock. Especially when she had hurt William too much.

The very thought of him at this minute was too much for her. What were all those other folk she had got herself into such a stew about compared to him – and Benedict's, and their love for each other? All the same, they did not live in a goldfish bowl, however beautiful it was. As John Donne had said, '*no man is an island*'. If, as he also wrote, any man's death diminished him, so must everybody else's unhappiness tend to diminish theirs – if they let it.

William had already sensed the danger. He had not tried to stop her doing what she felt she must to sort out whatever was wrong, probably because he knew it would be no good, but also because he did understand that the immediate difficulties had arisen in the first place from a gesture of friendship thought up by Eric to mark her birthday.

But for her something was rotten in their usually happy little state, and the time was out of joint. Like poor Hamlet, she felt it was cursèd spite that it was she who had, apparently, been born to set it right. How apt!

The quotation flashing with such rapidity into her mind as if waiting there like a Puck in the wings surprised even her; her capacity to summon words to her own rescue actually made her smile, and immediately she felt better. She must get up and do something. To sit there and think would still be too dangerous. She went into the kitchen, though without any idea what she meant to do.

She heard a noise at the back door and next moment saw that, Saturday though it was, Ned had come to light the sitting-room fire, and pile up enough logs to see them over the weekend. He came into the kitchen loaded with logs, and gave her a cheery greeting.

When he had the fire going, he came back to her, by which time she had the kettle boiling. As he accepted his cup of tea, his eyes strayed critically round the kitchen. 'Looks to me as if you're missing Soph' more'n you know,' he said. 'You could sow onion seed in the dust on that window-sill – and as for the Aga – and the floor! Do you want me to stop now and give you a hand to clean it up a bit afore she comes back a-Monday? You don't want Olive Clap-Trap going round telling everybody what a pigsty you're been living in while waiting for folks like her to come and clean it out for you, do you?'

He was drawing attention to all sorts of small details that Sophie would never have let slip, as Fran had done in the last month while having to do the housework herself. For a moment, she wanted to tell him to mind his own business, but she could never be cross with Ned! He was worth his weight in gold – one of the things that she could never be grateful enough for.

'I've had such a lot to do, Ned, and I hate housework! But you're absolutely right. I can hear Sophie muttering, "Pig's 'ole!" when she comes in on Monday morning and being ashamed of what she'd told Olive to expect. Will you really do a bit of hoovering while you're here? I'll dust after you.'

'Are you going to want to use the Aga to cook supper?' he asked. ''Cos if you are, I'd better give that a bit of a do first.'

Supper? She hadn't given it a thought! But now what she wanted more than anything else was to cook as good a supper for William as any Sophie could have done. That was something she loved doing and had rather resented having to hand over so completely to Sophie. She made up her mind. Let everything and everybody else wait till Monday. Now . . . what was there in the fridge?

So while Ned cleaned and polished, Fran turned her mind to her culinary skills. If there was anything William loved, it was a lamb stew, and she'd laid in some lovely neck-chops only yesterday while buying a chicken for the weekend. An Irish stew, then, with plenty of herby dumplings. There was still time! Dessert . . . apple pie? No! Pancakes. They both loved them. She flew round preparing vegetables and making batter to stand, as it should, till the hump of anxiety was beginning to shift from her shoulders.

Ned was whistling merrily, as he so often did when enjoying himself, and as soon as he had finished to his satisfaction, he accompanied her to the sitting-room, stoked up the fire, drew the curtains against the November dusk and went home. She heard him greet William at the front door.

He was aware, at once, of the homely smell of cooking, and his own disappointment faded as he realized that Fran herself must have prepared it against his homecoming. So she was not so 'low' as he had expected her to be, and been prepared for. He was taking off his coat by the cupboard under the stairs when she came to greet him. He turned, and opened his arms – and she fell into them. God was in His heaven, and all was right with their little world.

It was only after the last dumpling had been scoffed and he'd asked what was for dessert that either of them gave much thought to anything but each other. He told her what a pleasant time he'd had with Bob, even if it hadn't got them much farther with the bit of proof he needed to establish the book's authenticity, and explained to her why he didn't want Bob to know that he'd ever had any doubts about it. He knew he was playing a dangerous game by setting Bob up as his excuse for not telling Fran what he was really after, and vice versa. But if it worked out . . . what a triumph it would be for them all! Himself included. It was worth the risk.

She could see that he had relaxed a lot since she had left him early this morning, and blessed Bob. She was content to wait till he asked her what she had been doing. Instead, he was asking what she had ready for dessert.

'Pancakes?' he said, joyfully. '*Pancakes!* The Food of Love, of course. Sit still, I'll make them.'

And while they ate, they recalled the first time they had ever eaten pancakes together, and then the evening when they had made them for Beth and Elyot, and most of all the impromptu 'Love Feast' that Fran and Beth had arranged on Shrove Tuesday this year. They fell silent then, wishing they hadn't mentioned it, because it brought them back, inevitably, to Terry and Anthea. The promise of that lovely evening had looked as if it was going to blossom as they had all hoped it might – right up till last week. They dropped the subject. Too soon yet, to start dissecting Fran's problems.

They washed up together, and went to sit by the fire with their after-supper drinks. William sat down in his own chair, but got up again to go and sit at her feet with his head against her knee.

'Now tell me,' he said. 'And don't get yourself upset. We're in this together as we are in everything else.'

She gave him a short but fairly clear and concise account of her day. The strong emotions were threatening her again, and in spite of herself her voice quavered. He had been expecting this and opened her hand to put a kiss in the palm and fold her fingers over it.

'It's all so silly,' she suddenly burst out. 'The whole thing's reached a pitch of such idiocy I don't know how I can possibly face next Saturday! Birthday celebration? With everybody putting on false bonhomie, and absolutely hating every minute of it — because they all hate each other, as far as I can make out. None of them can escape, now, without losing face to the others. I mean ... everything I've done today has only made it worse. Nigel's still away, leaving everything to Effendi and Jane to cope with. What on earth does Nigel think he's doing? I don't suppose Jane minds, except that Bob will have warned her that it won't be easy. And Eric really worries me. He's not only the most miserable, but hating it worse than anybody else because it was all his doing in the first instance, and things have gone wrong that for once he can't put right. For neither love nor money, literally. He's at odds with everybody, except perhaps us, and Jess and Greg. And, sweetheart, can't you see? It isn't my fault, but it does all revolve round me! I thought perhaps that if I acted as go-between, I might take some of the sting out of it so that at least we could get the day over with some semblance of dignity and civilized behaviour. Now I doubt it. And I can't stop it, without giving great offence. I suppose I could take to my bed, so that it would have to be cancelled. Sophie will be back on Monday, thank heaven, so it could be possible for me to swing the lead. It's all so hopeless that the one thing I want to do now is to creep away and hide. They surely wouldn't hold the stupid lunch without me.'

And then she began to cry, not as he had rather been expecting, with anger, but quietly and helplessly, as he had rarely seen her before. She had been defeated, and nothing could have hurt him more than to see those hopeless tears.

But they had the effect of calling out the man in him: her protector, her defender, her lover. The flexible core of steel under the velvet scabbard of his disarming charm and courtesy showed clearly as he stood up, pulled her to her feet, and then sat down again in her chair with her on his knees. He cradled her wet face against his chest, and gently wiped it with his handkerchief.

'Now, my darling, cry it out if it will help. But what we need is to take a calmer look at it, and then see what we can do. I know

I've left you to it, because I thought you didn't want to involve me, and I wanted you to do it your way if you could. But I'm still here, my sweetheart – your husband and your knight, pledged to his lady's service before anything else in the whole wide world.' He turned up her face to him and kissed her. She lay passive in his embrace till the great surge of emotion flowing through her passed.

'Darling Sir Galahad,' she said. 'That's all I needed. Whatever got into me? Of course we'll go on trying.

'Come the three corners of the world in arms,
And we shall shock them.'

She was struggling to get up, but he held her tight.

'Don't move,' he said. 'We've got time for ourselves first, haven't we? That damned book of mine has been getting itself between us. I've been neglecting you. Forgive me. That was a lovely meal – something good to come home to. But not so good as this. We're both back home again. And on Monday, Sophie will be here as well. So we've got tomorrow to ourselves. We'll make plans in bed in the morning.'

'And by this time next Saturday, my wretched birthday will be over,' she said.

He kissed her again. 'It may be very different from what you expect,' he said. 'Why don't you leave it to the gods? You've done it before, if I remember correctly?' He looked down on her with one dark eyebrow raised, and the other lowered.

'Neither of us could ever forget,' she said. 'I'd already made up my mind to do exactly that. The gods with you to help them can't fail me.'

'I'll make you a promise,' he said. 'Stop worrying about this birthday, and I promise that next year's shall be the best ever.'

It was only the pressure of her considerable weight on his knees that finally caused them to move. He went out to make another drink for them both, whistling, sweet and true as a blackbird, 'Who is Sylvia?'. She followed him by the sound as he moved about the kitchen, her ear tuned to him only. Next came 'You are my heart's delight' as he poured the milk into the hot chocolate which was his favourite beverage when relaxed and happy. However, before he left the kitchen, the tune changed again to the dance rhythm of 'Love is – the sweetest thing', and she was already on her feet to meet him when he set the cups down and held out his hands to her.

But as they began to dance, he turned his whistled tune to the waltz from 'The Maid of the Mountains', and she got his unspoken message. He stopped whistling and they stopped dancing, only so that he could kiss her again.

Love would surely find a way.

*   *   *

Monday morning came, greeted with mixed feelings at Benedict's. They had enjoyed Sunday, but they woke early next morning, and knew why. This was it. Five days to *der Tag*.

William, afraid that Fran would start worrying as soon as her eyes were open, drew her towards him and said, 'Don't run to meet trouble. I know it feels like waiting for D-Day again, but that's all history now. Remember that even such a great scheme as that, a manoeuvre planned to the nth degree in advance, was in the end subject for success or failure on the weather.

'We're very much in the same boat about Saturday. We can't control what happens. All we can do is to wait and see what does, and keep hoping that if there is a bomb about to fall it may only be a near miss that doesn't succeed in blowing us all asunder. That's what you're really afraid of, isn't it? But it's only the same old dog with more hairs on, you know. The result of a period of change leading to chaos. There comes a time when even the Churchills of the world can't control the effects of change because of a sort of immutable condition: that though circumstances change, human nature doesn't, it only adapts itself. People remain very much as they have always been, but they have to react to

209

sudden changes in their environment. Which is what is happening here, as Eric keeps warning us.

'If we – you and I – could but detach ourselves from it enough to see Saturday as only one drop in the ocean of Time, and Old Swithinford as only one grain of sand in the landscape of history, we should be able to see how little significance all this has. We can't because we're too close to be able to see it in perspective. But it really is only a sort of hiccup. Don't let whatever happens hurt you too much, my darling. I sometimes think it's a comfort not to be young any more. It does give us a bit of perspective that youngsters born since the war don't have. Maybe this little upheaval will prove to be salutary, in the end. It was hardly to be expected that we could all go on living the life of Riley, as we have been, much longer without a hiccup or two.

'Let's trust that everybody will learn something from it, and make up their minds to make the most of what's left when Saturday's over. As for us, we'll take each day of this week as it comes.'

She chuckled, and his heart leapt to hear her. 'Thanks for the lesson, sweetheart, but actually I thought we had decided on doing exactly that yesterday, to wait and see what the weather's like before making the final decisions about D-Day. But today's only Monday – and if I'm concerned about anything, it's how to deal with today. Sophie will be back this morning, praise be, but even that's giving me a few qualms. As you say, she won't have changed much, but circumstances will. Olive 'Opkins will be here as well. Does that mean we have to be prepared to adapt ourselves to a new routine? Will Olive throw a spanner in the works?

'We don't know her, except by hearsay from Sophie and Mary Budd. Sophie says that she's "like a pea in a porridge, neither good nor harm". She's sort of taken Olive under her wing since Mary died and my guess is that she's been waiting for a chance to find Olive a toehold here, on the grounds that if she'd do for Saint Budd, she'd do for us. What's worrying me is what she may do to our relationship with Sophie.'

'Can't we hope that in her new role as "housekeeper", we can trust Sophie to take charge of Olive and keep her in her place?'

'I suppose so. We shall soon find out. That's what I meant. What shall we do – wait at the table after breakfast to greet Sophie like we've always done, with Olive standing by?'

'Why not? Of course we shall. Just be ourselves. As we've agreed, just wait and see.'

So there they were, still sitting over their breakfast, when the heavy tread of two pairs of feet announced that Sophie was taking no chances. William sprang to his feet as he would for any woman from the queen to – well, as was evident – a charwoman. Sophie approached the table with a determined step and the resigned air of a mother obeying her moral conscience to hand over one of her offspring she suspected of misdemeanour to the village policeman. 'This 'ere's Olive,' she said, shoving forward her somewhat reluctant protégée, a tall, row-boned woman with flat planes everywhere. 'If it's all the same to you,' Sophie went on, 'I'll show 'er over straight away and give 'er 'er orders, like, while you finish your breakfastses, and then come back to see as 'ow you want me to arrange things, like.'

Then she dropped her voice, and addressed herself directly to William. 'Do you sit down,' she said. 'There's no call for you to treat Olive like a lady, do she ain't used to it. And do you don't want her to waste time as you're paying 'er for, don't ask 'er no questions. Do, we shan't none of us get nothing done, 'cos once she start chelping, she don't know 'ow to stop. It's all on account o' 'er being so lonely, like, poor woman, heving to live with a man as never opens 'is mouth only to shove 'is meals in it. I'd rather live by meself, that I would. Heving a man like 'er 'usband playing silent donkey in my sight for years on end would ha' druv me to 'it 'im over the 'ead with a flat-iron years ago, I'm sure. But she just can't 'elp talking when there's anybody to talk to. So I thought as if me and Olive were to 'ev our 'levenses together, she could talk to me all she wants, without upsetting you. I'm knowed 'er since we was both child'en so it won't bother me. Will that do?'

William sat down, relieved that Sophie had lived up to her reputation yet again, and sorted out what might have been a slightly embarrassing situation well in advance. On the other hand, one glance down at Fran told him that Sophie's forthrightness in front of the newcomer had caught her on her very delicate funny bone. He was about to suggest that perhaps they'd better get out of Sophie's way, when the gleam of mischief in Fran's eye stopped him. If she wanted to enjoy her first experience of Olive, he wasn't going to prevent it. Especially this week.

'Put the kettle on again, darling,' she said. 'Let's have a cup of tea to celebrate Sophie's return to the fold, and to welcome Mrs Hopkins.'

Sophie scowled at her, shaking her head to warn Fran that she was taking the wrong line. Fran smilingly ignored her. She was proposing to enjoy Olive, as William had realized. Taking his cue, he turned on his most courteous male charm, and directed its beam first towards Olive, and then back to his wife.

'Whatever you say, my precious one,' he said. 'Your wish is my command.' He turned away to fill the kettle, knowing that if he caught her eye Fran wouldn't be able to suppress the laughter already bubbling in her throat at the way he was deliberately overplaying his part to please her. Sophie was showing her disapproval in no uncertain manner.

'Now then,' she said in a hoarse stage whisper, 'be'ave yourselves, do! Didn't I tell you as Olive ain't used to such wayses? It'll be all over the village come tea-time as neither the one nor the other of you is right in the 'ead. I'm used to your goings-on. She ain't.'

Fran suggested that Sophie should show Olive where to hang up her coat in the 'utility-room' that had once been the scullery. Sophie went grimly, and Olive followed meekly. Fran took advantage of their absence to let her laughter free, while William made the tea and got out extra cups.

'Sh!' he said. 'They're coming back.' But he went too close to Fran, and found the infection of her laughter catching. She stood up and hid her face in his chest, trying to muffle her gurgles in his shirt. He attempted to put his arms round her but was handicapped by a tea-pot full of scalding hot tea in one hand. So he took the only measure he could think of to stifle the sound of mirth from both of them: he bent and kissed her, carefully holding the tea-pot at arm's length. Such was the tableau that greeted the return of Sophie and her apprentice.

Fran caught sight of Sophie's face, which almost set her off again. She disengaged herself from William, found her handkerchief and began to cough vigorously. William set the tea-pot down and hit her hard on the back. As soon as she had herself well enough under control to speak at all, she said, 'Do sit down, Mrs Hopkins. I'm so sorry about that. A crumb went the wrong way, and when that happens I sometimes get quite nasty fits of choking. I think I'm all right now, thank you, William.'

He placed a chair for Sophie, and another for Olive. Sophie, not deceived, merely said, 'Thenks'; but Fran was proof against her for the next few minutes. She knew that Sophie had seen through her subterfuge, and was offended by the unnecessary lies it had occasioned. After all, said her unspoken comment, she had warned them to behave 'ordinary, like' till Olive got used to them.

So she sat bolt upright, and drank her tea silently, with her little finger cocked in reproof. Olive sat down gingerly, and took the tea offered to her. But she was incapable of Sophie's dignified silence; she responded, as Sophie had forecast, to Fran's explanation.

'I reckon as you must ha' lost the luker out o' your throat,' she opined. 'My sister married a man from a fam'ly out in the fens as none of 'em could talk proper, and one of 'em as was called Fred used to hev them choking fits so bad that in the end 'e went to the doctor about it. The doctor looked down 'is throat, and ask 'im if 'e'd ever 'ad the Dip Theria, and when 'e said yes, the whull hustle of 'em 'ad 'ad it when they was child'en, the doctor said as that must be the reason 'cos Dip Theria was a disease as took you in the throat, and if you 'ad it bad enough, your luker wouldn't never work properly no more, so you 'ad them choking fits when you couldn't get your breath. But come the time when that doctor died and they 'ad a new 'un, and 'e said e'd never 'eard o' no such thing. He reckoned it must be on account o' something altogether different and kep' asking Fred till 'e told the doctor as 'ow they'd all been bit b'dogs.

'"Dogs?" say the doctor. "All on you bit by different dogs,

213

d'yer mean, or was you all bit by the same dog? 'Cos do that were a mad dog as 'ad 'ad hyperthermia, it could ha' give it to all on you."'

She paused, and took another noisy sip of her tea. 'I *think* as that's what 'e said, only I ain't no good at calling long words to mind. Seems to me, now I come to think about it, as it was more to do with hens than dogs. 'E thought as they might ha' caught that there complaint as makes old 'ens 'old their 'eads up and gape all the while 'cos they can't swaller. It were some long word like tracky-hitus or some such. No, I tell a lie. I knowed as it were something to do with 'ens. Hencoffeelightus. That's what he said it might be.'

Fran and William were in difficulties again. Sophie growled at Olive, *sotto voce*, ''Old your tongue, Olive, do! Us as 'as knowed you all our lives knows you can't never remember nothing for two minutes together, try as Miss might to 'elp you. But 'im and 'er don't want to 'ear no more now about that queer tongue-tied lot o' fen-tigers as your sis married into. You're 'ere to work, not to run on about folks as they don't know – so you'd better get on with it.'

She turned to Fran, and to change the subject asked, 'Who's been a-helping you while I'm been away, cleaning the Aga and such? Ned, I'll be bound. This kitchen ain't 'alf such a pig's 'ole as I'd expected to find. But if you'll take yourselves out o' the way, I'll give it a real proper do myself, and Olive can do the same in the scullery and the pantry. What both of 'em needs most, I reckon, is a good breath o' fresh air through 'em. So goo you, Olive, and start by opening every winder as wide as you can.'

Olive stood up to order, but paused to say, 'Ah, I know who teached you that, Soph' Wainwright. That were Miss Budd, that were. I can 'ear 'er saying it now, that time as we 'ad 'ooping cough in the school, and she made us work wi' the winders open even when it were snowing outside and we was all nearly frez to death. If she see us shiver, she'd open the winder wider still, and say we 'ad to remember the proverb as we'd writ yist'day: "Ventilation's better than cure". She were a good'un though, Miss were, weren't she, Soph'?'

214

Fran and William were glad to escape before Sophie defended her beloved 'Miss' in case either of them should experience another 'fit' of 'the gapes'.

'Where on earth did she get a word like "luker" from?' Fran said, through her laughter. 'I wonder if it's a dialect word. I don't know it at all, except in the sense of "filthy lucre".'

'You're never too old to learn,' he said, grinning, 'even from a Mrs Malaprop like Olive.' He fetched a dictionary and at once, as is inevitable, got hooked on it.

'There's a noun here spelt "luke", which, according to Dickens, meant "nine penn'orth o' brandy and water" so that can't be it but . . . O I see! Of course. It's plain enough when you know. Whatever the doctor did say, he was referring to some difficulty in breathing that affected Fred's speech. It actually says here that in the seventeenth century, the medical profession derived the word "luctation" from the Latin verb "*luctari*, to struggle", denoting "a struggle for breath". It must have got into the dialect that way. How fascinating!'

They had retreated to William's study, leaving the door slightly ajar on purpose; but all they heard was Sophie's sergeant-major-like tones issuing orders, and the buzz of the vacuum cleaner and other such domestic utensils as mops rattling on buckets. It was clear that Sophie had determined that Olive should not be allowed to talk while working. Regretfully, they gave up listening, though sounds still penetrated their hide-out. Sophie might have succeeded in stopping Olive from talking, but not from tongue-wagging in a different form.

'What Sophie needs is a scold's bridle,' William said. He was finding the whole situation even more hilarious than Fran did, which was saying a lot. When Sophie remained stonily silent, depriving Olive of a listener who would respond to her chatter, Olive raised her voice in song. ' "O, Rose-Marie, I love you", ' rose loudly and hoarsely above the surrounding clatter, so off-key as to be barely recognizable. William began to laugh till he was out of breath, and had to find his handkerchief to wipe his eyes.

'Shut the door, darling,' he gasped, 'or I shall explode. How much longer is she going to be here now? And how often?'

'Mornings only,' she assured him. 'Get it over before Sophie brings us our coffee. I don't yet know myself what it is she proposes under our new regime.'

But Sophie made it clear that she could not leave her charge long enough to stop and discuss anything with them just then.

When at last they dared venture again into the kitchen, they could see why. She had certainly kept her word to 'give it a good do', and had prepared a light mid-day meal for them into the bargain.

'I'm now a'gooing to see 'ow Daniel is,' she said, nodding towards Olive to convey that her real reason was to make sure Olive went too. 'I'll be back to get your tea and put a meal in for you to have tonight. Olive's a-gooing with me, now, when I goo.' She was taking no chances.

Fran and William saw them to the door. Olive had the last word.

'I can see why it was as Soph' needed a bit of 'elp,' she said, 'with all them there big old rooms at the back to keep clean as well as the rest of an 'ouse as big as this is. Mind you, do it 'ad been me, I shouldn't ha' choosed to hev that pantry and that ol' dairy-as-was painted white. Reminds me too much of an 'orspital – too cynical, if you know what I mean.'

'Come you on!' yelled Sophie, from some distance up the drive.

Olive made her farewells to Fran and William. 'I mustn't keep Soph' a-waiting,' she said. 'But we shall see what transfers tomorrer.'

She picked up the front of her skirt and ran clumsily to catch up her impatient mentor, singing breathlessly, and more off-key than ever, her own muddled version of the lyric of 'Rose-Marie'.

'Well,' said William as they sat down to Sophie's meal. 'I must say this feels like home again.'

Yes. Benedict's was back to normal, and whatever else might have changed, Sophie hadn't, in spite of her new position within the hierarchy of the household. Fran, putting it into perspective as William had urged, came to the conclusion that that was probably because she'd had time to get used to the idea of the change, having had warning of it in advance. It was sudden changes that caused shock. That surely was a lesson to be learned.

William, watching her as she ate the simple meal Sophie had left ready, could almost read her thoughts, and breathed a sigh of relief at her air of general relaxation. He silently called down blessings on the head of Olive for making them abandon themselves to laughter. It had been a long time since they had laughed in unison like they had this morning.

'I wish,' said Fran, 'that a lot of other folks we know had as much sense as Sophie.'

'That's the spirit!' he countered. 'And our cue for Saturday. If we use our common sense, it will take more than a fit of the blues to make our friends forget it's your birthday. It began, after all, as a celebration just for you, my darling.'

He reached his hand over the table to her, and sang, '"O, Rose-Marie, I love you",' which sent her into another fit. He had tried to imitate Olive – but he couldn't have sung off-key to save his life!

*

Their sitting-room was warm and cheerful, and so were they. Comfortable and happy, William, noticing how somnolent Fran seemed, crept out to get himself a book, and found her fast asleep when he returned. If only she could keep this mood up, and he could persuade her to stay away from the centre of controversy, they might still find they had a circle of friends as close to them and to each other as they had ever been.

But he feared Fran's tendency to run towards trouble. She allowed those in trouble to batten on her – or so he had often thought, and said. She defended herself hotly against the charge. 'I didn't ask for it,' she would say, but when people in trouble turned to her, how could she send them away without at least listening and trying to help?

But now, through no possible fault or weakness of her own, she'd been caught like a toad under a harrow that she hadn't known was there, and one after the other the tines of friendship were knocking her over and wounding her. He was not as optimistic about the coming Saturday as he pretended to be; but he hoped she could keep up her spirits till the ordeal had to be faced.

It was not like her to be so low in spirits. He wondered now how much his preoccupation with his book, coupled with his reluctance to start on it, could be the primary cause of her slightly depressed and pessimistic mood . . .

What she didn't know, of course, was that he had a great secret which he was keeping from her; not, in the first place, for his own sake, but all for her delight if, or when, the time came and he could prove to his own satisfaction that what her ancestor had alleged was true beyond all reasonable doubt.

He wanted it to be true for his own sake – just how much, only he knew – but he wanted it even more for hers. Like Terry, he had been building dream castles in the air of the time when he could lay the finished book at her feet, containing within its pages the greatest present he could ever surprise her with. Now he wondered if this was silly, when at present she was needing something more concrete than abstract promises to uplift her.

No; he wouldn't go back on his plan. The steel in him came through its scabbard again, and he rejected the thought. He was doing it *for her*, and nothing of what was happening now was going to be allowed to spoil it for either of them.

He got up and went to stand beside her, looking down on her as she slept, and was overwhelmed by a blaze of love that reduced all other things to vague shapes in a distant haze of shadow. He wanted her to wake up, so that he could tell her so, and bent to kiss her – just as Sophie, bearing a tray with their tea on it, pushed the door open with her bottom and sidled in.

He sprang to help Sophie, and his sudden movement roused Fran.

'Sophie!' she said, delightedly startled back to the reality that things at Benedict's had returned to normal again. 'How good it is to have you back! What have we got? Gosh – hot buttered toast and chocolate cake? However did you manage that as well as everything else you've done today?'

Sophie beamed her gratitude. 'It ain't much of a tea,' she said, deprecatingly, 'only I couldn't use what we 'adn't got in the pantry, could I? But there ain't many folks as don't like toast as is soaked wi' butter, and the cake's what I'd made last night for Dan, so I cut it in 'alf, so as you could have it for your tea. I'll make him another tonight, do 'e want it.

'But 'e ain't 'isself. Been losing his dossity a lot just lately, Dan 'as, though for why I can't make out no'ow. They were all so 'appy together up at Glebe a little while back. Though I say it as shouldn't, I thought as once Thirz' was gone, Dan was 'appier than 'e'd ever been since he married 'er. You'd often come on him a-singing at the top of 'is voice to them cows, as 'appy as a lark, and very often George would be a-singing along of 'im. But there ain't no singing up there now. I know as they're all more disappointed than they let on to be at not being able to hev a proper party for their Golden Wedding, but as Dan says, there's nothing to stop 'em heving it a bit later on, once Rosemary's got better.

'But though George ain't said a word to 'im – and 'e tells 'im very near everything – Dan thinks George is got another worry o' some sort as 'e won't tell nobody. There's rumour flying about, for one thing, like what folks are a-saying about the doctor putting so much time as 'e is up Temperance, 'specially when Marge is there. Making it out as it ain't Rosemary as he goes to see at all. I don't know the truth o' that myself, so I shall say no more, but it ain't like Dan to say as much as that to me do 'e don't believe there's a bit o' truth in it. And if there is, and that's what's making George so quiet and miserable, it can't be wondered at, can it?'

Fran was flabbergasted with indignation, and pushed her tea aside. 'What absolute nonsense!' she cried. 'How dare anybody suggest such a thing! I know Dr Hardy's a dog with a bad name that some folks would hang if they could – but Marjorie? Who on earth has thought that one up! All George would do about a rumour like that would be to slap his sides and laugh. If he's brooding about anything, I'd swear it isn't anything so ridiculous as that. There must be something else.'

William sighed; it was just the sort of thing he'd hoped wouldn't happen. There were still four more days to go yet. 'This toast's something else, too,' he said. 'Don't let it get cold, Fran. It's probably the building up of worry about Rosemary.'

219

Sophie, realizing she'd upset Fran, looked at William gratefully. 'Tales will get about,' she said, 'do what you may. Them as lives longest'll see most. I'm off 'ome, now. Best place, this weather.' And away she went.

'So it is,' said Fran, and William, looking at her, smiled a contented smile. So she wasn't about to slide back into gloom again. He bit into another piece of toast and felt relief running over him like the butter down his chin.

*　　*　　*

The days crawled by like centipedes with half their legs broken, like Sundays used to when they were children. Grown-ups rejoiced in the 'day of rest and gladness', but impatient children, who certainly didn't want to rest and had their own ideas of what constituted gladness, miserably waited for Monday morning. Fran felt again as she used to then, not really being able to decide whose side she was on.

William had more or less decreed that they put the slowly approaching day of judgement out of mind, and had as little contact as possible with the other people involved. The weather was cold, dull and miserable; their house warm and pleasant. There was every inducement to stay there, and keep the rest of the world outside. But thought knows no boundaries, and insisted on intruding on Fran's peace. Neither she nor William would be truly at ease till this tortuous period was over.

Fran pondered on Sophie's report of the scandalous rumour going round. She hoped that Terry didn't get to hear of it, because he was too vulnerable at present to withstand even a pinprick in what *amour propre* he had left. He had been a victim of chance, but also of his own emotions, over which he had not exercised the control of common sense. But of all people *she* ought not to be blaming him for reacting to his heart instead of his head! Didn't she preach Love as the all-important ingredient for happiness? And she didn't mean 'lerve', she meant *caritas*, that all-inclusive loving-kindness for friends and neighbours and those less lucky than oneself, as well as the magic element of sexual love. The sort of Love that has an object outside the desires and devices of one's own heart.

The clock had moved about three minutes. Philosophizing wasn't much help just at the moment. It was enough to make her seasick, this constant swing from vague apprehension to hope. But who could have given birth to such a stupid rumour? The arch-queen of malignant gossip, Beryl Bean, had gone from their midst, so who was the new snake-in-the-grass they had to be aware of?

Sophie was being a bit tight-lipped since she had had to draw her horns in after reporting Dan's 'rumour'. She didn't stop to chat, or let Olive, either, which Fran rather regretted, because at least Olive might have kept her amused. The only amusement they got out of having Olive about was the way Sophie organized matters so that she was never where her loquacious nonsense would have whiled away a bit of their time. But slow as it was, time did still move onwards till Friday came and Fran began, with a good deal of relief, to put her mind back to small details, such as which articles of her wardrobe would be most suitable for an informal lunch amongst friends. It was bound to have a touch of formality, though, because Effendi the polished diplomat would be in charge, not Eric. And where on earth was Nigel? He wouldn't have come back without letting her know, surely? Suddenly, her real worries about it returned. There were too many unanswered questions.

She went to consult William. 'There are all sorts of things we don't know,' she said, 'though – or perhaps because – we are the chief guests, we haven't had any finger in the pie. We haven't even got an invitation card to refer to! I saw Terry's, and I'm sure it said "Lunch at 1.30 p.m." Does that mean we arrive exactly at one-thirty, and go straight in to lunch? What about the usual drinks first? Surely Jane and Effendi know enough about entertaining not to miss out on things like that? The invitations were hand-written, which could mean that they weren't all the same. Oh dear – can that possibly mean that Terry's was different? He was certainly

221

under the impression that he had been asked out of courtesy only, and was definitely not wanted. They couldn't possibly have been so nasty as that, could they?'

'Now don't be silly, and start inventing dramatic scenarios,' he said. 'Of course they couldn't, or wouldn't. There must be some explanation. I suppose we ought to find out what time they are expecting us. Better not let anybody else know, I think. I'll ring Jane, rather than Effendi. Now don't start running towards trouble till we know.'

She could tell by his brusque manner that he was both puzzled and anxious; but she was glad that he had so readily taken it upon himself to make the next move.

He came back smiling. 'Poor old Jane, I haven't half put her in a tizzy,' he said. 'Effendi did the invitations himself and as she said, she thought she could leave a little job like that to him! But it seems he waited too long for Nigel to come back and approve, and had to do them in a great hurry. Nobody's heard a squeak out of Nigel yet and they are a bit anxious about him. They have no idea where he is, and Jane asked if we knew. I told them you knew why he was going, but was vowed to secrecy, though not where. It does seem that there's a jinx on everything and everybody. Rest assured, though, my darling, that all the invitations are alike. She's just looked at one again, and realized it doesn't even say to whom the invitees are asked to reply. But all is laid on. They expect us by one p.m. for lunch at one-thirty. She'll ring round all the others to tell them.'

Comforted, Fran began again to think of what she would wear. The weather forecast was not too kind: 'dry but cold' was the outlook for the next few days. Warm soft suit then, and a wrap. She started to take clothes out of her well-filled wardrobe, but discarded one after another for different reasons till the pile on the bed was huge and the wardrobe more or less empty. Blue? No: that was Jane's colour. She wouldn't wear her newest blue angora. No, not black, however smart; nor green, because that was unlucky. She couldn't wear the one she'd worn for Jane and Bob's wedding – she held it up under her chin and wondered how on earth she'd ever got away with that colour. All it did for

222

her now was to make her look like a sallow old hag! She must be showing her age a lot more than she thought. She sat down on the bed feeling utterly miserable again. There was no time left to go and buy anything new now.

William opened the door and looked in. He sat down beside her and listened to her tale of woe.

'I seem to remember another occasion when we had to have a mannequin parade,' he said. 'On the evening of Mary's first horkey. You were in just the same state then, except that you would no more have let me into your bedroom to help you choose than you would have invited in a ravening lion. I remember sitting downstairs between your appearances in one frock after another till I fell asleep, and woke up to find you in just the right one. Something that you had pulled out from ages past and forgotten you'd got. I suggest I just make myself comfortable here while you rummage for something spectacular that you've forgotten and I've never seen. After all, look what the result of that evening was! I kissed you. Once. I don't suppose you remember, but I shall never forget. It's warm lying here, so you go and ferret in all the other wardrobes while I recall the details of that enchanted evening.'

The dark afternoon was drawing in as she watched him pull up the eiderdown under his chin, but he was by no means asleep when she reappeared. He sat up wide-eyed in surprise and admiration.

'Gosh,' he said. 'Do you mean to tell me you'd actually forgotten *that*! It's absolutely stunning.' She had to agree with him as she pirouetted before the dressing-table mirror. She had forgotten it absolutely, so long had it hung unused. Yet it fitted her as well as it ever had. It was a two-piece suit made of a very heavily brocaded satin: slim skirt and tunic with a high Mandarin-style stand-up collar. The black background only threw up the gold and many-coloured brocaded flowers and birds, and both skirt and tunic were slit vertically at the bottom to reveal a matching bright red, heavy satin lining as she moved.

She read everything she hoped for and more in William's appreciative expression. She had expected him to ask if it would be warm enough for a cold November day, which it would, because two layers of heavy satin was the main reason she had worn it only on two very special occasions before. It was too warm for most indoor evening gatherings.

Instead, he asked her unexpectedly, 'Have you still got those earrings? Those I bought you for the horkey?'

'Of course,' she said. 'You mean the ones you said made me look like a gipsy? I treasure them, but I don't wear them much because I thought you didn't care for them. You apologized so profusely for them being only cheap costume jewellery that I thought they might embarrass you if I flaunted them. But I loved them. They are rather flamboyant, and I've never had the absolutely right occasion to bring them out again. Why do you ask?'

'Wear them tomorrow, with that suit. Just to please me. I was afraid you wouldn't accept any sort of present from me at that time, so I didn't tell you the truth. In fact, they cost me more than a month's salary, but I knew you wouldn't take them if I told you that. I couldn't resist them. I knew, somehow, the moment I saw them in the antique jeweller's window in Cambridge, that some day they would bring me luck. It was a long time coming, but they certainly did. Go and find them. I want to fasten them on you again. For luck.'

She came back with them in her hand, studying them as she never had done before. She said, in an awed voice, 'Are you telling me that what I took to be only red glass beads are actually rubies? Set in Victorian gold? And you haven't let on all these years? Oh darling, I'm so ashamed at not knowing, or thanking you properly for them.'

'I chose rubies because they matched the raging fire in my heart,' he said, 'and I've been giving you rings and things to make up the set ever since – all rubies, because the fire's still burning as bright as ever. I won't promise you a full parure, because somehow I don't think you'll ever have need for a tiara, but there must be a bracelet somewhere to be found one day, and a necklace, or at least a pendant. All you need tomorrow, though, is a brooch at your throat.'

'I'll wear an unobtrusive gold one,' she said. 'No setting out in the morning to find me a ruby one. Promise.'

'I'll promise if you'll let me put your earrings on,' he said.

She sat on the side of the bed and he put the beautiful heavy earrings on, first pushing her away from him to see the full effect, and then pulling her back to lie in his arms beside him. He kissed her and asked if they were expecting Sophie back to get their tea. She shook her head, and the earrings rattled, so he took them off and dropped them nonchalantly to the floor. Then he sat up and looked down at her, stroking her face till his fingers moved to find the row of buttons on her tunic.

'Oh God, Fran,' he said huskily, 'have I told you lately how much I love you? I never know how much till I find out again by chance, at a moment like this. If this is anything to go by, Love must be in luck tomorrow.'

*

An hour and a half later, they sat facing each other across the kitchen table, neither face wearing the strained look that had been showing on both every day for the past week.

'I feel,' he said lazily, 'like the mean old farmer when his wife had had visitors to tea. He is supposed to have said, as he got up and made for his armchair, "Now I'm at home, and wish everybody else was as well."'

The telephone bell interrupted the conversation. Fran heard him say, 'Hold on. I'll get her for you.' He handed her the receiver.

'Nigel!' she said. 'Well, thank goodness. Where are you?'

She listened for what seemed to William an unnecessarily long time, before answering, a bit hesitantly, that she was sure it would be all right. If she hadn't rung him back in ten minutes, they could come.

'Nigel, in a bit of a mess. He's got Pansy with him, but she only agreed to come on condition that she could turn up at the lunch just as it was about to begin – not because she wants to be a "surprise present" but because she dreads having to be questioned by everybody till she chooses her own time to tell those she wants to know where she's been and what she's been doing. He had to agree, and they're both at Church Cottage now. He

225

hasn't given much thought to anything but getting her to agree to come home with him. It's only just dawned on him that she can hardly stay there all night unchaperoned, for his sake if not hers, even if there was another bed made up, which there isn't. So he proposes to bring her to us for the night – if we're willing.'

William grimaced. 'We might have expected something of the kind,' he said. 'It's lucky we made the most of this afternoon.'

She nodded. 'I wonder if either of them's had any supper? There's plenty of our steak-and-kidney pie left. I'll stick it back in the oven, and do a few more veg. At any rate it will mean we shall get a bit more gen from Nigel about the procedure for ourselves tomorrow. I wonder what Pansy's like now? The last to see her, other than Marjorie, was Eric, that day he took Marjorie to Deal. He said she looked an absolute wreck then, and she's been terribly ill since. Nigel, of course, didn't know her in her brash Bailey days.'

They scuttled around to clear away their supper and lay the table afresh, prepared more vegetables, and sat down to wait. It seemed for ever before Nigel banged on the old knocker, and William went to let him and his charge in.

They would never have recognized her. She was thinner, but healthily tough in appearance. The main change was that she was no longer a brassy blonde with puffed-out coiffeured hair, but a slighter, older-looking version of Poppy, though there were two marked distinctions. Poppy's hair curled round her face very much in the same way as Anthea's did, giving her a youthful, sprite-like air of anticipation that life could be even better for her than it already was. Pansy had allowed her hair to return to its natural colour and contour, framing a face that subtly suggested a bit of hard experience. But it was a face so serene that it signalled a greater change inside than out. Her eyes, no longer hidden under over-applied make-up, were clear and honest; there was no longer self-importance or arrogance in her manner, and her smile was genuine if bashful. She had a dignity now that no one who had ever seen her as she had been before could have believed possible.

William, who was taking her overnight case from Nigel, set it down, took Pansy into his arms, and kissed her. 'Welcome home,' he said. Fran, hovering close and feeling tears behind her own eyes that she dare not let show, kissed the girl's cheek and squeezed the hand she held.

'Have you had any supper?' she asked and was relieved to hear that they hadn't. They were both hungry and more than grateful for the offer of 'left-overs'. Food is always the best of ice-breakers.

So they ate and talked trivia till the meal was finished. Then Fran suggested she should show Pansy her room, and the girl asked if she might retire to it at once. She said goodnight to the two men, who had risen to their feet and were still standing, and followed Fran upstairs.

'Now,' said William, sitting down again and refilling Nigel's wine-glass, 'as soon as Fran comes down, you can tell us all.'

Nigel apologized for his long absence and his lack of communication. For one thing, it hadn't been easy to persuade Pansy, or to get her released from commitments she had undertaken. And he had thought to kill two birds with one stone while he was there, which had also taken time.

'I thought you would have guessed where Pansy was,' he said. 'With my two marvellous old friends at Canterbury, the same who had taken her in to care for when she was at rock bottom. A couple of honest-to-God saints, in its literal sense, but so human themselves that they understand human failings and make allowance for them. I think what is most impressive about them is their own abundant *joie-de-vivre*, though well into their eighties. But perhaps that's one of God's greatest gifts: to remain young in heart while bodies grow old and heads grow wise because of years of accumulated experience. I don't mean that they're sloppy do-gooders; both are capable of censure when and where in their opinion it's deserved. They trust their hearts to help first, as they did with Pansy. They just overlooked her submission to modern standards of morality, and gave her what she needed. Rest and security, care and comfort for her body; understanding and tolerance for her disturbed mind, and her regret and shame at what

227

she had done to her family; and above all, love to heal her spirit. It is no wonder that she didn't want to leave them to come home, partly because she couldn't face her family, and partly because just at the crucial time when she was being urged to return, my old friend was taken ill, very ill. Pansy saw it as a chance to repay in kind a little of what they had done for her, and took some of the ordinary, everyday chores off his wife's shoulders.

'As he said, perhaps it helped him to dodge the undertaker yet again to know that the shopping was being done while his wife was visiting him in hospital, the dog was being walked, the hoovering done and so on.

'Anyway, the upshot of it was that when he came back, convalescing, Pansy also proved herself to be a very capable and caring nurse. It put ideas into their heads for her future, and they encouraged her to get herself some training as an official "carer". So she has done a course and, Sod's Law, was just in the final week of it, assessment and all that, when I arrived out of the blue to try to persuade her to come home. She wouldn't have come, and they wouldn't have wanted her to, if I had insisted she came there and then. She couldn't leave till this afternoon, that was flat. I could have come home and then gone back for her; but I dared not let her decide unsupported. She would have chosen to stay where she was "safe". I had to be patient and wait, so I used my time to go and consult another old friend about a very different matter. I won't stop to tell you about it now, but I think you may be interested. I've got so many things on my mind just at present that I don't know whether I'm coming or going!

'Pansy was adamant that she wouldn't meet any of the family till she walked in on them when they were all there together. Perhaps that was good thinking. But just in case, I've had to promise that I'll take her up to the Old Glebe at one o'clock, and hang about long enough to make sure everything's OK before I leave her to it. Knowing them as I do, I can't imagine that there'll be anything but general thanksgiving and rejoicing, but human nature being what it is, it's better to be on the safe side.

'As soon as I got home to Church Cottage, I rang Eric, then Nicholas – Effendi – and then Jane. Got told off properly for not being here to do my share, or keeping in touch but, of course, under the circumstances, I could offer them no explanations, only excuses.

'However, I'm told that everything is well in hand, except that till I was home they couldn't finalize the details with regard to you two. They have arranged that everybody else must be there before the guest of honour makes her appearance, so while all the others are invited to arrive around one p.m., you are to be kept waiting somewhere to make a grand entrance when all the rest are gathered together, say at one-fifteen. They would have preferred five past one, but I had to say I couldn't guarantee to be there myself till at least ten past. So they had no option but to settle for that.'

Fran looked suspicious. 'What little game have you all got up your sleeve?' she asked.

'Never you mind,' he said. 'Don't do anything to rob me and Effendi of the first chance we've ever had to repay some of your wonderful hospitality. Heavens, is that the time? I really must go and see if I've still got a clean collar left.'

*   *   *

William remembered, as soon as he was awake, that it was Fran's birthday. He hadn't had time to pop into Cambridge to buy her a special present, but he hoped that the bouquet of bronze chrysanthemums he had ordered would be delivered before the end of the day.

He kissed her to wake her, and told her how he'd failed her. She didn't show any signs of disappointment, but told him not to be so silly.

'I'll take an I O U,' she said, 'for something that I both want and need if ever that time comes. At this moment there's nothing I can think of that wouldn't have been a waste of your precious time and money. Forget it. As long as today goes off all right, I shall be happy enough without my tiara.'

'I've given you an IOU promise,' he said. 'If it's possible at all, you shall have an extra-special present next year. A sort of two-in-one. Damn, who can that be ringing so early?'

He took the call himself, apprehensive of what the news might be on this day of days. It was only Nigel asking if they could have Pansy ready to be picked up in half an hour. He wanted to get her to Church Cottage before any prying eyes recognized her and blew the gaff.

William promised, and Fran went to rouse the sleeping girl. Nigel had said not to give her breakfast, because he'd prepare it while she got her things together.

Fran had to admit to herself, and to William, that that was the first small mercy of the day. 'Talk about cloak and dagger,' she said. 'This whole affair becomes more like a Whitehall farce with every hour. I'm getting to the state when, if I'm not careful, I shall lose all my middle-aged dignity and find everything and everybody so ridiculous that all I shall be able to do is giggle. But there, as George Eliot says somewhere, "*Ey, I like good laughers. Ill they may do, but they ain't bad 'earted, not if they laugh till it 'urts 'em.*"'

'I shall tell the assembled company how you came to lose your "luker",' he said. 'I shouldn't be surprised to find them all in a similar state, in view of all the heart-searching and looking askance at each other there's been.'

There were lots of birthday cards to be read and displayed. Fran began to quiz William as to the details he had given for the delivery of their bouquet to Molly. Sophie appeared, carefully carrying a large box which, when opened, revealed one of her own matchless home-made iced birthday cakes; decorated, of course, with pink sugar roses, and with Fran's age set out in little silver balls in the centre.

'I couldn't just let your birthday goo by wi' nothing at all to mark it, like,' Sophie said. 'Besides, I know you of old. If you get through this 'ere day without an 'ouseful o' visitors, I shall miss my mark. So as soon as you're gone out o' my way, I shall be back to get one o' them "buffet" suppers all ready, just in case. Will about enough for ten folks be enough, seeing as 'ow none o' the Bridgefoots'll be able to come? You'll find it in the fridge.

And I'm told Ned 'e'd better look in, come six o'clock, to see if 'e's needed, and if I am, to come and fetch me. I'm off up to see if Dan wants any 'elp now, and to take George and Molly a card from all our fam'ly.'

She produced an envelope of A4 size. Fran dared not ask if she might see the card, fearful that by the flicker of an eyelid she might spoil the fine filigree of Sophie's pleasure in showing her devotion to the Bridgefoots by buying as big and as sentimental a card as she could find. She expressed her genuine appreciation of Sophie's card to herself, and her forethought in setting herself the task of preparing the buffet, though to be honest she thought there would be very little chance it would be needed.

William went round the table to give Sophie a grateful kiss. Her face almost caused another bubble to rise in Fran's throat. Sophie had never quite cleared her conscience about letting another woman's husband kiss her. But Fran regarded her uncomfortably sensitive reaction to Sophie's scruples as an augury for the rest of the day; she didn't know whether to laugh, or cry.

Time was flying. 'I think,' said William, 'that it might be a good idea if we made ourselves a timetable. There are a lot more phone calls to come, I fear.'

He was right, but it made the morning she'd thought would seem endless fly by. She left herself plenty of time to dress with care, and was duly inspected after William had put on her earrings. He said that in every respect she was 'stunning'.

'You satisfy all my senses,' he said. 'You more than satisfy my eyes; and that satin suit is as soft to the touch as – what was it Pa wrote? – "as a wren's breast". I could trace you in a million by the scent of you, and your choice of perfume, and I must say you look good enough to eat. All I need is to hear your voice.'

'*Parles-toi d'amour*? What else is there to say, except that I love you? And that though you may only be wearing a lounge suit, you look like all my favourite film-stars rolled into one.'

Both were acutely conscious that they were deliberately keeping everything on a light and rather frivolous level. Emotions today were liable to get out of hand at the slightest provocation.

'Drat the thing! There's the phone again!' she said. It was

Terry. Without speaking, William handed the receiver to her. Her heart sank.

'Terry? Something's gone wrong. I can tell by your voice. Tell me quick. We're almost ready to start out.'

'I've had Jane on the phone. She wants to keep you out of sight until you are summoned, and suggests that as I'm only in the next room, you should come here to wait. I could hardly say no, but I warn you that I'm in a bloody awful mood and a raging temper. I don't think I can go through with it. No, there's no time to tell you. Just the last straw, something that happened earlier this morning. There's no point in me trying. I'm scared of letting myself, and you down. I'm in a state of utter panic. I'd got to the point of bolting here and now – being called away to an "emergency", when Jane rang. Yes, I'll promise to be here when you arrive, no more than that. Don't expect too much of me. Yes, of course I've thought it all out. I've got to face the music one way or the other? Do you think I don't know that? But I'll wait to say goodbye to you before I make my final exit, whichever way Fate tosses me. Will you be long?'

'We're on our way,' she said. He had given her no chance to find out what this last crisis was, but he'd managed to bring back her mood of depression and pessimism. 'William will be with me, of course. So you have about ten minutes to decide whether you're the man we believe you to be, or a moral coward running away from his own shadow.' Her voice was brittle with disappointment. She slammed the phone down before he could reply, and went with flushed cheeks to William. She was furious with Terry. He had no right to spoil today for her and those who had laid it on for her. She said so to William.

'I've had enough of him,' she said. 'I can't take any more of his grizzling. I can't bear to think what all the rest of you real men think of him. He might at least have held out for today, and gone with dignity.'

'Be fair to him, darling. You were asking a lot of him, you know. I'm sorry he's let you down, but keep a cool head, and don't make matters worse. He's had a raw deal. Isn't it possible that what happened this morning is that somehow he heard of the last bit of scandal? You said yourself that he was so vulnerable that a pinprick would bring him down in flames.

'Come on, we must go. We must have time to hear his side of the story. We said, you know, that our motto for today would be "Wait and see". Don't set yourself up as judge and jury before hearing the defence.' She gulped back her tears, and they left.

*

Effendi's house stood fronting the road. His part of it was more than twice the size of Terry's, but they had been left under one roof, to make it possible to put them together again if required. Effendi's side had a cottagey porch over the front door; Terence's had no such decoration, though it did have a brass plate, and inside it there was a small vestibule with two doors, one leading into Terry's sitting-room, and the other into his patients' waiting-room.

She saw at a glance when he opened the door to her knock that he had been telling her nothing but truth on the phone. He was as immaculately dressed as William, and her first thought was that she had never seen him look so manly or so handsome.

He was obviously under great stress, but he was not the wilting moral coward she had called him. His stance was such that he appeared to have a ramrod up his back, and though his face was white and tense, his head was high and his firm chin very much in evidence. He invited her in, and held out his hand to her in greeting, cool, aloof and excessively polite. Thinking back to the way she had stripped him down only so short à time ago, she didn't blame him, and did feel ashamed of herself. She hadn't got much moral stamina left either, but then, nobody was acting in character at present.

William had gone to park the car. Perhaps she had time to make her peace with him. She took the hand he held out, and felt it trembling. Then she leaned forward to kiss him, as was her usual greeting to her friends, male or female. He did not bend towards her, and suffered it, rather than responding to it. But it was enough for her to detect the tremors running all through his taut figure that he was endeavouring to keep so rigidly in control. He was as he had said: under the stress of almost uncontrollable rage and anger. She came swiftly to the belief that if their guess of its cause was correct, it was justified. He had been ready to do all he could to reinstate himself with his friends, and clear his name of the charges laid against him. This last had been one too many; he might be a dog with a bad name, but he was damned if he was going to stay around to be hanged. For once in her life, Fran was rendered speechless. She had no idea how to deal with him. Where was William?

At her side. He took in Terry's unwelcoming stiffness, and Fran's very visible distress. He said, urgently, 'May my wife sit down, Dr Hardy? I rather think she's going to faint if she doesn't.' Punctiliously, the rigid doctor pulled up a chair for her. She dug her nails into her palms, and tried to calm herself down.

William turned his attention to the doctor. 'Now you sit down as well, before you fall down, and I have two of you to cope with. I'll get you a drink. We have to go soon, whether you accompany us or not. I suggest very strongly that you do. There's no time to listen to what's got you into this state, but if the boot were on the other foot, you wouldn't hesitate to let into me and tell me what to do. All I do have time to say is that if I were in your shoes, I'd be shot before I gave whoever it is doing this to you the satisfaction of knowing that he – or she – had won. If you've really made up your mind to go, for heaven's sake, man, go out with a bang, not a whimper.'

There was just time for William to note the way his curt words caused the doctor's back to straighten, and his head to come up proudly to offer a retort, before there was a knock on the front door. William, thinking it to be their summons, raised Fran to her feet, holding her close to him to give her both physical and moral support, while Terence went to see who it was. From the vestibule, after a rather long silence, a voice they recognized came clearly through to them. 'Won't you ask me in, Dr Hardy?'

'It's Anthea!' gasped Fran. William pulled her behind the intervening door.

'Certainly, Miss Pelham, if that is what you wish.' Fran, her antennae now extended to the utmost, heard the quaver in his voice, closed her eyes, and prayed.

'It is. There are things I want you to know. Personal things. Won't you let me in, and make it easier for me?'

'With all my heart, if it means what I hope, that we may part as friends when I go.'

For the first time, Anthea's voice trembled as she replied. 'I can't promise you that, Terence, because it depends on you. I've come to apologize for my behaviour to you the last time we met, and to ask you to forgive me for hurting you so much. I truly didn't mean to. Will you forgive me, and tell me so?'

His reply, slow in coming, was huskily lower in tone, but the same as before. 'Will I forgive you? With all my heart,' he repeated.

'Terry, is that true – or is it only a figure of speech? Is it really your heart that's speaking, and not just gentlemanly courtesy?'

'How can you ask? And how can I know?' he said, his voice now breaking on a tinge of despair and warning that under such torture he could not hold out much longer. 'I have no heart. You have it in your keeping.'

'Then let me come in, properly. Because I have another question that I would rather ask you in private, than with the door half open to the street.'

They heard him close the front door, stand back to allow her to pass him, and then push open the door into the sitting-room. William made as if to move, to let Anthea know they were there, but Fran put her finger across his lips, and stayed him.

The pause grew long, and they held their breath. Then they heard Anthea's tremendous effort to control her quivering voice as she steeled herself to say what she had come to say.

'I'm not asking this of Dr Hardy. I'm asking it of the man I hurt so much. The man I love, and shall love for the rest of my life. So, will you marry me, please, Terry, before I die of a broken heart?'

In the dense, unbroken silence of the next half-minute, William felt Fran go limp in his arms, and sat down hastily on the nearest chair, holding her on his lap. For the first and only time in her life so far, she had actually passed out. She came round almost at once, to find Anthea sobbing on Terry's chest and he covering her face with kisses, completely oblivious of any spectators.

235

'Don't mind us,' said William, scared into a touch of sarcasm. 'Fran only fainted. But I think we may be summoned to the other side of the wall at any instant. Greg's seated at the piano, as I can hear, ready to greet the birthday girl in the traditional way. They're probably only waiting now till the last minute in the hope that two others who have been invited may turn up just in time.'

Fran, still feeling a bit woozy with shock and relief, made herself believe that she was seeing straight by taking in the vision that was Anthea. The 'uniform' today was made of deep crimson velvet, and at her neck snowy-white frills stood up round a face they'd never seen before; a face that had lost its undercoating of pain, sadness, and resignation, and instead shone to perfection with the varnish of happiness. She simply glowed, like a beacon fire on a cold frosty night to beckon her happiness home for good.

She turned, without taking her head from Terry's breast, and held out her arms to Fran while William lent Terry his handkerchief.

'We must go,' Fran said urgently. 'You'll have to go first, separately, and we'll follow as soon as you are inside. But, Terry, *you've forgotten something.*'

Terry was looking completely dazed, but he followed Fran's mime till he got her message. He fished in his coat pocket, fell on one knee, and took Anthea's left hand in his own. Then he slipped the amulet on to her finger, kissed it, and nodded when William asked if he could make an official announcement. Anthea slipped out, and went next door.

The summons came. Standing together with as much dignity as they could manage after such a scene. William and Fran heard Terry apologizing to Nigel for being late and holding up the proceedings. He left by the back door as they went out of the front.

They followed Nigel through the porch to Effendi's reception room, where at a baby grand piano, Greg and Beth sat side by side ready to break into 'Happy Birthday to You'.

Fran ruminated that night to William that 'Happy Birthday' must surely be the silliest, crudest and most corny bit of musical composition in the whole repertoire of available song. 'But after today,' she said. 'I shall think of it as hallowed. Second only to the "Hallelujah Chorus".'

*

They moved about among the gathered throng of their friends, Fran being hugged and kissed by all the men, and William gallantly saluting all the women in the same way. In Fran's philosophy, the sense that conveyed true friendship most was that of touch, which was why hand-clasps and kisses were so important to her. As soon as she was among her friends again, she went into her 'overdrive' gear, which meant that she could act on one level and think on another without missing a single significant detail of what was going on around her. She watched Terence and Anthea greet each other with put-on cool politeness, only really communicating with their eyes; she watched Elyot's eyes lovingly following his wife's tall, slender figure, on which a tell-tale bump was just beginning to show, desperately trying to appear relaxed – but she could almost hear the command to 'action stations' ready on his lips if Beth tripped, coughed, or caught her breath on her drink. Jane was being a perfect hostess, standing in for the two older men who had no other women attached, the bachelor clergyman and the suave diplomat who had buried much of his heart a long time ago in a middle-eastern desert. Then there was Greg the mercurial, Bob the extraordinary, Eric the bachelor businessman, with the duty of making the occasion go smoothly now paramount on his mind; and there was William, with whom Fran rarely lost conscious contact. And today there was Terry, valiantly maintaining that somewhat frosty, detached air, which she knew was covering a tumult of joy inside him. She was always in her own particular element in this sort of situation, with people she was fond of all round her.

A gong sounded, and they were asked to take their places at the long table. Apart from herself and William, she noted with approval that Jane had separated all the other couples, no doubt with Terence and Anthea in mind. She hugged her secret to her and began to foresee what had to be done before the lunch came to an end. She had a whispered conversation with William.

Effendi rose to welcome them to his house and his table.

Nigel, wearing only his dog-collar as *'the sign of his profession/ upon this labouring day'*, asked them to stand while he said grace. She caught Bob's eye, and they read each other's thoughts: to whatever God the gratitude was addressed, they both had too much to be thankful for to care what He was called.

The food and wine were of the very best; conversation was flowing easily. The nightmare Fran had been dreading was turning into a dream. It was all so wonderfully civilized, without being in the least 'stuffy'. For that, she knew, they could thank Eric.

The tables had been miraculously cleared of everything but fruit, cheese and *petits fours*, and new glasses filled with champagne. Eric banged the oriental gong in front of him for silence, and Effendi rose again to make a perfect little speech to their guest of honour, and propose a toast to her.

'Ladies and gentlemen, will you all please stand, and raise your glasses to Fran, to whom we offer not only our good wishes, but our eternal gratitude, and – our love.'

Fran, the only one left seated as the glasses were raised, looked up at the tall figure of William standing beside her, and he knew what he had to do. When they had all sat down again, he was left standing.

In the normal run of such occasions, his little speeches were gems; today, what he said would have to be extempore. It didn't matter.

'Friends, neighbours, countrymen,' he began, 'lend me your ears. I have something of importance to acquaint them with. But first I must thank you, on behalf of my wonderful wife, for this party, which is more wonderful than you yet know. And if I appear to be taking unorthodox lines, I beg you in advance to excuse me. There is a good reason. So first I turn for help to Eric, to ask if our glasses may be refilled for another toast. And while that is being attended to, I will do my best to explain.

'We have all, of late, been uneasy. Somehow or other our comfortable and happy lives have got out of kilter. Along with other matters, there has been a lot of trepidation among us that we were in danger of losing from our midst some we have grown to love and respect; be it my happy task to remind you of what the psalmist says: that "weeping may endure for a night, but joy cometh in the morning". He has been proved right. Morning has broken.

'Are your glasses filled and ready again? Then I shall ask you to raise them again in a moment to our dear friend Dr Hardy, who has decided not to desert us after all. But coupled with his name I ask you to drink also *to his future wife* – that vision of delight in the red dress sitting at your side, Greg – Anthea. May I ask you to change places with Terry, Greg? Thank you.

'Then it is with enormous pleasure that I announce their engagement. I can also disclose that neither of them knew anything about it till less than two hours ago. If you are stunned, so am I – or I should be making a better job of doing this than I am. But if you don't believe me, proof is, quite literally, "at hand". Just steal a glance at the third finger of Anthea's left hand.'

Terry raised Anthea's hand high for all to see, and then bestowed on her such a proprietory kiss that the stunned silence broke into laughter. William waited till it had died away and then, much more like the skilled speaker he was, asked for silence again.

'I ask you to raise your glasses again, this time to drink to the health, wealth and future happiness of Dr Hardy and the future Mrs Hardy – our dear friends, Terry and Anthea.'

'Terry and Anthea! Terry and Anthea!' rang from all sides of the room while the couple were passed from hand to hand, to be congratulated, hugged, and kissed.

Effendi had to ask Eric to gain him a moment's silence from the hubbub in which to say, 'Coffee is ready in the sitting-room. "Let joy be unconfined".'

It was. The rather dazed couple were besieged again, and in a few cases, cried over, especially by Beth, till at last they could all sit down with cups of calming coffee.

Then Fran, who had taken care not to let Greg out of her sight, urged him towards the piano again. As a classical pianist he was brilliant, but he knew that what was required of him now was to match his music to the mood. He had the ability to invest the most hackneyed of popular songs with a magic touch all his own.

He began softly to stroke the melody of *'Parlez-moi d'amour'* from the keys; slipped from that to *'La Vie en Rose'* and 'As Time Goes By'. Then, as the party fell more and more under his spell, and that of love in the air, he deepened the mood by sliding into one of Fran and William's favourites, the waltz from 'Maytime', usually remembered as 'Sweetheart, Sweetheart, Sweetheart'. William sought and found Fran's hand, and both knew that the other's heart was dancing, if not their feet. The others, enthralled, sat on as if mesmerized, until, as Greg began to play the first few notes of Elgar's *'Salut d'Amour'*, the silence was broken and they were brought back to reality by the door being closed behind Eric.

*

As the party broke up, William and Fran went to thank their hosts for what had proved such a successful and happy occasion.

Effendi was particularly pleased with the outcome regarding Terry and Anthea. 'He'll go ahead with the cottage, I suppose,' Effendi said, 'but I shan't press him to get out of his tenancy here. His plans may be very different now. It was never of any moment – certainly not enough to have caused all the fuss. And it matters even less now, because I think I may have found just the sort of clerical help I want locally: a middle-aged woman who has retired early from a job in Swithinford, and bought a bungalow in Hen Street. She's advertising for part-time work. If I think she'd suit me, are you interested?'

'It seems too good a chance to miss,' William said. 'Let me know. I'm not quite ready for the starter's gun, but I'm sure I could find her plenty to do till I am.'

Fran issued a general invitation to anybody interested to Sophie's 'buffet' supper at Benedict's later that evening. Laughing, she pronounced it as it is written, for Sophie always rejected the sound of 'boofay' as vulgar, substituting 'buffet' because it was English, and as she said it, it was.

They sought out Nigel, and asked how he had left Pansy at the Old Glebe.

'I was lucky,' he said. 'I thought I might have to take her in and stand by; but just as we got there so did Charles, with his wife and young Nick and Poppy. Poppy and Pansy flew at each other like a couple of magnets, and nobody after that bothered about me. So I sneaked away, because I was needed here.

'But I want a talk with you, William. I need your general knowledge of history. So maybe if I'm redundant here, I'll accept your offer to get my ears boxed by Sophie.'

It was a queer mixture who forgathered at Benedict's around seven o'clock. Nobody expected the newly engaged couple. Beth wanted to hear every detail, so she came alone, because Elyot had arranged to meet Eric before they knew anything about the supper at Benedict's.

Fran and William held a hurried conference in the kitchen. There was no way they could pretend they didn't know what happened when Terence and Anthea met, but it wouldn't do to let on that it was Anthea who proposed.

'So we have another secret "never to be told" added to our list,' Fran said. 'I shall have to find a bed of reeds somewhere, and whisper "Midas has asses' ears" just to be able to tell somebody. Otherwise I shall explode and scatter all the secrets abroad. That would put the cat among the pigeons!'

'Try the fens,' he said. 'We might go together. I've already got secrets whispered there to stop me from telling you.'

Bob rang. Jane was tired, so they wouldn't be coming. 'But we'd like to know how they got on at the Glebe today,' he said. 'So if you hear anything about it, give us a ring. I keep getting the idea that Charlie is sending me messages I can't quite get the right end of. My feeling that something's wrong there is getting worse.'

Jess and Greg, who had a permanent baby-sitter in Sophie's sister Hetty, arrived first, Jess anxious to know if Fran had any idea of Anthea's plans once she was the doctor's wife.

'We shan't expect her back at the hotel until after the honey-moon,' Jess said, 'but it's jolly short notice for us to raise anybody else to take her place, and Eric's no use at all. He's put on a "do what you like, but don't bother me" attitude. That's all very well, but somebody has to do it. Besides, it isn't a bit like him. Mind you, he's not his usual self by any means – though he seemed all right this afternoon till he suddenly got up and went out. I wonder what that was in aid of?'

'He says he's redundant wherever he goes,' Fran said seriously. 'I suppose it could be a too-successful businessman's syndrome; boredom setting in because things are going too well, and demanding nothing of him personally.'

'I don't know how he can think that,' said Jess, somewhat tartly, 'with all the problems that face us over Christmas.'

They were relaxed and contented to be so informally together again, and as soon as Nigel arrived, they did full justice to Sophie's preparations; but they were all emotionally worn out, and happy to bring the day to an early end.

'See you on Monday then, William,' said Nigel. 'Eleven-thirty at Church Cottage. Goodnight – and thanks for everything.'

*   *   *

'I take it for granted that what we discuss this morning will be in confidence, William,' Nigel began. 'I suppose I should have consulted my churchwardens first, but under the circumstances it would have worried George, and I can't and don't wholly trust Kenneth Bean. When I've told you what I have to say, you'll see why Effendi and Bob Bellamy must be kept in the dark, for the time being. It is a most extraordinary turn-up for the books, I must say.

'When I was forced to hang about in Canterbury waiting for Pansy I went to see another old friend who happens to be steeped in church history. Everything was happening at once, including the question of what to do about St Saviour's. It needs repair but doesn't warrant the cost. It robs me of precious time that I grudge being spent on an empty church. Even the cat I used to see there sometimes has deserted. So I went to see my old friend the Bishop for advice about the possibilities of closing it, selling it, or handing it over to a heritage trust or something.'

He paused. 'My word, did I get a shock! It isn't listed as a diocesan church at all – and as far as we could make out, never has been. Which means that the Church Commissioners have no authority over it. It has never been a benefice in the ordinary way, though somewhere along the line the de ffranksbridge family – lords of the manor, in reality if not in fact – more or less decreed that the incumbent of St Swithin's took it under his wing, on condition that they – the de ffranksbridges – should be responsible for its upkeep. Then, around 1880, the family ran out of ground for burial in St Swithin's churchyard, and had another vault opened at St Saviour's for the less respectable members of the family. They used it, in fact, up to and including the first war, but when Hugh de ffranksbridge died, his widow refused to fork out a penny for anything. Before that happened it had been restored by the wealthy eccentric who also did up the ruin of Bellamy's house, and who seems to have believed he owned the church. Nobody appears to know anything much about it, and it was left derelict again till land was needed so badly in the war that the Cambridgeshire War Agricultural Committee took it over. Since then, as far as I can make out, the church has passed as part and parcel of the farmland surrounding it. There was no time to spare during the war for looking up old deeds, even if they still existed. Anyway, there's no record of it in the diocesan archives. It's a mystery. And the sixty-four-thousand dollar question is: who owns it, or has authority over it, now? It has never been a parish church. Rules that govern them do not apply in this case.

'I wondered if you knew any details of its history that might help. It doesn't need an expert to see that its first origins are very old, but what could account for the present extraordinary anomaly? Take a practical point of view for a moment: was it ever properly consecrated, after it was restored to what it is now? If not, are Beth and Elyot Franks properly married according to the C. of E.?'

William needed time to consider all the implications of what he had heard, and was glad of a moment's temporary respite. He laughed, and said that he didn't know any more than Nigel himself did about the sanctity of that marriage from the C. of E.'s point of view, but he could vouch for the fact that Nigel needn't worry about Elyot and Beth living in sin. They were married all right. He'd been a witness at their wedding at the Cambridge Register

Office a few days prior to the wedding conducted by Beth's father in St Saviour's. That, also, was in confidence. Beth's father had been a very difficult customer to cope with.

He said he needed a few days, to look into it. 'Give me a week,' he said.

Nigel agreed, looking relieved, but added, 'In which case, I should perhaps tell you two more bits of information I got from the Bishop. He asked if I knew whether or not it had ever been a chapel, either in the old sense of a private chapel, or in the later sense of a meeting house for some dissenting sect that broke away from the Anglican Church, as the Wesleyans did. If that were the case, then the same conditions would apply to it as do to many redundant "free church" places of worship now.

'However, there's a rider to that. When such chapels are sold, say for conversion to a house, if there is a graveyard there are different regulations. The graveyard becomes a matter for the Home Office.'

'I'll do what I can,' William said reassuringly as he left, anything but reassured himself. Nigel had opened up a real can of worms! In the first instance, there were only four people all told who knew of the manuscript's existence. Bob who had found it, William to whom he had confided it, Fran, and Beth's father, the Reverend Archibald Marriner, thank heaven, at present well out of the way in Singapore.

As he put the car away, he made his first decision. At this, the eleventh hour plus, nothing and nobody would induce him to divulge the secret of the manuscript's existence, his main reason for his social interest in that particular church. He would have to prevaricate, and give Nigel only snippets of general information.

He must also warn Bob, but that presented him with a different set of problems. He had to consider those objectively. If what Nigel reported were true – and from his inside knowledge of the little church's history gained from the manuscript he had no cause to doubt it – *to whom did the church now belong?* Could it possibly be Bob himself? As a solution to their private concern, it was an almost incredibly lucky accident, the answer to all their problems.

But it was too hot a subject to handle without a lot of thought of its effect outside his and Bob's own interests.

He could imagine what indignation and militant anger would be roused in the breast of every member of the C. of E., from George Bridgefoot himself to the likes of Sophie, at any intimation that such a situation could ever exist. He could hear Sophie declaring that 'it was sin to rob 'Im Above of what was rightly His, and they all knowed as 'E didn't pay 'Is debts wi' money. Nothing but bad would become of it.'

'Kid' Bean, the people's warden, was still smarting at his own downfall when Effendi got the better of Bailey in the matter of Castle Hill Farm by securing it for Bob, which put an end to Kid's dreams of becoming not only well off, but a power in the community. He would be out on the warpath with all the guns of his fury loaded and ready to fire.

This would be his chance to 'get' Bob Bellamy and his father-in-law, and all the rest of them other stuck-up folks 'up Church End'. Who'd ever heard of such a thing before? Didn't them as had been born and lived there all their lives know as it had all'us been a proper church, same as St Swithin's? He'd have the law on them, that he would!

And with a sinking feeling in the pit of his stomach, William knew to whom Kid would rush, and thereafter leave to run his campaign of sweet revenge and envy for him. Who but Greenslade, the up-and-coming ambitious local politician. There were no flies on Kid Bean!

What a gift it would be to Greenslade, and what a problem to the rest of them! A threat to their whole environment! He must not let even a hint of what Nigel had told him leak, even to Bob himself. There must be a loophole somewhere. For the first time ever, he found himself wishing the damned manuscript had got burned to ashes in the fire that was told of in it. He must make doubly sure that Nigel understood why he must not tell anyone else what he had learned. It was as the sword of Damocles, hanging only by a hair of silence over all their heads. And, as Fran would say, yet another bloody secret to keep.

Not that there was anything very new about that. It was part and parcel of all history: plots and counterplots, conspiracies and feuds, lies and damned lies. A magpie squawked across his way from the garage to the door, and he reacted instantly, stopping to watch for another. One magpie meant ill luck. He was surprised, and a bit ashamed, to find himself as vulnerable to such omens as the majority of other country folk. All born of insecurity and fear, he surmised, and the need to peer into the future, just as he was doing now. Magic had a grip on them still, however modern they might be. Which took his thoughts back to Bob, who had magic built into his very being. Bob said there was sorrow about – and there was. William didn't need a magpie to tell him so. But wasn't that life? There was always sorrow for someone, somewhere, as there were weddings and births to balance it. In today's grasping society, there wasn't much room left for magic; greed for money wiped out all but the ephemeral illusion of happiness.

One for sorrow, two for mirth . . .

He mustn't forget that mention of mirth. It didn't take much to make commonplace events seem magical. Look at what had happened only yesterday! He must hope that Bob's fey magic wouldn't worm anything out of him, but if it did, he could trust Bob to keep it to himself. He knew better than to try to deceive Bob, but he would be sparing of what he told. Bob would accept what he said without question, though he could imagine the twinkle in Bob's eye as he answered in his broadest 'ol' fen twang': 'If you say so, bor, tha's good enough for me. You're the scholard.' So he would have to prevaricate again – even with Bob.

He would simply tell him that Nigel had so far not been able to find any answer as to what would eventually happen to the church, so for the moment it gave them a bit more time to go on searching for that evidence. But he could and would tell Bob that whatever the final decision about the building was, the graveyard was safe for a few more years.

He found Sophie with Olive in the background, discussing the extraordinary events of Saturday. He was in time to hear

Sophie say sharply and dogmatically to Olive, 'You 'old yer row! I don't care what you seed with your own eyes, or 'eard wi' your own ears. I shall never believe it, and more won't nobody else as knows you, Olive 'Opkins. Do you goo and scrub that dairy floor, same as I told you to half-a-hower agoo.'

William crept past them into his study, where at least he could think straight and use the telephone without being heard.

*

Sophie and Olive departed, still wrangling, much to William's relief, and almost immediately a car drew up on the gravel. It was Terence Hardy.

They noticed the spring in his step and the gleam in his eye as they opened the door to him, Fran flinging herself at him in greeting, and William holding out a hand and inviting him in.

'You've forgotten your stethoscope,' William said gravely as they led him into the sitting-room.

'Do I need it? What's wrong?'

'You don't need it for either of us, but by the look of you I wondered if we might have to reverse our roles. Too much excitement can be bad for you, you know.'

Terry laughed. 'A stethoscope wouldn't tell you much about the state of my heart this morning,' he said. 'You'd want the whole of Addenbrookes' cardiac unit. I know now, Fran, what a great part you played in it. I can't stay long, but I had to come and thank you, and tell you that Anthea and I want you two to be the first to know our plans.

'Luckily, I hadn't got round to cancelling the locum I'd booked, so while we get the cottage furnished and made ready, he'll move in with me. We shall slip away to be married when it suits us. After all that's happened, the last thing we want is any fuss – so no planning of secret parties for us behind our backs!

'But I felt I owed you an explanation of what happened on Saturday morning to tip me over the edge again. Then I would rather just forget it, and I hope that Anthea may never need to know.

'I can't, and shan't give you any medical details, but treating Rosemary Bridgefoot has become a bed of nails. She's a woman with a very strong character, and she's been in severe pain, but there was something holding back her recovery, and I became convinced that it was more psychological than physical. She's obsessed with gratitude to her in-laws, I gather because they rescued her from a ghastly childhood and gave her the love she'd never had before. When I advised her to stay on her back for a month or so after the accident she said flatly that there was no way she either could or would. She couldn't let the rest of the family down. She *mustn't* be ill!

'I hear that very often, from mothers of families who've been deserted by their breadwinner, for example, but as far as I could see there was no justification for her taking up such a stance, and said so.

'Oh, yes, of course I knew about the Golden Wedding. She'd promised Marjorie help, and must keep her promise. A poor excuse. We were all well aware that the old couple understood, and that any celebrations would have to be small. Marjorie was wearing herself out trying to be everywhere at once. I didn't say so, but I went oftener than I need have done to keep watch on Rosemary's state of mind. She was becoming more and more agitated till, to put it crudely, she was showing signs of becoming mentally unbalanced.

'It was as though she was genuinely afraid to be ill. I wanted more tests carried out, but she refused adamantly to cooperate unless I could arrange for them to be carried out under a veil of secrecy and pretence, with nobody but Marjorie in the know. We agreed to say that she'd been offered a cancellation spot at the RAF hospital at Ely at short notice, so there was no time to tell anybody.

'Marjorie got her there and back without anybody being the wiser. One didn't have to be a mind-reader to see that whatever the trouble really was, Marjorie was part of it. Rosemary dreaded my visits so much that I began to think she had taken a personal antipathy to me. Then one day her husband came in unexpectedly when I was there, ignored me completely, and asked her sharply what was the matter with her now, that she'd had to send for me yet again.

'I told him she hadn't, I'd just called, but he looked daggers at me and muttered something to the effect that if I'd looked after her properly in the first place, she'd have been OK by now. She was only making a lot of fuss about nothing. People had little bumps with a car every day of the week without all this palaver. She'd be all right if she stopped relying on my sympathy and pulled herself together.

'After that, she got worse. There were unmistakable signs of neurosis. It was my professional duty to warn her husband, but when I asked Marjorie how and when I could arrange to see him without letting the patient know, *she* threw a fit. She said there were things wrong worse than I knew, and almost in hysterics she begged me not to say anything to anyone but her. She'd be responsible – and redouble her care of Rosemary, if I would agree.

'This was a doctor's dilemma with a new twist. To load her, the patient's sister-in-law, with details of the case would have been unethical, amounting almost to professional misconduct. I suggested that it was time we had a second opinion.

'The effect on Marjorie was almost unbelievable. I had to give way at that time, because it was clear that if I put any more stress on her, I should have two patients on my hands instead of one. The feeble excuse was that the Golden Wedding mustn't be spoilt.

'When I left Temperance that day, the two women were clinging to each other in such floods of tempestuous tears that anyone would have had reason to think Dracula was at the door or that I had just pronounced a death sentence on both. What they were both so scared of I could not fathom.

'That was just previous to my being knocked out of my wits by Anthea's refusal. I was in no state to help those who wouldn't be helped. I made up my mind to wait till Saturday was over, and then, if I hadn't already cleared out, or taken an overdose, I'd hand the case over to one of my partners. Incidentally, I've heard since that Rosemary and Marjorie cooked up a tale of Rosemary having been diagnosed as being in the first stages of multiple sclerosis. It was news to me. I cut my visits down, because if ever I encountered Brian he was downright rude to me – though Rosemary and Marjorie's pathetic faith in me made me feel worse.'

249

Fran intervened. 'Brian's attitude doesn't actually surprise me,' she said. 'He seems to have a built-in phobia about doctors. We've been through it all once before with him when Charles was ill and didn't want to get better.'

William joined in. 'It's a sad streak in him – I guess part of the sudden change in the social standing of farmers when they began to make a lot of money after the awful years of the agricultural depression. They were climbing over each other to display the size of their bank-balances. One sign was that they sent their children to tin-pot "private" schools, and the other that they need have no truck with the National Health scheme. They could afford "private" doctors. Brian's an extreme case of such money-oriented snobbery. In his book nothing's of any value unless you've paid an exorbitant price for it. At the time Fran's referring to, it was his brother-in-law, Alex Marland, who took the brunt. He's a Harley Street man who rather unwillingly came to the rescue of Charles at Rosemary's pleading. But he made the mistake of waiving his fees because it was a family matter. I think Charles would have gone under but for Alex – and Bob Bellamy, who played a large part in the drama of Charles's eventual recovery.'

'He got no thanks from Brian,' Fran said. 'Think that over, Terry. It may be that Brian's terrified of a doctor in the house because of what happened then.'

'I suppose it's possible, but it isn't what you'd expect of a Bridgefoot. He's certainly got it in for me! Though I was no happier after you dressed me down, Fran, you'd made me see that for my own sake I must make some sort of a show of keeping my own end up till I could leave with a bit of my professional dignity intact. So I'd psyched myself up to be at your birthday lunch, whatever it cost me. I'd made a special effort to look my best – for your sake – before I set out to see the few patients who expected me. I thought that with Marjorie being up to her eyes at Glebe, I could possibly give Rosemary the sort of help and confidence she needed to get herself ready, and I was prepared, if necessary, to tranquillize her.

'So I turned up unexpectedly to find Marjorie already there, glad of my help. Rosemary was making a great effort and I decided it was Marjorie who needed my ministrations most. So I sat her down, told her to relax, and proposed that she should take a tranquillizer. I had to urge her to take it against her will, and was actually sitting on the arm of her chair putting the pill into her hand when the door flew open and in came Brian.

'I don't know that I've ever encountered a mad bull, but I understand that they signal danger by bloodshot eyes. I got that message at once, but had no idea what was wrong, or who he was about to let his pent-up rage loose on.

'I wasn't left long in doubt. It really was a most extraordinary scene. The two scared women clung to each other, and I concluded that he was drunk – that this was the mystery his devoted wife and sister had been keeping. Chronic alcoholism.

'It made sense, and I felt guilty that I'd been giving too much attention to my own problems, and not enough to theirs. But I was wrong. He turned on me, without the least sign of being drunk, and yelled, "What are you doing here again? *Get out! Leave my sister alone!*"

'Rosemary began to cry and Marjorie jumped up and faced him. "Don't be so silly, Bri. Dr Hardy's only trying to help."

'To my dismay, he turned on her. "Shut up," he ordered. "We've all had just as much as we can take of you and your affairs with men. Letting us all down, besides making a whore of yourself. Marrying a chap like Vic Gifford to start with – and as soon as you were free of him setting your cap at Eric Choppen. I shan't forget all that scandal when he gave you the push. Now the village is full of the tale of you being seen in broad daylight cuddling this new bloody nobody from Yorkshire. And as if that isn't enough, you start an affair with this philandering bastard who pretends to be a doctor. Don't deny it – he never comes here except when he knows you'll be here as well. I tell you straight – I won't have it going on under my roof. Your name stinks as much as your daughter's does, and all the rest of us are tarred with your brush!"

'I saw Marjorie was about to collapse, and went to support her, but he was beside himself and ready to attack me physically. For everybody's sake I decided that the better part of valour was discretion, and prepared to leave, rather than let the situation get any worse. He ordered me out of his house, with instructions never to set foot in it again. His last cut at me was that if Anthea hadn't taught me to clear out of my own accord, he'd see that I was struck off the register for making sexual advances to my female patients.

'I felt bad at having to leave those two poor women to it, but it was the very last straw for me. After that, there was no way I could stay and face the gathering at your party; but the phone was ringing when I reached home. It was Jane – and you turned up next minute.

'So I'm the one who's drunk now – with disbelief and happiness. But I shall have to ask one of my partners to take Rosemary's case over. I wish I knew, though, what happened after I ran away – and what it did to the party afterwards.'

Fran said, 'Oh, Terry, so would I! But what a glorious, glorious outcome there was to our party, whatever happened there.' And she flung herself at him, to be caught and hugged and kissed till she was breathless.

'Don't mind me,' said William, delightedly watching from his chair. 'Fran's only my wife, after all. No substitute for Marjorie Bridgefoot. You do know how to pick 'em, doctor.' He stood up and took Fran out of Terry's arms into his own.

'I'm a quick learner. I'm only emulating you,' Terry grinned.

William reached over Fran to extend both hands to the doctor. 'Then off you go to find Anthea,' he said. 'If you're half as happy as Fran and I are, you'll have plenty to thank your lucky stars for.'

*　　*　　*

Marjorie had spent the Friday night at Glebe so as to be up at dawn to start preparations. Yorky, who was feeling better, had been there all that Friday. He cleaned all available silver, then checked the arrangement of chairs round the dining-room table to accommodate little Georgina's high-chair, a mahogany and wicker relic of George's own childhood which was not, in Yorky's eyes, as hygienic as it might have been. So he'd scrubbed the wickerwork and washed down the wood with Dettol-laced water before polishing it.

Then, on Saturday, he was there again early. So was the postman, and Marjorie and Yorky sat down to witness George and Molly, over their breakfast, open all the cards. George slit them expertly with his old well-worn, horn-handled shut-knife, and handed them one by one to Molly for her to take each card out of its envelope and read the message and name of the sender. They were legion: from next-door neighbours and members of the church congregation to half-forgotten forty-second cousins spread out all over East Anglia. Molly paused as she took one card from its envelope, and wiped tears away as she offered it to George to read for himself instead of reading it aloud. *From Michael Thackeray and family.*

'Well . . . fancy them remembering,' said George, his mind on the little group of graves he tended, in which lay four of the Thackerays: his oldest friend, wife, and son, and that of their pyromaniac adopted child who had caused the fire that had put the penny in the slot for so many changes.

'Here's another,' said Molly, tears slipping unheeded down her rosy cheeks at this second reminder of the past. *'With love from Tom and Cynthia Fairey.'*

George, endeavouring to hide his emotion, said gruffly, 'I don't know as they need have bothered to put "Fairey" on it,' he said. 'There ain't a lot o' chance we should ha' forgot who Tom and Cynthia were – or young Robert. Put that one where Charles don't see it soon as he comes in,' he told Marjorie, who was trying to find a place to display every card as it was opened.

She was glad to turn her back on them to do as her father asked. Robert had been the boy whose death had first sent Pansy off the rails, besides causing the sale of Lane's End Farm to Bailey, the developer who had turned it into the Lane's End Estate.

Marjorie had been searching the writing on the envelopes in almost desperate hope that she might see Pansy's hand, but the pile grew smaller and smaller till it ran out. Nothing. Pansy had not even remembered. Marge gathered up the empty envelopes and took them to the bin in the kitchen to shed a few private tears of disappointment, and there Yorky found her.

'Nay, pet, tha must keep tha tears to the'sen today, for Gran's and t'Boss's sake. Besides, there's hell-an'-all to be done to get this meal properly coooked, so I'd better get steam oop. Ee-God-aye I had! Joost loook at t'clock!'

Marjorie, obeying, was powdering her nose when there came a ferocious banging on the door of what had been the kitchen. 'Who on earth can that be, so early?' Marjorie said. 'Nobody's expected for at least another two hours!'

Yorky peered out of the window of the new kitchen and reported: 'A delivery van, wi' a parcel. Ah'll go and tek it in, so's Gran don't see them tears. Don't let nowt booger-oop today, pet. We're doing it for them, nor for oursen, ain't we?'

He was passing her, and stopped to put his arm round her to give her a friendly squeeze. 'Tha's better, pet. Come tha now an' see what yon chap at t'door has fetched.'

He took in, and signed for, a large box-shaped parcel, then set it down in front of Molly. George fished in his trouser-pocket again for the indispensable shut-knife, and cut the high-class tape that secured a very smart parcel. A discreet, up-market label gave its source as *'Yesteryear': Antiques and Objets d'Art, Cambridge, England*.

'Whatever can it be?' Molly asked, looking scared to touch it. 'Are you sure it's come to the right place?' Marge went to help her, holding the box for her mother to lift out a large, heavy object swathed in layers of tissue paper. Molly looked helplessly at George, at Marge and finally at Yorky. He took the hint and extracted the swathed lump from its box, and helped her slowly to remove each sheet of white tissue till only one was left – revealing the shape to be that of a squat object with a spout and a handle.

'Show us, Mother,' George encouraged her, putting away his knife to stop himself from tearing off the last bit of covering. Molly found her courage and pulled at the flimsy paper – and before them stood an exquisite late-eighteenth-century silver tea-pot. There was an envelope tied to the ebony handle. Out came

George's knife again, and the small, elegant card was taken from its envelope.

'Read it, Mother,' George said.

'I can't see to read it,' she answered, 'any more than you can. You read it to us, Marge.' She did.

> *Congratulations to our dear friends and neighbours,*
> *George and Molly,*
> *with all good wishes and love from*
> *Nigel Delaprime*
> *Nicholas Hadley-Gordon*
> *William and Fran Burbage*
> *Bob and Jane Bellamy*
> *Greg and Jess Taliaferro*
> *Elyot and Beth Franks*
> *and Eric Choppen.*

As she got to the last name, Marjorie's voice broke. So did George's, as he said, 'Fancy them doing that when they can't be here to share today with us any more than we can share Fran's birthday with them. But I tell you one thing, Mother. We'll make up for it as soon as Rosy's herself again. The proper party's only put off, like, for a while.'

Then the florist's van drew up outside, and the room was filled with bouquets.

'You'll have to cope,' Marjorie said to Yorky. 'I simply must go and help Rosemary to get up and be ready.'

*

She found Rosemary was ready. She had managed to dress herself without help, but Marjorie saw that it had been a great effort.

'Where's Bri?' she asked. 'I thought he'd be bound to be here helping you this morning.'

Rosemary shook her head. 'He's in one of his moods,' she said. 'I can't do or say anything right for him. I'm sure he thinks

I'm putting this on just to aggravate him. He's been nasty to Charles – as usual about Charlie – and was very put out when he found that Alex and Lucy were bringing "that grizzling kid of their's" with them. You're about the only one who can cope with him at all when he gets like this. It's getting worse all the time.'

There was some truth in that. There had been a time when Brian had become so difficult, because his father wouldn't retire and hand over the chairmanship of Bridgefoot Farms Ltd to him, that his relationship with Rosemary had been in danger. Rosemary the docile had found herself having to choose between her husband and her son. She had stood up to Brian and had insisted on giving Charles her shares in the company outright. They had been her own in the first place, the only legacy from her own family. It had been a most unhappy time till George had yielded to pressure and retired – and to his own surprise, was thoroughly enjoying his changed status. An uneasy peace had ruled since the worst bone of contention, the marriage between Charles and Charlie Bellamy, was *fait accompli*.

Marjorie's relationship with her brother had always been unusually close. They were, in age, about as near as two siblings can be, but she had grown up in Brian's shadow, adoring him and unable to see a fault of any kind in him. He had succeeded in all the things she'd failed in: such as going to the grammar school, while she had 'been kept at home to help Mam'. There had been little choice for her to mix with any but the local youths, and she'd got married early – to the wrong man. Her brother had supported her through thick and thin, and so had his wife, who became a sister Marjorie loved as much as she did her younger sibling, Lucy.

Once Charles had married Charlie, in the face of his father's opposition, George had yielded and handed the reins over to Brian. There had been an end to open hostility; but once Brian began to feel the power of being first horse, he had begun to pull hard against all the others. Marjorie trusted him to keep his temper and his head down about any drastic alterations a bit longer. She thought he could not possibly wreck his father's new contentment – especially with the Golden Wedding in view.

Which was what Marjorie comforted her sister-in-law with now, telling her about the mass of cards, the flowers, and, above all, the silver tea-pot. Both had cheered up, putting Brian's bad mood this morning down to something on the farm that they didn't yet know of, when Dr Hardy appeared.

They knew, of course, about his rejection by Miss Pelham – such a thing could never be kept secret in a village – and his spruced-up appearance was attributed correctly to his having decided to attend Fran's birthday party in self-defence against the calumnies surrounding him. They approved of that. They liked him, and were glad he was prepared to face the village with a show of proper pride.

He congratulated Rosemary on making her own toilet unassisted; then he told Marjorie that though it was still early, the day for her was likely to be a long one and as she already looked 'all in' he suggested she should sit down, relax while she could, and take a mild tranquillizer of the kind he had already prescribed for Rosemary.

Then Brian appeared, and upset the apple cart with a vengeance. There was a dreadful few minutes after the door had closed behind the doctor. Brian raved and swore, and Rosemary sobbed helplessly in Marjorie's arms till Brian, remembering what day it was, began to make excuses for himself – though without withdrawing a single one of his brutal accusations against his sister.

He watched her turn white, then red, which he interpreted as shame. He began to declare that he had only said what he had said to put her on guard, so that nothing more was added to the scandal going the rounds of the village already.

But the worm turned. The pill she had taken was beginning to take effect. She no longer felt like crying. Her flushed face was by no means an indication of shame, it was the signal of an outburst of full-blooded anger from a too patient, too tired woman who was not prepared to take any more from him. She let go of Rosemary, walked up to face Brian, and said coldly, 'Take that back, or face the consequences.'

'Calm down,' he said in a bossy though slightly surprised and less belligerent tone. 'I only told you the truth for your own sake.'

'You beast!' she said. 'You selfish, arrogant, money-grubbing, pigheaded beast!'

He turned white with temper and clenched fists, but she got in first. She was a tall woman, who had been toughened by hard work, first as a land-girl during the war, and since then by always being at the beck and call of those she loved. She pulled back her arm, and slapped his face with all her strength. He staggered, fell into a chair, and looked murderous.

'I wouldn't, if I were you,' she said. 'I didn't put up with Vic Gifford all those years without learning a few tricks of self-defence – or what to do with a maudlin man afterwards. Oh, go on, cry if you must – it would be nice to think it means you feel guilty, but I know better. It's only frustration that you daren't lay me out. Grizzling'll get you nowhere today. So go and wash your silly face and pull yourself together. I give you ten minutes before we start to go back to help Mam and Dad celebrate their day. If you dare do or say one thing to upset them, I promise you that the rest of us, your wife and son included, will gang up on you and make you pay for it.'

By this time, cringing under her whiplash tongue, he sneaked out, cursing under his breath. Marjorie turned her attention back to Rosemary.

'Sorry about that, Rosy,' she said. 'But you know as well as I do that it had to come sooner or later. What's got into him I just don't know – except that he's up against something his money can't buy him – again. We couldn't have gone on much longer covering his tantrums up – or his downright cruelty to you. He's been getting too big for his boots for a long time and flies into a rage at the first sign of not getting his own way, now. But he will *not* spoil anything today. Apart from Mam and Dad, there are all the rest to think of. You've been a brick till now for his sake. Be one today for your own.'

Rosy held Marjorie's hand and took courage from it. 'There must be something causing him to be like this,' she said. 'Tell me the truth, Marge. Is it another woman?'

'No!' said Marjorie, shocked at the very thought. 'That I can promise you! But I am beginning to think he's up to something he doesn't want us to know.'

'I shall be all right,' Rosemary said. 'He'll quite likely be better tempered, once I'm myself again.'

He appeared, sulky but meekly pleasant. The women breathed deep sighs of relief.

*

It was almost one o'clock. The table was laid, and others had already arrived: Lucy and Alex and little Georgina, now at the most attractive toddler age. She alone would have made the day for George and Molly as she prattled and played peep-bo with Yorky.

The arrival of Marjorie back again was a relief to Yorky, though by this time he had everything well in hand. He had donned a white chef's apron and his curly black hair was covered by a rakish-looking chef's hat, but he had put on no subservience of any kind with his attire. He was introduced to Lucy and Alex by Molly, who told them in front of him what a treasure he was. Marjorie noted that he was in no way embarrassed, but told her his place was in the kitchen from now on unless she wanted him specially.

That was lucky, because he was not in view at all when Rosemary and Brian went in. All three of Molly and George's children were there now. They were just waiting for the grand-children, because Charles had had to go to Cambridge to pick up Poppy and her fiancé, young Nick. Drinks were being passed round, and Marge and Yorky were keeping anxious eyes on the clock.

There was a commotion outside, and everybody looked towards the door. It swung open, and in the doorway stood the twins, arms around each other's waists, while behind them, like a guard of honour, was Charlie between Charles and Nick.

There was a moment of dead silence while everybody tried to take it in. Then Marjorie, gasping, cried, '*Pansy*,' and the youngsters all went into a huddle round the girls and their mother, before the general family hubbub broke out, and George and Molly were submerged under hugs and kisses, congratulations and presents till the stunned old couple lost track of everything but that their family was complete. Wonderfully, marvellously, miraculously whole again! Released for a fraction of time while all the rest were admiring the tea-pot, George clasped his hands together, put his forehead on them, and silently gave thanks. Then Yorky appeared at the door from the kitchen, and said, 'Gran an' t'Boss, ladies and gentlemen, lunch is served.'

They followed him into the dining-room, each to his or her appointed place round the table, chattering and standing behind their chairs in anticipation of George saying grace – when a wail from Molly turned all heads in her direction.

'Don't sit down, any of you! You mustn't! With Pansy, there's thirteen of us. What can we do?'

For a second or two, they were all like the Wise Men of Gotham, each forgetting to count himself, but there was no doubt that the total was thirteen: George and Molly; Brian and Rosemary; Marjorie; Lucy, Alex, and Georgina; Charles and Charlie; Poppy and Nick; and Pansy.

'I'm the one you weren't expecting, Gran,' said Pansy. 'I won't sit down with you at the table. I'll help Yorky, if he'll have me, in the kitchen. Then there'll only be twelve round the table.'

'No,' said George. 'I know how Mother feels, and she'll worry herself to death if we sit thirteen round the table, but none of you is going to be the odd one out today. There's another way we can put it right. We can add one and make it fourteen. Yorky, come you and sit down and eat with us. You're nearly one o' the family anyway by now.'

Molly added her plea to George's. Yorky gave in with no fuss, only asking where he should set himself a place. Between Marge and Pansy, Molly said, and the seating was duly rearranged. Only Charlie witnessed the note of discord in the family harmony.

She had been watching all the faces, with her triple antennae tuned to their furthest extent. At work there was her love for all the Bridgefoots; her high intelligence, refined and cultured by long years exiled in one of the best high-class schools for girls in the country; and her fenland 'feyness' inherited from Bob. She understood absolutely Molly's superstitious fear of sitting down thirteen to a meal. Such feelings, she knew, were 'heired', as her father would have said, at least from as long ago as the Celtic Iron Age, though this particular one had been built on and given wide acceptance by being linked to the Last Supper. In Charlie's own opinion, it was much more likely to be a remnant of pagan ritual. She knew that it had been used throughout history for whatever purpose it would serve, as for example, in the seventeenth century, when a coven of witches was thirteen in all, twelve women with 'the Evil One' in the middle. Her fenland genes were uppermost at this minute, and she shivered, almost afraid. Standing behind her chair, she had seen diabolical rage on the face of her father-in-law pass like a dark shadow across the happy gathering at Grandad's ingenuous remark about Yorky being 'nearly one of the family'.

So he had taken against Yorky as he had taken against her; and though he had dissembled a lot lately, she knew his antagonism towards her still rankled. She noticed how pale and tense he had become, and how little he ate of the splendid meal that followed. Something was biting him again. She made a mental resolve to talk to her dad about it when next she had him to herself.

Time for speeches. To Charles, her husband, the only male Bridgefoot of the next generation, had fallen the honour of toasting the grandparents he loved more than anybody else in the world other than his wonderful wife. He made no pretence about anything: that was her Charles's gift, as it was his grandfather's. Surely that wasn't what was the matter with Brian – that he was miffed by Charles being chosen to make the toast? He couldn't be so childish!

George had no ability to be anything but himself. He rose to reply, standing tall and straight, head held high, hand on Molly's shoulder, with unashamed tears coursing down his face. 'In a few minutes,' he said, 'I shall ask you all to stand up again while I give thanks to God for the goodness and mercy that have followed me all the days of my life – but never more than today, when my family was so unexpectedly made whole again. I am grieved that so many dear old friends couldn't be invited to share our joy today: the Thackerays and the Faireys, and others like dear old

261

Daniel Bates, who's been at my side all his working life so far. And women like Sophie, who without being asked, has made us a Golden Wedding cake for tea-time. Then there are all them others who I hope are having as happy a day as we are, and whose names you can all read for yourselves on the label on that silver tea-pot over there; and all them who sent us flowers and cards: folk who have served the church, side by side with me, as their fathers and grandfathers did with mine. But if God wills, as soon as our Rosy's well enough, we'll still have that party. Sometime just after Christmas, perhaps. Let's look forward to that, as well as backwards for fifty year to the day I married the prettiest girl and the best wife in the world. He stooped and kissed Molly, while they all cheered. Then he held up his hand for silence, and they all stood with bowed heads while he called down blessings on them.

Yorky, with several willing youngsters to help him, served coffee.

'We shall be looking forward to that party, Grandad,' Charles said.

'Don't set your heart on it being in the barn,' Brian said, apparently addressing everybody.

'Why ever not?' asked Molly.

'Because I may have other uses for it.'

George, shocked though he was, said soothingly, 'Well, we needn't make plans for it now.'

But Marjorie had caught Rosemary's eye as they witnessed her prediction come true. In that moment all the others had stiffened, ganging up against Brian. They were twelve to one. He had overstepped the mark.

After another hour, the party drew towards its end. Brian said they must go home, his excuse being that Rosemary was already overtired. Her protests that she didn't want to leave yet were utterly ignored, and Brian went out to fetch the car to the door.

It was taken for granted that Pansy would stay wherever her mother was – Molly hoped at the Old Glebe. Marge was dropping with tiredness, more emotional than physical.

'Somebody must be up at Temperance with Rosy,' she said.

'She'll need some help tonight. I hope I shan't fall asleep when you need me, Rosy. I'm all in.'

Pansy ran to put her arms round her. 'Poor old Mum,' she said. 'Let me go. I've trained now as a "carer" and I know I can do anything Aunt Rosy's likely to need.'

'Oh, Pansy! Is that really what you've been doing all this long time?' Marjorie flung her arms round Pansy, overcome by guilt that she had never for a moment thought that Pansy's absence for so long had meant that she was trying to rehabilitate herself as she had. She hugged her daughter as if she would never let her go again.

Brian honked an irritated blast on the horn of his car, and all the rest prepared to escort a somewhat tremulous Rosemary to it. 'I don't want you to have to go yet,' Marge said to Pansy. 'Need you? Will you be OK, Rosy, if Pansy stays a bit longer and Alex brings her up to Temperance when they go back to the hotel?'

'Of course I shall. It isn't me who's in such a hurry to get away!' The horn was honked again, this time louder and more impatiently. They helped Rosemary into the car, and watched as an irate Brian roared away. An uncomfortable silence fell as they turned back.

'Grandad,' said Charles, 'Charlie's been looking forward to seeing the new bull today. Couldn't those of us who want to put our coats on and go now before tea? While it's still daylight?'

Nothing could have taken out the sting of George's disappointment at Brian's behaviour and early departure better than Charles's interest in his Golden Wedding present to himself: that new young pedigree Jersey bull.

Everybody wanted to go, except Molly and Marjorie, who said they'd stop indoors and prepare tea. Yorky said he'd help them but Marjorie told him to go: she wanted to have her mother to herself for a few minutes. 'Go and look after Pansy,' she said. So he went.

His acquaintance with the Bridgefoots had ripened fast, but till this day he hadn't had a lot to do with any but George, 'Gran' and Marjorie. He had gathered that her distress was focused on her 'missing' daughter, Pansy: 'the black sheep o' the family' who had insisted on straying despite all their loving attempts to bring her back into the fold. He had also tumbled to the fact that the blond, curly-headed giant called Charles, Brian and Rosemary's only son, was the apple of his grandparents' eyes and could do little wrong. Marjorie had been at pains to excuse her wayward absent daughter, explaining that her twins were not identical, and that where Poppy was mainly Bridgefoot, Pansy was too much like her father: different in looks and temperament – and character.

So when the twins had so unexpectedly burst in on the Golden Wedding day Yorky had been quite taken aback by their astounding likeness to each other. Amid the ensuing commotion of unbounded joy, mixed with Molly's wails of apprehension at there being thirteen of them, he had observed them, and understood that the difference now was exactly the reverse of what he'd been led to expect. They were as alike as two peas physically, but there could have been anything up to five years difference in their age when it came to maturity. Poppy bubbled with youth and happiness. Pansy, just as glad at the reunion, was much calmer and in control of herself. His warm heart went out to her, in the same way as it had done in the first instance to her mother. Such acceptance of Fate was only achieved at the cost of a lot of suffering, as he had good cause to know. He had not yet managed it himself – after twelve years, since his wife had walked out on him.

In all the excitement, he'd encountered Pansy first when she'd suggested that to allay her grandmother's superstitious fears she should act as his kitchen-maid and not sit down to eat with the rest. Her gesture was made more poignant by the fact that she could have supposed herself to be the most important, the returned prodigal for whom the fatted calf had been killed.

His appreciation of her had grown during the eventful lunch which followed, with him sitting, still wearing his chef's outfit, between her and her mother. Till then he had had no time to make the acquaintance of the rest of the family. When Marjorie had urged him to go with Pansy to see the new bull, he went – though he didn't know why.

The as-yet-unnamed bull was from the same local pedigree

herd as the cows, though from the previous year's calves. Consequently, he was registered in a 'C' year, not a 'D' like the cows, whose names therefore all began with 'D'. It had been a topic of conversation over lunch, Brian's only contribution to it being that he had never thought his father's determination to have a resident bull had made much sense, and only been done in any case to please Daniel Bates. He had little interest in his father's latest expensive plaything.

The others had ignored him, simply continuing to discuss the question of its name. As George said, while he had to keep its name as given on the pedigree, they could hardly expect Dan to get his tongue round a name like that!

'Let's name him properly, then, like they launch ships, with a bottle of wine,' said somebody, and Yorky gave his attention for the first time to Charles's young wife. He'd heard how absolutely besotted her young husband was with her and now he didn't wonder. Though the other young women, including Lucy Marland, pleased eye and ear, warmed the heart and challenged the intelligence, this girl stood out: a real jewel. How he could have missed her until now, he could hardly believe – except that he guessed she had deliberately chosen to play herself down for Pansy's sake. When they all trooped out to the newly constructed farmyard, armed with a miniature bottle of whisky, he was with them.

They found Daniel strawing the bull's yard, always with one wary eye on the handsome animal backed into the opposite corner. The man and the bull had not yet got to know each other well enough to establish any degree of trust. Dan indicated to them not to come too close to the iron-railed fence till he had finished his task. Wherever he turned to distribute the straw, the bull turned to face him, occasionally pawing the ground with one fore-hoof, and lowering his head with a gleam in his eye that could mean either mischief or anger.

But if he was prepared for either, so was Dan. The two-tined hayfork he was using had a six-foot-long haft, a very old and seasoned one, most carefully shaped to provide a safe, strong hold when expert hands needed to lift a heavy load with it. Dan took care never to be far from the fence. The fork had been carefully chosen: as a defensive weapon it would have been very useful; but by keeping close enough to the fence, the man could have used the seasoned handle as a vaulting pole and cleared the fence at one leap. (Or so he hoped. It would have been nearer the truth to say that he could have done once!)

'There y'are, mate,' he said to the bull as he opened the iron five-barred gate just far enough to let himself through. 'That'll do you till termorrer. You're got visitors. Come and let 'em have a good look at you.'

George, Charles and Charlie moved closer to the fence. The bull, inquisitive, came nearer too.

'What's his pedigree name, Grandad?' asked Charlie.

'Ask Charles,' he answered. 'It's one o' them fancy names meant only for the showground, I reckon. They don't expect folks like me to get their tongues round 'em.'

She turned a merry face to her husband, who put a protective arm round her, and escorted her close to the railings. 'Come on, Chol-mond-e-ly,' he said. 'Come and be introduced.'

The girl let out a silvery peal of laughter. 'Spell it,' she commanded, and he obliged. 'And are you telling me, my darling idiot, that you don't know how to pronounce it? It's one of those names like Taliaferro, pronounced Tolliver. Cholmondely is pronounced "Chumley".'

'Well, that makes things a lot easier, don't it, Chum,' said George.

'So shall we proceed to launch him now?' she said, disengaging herself from Charles in order to unscrew the tiny bottle of whisky. And, innocently, they all watched her approach the fence – then nip over it as agile as any athlete and stride across the straw till she stood by the side of the bull, close enough to touch him.

The fear engulfing the onlookers, especially Charles, was evident from their shocked silence. Charles possessed himself of Dan's hayfork, but made no other move. The bull raised his head and sniffed. Charlie stretched out a hand to him and, stepping silently in the straw, went closer and slid her arm round his neck. Then she rubbed the smooth but slightly longer-haired stretch between his horns.

'Oh, you beautiful, beautiful creature, Chum,' she said. 'Stand still. I'm going to name you.' She took the little bottle of whisky from her pocket, and removed the top. Still caressing the top of his head, she urged him a bit closer to the fence and the audience to whom she spoke decisively and clearly. 'Don't clap or cheer,' she said. 'Just in case you frighten him.'

She poured a teaspoonful or so of whisky into the hollow of her hand and announced, as regally as she could manage: 'I name this bull Chum. Every Bridgefoot expects him to do his duty, faithfully and well.'

And with complete aplomb she rubbed the whisky, warm from contact with her hand, on to the back of his neck. He lifted his head and attempted to back away, but she ran her hand down his face to his muzzle, stroked it, and whispered sweet nothings into his ear. He stood still, so she bent and kissed his nose just above the place he had been ringed for stronger control of him. Then she deliberately turned her back on him, and calmly climbed back over the gate.

Charles, white with tension, grabbed her and shook her. 'Don't you ever do such a foolhardy thing as that again!' he exploded.

She reached up and kissed him. 'Sorry, darling. Sorry, Grandad. But you do all know that I'm going to be a vet and that I've been handling farm animals since I was born. You have never to let them think you're afraid, even if you are, but I think I've proved that nobody's going to have much need to be afraid of Chum – unless they've frightened him first. He's absolutely gorgeous. I love him.'

'That's all very well,' said Charles, 'but you might just have thought about me! I die of heart failure every time I see you lead Ginger out of his stable, but if you're going to start sneaking out to visit Chum as soon as my back is turned, I tell you my nerves won't stand it. Book me some sessions with you, Uncle Alex, as soon as you can. I'm afraid I may need them.'

Charlie was looking very prettily contrite. George was waiting his turn to kiss her.

'You're a cough-drop, and no mistake,' he said. 'Now let's all go back to the house and sample Sophie's cake.'

Charles swooped, picked up his wife like a sack of potatoes, and threw her over his shoulder. 'I'll l'arn you, one way or another,' he said. She kicked and screamed and tried to reach a handful of his curly hair to pull, but as her head was halfway down his brawny back, and her legs pinned close to his chest, she gave in and let the pretended screams turn to peals of laughter. They all joined in.

So the happy group moved back towards the house. George brought up the rear, accompanied by Dan carrying the hayfork over his shoulder. Only Dan heard him say what he was thinking – that he had no right to grumble. Nobody could have everything.

When the time came to break the party up, Alex and Lucy were waiting for Pansy to drop her off at Temperance Farm.

'Are you sure you'll be able to manage?' said Marjorie, loath to part from her long-lost daughter.

'As far as anything I can do for Aunt Rosy's concerned, I'm quite sure,' the girl replied. 'I won't answer for Uncle Bri, though. He's like a bear with a sore behind. He doesn't need my sort of care as far as I can see. What he needs is a psychologist!'

'Right on the nail, Pansy,' said Alex, laughing, 'but if you want one in the night, don't send for me. I had more than my fill of him last time!'

George took Pansy into his arms, and held her there. 'Give us a big kiss before you go,' he said, 'and don't let it be quite so long next time before we see you again.'

He hugged her in silence as the rest looked on, and then kissed her heartily, saying gruffly, because of the tears in his throat, 'God bless you and keep you. And welcome home.'

*   *   *

Christmas was less than three weeks away, but nobody seemed to want to look forward. The events of last Saturday were still too much in everyone's mind. The village buzzed with rumours, garbled padding round a speck of truth.

Anthea Pelham must be pregnant, to have made Dr Hardy come up to scratch like that! Where had Pansy Gifford suddenly appeared from, and why? What was Marjorie Bridgefoot up to, that she didn't now go back to Monastery Farm?

Fran's mind kept returning to Terry's account of his visit to Temperance on Saturday morning, but she hadn't heard what had happened thereafter. Even accounting for Brian's dislike of doctors in general, and NHS doctors in particular, his attack on Terry for apparently pursuing Marjorie with the intent to seduce her was so wild as to be ridiculous – but sinister all the same. The revelation of Brian's attitude towards Rosemary's illness, and his obstruction of Terry's care was almost paranoiac. He'd been very strange and unhelpful when it was his son who'd been in danger. Fran knew that because she and William had both been involved, and the doctor in question who had got all the aggro that time was Brian's brother-in-law, Alex Marland. Perhaps the Bridgefoot family were accustomed to having to make allowances for Brian where illness was concerned? She'd go up to the Old Glebe to hear all about the party as soon as she could. She knew how welcome she'd be.

Meanwhile, she wondered what it could be that William had on his mind; he was as delighted with the outcome of her birthday as she was, but she had caught him several times since rather distrait, pondering on something not at all connected with the events of the weekend. She suspected it to be yet another problem to do with the book, about which even she knew only what he chose to tell her, and of which nobody but Bob knew anything at all. That in itself was almost miraculous, in a village where everyone knew everybody else's business before they knew it themselves. He had managed to keep the existence of that manu-script secret, perhaps because people were used to him writing books – history books. There was no reason to suppose that this was any different. That Effendi going to write one as well was news of a mild kind. It was common knowledge, as Sophie said, that he was going to start writing his 'rememboirs'.

Fran could hear Sophie in the kitchen, giving orders to Olive. Of course: Sophie must have seen Dan yesterday – Monday –

and heard all about the Golden Wedding party. She could tap the village grapevine via Sophie. Besides, William had told her what he'd heard Sophie say to Olive: that she wouldn't believe it whoever had 'seen it with her own eyes'. For no explicable reason, she'd associated that remark with Marjorie. She'd bring the subject up with Sophie at coffee-time, though she'd have to be extremely diplomatic. She knew her Sophie.

She began by asking if Sophie had seen Dan since the party, and if he had told her how it all went.

'Dan didn't tell me a lot,' Sophie said, 'and you know very well as I don't repeat things as I 'ear unless I can vouch for the truth of 'em. But I can speak after Dan, and seeing as 'ow you and 'im [meaning William] put your names to a beautiful card and a bunch o' flowers and that there silver tea-pot as Dan says I must goo up and look at, I'm sure he won't care about me telling you.

'Seems Pansy Gifford turned up, just as they was gooing to start eating. They was all so glad to see 'er, Dan said, that George could 'ardly tell 'im about it without shedding a few tears. It caused a bit of a to-do first though, 'cos Molly wouldn't let 'em set down thirteen at a table, do it meant that within a year one of 'em would die, like Jesus did after they'd set down thirteen at the table at the Last Supper. So Pansy offered, like, to be the one to hev 'ers in the kitchen wi' that Yorky as they call 'im; but George said if Yorky sat down with 'em as well, that would make fourteen and they'd none of 'em be in danger.'

Sophie sipped her coffee, but not before Fran had noticed the tightening of her lips as she had recounted the last bit. 'But Brian put 'isself out about it, and as far as Dan could make out, it could ha' sp'iled everything if any o' the rest had took notice of 'im. But they wouldn't and didn't, not even when 'e were nasty about other things an 'all. Dan says 'e don't look well, and I dare say 'e's been worried to death about Rosemary. But you know 'ow fond 'e is o' Marge, and no doubt 'e's putting 'issef out about that. Not that she ain't been goodness itself to Rosy, whatever else she choosed to do. It were just a bit o' bad luck, like, as Pansy made them up to thirteen and it 'ad to turn out as it did. Seems Marge stopped at Glebe that night, and it were Pansy as went to Temperance to

270

look after Rosemary. So changed as she is, Dan said, that they'd hardly a-knowed 'er if Poppy and the rest o' the young 'uns hadn't been with 'er when she arrived.'

As usual, Sophie had neatly sidestepped the real issue of the reason for Brian's 'putting 'isself out'.

'I'm sorry, Sophie, but you've lost me. What did Brian object to? And what had Marge to do with it?'

'Why, to that there chap from Yorkshire a-sitting down with 'em, do 'e was a'eady one o' the fam'ly.'

'Oh, really, Sophie! It's only a few days since Marjorie was being accused of seeing too much of Dr Hardy! If Beryl Bean was still about, I should put it down to her substituting Yorky for the doctor at short notice. As far as I know, Marjorie's interest in Yorky is no more than being glad of him as a great help just when she happened to need it. It must have taken the wind out of the sails of whoever made such a tale up to hear that after all Dr Hardy is going to marry Miss Pelham.'

Sophie was beginning to look grim. She set her cup down and looked Fran straight in the eye. 'Beryl mayn't be dead yet, do she don't live in Church End no more. There's others willing to do 'er dirty-work for 'er, same as Olive does the dirty-work 'ere instead o' me now. And as for that doctor, it's to be 'oped as 'e treats this one better than 'e did them as 'e married afore. Not as I'm got anything against 'im as a doctor, seeing 'ow good 'e was to Thirz', but there's still a lot o' truth in the old saying about men as like more'n one woman. "If one ain't enew, twenty's too few." We shall see 'ow long this one'll last.'

Fran bit back a sharp retort, and said gently, 'That isn't very Christian of you, is it, Sophie? You don't know any of his side of it. Doesn't the Bible say "*Judge not, that ye be not judged*"?'

''E can't be no Christian, not wi' four wives all alive at the same time. I'm sure I shouldn't want to face 'Im Above come Judgement Day if I'd forgot my Jelly as I was promised to, and then had three more 'usbands one after the other while they was all still alive.'

That notion was so ludicrous that for a minute or two Fran lost the thread of the conversation; but she was determined not

271

to allow Sophie to escape like that by diverting her to another topic.

'Sophie, stop going round the mulberry bush and tell me what it is that's being said about Marjorie. Whatever it is, you know it isn't the truth. You've known her all her life. She doesn't deserve any more trouble. I don't know and can't guess who it is doing the dirty-work, as you put it, but for all their sakes the silly tale should be stopped in its tracks now – before it does real harm to her. She doesn't go home to Monastery Farm to sleep because Rosy needs her at night, but she's been nearly working herself to death making sure she doesn't neglect Mr Choppen and the Rector, and she goes to Glebe every day, keeping an eye on her parents. To say nothing of bearing all the brunt of arranging the party for last Saturday. No doubt she's stayed at Temperance to make sure that Brian got as much sleep as he could, because he still has to work in the daytime. And the only thanks she gets for trying to help everybody is to be talked about in a way likely to upset her relationship with her brother and split the family. I'm going down to see them at Glebe myself later on today, and I'd like to be prepared before I go. So tell me what you've heard, and who's the one to blame. I'd bet my boots it isn't Dan.'

'No, it ain't. And it 'appened afore this latest news that the doctor's going to marry 'is lady friend after all. It were Olive as told me, and I told 'er as I wouldn't believe it, but there you are, seems Brian does. Don't, 'e wouldn't ha' put 'isself out like 'e did in front o' all them others at the party. But I ain't gooin' to be blamed for repeating nothing. I'll call Olive, and she can come and tell you 'er own self what she swears she seed with 'er own eyes.' And with that, a very disgruntled Sophie, on the verge of tears, rose, opened the door and yelled for Olive to 'come 'ere, quick'.

The peremptory call seemed to have robbed Olive of what sang-froid she normally possessed. She appeared in the doorway, looked at both unsmiling faces, and words burst forth. It wasn't her fault as she'd been so long doing them pots and things, it was all 'is'n: Mr William's. He'd been a-questioning her about them times when she'd lived down the fen in China Row along the bank as you went to Woodwalton, when wages was so low as families with a lot of children would have starved if it hadn't been for eels and things in the Catchwater and the men going a-poaching on Lord de's land.

'And I were just a-gooing to tell 'im as how it 'appened as my Job got in with the gang of 'is cousins as led 'im to get catched poaching 'ere by Old Bartrum when you screeched out like that for me – so as he come to be struck dumb like that there man in the Bible what wouldn't believe the hangel as told 'im 'is wife were like to 'ave a child, and he said 'e knowed as that couldn't be the truth whatever God said, 'cos his wife was well past the change – only they don't call it that no more, they call it the "menopaws" or some such word. I never can remember, try as I may. But that story I do remember, 'cos Miss Budd told us 'ow God punished the old man for not believing 'im by turning 'is wife into a pillow full o' salt there and then, and struck 'im dumb. And 'e never spoke again till that child were born, and then he said as his wife 'ad got to call the baby John the Baptist.' She paused for breath.

'It weren't nothing o' that sort as we wanted you for and you ought to be ashamed o' yourself in any case, talking to a man as ain't your own 'usband about such things as that. I want you to tell Mis' Burbage what you telled me about seeing Marge Bridgefoot with that man as is doing the decorating and such up at Glebe.'

It wasn't often that Olive was actually invited to talk, but she had been warned strictly by Sophie never to be heard repeating that tale again. However, after a glance at Fran's face, she launched into it with gusto.

'It's as true as I stand 'ere, Mis' Burbage,' she said, 'whatever Soph' say. I seed it with my own eyes, and I told 'er out o' my own lips, do she still wouldn't believe me. It were that day not long agoo when the fog come up sudden. I were gooing down the village when I thought to walk on to see Beryl Bean as I used to work for as now keeps a shop in Hen Street for few things as I wanted, like, for Job's tea, 'cos though 'e don't say so, he do like a tin o' baked beans on toast, but it were getting dark early and I could see as it were gooing to be so foggy as I shouldn't see my way 'ome. I'd got nearly as far as the gates o' the Glebe, and stood there wondering whether to keep gooing or goo 'ome and give Job a slice o' bacon and a hegg and some fried 'taters instead o' beans when a car as was stood outside on the road flashed its lights on, so I dropped back against the 'edge while I made my mind up. And I hadn't been there mor'n a couple o' shakes when another car with its lights on drawed up behint the other and showed me who were in it. He got out and I seed 'im as plain as I can see you now, that chap as they call Yorky. And it come to me in a flash as if I could see 'im, 'e could see me skulking there as if I were up to no good, so I got on the road all in the fog, and walked by them two cars. The car as were behint 'is'n were Marge Bridgefoot's, and she set there in it awaiting for 'im – must ha' bin, 'cos she didn't make to get out. But 'e did, and got in aside of 'er, and there they set – and may God strike me dead if I tell a lie – close together they was, him a-cuddling 'er and a-kissing 'er, as bold as brass. In broad daylight – no, I tell a lie, it were getting dark and the fog so thick as you couldn't see your 'and in front o' your o' eyes. But I seed what I seed, and nobody shall say me nay about that.'

'If you were the only one to see it, nobody else is likely to contradict you – certainly not me. As it happens, I already know the other side of that story. Mr Postlethwaite called here on his way home to tell me. Marjorie was very upset about something, and had stopped in her car to cry it out because she didn't want her mother and father to ask her any questions. But he was having one of his bad turns that day, and had only been waiting for her to come because they'd agreed to talk about arrangements for the party. She was in such a state that he stopped to comfort her, but by that time the fog was so thick and he felt so bad he was afraid he wouldn't get home. So he stopped here and asked me to let Marjorie know why he might not be there to work the next day. As you said the other day, Sophie, that's how tales get about. What beats me is how anybody else got to know anything about it. Did anybody else but you see it, Mrs Hopkins?'

There was definite accusation in her voice, but to her surprise it was Sophie who came to Olive's rescue. 'Dan never seed it 'isself, and said so, but 'e knowed as it were the truth. Seems Brian 'ad slipped over to get something out o' the barn, and were in the yard ready to goo 'ome and when 'e switched 'is lights on, 'e seed exactly the same as Olive's said. 'E told George about it next day, and George told Dan. Brian were so put out that 'e more or less give 'is dad orders to sack that Yorky there and then. 'E – I mean Brian – does get a bit above 'isself a lot nowadays. 'E's never forgive Marge for the way she be'aved the day as Vic Gifford were buried.'

'Now that is the truth, as we all know,' put in Olive. 'But then she never had ought to ha' let 'em down in the first place by marrying beneath her sex like that.'

'Thank you, both of you,' said Fran hastily, anxious now to get rid of them and report to William before she forgot Olive's gems. But the puzzle remained. How had such a simple incident got blown up to such dangerous proportions? If only Olive and Dan the faithful and, because of Brian, the Bridgefoots themselves knew of it, how on earth had it raced like wildfire all round the village?

She went to find William, and was quite disappointed to find Nigel sitting with him. He was Nigel the Rector this morning, wearing cassock, dog-collar and also, for him, a rather worried expression.

William was getting him a drink. 'Come on, padre,' he said. 'Drink that and tell us what's the matter.'

Nigel appreciated a good whisky. 'Nothing more than everything,' he said. 'Just shows what can happen if you don't look where you're going, and then desert your post to chase one vanished lady, and be late getting back to host a party for another. Now that's all over, Christmas is upon us, and we have nowhere to celebrate it. The builders have notified me that St Swithin's will simply not be safe for any Christmas services to be held there. I shall probably be run out of the parish by people like your Sophie and Daniel Bates, who haven't missed Christmas Morning Communion there for at least fifty years. Eric's mad with me for not foreseeing what would happen, because he did, and warned me, but I took the builder's word. It means Eric has to inform all his regular Christmas clients that what they have enjoyed the last two or three Christmases won't be the same this year – and in any case he can't yet find a substitute for Miss Pelham on the language front. Not much fear of her being on duty this Christmas Day, I hope! But it did occur to me that if the weather is not too inclement, it would hurt none of the faithful communicants to walk up as far as St Saviour's. That's what I really came to see you about, William. Have you had time to find out anything about its history?'

'Yes, though I already knew quite a lot. I won't go here and now into any great detail, but I can give you a very rough sketch.

'The two religious houses of Ely and Ramsey were at each other's throats from the beginning. In the twelfth century, Ramsey got the worst of Geoffrey de Mandeville's raids. He looted a lot of their treasure, and deposed their Abbot for a while to take the Abbey and all its goods into his own hands – maybe with Ely's connivance, but that's only my guess. Mandeville soon overreached himself, and got his come-uppance at Burwell soon afterwards. Then Ramsey set about putting its house in order again, always with one eye on Ely. Ely was a bishopric and Somersham part of his banlieu, though whether this means the Manor of Somersham or "the Soke of Somersham" I haven't yet decided. It was a well-wooded area for this part of the world, and boundaries were always in dispute, probably because of the vagaries of the Ouse and its tributaries. There don't appear to be fixed boundaries to the banlieu of either Ely or Ramsey, especially where from Earith one tributary of the Ouse flowed south to north. On old maps it's called the Chaire. Ramsey lay to the west of it, while Ely was on the main river to the north-east. The fens round Ramsey were, if anything, lower than those round Ely, so any bit of land above sea level was grabbed by one or the other.

'This ridge of slightly higher ground, which didn't flood as often as the lower fens all round, was coveted by both houses. Ramsey must have got here before Ely claimed the whole of the Soke of Somersham. The monks of Ramsey were scared of another barons' raid, and of Ely getting too big for its boots. Ramsey needed to hide its treasures at a good distance from the Abbey itself, and have a watchtower from which they could keep a sharp eye on Ely. They set up a monastic cell on Carr's Hill, the high ground we now know as Castle Hill, with a splendid Lady Chapel; but for places to hide men, and their famous library in another emergency, they had to have somewhere with secret hidey-holes, underground passages and the like. What could be more innocent than a church, to all intents built to serve their lay brothers and other dwellers in the fen islands around?

'It must have been a hive of activity during the Reformation, but at the dissolution, Ramsey Abbey and its possessions were lost – to the Cromwell family, mostly. They acquired a great deal of what had been church property then, including Carr's Hill. The Lady Chapel was turned into a grand house and the church was robbed of everything worth having. You'd have thought they might have demolished the church, but not all the Cromwell family were against the Reformation, and several branches of it became members of the King's Anglican Church. Those who took over Carr's Hill must have been that sort. They set up a living to go with the church – a nice little job for one of their younger sons. But it was a case of "easy come, easy go". The Cromwells overspent on building and lavish entertainment, and were soon forced to sell. That's what must have happened at Carr's Hill. During the civil wars and the interregnum, the church was probably used as a meeting place for any of the so-called "Puritan" sects.

'After the Restoration, all was confusion again, and we can only guess what went on here. The church still stands, whole enough to serve your turn at Christmas. I'll try to find out more about the graveyard. I'll tell Bob Bellamy that much. I think the best thing for all of us would be to keep our heads down, and persuade you to go on as before – on condition that those of us who can afford to help with urgent repairs agree to do so. It really wouldn't hurt any of us who want to keep it going for sentimental reasons. What do you think?'

'Much as *you* do. I must be off – to see George Bridgefoot and find out what the chances are of using his old barn for a

Carol Service on Christmas Eve and a watch-night service on New Year's Eve. They seem to have had quite a successful lunch on Saturday, from what I hear; the unexpected homecoming of Pansy being almost a match for the so unexpected dénouement at our parallel party. Never a dull moment here, is there?'

*

Two hours later, a very embarrassed and distressed George stood before the Rector, who'd called at the Old Glebe on his way home from Benedict's to request the use of the barn for those Christmas services normally held in the church.

George had welcomed the idea heartily, but remembering the rebuff he had got from Brian when he had so hopefully suggested a horkey after Christmas was over, said that he had better just check with his son, who was the virtual head of their company now, before giving his consent. Nigel had said he would come back.

George had found himself up against a blank wall. Brian, in what seemed a filthy temper, had bawled that he could tell the Rector that the barn wouldn't be available for social gatherings of any kind from now on. They all might as well get used to the idea. The barn was now part of a farm in his charge, and in future it wouldn't be cleared or used for anything but purely agricultural purposes.

'But there's been church and village do's in it for nigh four hundred year, and family do's as long as I remember,' George protested. 'That's why I had it done up as soon as I could afford it. You can't stand against things as have always been, my boy, especially when it's the Rector asking, 'cos he needs it. Why shouldn't he use it?'

'I don't know that I'm obliged to give him, or anybody else, any reason. You made me chairman of the company, and I intend to run it as I like. If you're still prepared to suck up to the Rector and the rest of that old-fashioned lot, I'm not. As far as I'm concerned the church can fall down as soon as it likes, but that barn is a valuable bit of property, and it's in my charge now.'

George couldn't believe he was hearing aright. In the past, he'd several times had occasion to take his son down a peg or two, and he tried now to maintain his dignity as Brian's father, and as the head of the family, even if Brian was chairman of the family firm.

He drew himself up to his full height, and kept his temper. 'Don't overdo it, Brian, my boy. You may be the chairman of the company, but it's still my land.'

'It may be, but you've lost control of it. That's what I'm trying to tell you, you silly old fool. You gave authority over it into my hands – and by God, I'll do as I like with it.'

'Don't you dare swear at me,' George roared, his composure broken at last.

Brian snapped his fingers, literally, under the old man's nose, and said, 'Just you try to stop me!'

It was at that moment that the Reverend Nigel drove up again to get his answer. He heard the last exchange, and watched Brian roar away in his latest powerful car, while George stood like a stricken tree. Nigel had never seen his grand old churchwarden so piteously helpless before. He went to him, and led him to sit down somewhere before he fell.

George was looking desperately round him for a place to hide till he could recover his composure. Till now, there would have been two places of refuge close at hand: his pew in the church, with its white churchwarden's wand at the end, or his special little corner in the barn, where to please himself he had often sat with his unfilled pipe in his mouth to enjoy 'mozing' on how good life had been to him. As he sat there on his comfortable seat made of a bale of straw covered with clean cornsacks, smells would come to his nostrils of harvests past, of old wood soaked for hundreds of years with the scent of ripe corn; of linseed cattle cake; and (in his memory) the tangy smell of mangolds coming in long yellow strips through the mangold pulper when, as a child, he'd cranked the handle. Such old-fashioned implements were rarities now, but he had kept his for old times' sake. It was there he sat whenever there was a problem or a proposition to think over: such as when Charles laid before him his plans to buy Danesum from John Petrie and marry Charlie Bellamy as soon as he was twenty-one (though she was only twenty and about to go up to Cambridge to read for her first degree on the way to becoming a vet). The memory of that day was like a dagger in George's side, because he wanted that familiar refuge now, since the church was denied him – but he dared not try to open the barn door. He guessed, correctly, that not only would it be locked against him, but that all his old treasures had been cleared out while he had been giving his attention to the plans for the Golden Wedding.

The December day was cold, and the old man shivered. Nigel knew that it was not the temperature making him shudder. It was shock and despair.

They were both old, both tall, both still splendid specimens of the sort of men who had made Britain great. One from the very top drawer, who had been through the hell of desert war with his men, had risked his life alongside Eric in Europe and survived, still whole in body, mind, and spirit. The other had been born poor with regard to worldly wealth, but a countryman to the marrow. Fed only on what his father's farm could provide, owning only one set of respectable clothing for Sundays; but nevertheless with as much pride in his ancestral acres as ever a Delaprime had had in his high birth. Two of a kind.

There was nowhere they could sit down, so to help him maintain his balance till the shock passed, Nigel held out both his hands. George clung to them, slowly gaining control of himself.

'He's still my son,' George said. 'He's changed a lot – and he's never been a real Bridgefoot – but he's still my son. Whatever he is, he is still my son, and he has given me Charles, so I have a lot to thank him for. It's Charles as I worry about. I ought to have seen what it would do to Brian to have control – and I ought never to have put Charles's future into his hands. Charles is a true Bridgefoot, if Brian never was. But I must keep going now as well as I can for Charles's sake.'

'Head up, old friend,' said Nigel. 'Heart up, too – for "underneath are the everlasting arms".'

'Let's go in and see Mother,' George said. 'I shall be able to explain to her better if you're there as well.'

They found Molly sitting at the table, and by her side a very disconsolate Marge. Somewhere in the background, Yorky was clattering utensils and whistling. Marge jumped up and called to Yorky to put the kettle on. Nigel said that though a cup of tea would do him nicely, he rather thought George might be better for something a bit stronger.

George could not hide his distress, in any case. Marjorie looked from him to her pale-faced mother, and asked, rather grimly, who it was that her brother had got it in for this morning, besides herself and Rosemary.

'I don't know whatever can be the matter with him,' Marjorie said. 'Rosy hasn't got over his behaviour on Saturday yet, but he's being a devil untied to her again this morning, shouting at her that if she was well enough to cope with all that, she's putting it on today so as not to have to make any effort for herself or him. He was so nasty to me that I couldn't stop there, honestly, Mam. He had a snide go or two at Pansy, but bless her, she just ignored him. I'm at my wits' end. I can't and won't let Rosy down while she needs me, but I don't like leaving Pansy there with him while he's in this awful mood. Besides, I want to see more of her now she's come home at last. It isn't fair to her to have to stop where I can't see her.'

'He's got rid of his bile on me this morning,' George said, and gave them a brief, edited version of what had passed.

'It may mean no more than that he's out of sorts,' Nigel said soothingly. 'Perhaps he's finding being the boss rather more than he bargained for. Don't let it upset you too much, George. He'll be all right when he gets over this mood, I dare say, but I'm afraid that doesn't help me much. Christmas won't wait. I've got to find somewhere else, or cancel the Christmas programme altogether. I think I'd better get home quick, and consult Eric.'

'Don't take it so much to heart, Dad,' said Marjorie, 'or you either, Mam,' seeing that Molly was about to give way to tears. 'There must be some reason for him being so nasty. Pansy said he ought to see a doctor, but we all know what he's like about doctors – and he'll never have Terry Hardy in the house again. That's no matter. There are plenty of other doctors besides Hardy. As long as Pansy's willing to stop and look after Rosy for the time being, we shall manage somehow, but if Rosy's going to need help for longer, we shall have to try and get assistance from somewhere else. Brian won't get anything more out of me till he's apologized. No, Mam, don't ask me. I'm not going to tell you, except to say that somebody's putting tales about again. Dangerous tales, full of spite against me. I can't imagine who it can be, but whoever it is makes sure that Bri hears every whisper. And he believes it.'

'Why don't tha' all coom and have dinner,' said a voice from the kitchen. 'It's only leftovers from t'party but good enough fo' t'queen. Tha'll all feel better for it.'

They didn't want to eat, but Yorky insisted. As time passed, and Molly realized the full implications of Brian's attack on George, she began to wilt, and was cosseted by Marjorie till she agreed to go and lie down.

George went to find Dan and take solace from the Jerseys and his new bull. Marjorie was left alone with Yorky.

He sat down beside her. 'I doan't know what upset thee at tha brother's house t'other day, pet,' he said, 'but I could see it were summ'at bad. And I can tell thee a couple o' truths, aye-by-God, that Ah can! One is that Ah'm glad tha isna giving in wi'out a fight. Besides, tha looks grand, pet, with tha dander oop, I tell tha! And t'other is that whatever else is wrong wi' him, he's took again me, and was going to mek sure I understood. There'll ne'er be any loove lost between him and me, that's for sure. He can't bear to think of me having any part to play at all in this family, even if it's only as t'one who meks Gran's tea. He's jealous o' everybody as gets took any notice of. That's why he's set hissen against t'Boss. He's jealous if anybody teks more notice of his wife than of him, though he don't bother to tek notice of her hissen. You're his slave, so nobody must look thy way, specially low-down boogers like me. Worst of all he's jealous o' his own son, 'cos he knows he's never come nowhere near to being as dear to t'Boss as young Charles is. Now, pet, tha's nothing tha can do to right any o' that. He's putting everybody's back oop and soon won't have nobody but hissen. That'll teach him. Just try to tek no notice till he cooms to his senses.'

282

'I can't leave Mam and Dad by themselves tonight,' she said. 'But I must find out if Pansy's all right up at Temperance. She's got no transport, and she'd have to leave Rosy alone with Bri too long to walk here. Besides, I want to see her. It's so long since I did, and she's had such an awful time – I know she has. But she's come through it so changed that I've got to get to know her again. She's more like a true Bridgefoot than she ever was before and I want her – and I want her to know I want her, but if I ring up to speak to her, Bri slams the phone down on me.'

'Get Poppy to ring her and find out for thee.'

'Yes. I'd thought about Charles, but it would be better if we could keep what's happened here today from him. He's never got on all that well with his Dad. Thanks, Yorky. I don't know whatever we did without you. Don't leave us in the lurch, will you?'

'Not till Adam gets back from Doombarton,' he said. 'Tha need'na woory about that, pet.'

*

That was the situation Fran found when she got to the Glebe. Marjorie was alone, and Yorky was busy in the kitchen. Marjorie made a great effort as Fran admired cards, flowers, Sophie's (much reduced) cake, and the tea-pot, but as usual she picked up the atmosphere.

'I mustn't stop long,' she said, 'but I did want to hear how the party went. Are your Dad and Mum about?'

Marjorie shook her head, burst into tears, and out came all the story. If there was anyone in the village who would sympathize and then keep her mouth shut, it was Fran.

Fran was horrified. She had known, of course, from Terry, what had gone on up at Temperance while he was there – and, from Sophie and Olive, what the rumour was about Marge and Yorky's relationship. Moreover, that Brian also had seen what Olive claimed to have seen. She thought it had all the marks of a tale going the rounds of a village too long starved of juicy gossip, but it shocked her, all the same.

That Brian should deliberately obstruct Nigel's plans for Christmas was incredible enough, but that he should turn on his

283

father as he had was unthinkable. It hurt her to the core, because of the genuine love she had for George, and because she felt the general rapport between them important to everybody in the community, especially just at present. She had a feeling that it went deeper than any casual friendship set up between Benedict's and the Old Glebe since her return to Old Swithinford. She felt that their understanding and appreciation of each other had roots somewhere deep in the past, and that they had been intertwined for centuries.

She tried to comfort Marjorie, telling her how she knew about Pansy's return, and giving her Nigel's report on what a wonderful girl Pansy now was. Marjorie was not to be comforted.

'Let her cry hersen out,' was Yorky's advice. 'I'll stop with her till t'Boss cooms in, and Gran gets oop.'

Marjorie caught Fran's hand as she was leaving, and said, 'Please will you ring Eric for me and tell him why I can't leave Mam and Dad to go and do what I ought up at Monastery Farm?' she said. 'I can't ring him myself, in this state.'

'I was on my way to see him,' lied Fran. 'If I can find him.'

*

She went straight to the hotel, and found Eric in his office, bored and restless, but at the same time, for a man of his boundless energy, listless. He made no bones about being pleased to see her. 'For one thing,' he said, 'because I needed to.

'The business of this coming Christmas is getting me right down. It got out of kilter when I was obliged to hold the stakes while Terry and Anthea sorted their affairs out. I couldn't persuade Anthea to carry on, before last Saturday, and I daren't ask her to now. They're taking over Heartease from December the twenty-first, by which time, Terry assures me, it will be furnished and ready for them. Reading between the lines, I guess that means a honeymoon somewhere at Christmas time, and a new home waiting for them when they come back in the New Year. No skin off my nose, except that it begins to look as if I shan't get any sort of break at all. For once Jess is not being as cooperative as usual. All the Taliaferros can think about is the school concert at Fenley, which Greg is up to his eyes in, and for which Jess, with

284

Jane to help, is making – or at least providing – all the costumes. The concert takes place the last Friday before Christmas, and Jess tells me we are all expected to be there.' He grimaced. 'It hardly seems up my street, does it? I think I shall have to be too busy.

'I shall probably have to move back up here for all the Christmas–New Year period, playing mine host. We made such a hit with a group of middle-aged to elderly folk the year of William's challenge to Bailey of being at church on New Year's Eve, that they've been coming back ever since. People like Alex Marland's parents, getting to meet new people and enjoying the very last remnants of what rural England once was.

'We shall have to let them down this year as far as church-going and carol singing and such relics of the past are concerned. The church isn't safe, so Nigel tells me. I haven't been needed as a permanent host here before. I've been able to spend most of my Christmas with family and friends.

'It seems a long time since we spent that happy Christmas Day together up here, doesn't it? Before the love-bug got all of you except me, so that those who hadn't already got happy homes soon set them up. It made me want a home of my own as well as my executive quarters here – and I got it; but I've never had more than half of what the rest of you have. I'd more or less made up my mind to leave the hotel this year to my very competent staff and steal off to Cambridge to share Monica and Roland's Christmas – to be with my grandchildren and my two adopted "nieces". But of course, that's all off now. I tell you, I'm not wanted anywhere.

'Perhaps it really is time for me to seek fresh woods and pastures new. Start all over again. But I shall always regard Old Swithinford somehow as "my baby", the new village I made out of the ruins of the old one, keeping the right sort of balance between old and new, and between modern materialism and old customs and tradition. Keeping the "Englishness" of it that we fought for in the war – things no amount of money can buy. But my job is done.

'I should probably have made up my mind to call it a day before now but for the fact that I can't face the inevitable result of seeing all I've done being undone, and my restoration of Church End nothing but a high-class suburb of Swithinford New Town. We shall see.'

Fran had followed what he was saying with complete understanding and agreement. She didn't like the look of the future any more than he did – especially as she had gathered that Elyot's feelings towards local politics were barely lukewarm now, whatever the reason. But all her other reactions were swamped by something Eric had just said that had filtered through the rest and come to the top.

'Wait a minute, Eric,' she said. 'What did you mean about your idea of spending Christmas with Roland and Monica being "all off now"? I haven't heard of anything like that. I'd been hoping that they'd all come to us for one day – you included, of course. I haven't invited them yet, because I'm not sure what's happening to my other family – Jeremy and Kate are probably leaving for a job overseas in the spring, so I was giving them first choice this year.

'Eric!' Her voice sharpened with apprehension. 'There's nothing wrong between them – Roland and Monica – is there? His wife hasn't suddenly turned up again, or anything like that?'

He was quick to reassure her. 'No, Fran, no! Nothing like that! Though I don't wonder at you jumping to the worst possible conclusion, seeing how everything else has gone wrong just lately. No – when I rang up to tell Monica I was fed up with feeling so much the odd one out here, and suggested spending Christmas right out of it, at Cambridge with them, she was terribly embarrassed and said that both she and Roland had been working too hard, and had made a sudden decision to take a whole month off and spend it in a friend's beautiful holiday home on the Cornish coast. It's all fixed up. Topaz and Sapphire will go along too – they're sixteen now – and take the brunt of doing the chores and looking after young Bill and little Annette. Monica said it was to be the honeymoon that she and Roland never had.'

He added, a little sardonically, that perhaps that was why there had been no hint of an invitation for him to join them.

Fran was so relieved that she found dozens of excuses for

them as far as she was concerned, and a ready one on her tongue for their not telling Eric. 'They know how up to your neck you usually are at this time of the year,' she said. 'I don't suppose such a thing ever occurred to them. But they might just have told me. It looks to me as if we're all in for a very dull sort of Christmas.'

He nodded. She registered that he really was very low in spirits. 'Spend as much time with us as you like,' she said. 'It looks from here that the usual merry-go-round won't be working this year. And I must go home now – I hope William isn't champing at the bit. I told him I should only be about an hour. May I give him a ring? It's past lunch-time already.'

William was quite himself, if a little anxious about what she might have found at the Glebe. She didn't want the Bridgefoots mentioned in Eric's hearing, and was so careful with her choice of words that he chuckled. 'OK, darling. I've got the drift. As Sophie would say, "A nod's as good as a wink to a blind horse." Where are you ringing from?'

'Eric's – at the hotel.'

'Good,' said her husband. 'Get him to give you lunch. I've had a picnic of what I could find in the fridge, because I've arranged to meet Bob. Do you mind?'

'I've outworn William's patience,' she said to Eric. 'He's had his lunch without me. I suppose you've had yours?'

'No. I didn't propose to bother with any,' he said. 'But if I can have the pleasure of your company, that puts quite a different complexion on it. I want to talk to you, anyway, about Elyot.'

All he had to do to produce a cordon-bleu lunch with wine to match in record time was to press a button on his desk.

Chatting amicably over the delicious meal like the old friends they were, both relaxed. They always had their joint ownership of Monica and Roland's twins to bring up to date, together with the good prospects for Roland's firm of up-and-coming architects, and Monica's ever-increasing reputation as a couturière in the very top rank of 'the rag trade'.

'She's hoping that the two Petrie girls will agree to train for the catwalk at her expense,' he said. 'They're both absolutely cut out for it. I think I've never seen a more beautiful couple of girls, still so much alike that I can hardly tell one from the other. They haven't got quite the extraordinary colouring of Beth and Elyot's two, nor, perhaps, quite the maturity for their age that Emerald and Amethyst have; but they do have brains as well as beauty, and Monica says that's an asset she's not prepared to let them waste. Models have a reputation for being all body with very little up top except the "diamonds are a girl's best friend" mentality. Monica says that's why so many fall by the wayside. But her clothes demand more than a come-hither look and a display of beautiful legs and bosoms. They are designed for discriminating people who have personality as well as money, and should be displayed by models who can get that over to the buyers. She wants them to stay on at school and do their A-levels, and then go straight on to the very best model-training establishment she can find.'

'Sounds a marvellous plan to me,' Fran said. 'I wish there was some way we could let John Petrie know how well his brood of orphans have fared. He couldn't have hoped for anything half as good.'

'It's partly the result of him being what he was, and partly because of what I was saying to you before lunch. Chance had led him to a community that still retained a lot of pre-war values, though intermixed with new. Caring for the poor and helpless was accepted as their duty by folk who lived in such isolated places as Old Swithinford was in pre-war days. They had to be independent when no other help was available, and interdependence was part of their way of life. They had no one but each other to rely on.

'Nigel could explain it better than I. He's never managed to convert me to Christianity, but he did show me a lot of its characteristics by example when Annette died and I was against the whole world and everything in it. I'd been so cocky and independent till then. I found out how much I needed somebody else to depend on.

'He visited me here a lot in those early days, and I began to see the village – which I was intending to destroy just to make more money – through his eyes. A sort of repository of good old

English rural life, especially after you arrived, Fran. Nigel cites you and Sophie as the perfect example of "interdependence" that has no truck with what we now call "class". There wasn't much class in such a community in the time between the wars. Except for the remnants of local aristocracy, there was only a ladder of hierarchy on which people continually changed places. "Like the angels on Jacob's ladder," he once said, and I had to ask him what he meant! I remember thinking what a strange man he was, in spite of knowing him so well, because he had to explain that he believed wholeheartedly in "angels", even if they were nothing more than beautiful symbols of the best of human thought and aspiration. People, he said, went up and down the ladder. The top of it was out of sight, but God was always waiting there.

'I didn't believe in any god – but how I wanted one! I had to cling to somebody, so I clung to him. He gradually and tolerantly pointed out to me that I wasn't half the hard-headed businessman I prided myself on being. He knew, I suppose, because he'd been through a lot of the war with me, and said that such success as I'd enjoyed in the army was due mainly to my understanding of men and what made them tick. He convinced me that I hadn't lost that gift because I'd become an embittered widower. And he was right. He gave me my confidence back. I changed my tactics – and it worked.

'I'd never expected to be happy again, but I soon began to learn. It boils down, I think, to that: learning how to be "a good neighbour". It means understanding all sorts of people – very much like in the army. And being ready to take the lead when it was necessary, which wasn't often, because there were so many others equally capable of knowing what to do and when to do it.

'The Petrie orphans are a case in point. Where else but in a community like this could homes have been found for seven out of the eight of them, all homes that Petrie himself would have provided for them if he had had the health and the means?

'Looking back on all that now, it gives me a lot of pleasure to know what an essential part I played behind the scenes in the rescue of those kids. By saving not only the bricks and mortar of the old village, but restoring its flagging spirit as well. But for what I had done, when that time came, and without you and William, and the Bridgefoots, they'd have had to be split up and taken into care.

'You'd been planted in the soil here and had managed between you – with help from people like Miss Budd – to stand firm against the pressures of modern society, and the culture of "business" people like me. You, or the Bridgefoots alone, might possibly have held the salient, but with two gun emplacements, you stood more chance. Luck sent a third reinforcement in Elyot, and even a fourth in Bob Bellamy, because though he didn't belong on the spot here like you did, his general background was similar.'

Fran was frankly surprised. 'I didn't realize you were such a philosopher, Eric,' she said. 'I see what you mean. I was only thinking earlier that some of my attachment to the Bridgefoots in general and George in particular must go back a long way, before either of us as individuals was born. And I suppose what you mean is that the more guns you have, the better the chances of holding your salient. One gun and its crew can only hold out till the last man is dead. And the enemy we're trying to keep at bay is a society with modern, materialistic values? People who make money their god and their motto "Every man for himself and the devil take the hindmost." What's made this all so clear to you all of a sudden?'

'My solitude,' answered Eric unhesitatingly. 'I never knew how lonely I could be except perhaps for the awful time just after Annette was killed. I threw myself with all my might into work, with the intention of becoming a business tycoon. I've now got used to the loss of Annette, as long as I don't dwell on it too much. The friends I made here helped, but now, for some reason, I seem to be losing them all again. And I'm lonely, Fran. But at least it's given me time to think.

'Nobody can truthfully say they were "happy" doing their war service, but looking back on it, I can see what I enjoyed about it most. It was the planning, the strategy, the tactics. Once in action, you lose the ability to think in doing your best to stay alive long enough to achieve your objective. The thinking has to be done beforehand. At present I seem to be the only one trying to plan forward with regard to the proposed new development. Unless somebody's willing to stand, and be seen to stand, in opposition to Greenslade, it'll be a walkover for him, and believe you me, he's a real crafty politician in his way. What he's working for is to get such a majority that he will have what he calls "a mandate" to make his own position safe and self-perpetuating. While he lives we shall never have another chance to oppose him. We've got to do it now – or lose the chance. I honestly believed we had found the right sort of man in Elyot, but he's cooled off, and is about to run back on us. I don't know why, and can't find out. He won't even find time to talk to me about it any longer. It puzzles me. Let's go and sit somewhere more comfortable.'

They went next door into the room which, when he had lived there permanently, had been his sitting-room, and into which he occasionally now took business consultants, as well as his close friends. He sank into his own armchair and, looking at her for permission, produced his pipe, filled it, lit it, and puffed at it. He was now more himself than she had seen him for what seemed a very long time.

She sat down a good deal less agitated than she had been when she had arrived. The great hurdle she had feared had been cleared. He'd mentioned the Bridgefoots first, before she'd had to.

She made a swift decision to come directly to the point. 'I came here straight from the Old Glebe,' she said. 'They're in deep trouble. You weren't mentioned, except that Marjorie, who's in a dreadful state, asked me to let you know she wouldn't be up to Monastery Farm this afternoon as usual, or to Nigel's, either. So what's gone wrong between you and the Bridgefoots?'

'I've been hoping you'd be able to tell me,' he replied. 'I've no idea.'

'But you've heard rumours. Don't pretend you haven't, because you've let it out by mistake once or twice.'

He was silent, and she didn't press him; but after a minute or two, he asked, rather solicitously, she thought, what was the matter today. She hesitated before telling him, but in the end chose a middle way.

'There's a lot of spiteful rumours going around aimed at all the Bridgefoot family. I'm afraid Marjorie is getting the worst of it, because whoever is starting the tales and broadcasting them makes sure that Brian hears them with every little detail made plain, like every leaf in a pre-Raphaelite painting. The consequence is that he turned on Marjorie, till she could stand it no longer and retaliated.

'She doesn't go to help Rosemary any more, but you must know as well as anybody how fond she's always been of Brian. You must have heard from Nigel that Pansy is home – and she's standing in at Temperance for Marjorie, caring for Rosemary – to whom, according to Marge, Brian is being quite diabolical.

'This morning, it all blew up in poor old George's face. I don't know what they would have done if Nigel hadn't been there, but he's got far too much on his plate to give them the attention they need. Both George and Molly are simply flattened, and Marjorie almost beside herself. Nobody can do much to help for fear of making things worse. Their prop at the present is the man they call Yorky: to be relied on for help in any direction when he's well, but he's liable to awful panic attacks himself, with no warning.'

She watched Eric's mouth twist, and hoped it wasn't either disbelief or derision causing it. She leaned across to him and took his hand.

'Eric,' she said. 'It's absolutely essential that we find out who's starting these tales and see to it that they are stopped. If that doesn't happen soon, the main support for your village will collapse before your eyes. Without the Bridgefoots, other bits would fly off till there was no real community left. Please do a lot of thinking before you take any hasty decisions to leave us to it.'

He got up, and walked rather agitatedly round the room, pondering his answer. 'Marjorie declined all help from me,' he said. 'I did try. Can you explain that at all?'

'Yes, as it happens, I can. Brian has been getting at her about her conduct "letting the family down". First by marrying beneath her, then being so "callous" when her husband was killed, and the consequent scandal when she became your tenant. The emphasis on that has been changed. The story now is not that you were having an affair with her, but that she's been doing her level best to seduce you, and failed to such an extent that you've "given her the push".

'The next instalment has her chasing Terence Hardy, which supposedly was the cause of Anthea turning him down; and the last, so far, is that Marjorie has added insult to injury by being seen kissing and cuddling Yorky in the car outside the Glebe. You pays your money and you takes your choice – but you know that all of it is a complete fabrication. You should understand why she's hardly dared to come anywhere near you.'

He swung round on her. 'Is she fond of this man from Yorkshire? I've heard that story several times, every time with more detail. It would account for her not wanting to accept any help from me.'

Fran had to tell the truth. 'He's an attractive man,' she said, 'though younger than she by a few years. He's also a no-nonsense man when it comes to anybody putting on the dog – she feels a sort of affinity with him on those grounds, I think, to counter the charge of her disgracing the family by marrying a man like Vic Gifford. But he's also a very, very soft-hearted man, and a tactile one. The sort who, like me, thinks that to hold somebody's hand when they're in trouble is worth an ocean of words, and a hug and a kiss the best medicine for most wounds to the heart. I happen to know the real origin of that tale of her being seen in his arms in the car. If I'd been in her shoes that day, I'd have been glad if the milkman had comforted me like that! And you needn't talk, because you've confessed that you've had to comfort Jess occasionally – and I've had to comfort you! I won't say it doesn't mean anything, because such loving kindness is a most precious gift to both sides when it's put to proper use. But it has no sexual connotations, as you know very well. Somebody is going out of their way to rub Marjorie's nose in the dirt. Somebody with a nasty, cruel and jealous mind. Who on earth can it be?'

He was looking very thoughtful. 'You're right, Fran, as usual,' he said. 'And you've given me a clue as to what may be the matter with Elyot.'

She was all ears, but before she had time to ask what he meant, the internal telephone rang, and he answered it. 'Yes?' he said. 'Who is it wanting me so urgently? Oh. Yes, that will do – I'll come directly.'

'Then I must go,' said Fran hurriedly. Please stay in touch with us.'

She kissed him and left.

*

William had found Bob waiting for him in the church, as usual. The December afternoon was bright, but the keen wind was keeping the temperature low. The church was cold, so they wouldn't want to sit there too long.

On his way, William had changed his mind; in all fairness, he had to disclose Nigel's assessment of the situation, and ask Bob if he could add anything from his knowledge as tenant farmer or titular owner.

Bob listened, as he always did, with intelligent understanding. All that William told him about the early history of the church made sense to him, because he spent a good deal of his leisure time, especially in summer, "wisening out" why it had so many strange, out-of-the-ordinary features.

'Have you always farmed these fields round the church which I've always supposed till now to be glebe land?' William asked.

'Yes, but I took it for granted. As you know, I never intended to farm here. I took it on a five-year lease to please my son, and when he let me down I had to farm it myself, but I intended to go back to the fen the moment those five years were up. So I never bothered myself to find out much.'

'But you must have some idea of what land you were hiring, and what it comprised. Explain to me how you came to get it.'

'It was advertised. At such a low rent it was worth a gamble, because John, my son, saw the possibilities of high-land farming when modern mechanical implements were getting easier to come by after the war. The war had been over a long while then, but only a few fields here had been ploughed up, because they weren't worth the trouble when you couldn't get proper implements. The Cambs. War Ag. had taken control of it during the war – every little helped – but the college it had been left to wanted to get rid of it to anybody who would take it off their hands. You asked me once how it was they were able to offer it for sale. I told you they wouldn't talk to me about it because they thought I was a fen-tiger bumpkin who didn't know a big A from a bull's foot.

'I reckon you've just solved that bit of the puzzle. You say the Rector told you that the chap who restored the church and my house thought he owned it. If he left it to the college, you may depend that during the war their affairs got into as much of a muddle as everybody else's. They were glad to let it at any price, and be able to sell it if ever they had the chance. It would only be at that point they'd begin to look either at, or more like for, the deeds. It was all the more complicated by the War Ag.'s part in it. There's bits of land all over the place as were commandeered by the Ministry of Defence in wartime, and never used. I know of several good fields as were let along with the land they joined, and once the war was over, the tenant claimed them as his own and got away with it. When Effendi made a bid to buy this – as a wedding present to me and Jane – his solicitors treated with the bursar of the college. I had nothing to do with it. But when I wouldn't accept it and he had to become my landlord until he became my partner, his solicitors in London did all the business – all I ever did was to sign on the dotted line where they told me to. I've never seen the deeds. I should think they're still in a safe in London somewhere but a completely new set may have been drawn up for all I know. A lot of people did, after the war. Do you want me to ask Effendi to get them out, so we can know for sure?'

William thought fast. 'No,' he said. 'Not at present. Let sleeping dogs lie – at least till St Swithin's is safe again. As Sophie would say: "What the eye don't see, the 'eart don't grieve over". You go on as you've always done, using the fields. Nobody's likely to challenge you about those as long as the Church Commissioners have no right to and nobody such as the Association for the Preservation of Ancient Churches gets wind of it. Nigel will go along with us for a while, at least, and we might even have a chance to keep the status quo, if we give it enough thought, and raise some money. The tower here's safe enough as long as nobody tries to ring the bells. So it gives us a bit more time than we thought we had to keep looking for that evidence I need.

'The graveyard comes under different rules from the church building. It can't be disturbed or dug up till at least forty years after the last burial. And if I remember correctly there are one or two fairly recent headstones in the front where the path comes through to the porch door. And that's a wilderness.

'It's all got to be kept secret, just between us two. Whatever you do, don't let a word of it slip out to anybody else – even Jane or Effendi. Fran knows nothing at all, and Nigel will keep his mouth shut for his own sake, at least until Christmas is over.

'Now I must go, because I haven't seen Fran since breakfast-time, and she's more than concerned about something that's gone wrong at the Old Glebe.'

'So am I,' said Bob. 'Every time I look over that way there's a bird of prey waiting to swoop. I hate it. My Charlie's a Bridgefoot now as much as any of the others, though common sense tells me that whatever warning I have is meant for somebody with Bridgefoot blood. But I wish Charlie wasn't quite such a madcap on Ginger.'

'She won't have a lot of time for Ginger during this vacation,' William said, 'with her finals coming up in May.'

*   *   *

The next day Fran received a telephone call from Terence saying he wished to come round at once. She had an awful feeling that it was yet another chapter about the Bridgefoots. When he arrived there was a stranger with him.

'Gosh! What a looker!' said Fran to William, seeing them through a window. 'Must be his locum.'

'Very high-caste Indian – a Rajput, I imagine,' said William. 'He'll put the cat among all the female pigeons under thirty.' He let them in, the young doctor waiting with the polished manners of a courtier to be introduced.

'Fran, may I present to you Dr Jehan Chandra? Jehan, these are two of your patients for the next month, though they won't need you, but I suggest that if you find yourself a bit lost, you may need them. Dr William and Mrs Fran Burbage.'

The young man took Fran's hand in his own exquisitely delicate, long-fingered one, bowed over it, looked up at her, and smiled. Terry and William looked on with amusement as they watched her respond to his charm. He was tall and very slim and, Fran thought, like a beautiful piece of porcelain or a Rajah who ought to be sitting on a throne of gold. She was used to handsome young English doctors, had met many of the hearty, rugger-playing variety, and entertained a lot while they were still in the chrysalis stage of their studentship; but this was a one-off. His beautiful presence was magnetic, especially his hands, his finely moulded mouth – and those huge, jet-black, wonderful eyes. She made him welcome and suggested tea, but Terry said they had very little time and he'd come for their advice.

'First, though, I'm to deliver a message to you from Anthea. She's gone off at short notice to her parents to tell them the news. She sends her love and apologies for having to go without seeing you.

'Now that Jehan's here, I'm officially off duty, but naturally I had to introduce him to patients most likely to need him. He'll be able to call on me in an emergency, but I've got a hell of a lot of things to see to in a minimum of time.

'It's been a traumatic morning for him, though – not at all the easy, gentle English country practice I'd lured him to as a change from a busy London hospital. Not that he doesn't know England. He was born here and educated here, but in much more sophisticated surroundings than these. But I've landed him, and myself, into a mess that I've never met before, and don't know how to deal with. Temperance Farm.

'My leave began from today, and any of my partners at the Health Centre would have covered for me. But I'd better start at the beginning.

'Last night, John Postlethwaite came to see me, much shaken by an incident he'd been part of at the Old Glebe. He's not yet well enough to take much stress, but it seems he'd promised Marjorie that he'd stay with her in case she needed help.

'Sure enough, after it got dark, Pansy Gifford rang from Temperance wanting to speak to her mother. She'd got more to cope with on her hands than all her training as a carer had prepared her for.

'Rosemary was feeling the effects of the party, and didn't want to make the effort to get up. So Pansy made her comfortable and gave her one of the pills I'd left her. She dropped off to sleep, and slept on and off during the day, while Brian was out. When she heard him come in, she asked Pansy if she could have another pill, and did. She went to sleep again, and Pansy just let her.

'Then Pansy went to get Brian's meal ready. She thought he was in his office at the back of the house. She began to be a bit anxious when he didn't come so she went to look for him to tell him his tea was ready.

'What she found was a man gone all to pieces, worn out with crying. He told her he had the most awful headache he'd ever had in his life but didn't want Rosemary to know.

'She dealt with him as well as she could; gave him aspirins and made him eat something. He told her he'd had a row with his father and he didn't want her to leave him alone. She went to tell Rosy where she was, only to find that she couldn't rouse her. So when Brian went back again to maudlin tears, she slipped away pretending she had to go to the toilet, and rang her mother.

'Marjorie was having to deal with her parents – the story of the row was true – and she couldn't and wouldn't leave them. Nor could she leave young Pansy to cope single-handed at Temperance. Yorky, keeping his word to stand by, offered to go to Pansy, but Marjorie forbade that. So he told Pansy to phone him again if things didn't soon improve, and came to see me instead.

'Well, of course, he's my patient too, and the last thing I wanted was for him to flake out on them with one of his terrible panic attacks. But I knew the situation at Temperance – I had been shown the door and told never to set foot there again. Yorky was convinced he'd get the same treatment if he went near. I rang Temperance and mercifully Pansy answered. Rosemary was still fast asleep, and looked as if she'd sleep till morning; Uncle Bri was now also asleep in his chair. She guessed the aspirins had worked, and that he had worn himself out. His breathing was heavy and a bit noisy, but regular, though he "looked awful". A funny colour, sort of grey, she said. I had two choices: I could send the stand-by colleague from the Centre, or wait till this morning and send Jehan. I chose the second, as I thought it better for all their sakes.

'It was still only about six. I told Pansy to cover Brian up with blankets, and not try to wake him, if she was sure she dare stay there with both of them comatose till morning. I said sleep would do both more good than the awful scene that might ensue if I showed my face there when Brian was awake. She was a brick. She said she'd sit up all night herself if she had to – as long as Yorky did the same at Glebe, so she knew she could get him and her mother to her double quick in any emergency.

'Then I got on to Yorky at Glebe and explained to him; he said he already felt better and it was nothing new for him to doze in a chair all night. I promised him and Pansy that a doctor other than myself would be there by ten-thirty this morning, if I had had no more calls from them in the night.

'Jehan and I did a mercifully easy surgery together, and then I briefed him and took him up to Temperance, but stayed in the car on the road while he went to introduce himself.' There was a long pause.

'What happened?' asked Fran, almost scared to hear the reply.

The elegant young stranger answered. 'I'd been prepared for an irascible farmer who didn't care much for doctors, not for a raving maniac with a medico-phobia, if there is such a thing. At the first sight of me, he attacked me physically, yelling abuse which I won't repeat in front of a lady, and literally threw me out, bag and baggage, head over heels.'

'I should have known better,' Terence said. 'I'd never given it a thought that Brian might be a rabid racist! I rushed to Jehan's defence, and we got Brian back inside, and into his chair, still shaking with rage and growling unrepeatable abuse. We stood by till the worst was over, then I asked whether he would allow me to give him something to calm him down, or send for an ambulance to take him to hospital; I told him I thought he must be ill, and offered to get another of my partners to him at once.

'He told us both to get out, and to mind our own bloody business. He was never, as long as he lived, going to have a doctor across his doorstep again, nor go to consult one. By this time he was reasonably calm, but adamant. To have a doctor who wasn't English was the very last straw. He swore by every god in the pantheon that he meant every word he said – and that he would have his double-barrelled gun handy if I dared to go near the place again or send anybody else. He'd had enough of doctors when Charles was ill to last him for ever.

'He was more rational by then, and said grudgingly that he supposed he'd have to go on enduring his brother-in-law, Alex Marland, but that was his limit.

'So we retreated with our tails between our legs. Then I left Jehan to do a few more calls while I saw Anthea off, but by this time I had realized what a dilemma we all faced. In a case of a life-threatening condition, a doctor has the law on his side if he overrules the wishes of his patient, for example in the case of an unconscious Jehovah's Witness who must have an immediate blood transfusion, or die. But I don't know exactly how the law stands with regard to someone who refuses flatly to see a doctor professionally at all. I'm convinced that whatever else is wrong with him he also needs medical help, but I believe his civil rights protect him from having treatment thrust upon him unless he is a danger to others. Maybe Alex Marland will advise us – though I hear from Pansy that he's already said he'll have nothing to do with it.'

Dr Chandra spoke professionally for the first time. 'He said he would never have another doctor near him as long as he lived. I'm afraid my first clinical pronouncement would be to say that I think that may not be for very long.'

His words fell on the ears of the others like the tolling of a muffled bell in the stunned silence. Fran took in first the full implication of what the young doctor had said: that Brian might be really *ill* – and what his possible death could mean to everybody, as a ship running aground on a hidden shoal threatens not simply the captain, but the crew and all the passengers.

As always, she strove to hold off the moment of agony of understanding by reaching into her mind for words, but the warning bell went on tolling, like Kipling's 'Buoy Bell': '*Clangs the bell. "Shoal! 'Ware shoal!"'*

Her strained voice broke the silence as she quoted softly:

> '*By the gates of doom I sing*
> *On the horns of death I ride.*'

*   *   *

Fran's emotional reaction to Dr Chandra's remark surprised all of them, even William. He was used to her reliance on words at crucial moments, but he hadn't followed her quickly enough into what she called her fifth, or 'overdrive' gear. This wasn't at all the same as Bob's and (to some extent) Charlie's fey sixth sense. It was only that when she was already in an exalted, or conversely, a very low state of spirit, it seemed that all her senses were suddenly sharpened, and her mind made to work at excess speed.

She had been a bit worried at some of the things Eric had revealed yesterday, but unexpectedly and delightedly uplifted by the charm of Terry's locum, only to come crashing down again when he had made his casual suggestion that Brian might be ill – *clinically* ill. He, of course, could not possibly know the entire background to his first case, but she did, and her mind flew to the disastrous effects his diagnosis, if correct, could have. Not only to the Bridgefoots as a family, but as *the* family that Eric had said was the main pillar of stability in their village and community.

Without the Bridgefoot family at its centre, it could change as drastically as it had done after the fire at the Old Hall. Suppose Brian *should* be really ill, too ill to carry on farming? That would be the end of George, and she couldn't imagine Molly living long without him.

There would be only two options open to Bridgefoot Farms Ltd: to sell up, as the Thackerays had done, or for Charles to take the whole weight on to his young shoulders; which in turn would mean that his and Charlie's dreams would have to be abandoned, just as they were about to reach fruition. What would such a blow do to them – so heartwarmingly in love from the moment they had set eyes on each other – if Charles's sense of tradition and duty to his family pulled one way, and his love for Charlie and all they had planned for together the other way?

Would the dislocation of Bridgefoot expectations have the same effect as when tragedy had struck in the past? The only Thackeray left after the fire had never been seen in Old Swithinford again. It had been judged that he had had good reason for such complete abandonment of his roots – even George had thought so; but Tom and Cynthia Fairey, knocked out by grief at the death of their son Robert, had sold out to the unscrupulous developer, Arnold Bailey, who had built Lane's End Estate, and who had firmly intended to urbanize the rest of the village. His plans had been resisted, and he'd been beaten back, but his influence was still threatening all who wanted to keep their country style of living alive.

Brian would take the same route as the Faireys, if the decision were left to him. Faced with the possibility of having to give up the reins now that he had once felt them in his hands, he wouldn't hesitate. During his short flirtation with Bailey and 'business' (as opposed to farming), Mammon had gained a tight hold on him, and wouldn't let go. Charles, she knew, would fight side by side with his grandfather. Fran couldn't bear to contemplate such dissension in the family that had been, till now, a byword for its unity.

Nor would the rot stop there. When such tragedies struck, they were like ink spilt on blotting-paper, the stain spreading farther and farther.

Robbed of her dreams, would Charlie turn to Bob? How would that affect Effendi, and through him, Nick and Poppy?

Eric was unsettled already – and Elyot not proving himself the strong man they had thought him. Who else but he could champion Old Swithinford, threatened as it was now by bigger and more organized forces? How, without a strong man to lead them, could the Sophies and Dans, whose roots here probably went back to the time the Danes had come to Dane's Holme to bury their dead, and who still formed the base of the pyramid of traditional country life, be expected to stand against such go-getters as Greenslade, with his plans to modernize their environment?

This was Fran's 'overdrive gear' in reverse; when, as William said, she *would* 'go to meet trouble'. She always denied that, saying it came towards her, which William knew in essence to be true. She did attract people who were trouble, because she happened to love her fellow mortals. She reacted with her heart first, before giving her head a proper chance. She felt for those in distress so keenly that she suffered with them, and when there were too many of them and her load grew too heavy, it was often William who bore the brunt. He watched her showing signs of wilting, and was glad when Terence and Jehan took their leave, both quite uncomprehending of Fran's tragic-sounding outburst. They had different matters in mind.

As soon as he had closed the door behind them, William went to her and tried to comfort her, asking, because he truly had not understood, why she had sounded so anguished. She explained the chain of her thought.

'My darling,' he said, 'aren't you jumping the gun a bit? Young Chandra was rattled, or he wouldn't have expressed such an opinion to strangers – though one can't exactly blame him. It must have been a facer to find himself up against such virulent racial prejudice on his very first call.

'But you must keep it in proportion, sweetheart. His remark wasn't meant as a diagnosis, it was just a gut reaction to hit back. Brian isn't even ill, as far as we know – let alone dead. He's just having another fit of nastiness, probably because he hasn't yet been able to get all his own way. Wait and see what happens in the next few days before you toll the bell for him and all the rest of us. Come on now, promise me?'

She nodded, but told him he hadn't yet heard what else was making her feel down: Eric's disclosure that, without a word to her, Roland and Monica and the grandchildren were going off for a whole month over Christmas, doing her out of the family gathering she had hoped for. Kate and Jeremy would be taking their other grandchildren overseas – after which, if they saw them twice a year, they'd be lucky. But that was the fate of parents: children grew up and left, or stayed around, like Brian, and showed you how little you meant to them.

'It's at times like this,' she said, 'when poems that have stuck in my head make me realize how often such things happen. I recalled Henry Beeching's poem about "Fatherhood". The nonchalant way children leave or turn against parents who, as he says, "*would go through fire and water for their sake*". Or lie awake all night "*if but their little finger ache*".

'And what if such a parting is for ever? Then there's no way the parents can assuage their grief, no monument that will serve. That's the core of that poem, the grief of King David in the Bible, whose son rebelled against him and was killed. The father's grief is remembered to this day, not because of the huge pillar King David set up to be a memorial to his dead child, which crumbled to dust thousands of years ago, but because the King in his anguish cried it until the day was done. "*O Absalom, my son, my son!*"'

William sat down with her, and let her cry on his shoulder, stroking her hair and wiping her tears away. For some things, there is no comfort.

It was one of his greatest private griefs that his family line would end with him, but he had never till that minute actually felt the pain of what might have been, especially if a lost son of his had been Fran's as well. But what of all those other parents who lost sons in two world wars ... splendid young men like Mac who had been his special friend? No. He dared not let himself think of what Mac's parents had felt, or of what he had lost. He just held on to what he'd got, and in the growing dusk let her cry herself to sleep in his arms.

*   *   *

It was not to be expected that what was going on in the Bridgefoot family would escape the notice of the village, and not be added to the raft of rumour already afloat.

George was sunk in such distress and apathy that he could hardly bear to drag himself outside to talk to Daniel; Molly was in tears most of her time, which was so unlike her that Marjorie began to fear for her, and lost heart with every hour that passed. She also felt guilty at her neglect of Rosemary, but she couldn't forgive Brian, and stayed away from him so as not to make matters worse. She was also grieving because Pansy, for whom she had been yearning so long, was forced to stay away from her, instead of being where they could heal their long breach.

Pansy had gone willingly enough on Saturday to care for her sick aunt, but no one expected her to have to stay there indefinitely, especially with an uncle who was either in a vile temper or so sorry for himself that he took more looking after than her aunt did. Doctors had come to try to help, and had received unbelievable treatment. Any or all other medical help was banned.

But she was trapped at Temperance Farm; she often had to stand between her invalids, and didn't dare risk leaving them together even to visit her mother and grandparents, having no means of transport other than Shanks's pony. Besides, she didn't know how much of what went on at Temperance she ought to tell them at Glebe, for instance what had happened when the doctors had visited.

She knew that any of them with a car at their disposal – except her mother – would understand her predicament, and be willing to take her place for an hour or two; but anyone else in his house threw her uncle into a violent temper. Any mention of the uninvolved but helpful Yorky inflamed him to uncontrollable anger. She had to let sleeping dogs lie for as long as she could hold out, and though it already seemed ages to her, it was in fact only a matter of a few days yet. But it was not the homecoming she had envisaged.

Her mother had said not to let Charles know, if they could possibly keep it from him till things cooled down a bit. He'd never got on well with his father, and would take his grandfather's side. Better, Marjorie had considered, to let the matter blow over than have the family split right down the middle; but Marjorie had known it couldn't be very long before Charles turned up at the Old Glebe. How much she then dared tell him, she couldn't decide.

Luck was on her side. Charlie was going to be at home for a whole month, instead of just at weekends. They had given out that they would have to ration social events this Christmas, because Charlie needed time to revise, and they were also at the stage of having to set up the next phase of their plans, such as what alterations they would have to make at Danesum to provide living accommodation for a qualified vet as well as meeting all regulations for starting up a veterinary practice there.

George was yearning for a sight of his grandson, but hoping at the same time that Charles would stay away a bit longer, till things settled down. Time was, after all, very young since the barn incident, and he couldn't help hoping that Brian would come round. It did no good to brood over one trouble long enough to hatch out a whole clutch of new ones. The friction between his son and his grandson needed to be smoothed over, not roughed up by anything fresh. He tried not to grieve too much, but the spring was lost from his step, and the twinkle had gone from his eye.

Danesum, being the most isolated of the family's homes, was the least likely to hear gossip by chance. To Charles it was paradise when Charlie was there, and he had no particular wish to leave it for a single minute longer than he had need to. If Grandad or Gran wanted him for any reason, they'd ring. His ignorance of what had happened since Saturday consequently left him in bliss. But not so Charlie.

She'd picked trouble out of the air at the party on Saturday, and as four days went by without contact either way, she grew more and more uneasy. Then, on the Thursday morning, while Charles was out, there came a telephone call from a distraught Pansy, begging for help and advice. In Pansy's opinion, it was high time Charles took a hand.

Charlie knew only too well that she herself would be the last person Brian would have any time for, and she longed to protect Charles from involvement, at least till the worst of the heat had gone out of the quarrel. She sympathized with Pansy, and promised to do all she could to help; but in turn asked Pansy to stick it out at Temperance for a few more hours while she thought out the best way of dealing with it.

Pansy agreed on condition that 'a few more hours' meant sometime later that day. She said that things had been slightly better at Temperance, insofar as Uncle Brian's headaches had subsided a lot and he had been out once or twice, though, as far as she understood, nowhere near Glebe; and while he had been out last night, she and Aunt Rosy had played Scrabble together quite happily. However, this morning, he was like a bear with a sore behind again, and so nasty to Aunt Rosy that all she could do was to sit and cry.

'I'm sorry to bother you, Charlie,' Pansy said, 'but Mum's got more than enough on her plate with Gran and Grandad, and I can't take much more of this by myself. After all, they're Charles's mother and father, not mine.'

Nor were they Charlie's. She knew how difficult her father-in-law could be. Charles's mother had bowed to her husband with regard to his objection to Charlie as their son's wife, but Charlie remembered that when the crunch came, she had taken her son's side. So Charlie could forgive and forget, but the wounds he had received from his father at that time had gone too deep for Charles to be as magnanimous. However, there had been peace and good-will among them on the surface, and all had been tolerably happy.

Charlie made up her mind. She wanted to know what her own father would advise. So that afternoon she left Charles a note, to the effect that on such a fine day her books could wait, and she was going to take Ginger out for a bit of exercise – probably up to Castle Hill.

She came upon Bob in the churchyard, leaning on a scythe. He was so obviously relieved to see her that she wondered at once what new bee was worrying him now. For an early December day, it was mild, bright and sunny, with a clarity of light that showed up all nature's winter beauty in every sharp detail. The trees were bare and, as Greg had said when he had painted his now famous picture of Aunt Sar'anne, at the peak of their essential beauty. Rooks, hanging in the air against the pale blue of the afternoon sky, looked as if they had been painted there; and the long grass around Bob's feet was just moving in the slight breeze, as if caressing the blade of the scythe: the victim on the scaffold, feeling the edge of the headsman's axe. Bob stood still, and waited for his daughter to come to him.

'What on earth are you doing here with a scythe at this time of the year?' she asked him.

'What are you doing here at all?' he countered.

'Wanting to talk to you,' she said.

He made no comment, but propped the scythe up by the wall of the church porch, found the key among the ivy, and invited her in to sit with him in his favourite spot, just where the sun came through a clear glass window where once there had been a magnificent picture in medieval stained glass.

'You begin,' he said. 'I was only tiffling about, 'cos I like to be here in the afternoon when the rooks come home, and nothing else is spoiling. What's the matter?'

She told him. 'I ain't surprised,' he said. 'I'd heard something o' the sort. Jane's busy helping Jess and Beth with this concert at Fenley School, and I took her down to the Old Rectory yesterday so as I could bring the littl'uns back out of her way and look after them myself. Beth and Jess were full of what they'd heard about the goings-on at Glebe – no doubt with a few extras as usual.

'That's what bothers me. How do such tales get out? There's a traitor in the camp somewhere, but for the life of me I can't imagine who it is as knows everything in the first place, and then makes damn sure that Brian knows as well. That chap they call Yorky's the obvious suspect 'cos he very nearly lives up at Old

Glebe, sitting up all night, they say, in case Pansy should need his help at Temperance. But it don't hold water, to me. He hardly ever leaves the Glebe, and don't know folks round here to gossip to. That cock won't fight.

'Then there's that woman as works up at Benedict's now, but why on earth should she want to cut her nose off to spite her face? That don't make sense, either. Gossip's one thing, but this ain't just gossip for the sake o' gossip. I reckon as somebody's got it in for the Bridgefoots, and wants to down 'em, hook, line and sinker. Ruin all that they stand for, and take 'em down a peg. But why?'

He sat quiet for a while, communing with himself and what he usually referred to as 'his ghosts'.

'I'm worried,' he said, ''cos you're a Bridgefoot now. And I'm having bad dreams – very near nightmares, every time I drop off to sleep. It's so mixed up yet as I can't make head nor tail of it: Bridgefoots and Elyot Franks and a bird of prey and Ginger. Anybody with one eye in the pot and the other up the chimney can see as Beth Franks is worrying herself to death about Elyot. Is there some scandal about him mixed up with all the rest?

'Effendi interviewed a woman from Hen Street about this typing job for him and William and says she spent most of her time quizzing him about Elyot.' He grinned. 'She didn't know who she was dealing with. Effendi smelt a rat, and he's a lot cleverer at asking questions than most folk. He gathered that she was campaigning for that chap Greenslade. Effendi decided on the spot that she wouldn't be suitable for him. Not that that matters – there ain't much sense in either him or William setting themselves up to start writing till Christmas is over. It's 'cos of what William told me as I'd got the scythe with me. Besides helping Dobson to please myself, William said as the Rector's worried 'cos they ain't going to be able to use the church at Old Swithinford for Christmas Morning Communion, so he'll perhaps hold it up here. William's all'us ferreting about in libraries and such about this little old church, 'cos we don't want to see it bulldozed down. One thing as interested me was what he said about the graveyard having different rules from the building.

309

Depends when the last burial took place what you can do with it. So seeing what sort of afternoon it was, I thought I might as well spend it tidying up the front bit o' the churchyard where the latest graves are and seeing what I could make out from the headstones, besides making it tidy for them as may have to come here a-Christmas Morning while I were about it. We may be up to our hocks in snow by then.'

He sat in profound silence, which Charlie understood too well to speak again until he did. 'There's two things as I reckon have got to be seen to straight away,' he said. 'One's only a bit o' plain common sense, as I see it. I always have thought as people like me and old George and your Charles as work outside, with our feet on the earth and our heads under the trees and the sky, think a lot clearer than them as sit at desks staring at books with their heads in a bushel o' figures and business and politics and such. Somebody's got to find out who it is as is making such a hormpolodge about them at Glebe, and what it is they're after.

'Seems to me as Eric Choppen's the man to find out. He ain't altogether a countryman, but he ain't really a "furriner" either. And I take Fran Burbage's word for it that though the Bridgefoots seem to be off hooks with him, he ain't the man to wish 'em any harm. But whoever is there as does? Still, there's no mistake as somebody does, and we're got to find out who it is.

'Then there's my nightmares. Seems to me as I'm being warned that however bad it is up Glebe now, it's got to get worse afore it's better. There's that old bird circling round over Glebe, big as a buzzard or a kite, only there ain't been nothing bigger than a sparrow-hawk round here for many and many a year. But it's gliding about in circles, like they do, else it's hovering high up ready to swoop on somebody when the time comes. Might be you.

'When I heard about you showing off a-Saturday like you did with that new bull, I nearly had a fit. I woke up in a sweat, next night. I thought as the big animal as was all'us there as well as the bird had to be Ginger, and I ain't sure it ain't, yet. So no more risky tricks like that, my beauty, for my sake. How did you come up now? On Ginger?'

'Yes, Dad, but for heaven's sake, you needn't worry about that! I saddled him and just hacked up here. Why?'

'I wish you'd promise me not to ride him at all between now and Christmas.'

She protested, hotly, 'Don't be silly, Dad. You know he's as sure-footed as a cat, and he's got to be exercised. Besides, I'm not a real Bridgefoot, only one by marriage. Why should I be in any danger?'

'Because you're a mad-cat who ain't afraid of anything. And 'cos you and Charles are the Bridgefoots I care about most. I'm asking you not to take risks till I'm sure what's happening. Get somebody else to exercise Ginger.'

'And let them take the risk? Come on, Dad, that wouldn't be fair! Besides, you know I can handle a horse as well as anybody round here, man or woman.'

'Yes – that's what I mean. You're the one who'll take one risk too many, if I can't stop you while there's still time. I feel sure you'll be mixed up in something to do with a farmyard. Ginger comes to mind 'cos you're too sure o' yourself where he's concerned. He's only got to put his foot in a rabbit-hole. I'm just asking you to be careful.'

She cuddled up close to him, and sat silent as he waited for her promise.

'You know I believe in your dreams,' she said. 'In fact, it was something like that that sent me here to see you this afternoon. I wanted to ask you whether or not I ought to tell Charles all that Pansy told me.'

'Yes.' His answer was pat and positive. 'And tell him I told you to. Tell Charles his grandad is yearning for a sight of him, but I urge him to keep out of the row as he can and not take sides too soon.'

Charlie kissed him. It was one of her great delights that she'd never had to choose between her father and her husband. They'd understood each other from the very beginning, linked by their love for her.

'I've got to ring Pansy when I get home. She says Charles's mum doesn't really need her now at nights, but wants her to stay in case his dad flies into one of his rages. She's hardly seen her mother yet, but she hasn't got a car and has to walk from Temperance to Glebe . . . Dad! Why don't I lend her Ginger? She knows what to do with a horse nearly as well as I do, so I can trust her with him. Besides, she's so different from what she used to be, calm and dependable, but sad. I wonder if riding's one of the things she's been missing?

'I think she wanted more time before she had to come back. She has to show that she's independent, and get some of her Bridgefoot identity back. Make people forget that she was ever so much mixed up with the Bailey gang as she was.

'Think, Dad! If you're afraid to let me ride Ginger, I won't, but he needs exercise and I think he could help Pansy. Oh, Dad, do let me try. Charles's dad mightn't be so nasty to his mum if there wasn't somebody else there all the time. He may have got it into his head that he's being spied on! Charles's mum's convinced that he's got another woman, and I must say he does seem to have sex on his mind! Why, unless he has something himself to hide?'

Bob stood up. 'I reckon you've got our old fen feyness more than I thought,' he said. 'Yes. Let Pansy have Ginger. That makes sense. Are you going? I'll come and see you off.'

She leaned out of the saddle to kiss him, and he watched her ride away. He felt better. Charlie was a girl in a million in so many ways. He could stake his life that she would never break her word to anybody she loved.

*

Charles was waiting for her when she arrived home, and took Ginger from her to stable him. By the time he came in again, she was ready to tell him the whole sad tale.

His first reaction was one of fierce, raging anger. It was the bursting of the dam of antipathy towards his father that he had had to suppress so many times in the past for his mother's sake. But he was not just their son any longer: he was a man, with a farm and a home and a wife of his own, besides being the next Bridgefoot in line to inherit the land, the reputation, and their place in the Old Swithinford hierarchy.

312

Angry as he was about the way his mother was being treated, it hurt him more to know how his idiot of a father had turned on his beloved grandfather. That was more than he could take. It had been such refined cruelty, to strike at the very roots of George's place in the community: his long and faithful service to the church he loved.

'I'm going up to see Grandad,' Charles said. 'You can tell me all the rest when I come back.'

She caught his hand and held him back. 'No, darling. Wait and hear the rest of what Dad said, now.'

He looked down at her, and gave in. 'All right, my lambkin,' he said, sitting down beside her. 'I hardly know what I'm doing, but I'll try to listen.'

She gave him a word by word account of her conversation with her father. Frustrating as it was to Charles, whose one desire was to get to his grandad there and then, his affection and respect for Bob held him in check.

'He's probably right,' he said. 'He says we must find out who it is that's got it in for us Bridgefoots so bad that he'll stoop low enough to kick Grandad when he's down. If I had any idea who it could be, I'd go and wring his neck this minute!'

She cleverly turned the point, telling him of her father's nightmares and her suggestion of lending her horse to Pansy. 'It seems that this Greenslade man isn't one to let the grass grow under his feet, and Dad says Elyot Franks is nearly off his head about something. Dad can't imagine why, but he'd been thinking about it because Beth is showing signs of distress, and she's expecting a baby – you know what an old softy Dad is! He thinks Eric Choppen's the chap most suited to do a bit of detective work and find out who the troublemaker is. Dad's pretty sure it's real underhand skulduggery, not just gossip got out of hand.

'But he's having premonitions about things. That's why I've made him a promise that I won't go mad on Ginger till he tells me it's all right again – so you needn't worry about me.' She gave him the sort of smile that would have made a basilisk smile back at her. 'He's not at all pleased with what he's heard about my little

313

harmless escapade with Chum. Been having nightmares ever since, he says.'

Charles had calmed down a lot. 'It was never intended that Pansy should have to bear the brunt of looking after Mum, let alone Dad as well, when she offered to go to help Aunt Marge out on Saturday night. I'd rather you didn't ride Ginger, either, if that's the way your dad feels. Ring Pansy and tell her while I change to go out.'

She was on her feet in an instant. 'Charles – not to Glebe, yet! Dad begged you not to!'

'No, lambkin, but I've got to do something. I can't just sit here and think. When I've been in this sort of trouble before – twice – I've headed for Benedict's, and got all the help and advice I needed there. Come with me.'

*

Fran and William, pleased if surprised to see them, listened with patience and a great deal of sympathy to the narrative as told by both at once, Charles in alternating moods of anger and distress at what his grandfather must be thinking of him, and Charlie putting him right when feelings caused him to exaggerate, but never for a moment losing her cool appraisal of the damage to all of them if unity among them were not soon restored.

Fran and William thought it wise not to let Charles know the extent to which they were already apprised of the situation, and let him talk: but they were quick to take in that Charlie understood it all a great deal better than her husband did.

They backed her up entirely in her wish to keep Charles from rushing round to see his grandfather straight away, and praised her for agreeing to her father's request about not riding Ginger. To let Pansy have him was a splendid idea.

'Don't act on impulse over this, Charles,' Fran said. 'There are so many other people's feelings to be considered besides your own. Think of your gran, and Aunt Marjorie, as well as Pansy – but most of all, your mum. She's probably suffering worse than your grandad. If you go round there tonight, as upset as you are now, you'll make things worse. Sleep on it. Tomorrow is another day.'

'Besides,' added William, 'I think that Bob's on the right track.

If we can get any sort of clue that it is really a deliberate bit of sabotage, and who's behind it, we should at least have something for Eric to work on – if he'll agree to be used as our private investigator. Bob's right about him being our best bet. So hold your horses for the rest of today, cool down a bit, and go to see your grandad in the morning.

'When you were determined to die, and we were determined that you shouldn't, we found out the hard way how difficult your dad can be about doctors. It may be a genuine phobia, you know – and people with phobias simply can't control their reactions. They don't mean to be sick on the carpet at the sight of a beetle, or jump screaming on to the table at the sight of a mouse – reason doesn't enter into it. Give your dad the benefit of the doubt. You may find he's already been to put things right with your grandad. Give us another twenty-four hours to see if we can come up with any sort of reason behind any of it.'

'Yes, that's sound advice, Charles,' Fran added. 'Take him home, Charlie. If there is anything we can do to help, you know we'll do it.'

It amounted almost to a dismissal, but the two youngsters left, soothed if not satisfied. Fran had gathered that William was playing for time and had aided and abetted him. The car was barely through the gates before they were asking each other how to set about the task they had imposed upon themselves.

William was for ringing Eric at once, and asking him to come round. Fran said not till they had tapped their hotline to Glebe through Sophie and Dan. Ring Eric by all means and ask him if he could possibly spare time for a private conference, but next morning, after Fran had had time to glean more from Sophie. William agreed, and Eric was willing. He didn't ask questions, from which William deduced that he was on the ball as to what it was about.

*

Next morning, Fran found that Sophie, as always, was unwilling to reveal anything till she had made her obligatory speech denying that she ever repeated anything she didn't know the truth of. For once, Fran was short with her.

'This isn't just gossip, Sophie. It's serious. Somebody's trying to wreck the whole Bridgefoot family. Charles only heard about the row yesterday, and Pansy's very upset, too. We haven't heard from Marjorie but we can guess the state she's in. Now: Dan's there all the time, and if George has turned to anybody in his distress, it will be Dan. We want to help if we can. Will you help us to help them, and tell me what you know if I ask you a few questions?'

The tears were already running down Sophie's face at the thought of what Dan had described of George's despair and Molly's overload of grief. She nodded, and Fran breathed a sigh of relief.

'We guessed that Dan would want to tell somebody, and who would it be but you? Brian's been difficult before, but never like this. Can you remember when he began to be so nasty to his father? Was it before or after Rosemary had her accident? He seemed then to be very worried about her.'

Sophie sniffed. That told Fran a lot. 'No. It started afore that. Soon as George told 'im that 'im and Dan had decided to hev a bull o' their own, instead of relying on that there artificial insemnification. Dan never did care to trust that. Brian put hisself out time and time again with 'is father, but George took it all in good part.

'"I'm spending my own money, ain't I?" he'd say. "I don't interfere when you buy new cars." But, as Dan said when 'e were telling me, tha's where Brian and 'is father is so different. Since that time as Brian got mixed up wi' Vic Gifford and them Baileys, seems the only thing 'e cares about is money. Dan 'eard 'im mutter under 'is breath as that were it, there weren't no call for George to spend no more than he need, 'cos time would soon come when everything would be 'is'n, and 'is dad hadn't got no right to rob 'im of a penny afore 'e ever got it. Dan never told nobody but me about that! It's just what the Bible says, though, ain't it, about the love of money being the root of all evil? Then – still afore Rosy 'ad that there haccident – George put in 'and them alterations to the farmyard cluss to the 'ouse, so as to hev a proper up-to-date place to put a bull when he found one as he liked.

'Brian 'ad words with George about that an' all. George said as 'e was only doing up some o' the old buildings as they'd agreed he was to have with the bit o' land as 'e kept for 'isself and Dan to tiffle about on. And Brian swore – on 'is Bible oath, Dan said – as 'e'd never agreed to no such thing. All the buildings, especially the barn, was 'is'n. And if George done as 'e said 'e was a-gooing to, and made a place for the cows and another for the bull there, 'ow did he think 'e was to get his big new implements and things as 'e'd ordered past it down to the other big yard and the barn and all the rest as was 'is'n now?

'Seems Brian said as 'ow 'e'd ordered a great new combine harvester – from Russia! Dan never believed 'im. He thought Brian was just a-showing off, like, 'cos that big farmer the other side o' Swithinford whose daughter 'e'd set 'is 'eart on Charles marrying is just got one from Russia as cost *thirty-five thousand pound*!

'So Dan reckoned as it were all bravoation, and Brian were only a-bragging to show Charles what 'e missed, by marrying Charlie Bellamy-as-was like 'e did. Dan ain't 'eard no more about that combine since. Then come that haccident, as weren't Rosemary's fault at all, though she 'ad to stop abed. Well, you know as well as I do as Marge'd hev laid 'er life down for Brian till then, and she left 'er own 'ome to goo and do every mortal thing as she could for 'im and Rosy. But it weren't long afore George were telling Dan as Brian was a-losing 'is temper all the while with Rosy, shouting at 'er as there weren't nothing wrong with 'er bad enough that she couldn't get up and do for 'erself and 'im if she would.'

Sophie dropped her voice again, along with more tears, but she went on. 'Dan said George said as 'e couldn't but believe as Rosy was frit at 'er own 'usband! Them as 'ad been so 'appy together for so long. Marge 'ad to stop down at Temperance day and night 'cos Brian put 'isself out so when 'e wanted to go out of a hevening, and bawled at the top of 'is voice as neither 'is wife nor nobody else'd stop 'im gooing where he wanted to when he wanted.

'Marge 'erself told Dan as Rosy asked 'er if 'e'd got another woman! Marge wouldn't hear nothing o' that sort against Bri, as she all'us calls 'im, but she did think as it could be that if Rosy 'ad got such a thing into 'er 'ead, it was that as was 'olding 'er back. Y'see, Dr Hardy couldn't understand why she were so low. Marge could ha' told 'im, but she'd promised Rosy as it should never pass 'er lips – though come to think on it, she did tell Dan.

'And then Brian turned nasty with the doctor, as was doing all 'e could, making out first as there were no need for 'im to visit as often as 'e did and he only went 'cos 'e was sweet on Rosy 'isself. Then 'e changed 'is mind and said as it were Marge as the doctor went there to see. There weren't no truth in none o' that – and whatever Brian were a-doing it for, we shall never know.

''Owsomever, there were that there Golden Wedding a-coming up and, well, you know what went on that day, and 'ow Brian sp'iled it when 'e wouldn't goo and look at the bull, and made Rosy goo 'ome afore she was ready. Then Marge was so tired and upset she couldn't face gooing up Temperance, so Pansy as 'ad come back all so hunexpected went instead. Fancy 'er a-coming 'ome so changed as all that! George told Dan that whatever Brian 'ad said or done to 'im that day, nothing could sp'ile it for 'im. With Pansy back, 'is fam'ly was whull again, and 'is cup runneth over.

'But it didn't last long. Bri set for Marge one morning about 'er goings-on wi' men till she couldn't put up with it no longer. She give 'im as good as she got, and Dan says nothing'll never be the same atween 'em again.

'What'll become of it all – or any of us – I don't know, seeing as 'ow we shan't even be able to go to church come Christmas. I don't know what the world's a-coming to, that I don't.'

Fran had found Sophie's story enlightening, though she had noted two rather pointed omissions. Sophie had said no word about Yorky, nor had she referred to Brian's behaviour at the sight of Jehan Chandra. Was that deliberate on Sophie's part?

Fran knew that if her tale included even the remotest allusion to anything of a sexual nature, Sophie would get round it if she could. She interpreted the omission of any reference to Yorky as proof that Sophie believed 'there was something in it' between Marge and Yorky, and that she certainly didn't approve of it.

They were interrupted by William and Olive, bearing cups of coffee. Fran nearly laughed aloud. She couldn't decide whether William's curiosity had got the better of him, or whether it was Olive's incessant gabble that had moved him to bring coffee-time an hour forward.

'Can we stop and drink our coffee here?' he inquired. 'Mrs Hopkins has been telling me something I think may be to the point.' They all turned towards Olive.

She was drying her hands over and over again on her apron, till Sophie lost patience and ordered her sharply to say what she'd got to say if she must, and then get back to work. ''Ow come you to know anythink about what goes on up at the Glebe?' she asked. 'Seems to me as you're all'us about wheer you can 'ear somethink as you can talk about afterwards. What was you doing 'anging about outside Glebe this time?'

'It were nowheer near Glebe,' said Olive, bridling, and for once sticking up for herself. 'It were night afore last, and when I went from 'ere I walked up to hev a word o' two with Beryl as I used to work for, but she said she hadn't got no time for me 'cos 'er Ken was coming 'ome from work early to 'ev 'is tea and be ready to goo to the meeting. So I arst what meeting, and she said one as was called special in Hen Street 'cos it were to do wi' the henvirament. She was real excited about it and said as if they got their way, 'er and 'er Ken would likely get back all as Bob Bellamy and that hundertaker as is 'is father-in-law had stole from 'em a year or two ago.

'The proper man as did ought to ha' took the meeting weren't well, so that there Mr Greenslade as'll be a-taking 'is place come May were going to be the chairman. From what I could make out, they are got to make Swithinford bigger – and what they want to do is build twenty-five thousand new 'ouses round 'ere. Making it all one with Swithinford, is what I mean – 'specially as there ain't no church now this way as folks can go to if they want to.

'"Urbandize" is what I think Beryl said they wanted to do to it, but I never could remember new words. Miss laughed at me once when I were at school and it come to my turn to say the Lord's Prayer, 'cos though I knowed it well enough, seems as I said, "Lead us not into Thames Station" and Miss stopped me and asked me if I thought it were the next stop along the line from Swithinford Station. I remembered that 'cos she made all the others laugh at me. 'Ow was I to know wheer it was? To this day I'm never been on a train further than from Swithinford to St Ives. But whatever this 'ere urbandizing is, there's a lot o' folks as is against it, and tha's what the meeting were all about. As I 'eard it, if such as Beryl and Ken get their way, and Ken plays 'is cards right, they'll get the contracts for supplying the materials, and we should get all the fass-fass-fassinations – no, that ain't right – the fassillything-me-bobs as we all ought to hev now, same as they do in towns. Like bingo 'alls, and them big shops as sell everythink – soupmarkets or some such – and proper schools as 'ave swimming pools, and buses laid on for the children to goo to see football matches in London and I don't know what-all. Well, so Beryl said. And then she said as if I liked I could come 'ome and tell Commander Franks as 'e could put that in 'is pipe and smoke it, 'cos it were all cut and dried without 'im interfering – though what it's got to do with 'im, she never said. And just then as I were a-coming out o' Beryl's shop, her new friend as is called Gwen Bonnet were going in, so I 'eld the door open for 'er and listened to what she were a-telling Beryl. She's comed to live in Hen Street lately, see, and they are got very thick. She 'eard what Beryl said to me about Commander Franks and laughed. She said she'd found out a lot about 'im from wheer she'd been – to see some posh old fogey as she's applied for a job with and 'ad arranged a hinterview afore she'd been give the job as Mr Greenslade's champagne secretary. So she'd gone to see 'im and made it 'er business to quiz 'im about Mr Franks. Beryl said as she needn't a-took all that trouble 'cos there wasn't much she couldn't tell 'em about the Commander herself – only then she catched sight o' me still there, and asked me what I were a-standing gawping at, 'cos what her and Miss Bonnet was going to talk about was private.'

320

'So is what me and Mis' Burbage is talking about private,' said Sophie severely, 'so goo you and get that kitchen made tidy.'

Olive went, and Fran told Sophie that they were expecting Mr Choppen around eleven o'clock. As it was nearly that now, would Sophie please make sure Olive was kept far enough out of the way for her not to hear anything that was said? She thanked Sophie for telling them what she had, and assured her that if they did have to pass on anything she had told them, they would keep her name out of it. She was satisfied, but stalwart in her stand for the welfare and reputation of the Bridgefoots. 'I ain't told no lies,' she said, 'and I don't care who you tell as long as it'll help George an' them. It's liars like Beryl Bean and them as you hev to be ware of. Lawks, what is that woman a-doing of now?'

It was only Olive's voice raised in singing – having nobody there to talk at. William cocked his ear. 'Good heavens!' he said. 'She must be excited! She's giving poor Rose-Marie a rest! Unless my ear and my memory fail me, she is now serenading Rio Rita!'

He let Eric in, still smiling.

*

While William produced drinks, Fran explained. Things were getting worse by the hour, shattering the Bridgefoot family and, as they had already agreed, in a way liable to affect the entire community. 'It's like a deadly virus,' Fran said. 'Everybody passes it on to everybody else, and nobody knows how or where it started. So we're no nearer to the truth, or who it is that's doing his best to bring the Bridgefoots down – and for what possible reason. But we have got a few more details, via Sophie and Olive 'Opkins, this morning, as well as gleaning a bit from Charles and Charlie yesterday.'

'I don't hear any details,' Eric said. 'But I think perhaps if we pool all that we've heard, we may be able to see some sort of pattern in it. As you know, I've been elbowed out of the family circle, as it were, just lately. So you start, and I'll listen.'

They told him, as briefly as possible, of what Fran herself had heard from Marjorie; of Pansy's outburst to Charlie; of Charlie's visit to Bob and his presentiment that something was seriously wrong at the Old Glebe. Then they gave him the gist of Sophie's confidences, and the rather unexpected entry of Olive into the picture, along with Ken and Beryl Bean, and the new female who had 'quizzed' Effendi about Elyot. Eric sat silent, listening intently.

'What beats me,' said Fran, 'is what on earth it's all for, whoever the quisling turns out to be! Why should George Bridgefoot buying a bull set us all back on our heels like this? Why has Brian turned on his sister, who's been his best ally till now, and make out she's a middle-aged woman gone sex-crazy, a danger to any man who happens to drift into her orbit? We know – or at least I know, from Yorky, directly, the truth of the tale about him comforting her and how by sheer chance Olive saw and reported that incident. But I'd stake my life that it isn't Olive who's stirred the rest up. She hasn't the sense to add two and two together, never mind setting up a formula for making mischief. I'd go bail for Yorky myself – I grant that he's there in the middle of it and knows everything as it happens, but where could he spread such tales? He knows so few people here, and hardly moves from Glebe because he's given his word to Pansy to be on hand if she should need help. Who else is there that can possibly know what's said and done well enough to broadcast it all over the place? And why, why, why?'

'Don't get distressed, my darling,' said William. 'That's what we're here for: to see if we can find the answer to questions like that. I've been thinking about Brian. I had a good deal to do with him when Charles was ill. I think we have to take his nature and his place in the family into account before condemning him – even for standing up to his father in what is after all only a clash between old and new.

'How old is he? Somewhere around the fifty mark now, I should think. Is he having a male mid-life crisis? Afraid of losing his virility, at a time when his wife has been knocked out of action? He's never seemed a very happy man, at least since I've known him, and he's always seemed a rather jealous one. That's what I mean about taking some notice of his past life and its effect on a personality like his before making too much of his bid for freedom from family tradition. After the awful pre-war years of the agricultural depression, farmers made too much money, too fast, in the boom years of the war. It went to a lot of heads besides his.

'But farming now isn't what it has been, and he's worried by that, as well as finding himself an odd-man-out in his family. His father isn't money-minded, and his son has no need to worry about it now if he ever was, which he wasn't. So Brian's taking his frustration out on them – and the village is making the most of it. Isn't it just one of those things that time will cure?'

Fran said, looking thoughtful, 'I told George, about a couple of years ago when he came to me in distress, that however much it went against his grain and the Bridgefoot tradition, it was time he handed things over to Brian. To be the heir to the throne when you're past fifty and still with no prospect of succeeding can't be a very happy position to be in. When at last Brian did get the reins into his hands, Charles was twenty-one and made a partner, as well as becoming his own boss at Danesum.

'That riled Brian, I know. He'd had so many years of being pig-in-the-middle between his father and his son – but Charles stepped right over that stage. It irked Brian all the more because it was through Rosemary insisting on giving her shares direct to Charles that he became so independent. It's still galling him. So is the fact that Bob Bellamy, his spurned daughter-in-law's father, is now his farming equal. To sum Brian up: I think he's suffering frustration because his expectation of being absolute boss is now no longer achievable. I suppose that's at the bottom of this business about the bull: his father is doing as he likes without reference to him, and so is his son. But that doesn't give us any clue as to why he should turn on Marjorie. She'd have been on his side.'

'It's the personal details that get in the way of that theory, sweetheart. Rosemary thinks he's having an affair with somebody else. Sophie reports that he flies into a temper if he can't go "hout of a hevening" – but where does he want to go? Pansy says he sits and cries, which doesn't sound at all like a Bridgefoot!

'And somebody is kicking all these tales around in the village, upsetting everybody. That's why Bob suggested that you might do a bit of detective work for us, Eric. You have your ear to the ground, and you know what it is that makes men tick. If we could put a stop to the rumours, and prevent them getting worse, I think it would probably die a natural death, and perhaps even bring Brian to his senses.'

Eric was looking a bit worried, and when at last he spoke, his words were hesitant, but serious. 'I think everything you've said may be perfectly true, but I'm afraid I don't think it's the whole answer. As to my becoming your detective – some of that role has been forced on me already, or I wouldn't even consider it. I'm too fond of the Bridgefoots for one thing – but whatever excuses you make for Brian's other behaviour, I regard this attack on his father as insufferable. I can only put forward three possible reasons for it. One is that the "other woman" theory may be the right one and, if so, he's wallowing in guilt and an awkward situation he doesn't know how to get out of. Then there's a possibility that he has been going slowly round the bend for a long time. Nobody will admit how seriously off-beat for a Bridgefoot his behaviour is, and was when Charles was so ill. His tantrums lately aren't those of a reasonable man with the least scrap of love or respect for his family.

'But there's still the third possibility, which is that he has some deep ulterior motive. Fran asked the crucial question: how comes it that our quisling – good word for it, Fran – always manages to be able to vouch for the truth of the rumours? That whoever it is, Brian is willing to listen and believe what he hears? Leaving out Bob's bit of intuition, what do you two make of it?'

'Complete mystery,' Fran said, shaking her head.

'Not to me,' Eric replied, 'but I'd rather you had worked it out than left it for me to make what amounts to an accusation. Ask yourselves who is most likely to be bettered by changes in the Bridgefoot tradition – and who manages to be somewhere on the spot whenever and wherever an incident takes place? The constant factor?'

William, more willing than Fran to follow Eric's reasoning, said, slowly and reluctantly, 'Of course. Brian himself. But for God's sake, *why*?'

Fran was quiet, too stunned to speak, but with growing fear that Eric might be right. She swiftly ran over all she knew, and saw that it made sense. The only two things that didn't tie in were Elyot's changed attitude and Olive's bit of gossip about the 'henvirament' meeting called at such short notice in Hen Street.

She said so. Eric, having made his point, was relieved to see that they were not set on defending Brian; but at the same time, he was hesitant to push his theory too far in case all he did was to put two more valued friends against him.

'You summed up Brian's character pretty well, William,' he said, 'including the fact that he has a jealous streak which the rest of the family don't show. I'd put it stronger, and call him envious rather than jealous. Envy includes a dog-in-the-manger element. Envious people don't just think how nice it must be to have what others have got – that's jealousy. The envious take it farther. If they don't have what others have, they do their best to make sure that nobody else has it, either. Envy is positive, not merely negative, like jealousy. For example, in this particular case, Brian knows he has no chance of inheriting the love and respect that George has earned himself – for one thing he hasn't now got time enough to earn it. So he wants to rob his father of it. The same could be said about Charles. He's envious that Charles has got to where he is so young, when *he* had to wait. He can't put the clock back and have his own way over that now – but his resentment is so great that he wants to spoil it for Charles. Where Marjorie fits into it, I can't see, but it may be that he has an overall ulterior motive – and I'm afraid that without in the least intending to, I've already picked up what that might be.

'I've told Fran that I'm restless through not having enough to do. And whatever else I've become, I still came here in the first place as a developer, who keeps one ear to the ground whenever that word is heard again. Olive's bit of tittle-tattle happens to be correct.

'Our District Council has put forward a proposal to erect twenty-five thousand houses in and around Swithinford in the next three years. It will be done largely by infilling, and reusing old sites in villages round about. The long-term effect will be that they will become suburbs of Swithinford New Town. That means getting land to build on.

'Now think. Whose land round here lies most conveniently between Old Swithinford and Hen Street? Ours – my firm's – and the Bridgefoots'. Then look back. There was a time a short while ago when Bailey thought he had Castle Hill in the bag, to cover it with another estate, as he had done at Lane's End. *Vic Gifford and Brian Bridgefoot were up to their necks in that project with him.* Brian's envy of Tom Fairey was so strong that he would have robbed his own son of the chance of farming Bridgefoot land. Custom and tradition had no pull on him, but money did, and still does. Besides, to see Bob Bellamy turned out would have given him a lot of pleasure. He hasn't ever got over Effendi and Bob getting the better of Bailey and putting Bob on an equal farming footing with him.

'Then there was that piece of land opposite to the hotel on the Swithinford road, part of Bridgefoot Farms Ltd through Rosemary. Bailey had plans to set up a livery stable and riding-school there. You can bet your boots that Brian promised Bailey he should have it as soon as he was the boss. The riding-stable bit was only a ruse on Bailey's part to get his hands on it to 'develop' in the course of time, of which Brian would be well aware. His object was to sell it at a high, "developer's" price.

'I should have fought him tooth and nail myself over that – for one thing because if anybody was going to set up a riding-school so close to the Sports Centre it had to be me, and for another we certainly didn't want another Lane's End between the hotel and the river. As it turned out, of course, I didn't have to lift a finger.

'Now Brian knows of another chance to sell land for development. Agricultural land is not at nearly so high a premium today, and the need to produce more houses for 'nuclear families' inclines planners towards developers as never before. Brian wants big money as badly as he doesn't want land that will keep him only a fairly well-to-do, hard-working farmer instead of a rich pseudo-gentleman living in luxury somewhere on the south coast like Tom Fairey. But it isn't yet his land to sell. It's still Bridgefoot Farms Ltd's, with his father still owning the lion's share. None of the others, except perhaps Marjorie, would have considered letting a square foot of ancestral land go without a fight.

'When I heard that there were people in the Lane's End and Hen Street area saying "No bingo halls in my back yard" and demanding public meetings with regard to the District Council's proposals, I made it my business to be there. Greenslade, confident of being our next District Councillor, if not our County Councillor as well, stepped into the breach as chairman when our proper representative failed. It was only a public protest meeting and anybody could have set it up. In the event there were very few there – but at least we know where it was that Brian wanted to be able to go in the evening without having to disclose his destination. Oh, yes, he was there all right, hand in glove with Greenslade. Thick as thieves!

'That's when I began to put two and two together. Brian stood no chance of selling Bridgefoot land for development, however much it would make, until his father was dead, which could be a long time yet, long enough for this opportunity to be lost; but what if he could make life here for them so untenable that they would be willing to give up? It sounds far fetched, but could he have planned it, in cold-blooded cupidity?'

'I don't believe so,' Fran burst out. 'It's absolutely incredible. You're as good as calling him a murderer! And what about these crazy tales about Marjorie chasing every man in sight – how on earth do they fit in? Are you saying that if it hadn't been for Olive Hopkins happening to hear about it, nobody at this end would have heard that such a meeting was being held? And why is it a danger signal? Why is Elyot involved?'

'My dear Fran, what do national politicians do to gain advantage for themselves? Victimize their opponents by hitting below the belt at their private lives. A one-night stand with a chorus-girl has brought many a good man down. There's no nation so moral as the British when it comes to condemning people in power for doing what they do on the sly themselves all the time. It's a leftover from Victorian times, when a man wasn't even allowed

327

to see his wife's ankles till he was well and truly tied to her. But there may be more behind this dust-storm than appears on the surface. We may have been responsible for tipping Brian over the edge of reason. At our conference on the school issue, it was voiced that if we were seriously going to consider putting up a prospective candidate, *Brian wouldn't do.*

'I don't suppose he heard that, but it's significant that we all recognized a flaw in him. And when it came to his knowledge that Elyot had been asked, his resentment would know no bounds. He would have expected to be the first to be regarded as the leader of a farming community. I fear it may have caused him to flip.'

'Which is why Elyot wants to withdraw?' asked William.

'I don't know. But because I accept a good deal of the blame for not thinking how Brian would see it, and pushing Elyot forward, I propose to find out. I shall go and tackle Elyot face to face as soon as he will agree to see me.'

William and Fran both attempted to speak, but Fran wanted to hear what William would say, and waited. What he did say, slowly and with an air of conviction, was beyond her comprehension.

'Ward-room etiquette and Brigade of Guards mess rules, that neither Brian nor Greenslade would appreciate in their own right, offer them a chance to get at a man who has spent most of his life in the Navy?' William asked, cryptically.

'You don't miss much, do you?' said Eric. 'I risk his friendship, and his backing as the biggest investor in my firm, but I think we must know.'

'He's a gentleman first, and a first-rate chap as well,' said William. 'I'm with you. Good luck.' Fran was baffled as they solemnly shook hands, but she was also distracted, still thinking of what Dr Chandra had said.

*   *   *

Yorky was finding the new situation at Glebe very stressful, and afraid it might bring on a serious panic attack. He had, till this week, felt better there than he had done for months – even years. His rapport with the Bridgefoots – those he came into contact with in the main farmhouse – had been instantaneous. There had been no need to establish relationships with them, either individually or as a household.

The Golden Wedding had changed things. For the last three nights he hadn't been to bed – but had dozed uneasily in Gran's chair, watching the hands of the grandfather clock jerk noisily from minute to minute, and waking from any spells of sleep when the clock's loud but tuneful bell roused him tense and sweating from a recurring nightmare.

Lack of sleep usually triggered off dark moods of introspection, which had been the cause of the nervous breakdown and panic attacks and had first sent him to consult Dr Hardy. It had been wonderful the way that this doctor, only his own age or there-abouts, had seemed to understand him. Instead of handing out anti-depressant tablets and warning him yet again not to smoke or drink too much, he had found time to talk to him. And when the chance came, had winkled him out of the solitary false security of his top-floor flat and plonked him back into the middle of a welcoming family.

As the warmth of the Bridgefoot kitchen had thawed him physically, the atmosphere of being part of family life again had poured balm on places still very sore and tender. They had been there since his mother had died, leaving him, aged eighteen, one of the youngest of seven brothers coping with a father they both feared and despised. Her death had been devastating for him. She had been the core of their lives, the one who had held them together, besides keeping them from starvation. He had been born just after she had lost her only daughter in one accident and a young son in another, in the same year, which was perhaps why his relationship with her had been extra close, till a lingering cancer had overcome even her stoic spirit. By this time he, the brightest of a bright family, had won his way to a distinguished grammar school; but he had left it as soon as the law allowed him to, so as to be able to work and hand over his wage packet to his mother at the end of the week. He had not enjoyed school, anyway. It had been too far out of his ken to be learning Latin and such while at the same time being treated as a social outcast because of his poverty-stricken background. But he had been happy working on the railway.

Without Mother, the family fell apart and scattered. Each of the brothers went his own way. John had been the one to suffer most. He missed his mother both as the person he loved most in the world, and as the only breath of womanhood in a houseful of males. What, under such circumstances, would any boy have done but try to find a substitute as soon as he could?

He had tried, and it had resulted in a dismal failure of a marriage that had lasted only a matter of weeks. So he left his job on the railway and became a rover, trying his hand at any job, moving from place to place and earning a good living, without ever being really happy. He was a very attractive young man – working-class to the core and proud of it – but nevertheless carrying the bit of gloss his time at the grammar school had given him. He was different; hard physically, but with a soft centre that was sensitive to atmosphere and to beauty in any form. Women threw themselves at him, and being young and virile he took his fun where he found it. No woman, though, ever filled the empty, aching spot his mother had left, till, when he was coming up to thirty, he'd found one who did: a teenage girl. It had been so good while it had lasted. In spite of a loving relationship that had produced three children, they'd never got round to marriage. He wondered now if that had been the mistake which had caused the break-up. He hadn't minded not being married at the time, feeling the relationship secure as it was. But that had made their parting, when it came, all the worse, especially as there had been nothing dramatic about it, and as far as he could see, no real reason for it.

Her only excuse for leaving him, and taking his children with her, was that she had had no freedom in her teens such as her contemporaries had had and she wanted some of her lost youth back before it was altogether too late. They had remained 'friends', and he saw her often, and his children, but he had never recovered wholly from the blow. The emptiness he had felt when his mother had left him returned intensified, and the loneliness of a man without a stable relationship with any woman had grown till he had slipped into clinical depression – and had consulted a doctor. Which had landed him where he was now: back in the stuff that dreams are made on; but dreams can turn into nightmares. The warm, soothing bath of loving kindness and fun that Terence Hardy had pushed him into had turned to ice, alternating with scalding jealousy of the doctor who had, at last, found for himself the magic cure for loneliness.

He moved restlessly in Gran's chair. It was still only three a.m. There were at least three more hours before it would be light, but he feared to sleep again. He would only go back to his nightmare: that he was lost, wandering endlessly over miles of familiar territory that had been reduced to rubble. He was always looking for a tall building with its doors open and a lift waiting to take him to the security of a top-floor flat. When he reached it, though, all he could see from its windows was the desolation of what had once been a wonderful view. When he turned to go down again, both lift-shaft and stairway had disappeared. There was no way down, and he was trapped in his isolation.

He was dripping with sweat, and in a panic that was reaching uncontrollable levels, when the clock striking four woke him again. He got up and went to slosh his face in cold water, tidied himself up, made himself a cup of tea, and lit a cigarette. That and a breath of fresh air at the back door restored him somewhat, so he sat down again and tried to think. His urge was to run back to the enclosed if lonely security of his flat, where at least the troubles were all his own. But it was too much like his nightmare tower. What if he discovered that from there, as well, there was no way down?

Besides, the family which had trusted him so implicitly was

now in trouble itself. He couldn't let them down, whatever the cost to him. He was feeling better, so he continued to sit and reflect. From his first visit here, he'd felt part of a family again. George and Molly had more or less adopted him. Then he had met Marjorie – or, as she was usually called at home, Marge – and found her on the same wavelength as himself. They hadn't had to get to know each other any more than true siblings do. He liked her, and appreciated in her the feminine qualities he was missing, and which for so long he had not encountered among the sort of women he met on his rare social outings. She'd been harassed and overworked, and had turned to him for help and sympathy. He was flattered, and pleased to be back on increasingly familiar terms with what he called 'a real woman', and one who was undeniably extremely handsome, unattached, and good fun in the few minutes when they all relaxed together at tea-time over Molly's home-made scones.

He listened to her confidences with regard to her missing daughter with genuine sympathy and did his best to support her in her attempt to look after everybody till she had worn herself down to breaking point. But even when he'd had his arms round her that day in the car, there'd been no sign anywhere in him of a sexual interest in her, nor in her towards him. She was, in many ways, all that he had been subconsciously looking for: someone with whom to set up a truly permanent relationship – but he didn't want only a mother figure. He wanted a wife as well, to replace the 'magic' of his years with Debbie.

There was no vestige of that sort of magic in his relationship with Marge, even if he had aspired to consider it, which he didn't because he knew that financially she was quite independent, while he had nothing but himself – a nervous wreck at that – to offer any woman. Yet being part of a family again had rejuvenated him, and brought back a longing for the sexual sort of magic as well. He'd concluded that he was asking the impossible – there were so few women about now who possessed both the mature qualities he appreciated and sexual attraction. They had plenty of sexual experience – but sex was sex and marriage was marriage. They no longer went together 'like a horse and carriage', except in exceptional cases such as he had been made aware of last Saturday.

He'd found himself in the company of three young, modern women, all beautiful, but by no means all alike. Poppy was too young to interest him, even if she hadn't been absorbed by her fiancé, Nick Hadley-Gordon. A man with problems of his own, as he'd heard from Marjorie, but now settled and with all the care as well as the cure he needed to get over them. Pansy: so very much like her beautiful twin sister to look at, but – but what? She had all her mother's qualities, and youth into the bargain, but there was a sadness and an air of silent suffering about her that had reminded him of his own mother, and brought out in him a protectiveness he hadn't felt since Debbie had left him. He was drawn towards her instinctively, as he had been to her mother, but there was no sparkle in her, only a calm self-discipline that made her seem older by years than her sister. Two lovely girls like that should be enough to set any man's blood afire; but though Pansy particularly offered all the things a man could want, she lacked the magic ingredient: the verve that promised fulfilment in sexual consummation. And, in contrast, there was Charlie.

She was deliberately being demure, but she still lit the atmosphere like a firework. What a lucky young devil Charles was! It was plain that she loved and was loved by all of them – except her father-in-law – and that for Charles she was the sun and the moon combined. As he was to her. It almost hurt the aesthetic that lay beneath Yorky's practical skin to see anything so beautiful as those two perfect flesh-and-blood symbols of married love. That's what he had always wanted, and that's what he was still looking for – but there was only one Charlie.

He had watched the incident of the taming of the bull with awe, holding himself ready at whatever cost if Charles had needed help to rescue that glowing source of magic. Poppy's emotions were turned inwards towards her family and Nick. Pansy's emotions were turned outwards, towards other people, and her calm restraint for some reason saddened him. She was quite as beautiful as her twin – if anything, the depth of suffering left in her eyes made her the more appealing of the two. Yet, she showed not a single sign of the magic sexual sparkle that, in spite of Charles being at her side, he felt just looking at Charlie across the table. She was so full of *joie de vivre* that it was catching.

Thinking backwards to Saturday had cleared away much of his impending panic and he noted with relief that, while he had been musing, dawn was breaking and the eastern skies lightening to greet another day. He sat watching them, enjoying the dawn stillness, till it was broken by the unmistakable sound of clattering hoofs. Galloping hoofs on the road, at this time of the morning? He guessed it must be a horse broken out of its stable. There was nothing he could do to stop it before it would reach the main road, but he comforted himself that it was too early for there to be much traffic.

He sat up, alerted by the change in the rhythm of the hoofs as they neared the gates of Glebe, and was on his feet when it became obvious that the animal was slowing up to turn into the gates. In fact, the sounds told him that it was now only just outside the door. He went to look, and there, just outside in the yard, was the horse resolutely showing off its objection to having its lovely gallop brought to an end by frisking and cavorting, till it was finally brought to a stop by its rider: a girl, preparing to dismount, but first soothing the horse with caressing hand and voice. An experienced horsewoman whom to his knowledge he had never seen before. Yet when she spoke, her voice was familiar.

'That was good for us both, wasn't it, Ginger? You'll soon get used to me instead of Charlie. Now, now, that's enough. Calm down, because I don't think anybody'll be up yet – so I won't be a minute before we go on for another good gallop. Oh! Somebody is up!'

She slid to her feet in front of him, and raised her face so that he could see it. It was Pansy, but what a different Pansy! Her eyes were alive with excitement and pleasure, her face so full of life and animation that Yorky could hardly believe it was the same girl. She giggled, a youthful, saucy giggle, at the shock on his face.

She hitched Ginger to the nearest gate, and said, 'Morning, Yorky. Don't look so surprised. I know Charlie's old riding togs don't fit me as well as they might, but maybe Mum has kept some of my own somewhere. She isn't up yet, is she? Good. Can I have a cup of tea?'

He was dazed. A cup of tea? Was that all she wanted? In those few seconds he'd given her his heart! There she stood: all he'd been longing for in one. Her mother's comforting presence and all-round capability with an added bit of spice he hadn't detected before. Nothing in her past had succeeded in depriving her of an ebullient youthful vigour of the kind he termed 'magic'.

'Charlie's lent me her horse,' she said by way of explanation. 'But it isn't very flattering of you to be so amazed! Didn't anybody tell you that I'd ever been on a horse before? No wonder you were scared!'

He'd set a cup of tea before her, and she sat looking down at it in a bemused sort of fashion before picking it up to take a sip. When she raised her head again and looked at him, he saw that her eyes were brighter than ever with unshed tears.

'Gosh!' she said. 'That was all I really needed to make me feel properly alive. I'm *me* again. Not the me who went away, but the one I used to be before – before Robert died. I'm Poppy's twin and Mum's daughter and a proper part of Gran and Grandad's family again. I want Mum. I want to tell her what a gallop on Ginger has done! I'm home again – at last.'

There was no need for Marjorie to be called: she'd heard the horse in the yard and come down to see what had brought Charlie, as she thought, here so early. Yorky tiptoed into the kitchen to make a fresh pot of tea while the real reunion between Marjorie and her daughter took place.

*

Eric left Benedict's late in the afternoon in a more cheerful frame of mind than he had arrived, having expected, at least from Fran, some rather aggressive opposition to his theory, and a defence of any Bridgefoot on the principle of 'my friends, right or wrong'. He had trusted William to see his point more clearly from the social angle, as indeed he had. But as he drove down the avenue of bare trees that linked Benedict's with the road that went one way to the village, and the other towards his hotel and Swithinford town, he knew that as far as he, personally, was concerned, he had reached the point of decision with regard to his own future.

Was he going forward with his opposition to Greenslade and his plan to gather the old village into Swithinford New Town? Or was he going to retire from the fray, let it happen, and then make plans to begin again somewhere else?

He was more aware than any of the others of the old brigade of friends that they would have no legal leg to stand on with regard to ribbon development. Swithinford itself had grown up as an outshoot of what was now Old Swithinford, with the coming of the railway and a bit of building round the nearest halt in the days before Town and Country Planning became a political issue. Hen Street had been a spurious growth between the wars, and Lane's End more recent still; but the designation of Swithinford as a 'new town' had swapped their respective importance. Old Swithinford was now within the official boundaries of Swithinford New Town, which, like all others of the same nature, was designed from the first to expand.

So he had to decide, here and now, whether to withdraw altogether, or to put himself into the front rank of opposition. The first step towards that was to find out why Elyot was letting the side down. So which way would he turn, when he reached the end of the Benedict's drive? Towards the hotel, choosing to leave the old village to its fate, or towards Church End? Whatever he decided, it would take time for him to wind up the company, find new projects and new surroundings for himself – and new friends. That was where the hurt lay. So much had happened to change his outlook on life since he had arrived here, to make him happier than he'd ever thought he could be again. The best part of it all had been the old-fashioned concept of working again in a community, with friends and neighbours instead of with colleagues and executives, or his men, during the war. He turned his wheel, abstractedly, towards the village, and accepted what he had done as the casting of the die. What was to be would be. He drove slowly, taking in everything he'd had a hand in restoring as he went. Passing Heartsease, he noted a furniture van standing outside. So Terence was moving in! When he reached the scaffolded church, most of the village centre came into view: his own Elizabethan home at Monastery Farm surrounded by the other houses and buildings that were now part of his complex, including the big, beautiful barn that still stood as his son Gavin had left it when the band he led had set off to seek greater popularity in America.

Good Heavens! Why on earth hadn't he thought to offer that to Nigel for secular occasions over Christmas? It had far more modern facilities than George's, though it lacked the inapprehensible component of any previous connection with the church. He made a mental note to see Nigel about it before the end of today.

Oh, so he did care enough about what happened here to want to help? In which case, he'd better get round to the Old Rectory as soon as he could, and not flinch from bearding 'Lord High Admiral Franks' in his own quarters. Of all the houses he had restored, the Old Rectory gave him most pleasure. He was still thinking so when he drove across the paved 'quarter-deck' in front of the house, so called by all who had witnessed William and Fran's triumphant dance performance on it by moonlight on the night they had routed Bailey and Co. for the first time.

Emerald Petrie opened the door to him, with Beth and Elyot's first child on her hip as usual. Yes, Emerald told him, the Commander was at home; Mrs Franks had seen Mr Choppen arrive, and had told her to ask him in, find out what the Commander was doing and if it was convenient for her to take the visitor to him.

Beth greeted Eric with her usual warmth, but he didn't need telling that it was more than pregnancy that was making her look less overflowing with the joy of life than usual. Emerald came back to say that Elyot was in his study, and she was to take Mr Choppen there.

At least they would be private. Elyot rose to greet him from the depths of a huge leather chair, and waved Eric towards another on the opposite side of an occasional table that bore bottles and glasses. Eric was disturbed by the strong smell of alcohol. It was too early for 'evening noggins' before supper, or whatever they called their evening meal. It worried him, especially if Elyot was drinking alone because of whatever was bothering him. Well, he was here to find out what that was – and there was no way he was going to back out of it for his own sake now. After all, he was the one with least to lose if, in the end, circumstances turned against him.

Elyot offered him a drink. 'Too early for me,' Eric replied. 'Besides, I'm not here only in the role of a friend, though I hope I shall still be able to call myself one when I leave.'

Elyot did no more than raise his eyebrows, so Eric sat down and launched into the explanation for his visit, asking point-blank to be told if the rumour that Elyot was about to withdraw his promise to be their candidate for the Council vacancies was true, and if so, why.

Elyot was equally blunt. 'It is true,' he said, filling his glass again. 'But the reason for my doing so is my own affair, and I see no obligation to tell anybody what that reason is.'

Eric stood up, and over him. 'Then I think you force me to tell you what I know, and because of all the gossip, what I deduce from it. I warn you it's a nasty bit of business whichever way you look at it; and though only at present a bit of local skulduggery, could be an important turning point. If we are to save this bit of countryside and its way of life, we have to act now.

'The worst of it is that local politicians are taking their cue from the central government, except that in this particular case they think that they can get away with any underhand business because their opponents are either village idiots or smug, ignorant, too-well-off tom-noddies like us. But they recognize the pull you've got, and the thought of you putting your oar in has frightened them. So somehow or other you have to be prevented from going on with it. That's the part of it I can only guess.

'Do you want to hear the rest, or don't you? Because I'm going to tell you, anyway. You'll be involved in the long run, one way or the other. I've made my decision. If Greenslade is allowed to get his way without opposition, I'm quitting altogether. You'll have to find a new home for your investment, and get used to the new lifestyle he and his sort will force on you in the course of the next few years.'

'Go ahead,' said Elyot, reaching for the bottle.

'No,' said Eric firmly. 'You go and put your head under a tap first. This is serious. It's going to need a clear brain and your usual ability to make snap decisions.'

Surprisingly, Elyot got up and went. Eric took advantage of his absence to move the table with the bottles on it out of reach of Elyot's chair. He guessed his last shaft had gone home. So when they were seated again, facing each other squarely, Eric began to talk, and Elyot to listen.

Eric told him of his theory that what Fran had termed their quisling was none other than Brian Bridgefoot himself, whose purpose was to reduce his father and his son to 'has-beens' in his power. He gave Elyot a brief outline of his own opinion of Brian, like so many others playing at politics: a nice man flawed by an envious nature. That was what had embittered him in the past, and having at last succeeded to executive power, he was being totally frustrated by his father, his son, and his wife. And custom and tradition.

That was why he had had no scruples in giving his support to Greenslade. 'I think,' said Eric, 'that we probably wounded his pride to the quick by not turning to him as the natural leader of the old agricultural community.

'His other great weakness is his cupidity. He wouldn't have wanted to serve under Greenslade, but Greenslade's ideas would have put all the money he could ever want into his pocket. The chance to sell land at an enormous figure doesn't happen every day of the week – and Bridgefoot Farms Ltd holds most of the land suitable for development other than Manor Farms Ltd does – your ancestral acres, backed largely by your money, under my administration. Which brings it down to the question of personalities.

'Greenslade's a local man. I understand he started out in business selling fish and chips. There's nothing wrong with that – I sell fish and chips myself, under fancy names and at four times the price. But he was keen as well as ambitious. He offered to the first lot of London overspill what they were used to in towns when they came off shift-work: 'take-aways', which are not bound by English fish-and-chip laws. So he made his pile – and got bigger ideas. He wanted power, and that's what he's now making his bid for. He thinks he's got this seat on the District Council in the bag, but I doubt his judgement. I think he may be miscalculating. It's quite a time since the rise of Swithinford to its "new town" status, and those of the second wave, the sort who colonized Lane's End, for example, came of their own choice: commuters still working in London but living in the country. Not like the first wave, out of sheer necessity to have a roof over their heads somewhere. I can't see Lane Enders voting *en bloc* for town facilities in their own backyards. He also seems to have let success rob him of his knowledge of dyed-in-the-wool country folk. They hate change, especially if it's forced upon them. Custom and tradition pull hard, even with youngsters. I found that out for myself the hard way. All institutions have some sort of hierarchy of command. Anything else would be chaos. Country folk understand the way the countryside's hierarchy works. They accept people such as you as "leaders" without being bolshy about it, but take orders from a townee fish-and-chipmonger? Not bloody likely! So why are you letting them down?'

Eric waited – but in the end he had to pick up the gage Elyot's silence had thrown down. 'All right. If you won't talk, I must. I'm afraid you won't like it, though. As I said, I think they've deliberately set out to dispose of the challenge you offer. One only has to consider what happens in national politics if those in power decide to get rid of anybody they fear. They ignore all his worth as a conscientious representative of the people, and attack his private life – especially if they can unearth any sexual peccadilloes, however small and however long ago. Even an unsubstantiated allegation that he may have committed some "sexual misdemeanour" is enough for him to be declared as "not fit to be a Member of Parliament". There's no other way they can put you on trial – especially with your war record.

'Ah! I can see that I've hit the bull's-eye first time – and I've been listening to gossip. Don't answer till I've had my say, and then it will be up to you. If tradition holds anywhere as hard and fast as it does in country villages, it's in the Royal Navy and the top regiments of the army. One absolute shibboleth is the mention of a lady's name in the ward-room or the mess. Yes, I know what you're thinking. How can anybody like me, only a wartime soldier "up from the ranks" know about such things? I'll tell you how: my Annette's father was from an aristocratic military family. Her father was a Major-General in the Household Brigade. Killed in action.

'So my guess is that the rumours going round are built on a tale of a de ffranksbridge coming back to lord it over his heritage and seducing the parson's innocent daughter. You won't consider lowering yourself enough to deny it, so you let them win, and the rest of us suffer. Am I right?'

Elyot, face suffused with anger, exploded. 'Of course you're bloody well right! *But I will not have Beth's name bandied about by such filthy opportunists as Greenslade and Kenneth Bean whatever the outcome!* To attempt to deny it would be just what they want, and in any case, I couldn't. I suppose what they've got hold of and added to was what happened in the short period just before we were married. But how in God's name they could have found out about it is beyond me. Did you know?'

'No, but if I had cottoned on, my only reaction would have been admiration touched with a twinge of jealousy. I watched you the first time you met Beth, at Fran's party. I was the only man without a partner. And how the village found out so long afterwards isn't much of a mystery if you use your head instead of your pride, and put two and two together. The actual informant is Brian Bridgefoot. How did he find out? And how is he able to vouch for whatever it is they've got hold of?

'Don't I remember that when you first moved in here, you employed Thirzah Bates as your cleaner? She would have had eyes and ears everywhere for any sign of a woman in your bachelor establishment. Beth's father, the Rector of the time, was engaging in an anti-sex campaign, which suited the likes of Thirzah, and gave her a righteous reason for retailing any suspicion she might have conceived. To her husband, Daniel Bates, first, of course, who passed it on to George. I can imagine George slapping his side and having a good laugh about it – maybe Brian, too, then. But as we now know, Thirzah was in the early stages of senile dementia already and as it developed she became obsessed by sex. Perhaps she always had been. It's well known that people with a repressed sex-urge often just let go when old. What Thirzah made of Beth's visits to play your piano one can only guess at! And you did drop a bombshell on most of us when we heard that you'd married Beth with so little warning. There's no real mystery about how such scandal grows with keeping – especially if somebody has an axe to grind in resuscitating it with knobs on. So now we know where we are, what do you propose to do?'

'What can I do? Except keep out of it and let it all die down? Eric, look at it from any point of view but that of the friend you are. Beth *was* the parson's daughter, and I was already fifty-six, till then a confirmed bachelor. I was inclined to be horrified myself. I tried to cut and run when I discovered what it meant to be really in love. It was William who prevented me. He knew the whole story, and having failed to persuade me what an ass I was making of myself by "being a hero", went to Beth and told her it was up to her to save me from suicide, which she did *by coming and climbing into bed with me*! In spite of what she was already being accused of by that awful half-mad father of hers who was obsessed about modern sexual promiscuity. What courage – and what love that must have taken!

'But, by God, I never thought such happiness could be! Which is making it hurt all the more, because in the end Thirzah and that frightful father of Beth's have caught me out. Perhaps I ought to have had more sense than to let Beth change my mind. I feel such a cad – if that old-fashioned word still means anything. Do you know that I've just had my sixtieth birthday and I have a wife not yet forty, with one child at toddler stage, and another soon to be born, besides two beautiful adopted daughters I've made myself responsible for? There's no question of means, as you know very well, but reputation is another matter. The thought of having fingers pointed at me for sexual misbehaviour, of apparent proof of what a lecher I must always have been and apparently still must be, old as I am, being bandied about is more than I can take. If I agreed to go on it would be no good. I wouldn't stand a chance. And I'm too angry to be sensible. If I could I'd hang

Brian Bridgefoot and Greenslade from the yard-arm, and order Kid Bean and Co. five-hundred lashes, I would! If *you* want to quit, how do you think I feel?'

Eric got up and passed the bottle to Elyot and was glad to see it refused. He had followed Elyot's tirade with enormous sympathy and was seeing even further into the wood than he had done before. Elyot's last words had gone home to him. If he was ready to quit, why should he expect Elyot to ride the storm out? Suppose both quit: what about the others? Greg had 'made it', so the loss of Jess's job wouldn't matter very much – but how they would hate having to live in a tarted-up suburb, even if, for instance, they moved from their modern house into the Old Rectory. Why shouldn't they, too, move elsewhere? Jess had only returned to her roots slowly. But what about William and Fran, the remnants of the Bridgefoots and a lot of others not quite so high up the old-fashioned but still recognized hierarchical ladder?

It was not to be thought of. He said so. 'But I'm not asking you not to withdraw, Elyot. I agree that you must, but with the absolute dignity that is your birthright. As if you'd never heard of this scurrilous attack on you. Shove it back down their throats by being the man you are, with nothing to hide, but too many other things to do to spend time at their endless meetings. Good God, Elyot, what *have* you to hide but what should be within the reach of every man? As for admitting you're an old lecher just because you married late – hadn't you been at your country's service in the Royal Navy since you were thirteen and during the war, while Greenslade was growing up to make his fortune selling fish and chips? Your age gives you the first and best reason – I refuse to use the word excuse – for having to decide that you can't take anything else on. Couple it with a hint that you're satisfied with Old Swithinford as it is; you want your wife to live and your children to grow up in a disciplined world – as you did – and be able to think for themselves. To that end, you must give whatever time is left from your other duties, such as being a magistrate, to them. You haven't yet submitted your name as a prospective candidate. We'll let it be known that you never did have any intention of doing so. Let them prove otherwise if they can.'

Elyot looked like a man reprieved while mounting the ladder to the scaffold. He stood up and drew his shoulders back with a huge sigh of relief, but he still looked worried.

'Fran told Beth of that unofficial meeting of yours about a school for young Jonce and Stevie Noble. She gave me to understand that I was about the only suitable candidate. So I shall be letting all the rest of you down on a purely personal point. I hate the very thought of all we stand for being swallowed at a gulp and without a fight. Defeated before we begin because there's nobody who'll stand up for us.'

'Oh, I wouldn't be too sure about that. I think we may yet find somebody.'

'Honestly? Who else other than William – who I understand stated his case for refusing the honour very firmly – can you possibly have in mind?'

Eric was also standing up by now. He gave the Commander, who was rapidly becoming his normal self, what could only be described as a cheeky grin. Saluting briskly, he replied, 'Me, sir.'

Elyot collapsed back into his chair. 'You, Eric? Are you sure? Are you putting yourself forward in my place just to save me?'

'Aye aye, sir. Do I have your permission, sir?'

Elyot eyed him up and down before standing up, extending a hand and replying, 'Permission granted, Major Choppen. You can thank Nigel for letting that out!'

They stood with clasped hands while each treasured the moment of mutual admiration. Then Eric said, 'At that unofficial meeting, Bob Bellamy pointed out that some of us – him and myself included – weren't eligible to be the candidate to stand on a "rural conservation" ticket, because we were "furriners" with no family roots here. You had all the qualifications. I still haven't, but we shall have to risk it. It's my one reservation; but I shall go into it to win, slight as my chances may be. I shall need every bit of moral support I can get.'

'I'll pledge you mine, here and now,' said Elyot. 'Do you want me to swear an oath on it?'

Eric shook his head, replying that he had no faith in any oath. Like promises and pie-crust, oaths were mostly made only to be broken. 'But I'll accept a personal pledge from you,' he added. 'Your word that if I do stand in your place, and win, and Beth's baby turns out to be a girl, you'll keep your word to call her Arethusa Bellona Calliope.'

Elyot looked absolutely stunned. He knew Eric was joking, but there was a strand of seriousness there all the same. So he swallowed hard, grinned, and replied, 'I swear in my own name, and for Beth, too.'

Eric let out a deep chuckle. 'Then I shall have a good reason to put everything I have into my campaign,' he said. 'If ever I waver, I shall listen in my head to Nigel's voice saying: "I baptize thee, Arethusa Bellona Calliope". But don't let it worry you, old fellow. I haven't won yet, and if I do, you can always shorten her name to "Cally". She's bound to be a winner, whether I am or not.'

*   *   *

Eric was happier than he had been for a long time. It had been brought home to him that what he had been thinking was a purely personal rejection of him was nothing of the kind. The village had 'gone bad' from inside, as pears do. He blamed himself more than anyone else for not realizing what was happening. People like William and Fran had been occupied with other matters, but he'd had too little to occupy him. He'd had too much time for introspection, and had reached the conclusion that it had all been aimed at him personally.

At the centre of it was the Bridgefoot family, for whom he had enormous respect and affection. Now that he was assured that others beside himself were concerned to discover what was wrong, he had no hesitation in choosing to stay and use what expertise he had in trying to restore the status quo ante.

Remembering his intention to see Nigel about the use of his

345

barn if it would help at all at Christmas, he drove from the Old Rectory directly to Church Cottage. There was, at least between now and Christmas, more need for discretion than for valour. It could still be that Brian, finding himself checkmated, would change his tune and make it up with his father. Meanwhile, he was rather at a loss to know how much to tell Nigel of the conclusions they – meaning himself, Fran, William and Elyot – had reached by putting together all the various sherds of evidence they'd discovered by digging deep over a wider area than Church End itself. There was no proof yet that what they accused Brian of was anything more than suspicion backed by hearsay. He decided not to say anything to Nigel yet; nor was there any need for Elyot to do anything. Christmas would be over before formal application for candidature would have to be made. It would be much more sensible to keep it dark that they were intending to take part in the game till the other side showed their hand. He made a mental note that he must warn William and Fran, and Elyot and Beth, to keep their heads down for the present.

He found Nigel at home, confessing to being tired and hungry, having had no time to eat anything but a snack at lunch-time. Eric said that he'd also been too busy to bother about food, and suggested they both went back to the hotel for a meal. Everything else could be shelved for today, while he listened to Nigel's difficulties.

Nigel was, both literally and figuratively, wearing his clerical collar. Apart from his practical problems, he was having to act in a pastoral role to one of his churchwardens, and was keeping a wary eye on the other, Kenneth Bean, at a time when he needed both at his side helping him. So Eric listened and sympathized as they ate. Then he launched into his offer of Gavin's barn to Nigel if it would ease any of his practical problems over Christmas and the New Year. Nigel was intrigued, and asked when he could inspect the barn.

'Not tonight,' Eric determined. 'You're too tired, and I still have things to do. Besides, it's ages since I even looked into the place. It may need more work on it than it would be worth to you. Leave it till the weekend now and go home to bed.'

Nigel, for once looking his age, took his advice; but as he was being deposited at his own door, he asked, 'Does it have a piano? Because if it does and we need it, we shall have to get it tuned after standing so long unused, and if there isn't one, I'll have to see about getting one somehow. And there's so little time. Find out, and let me know as soon as you can. It may be the deciding factor. Goodnight, and thanks for all your support and help.'

Eric drove slowly away, now immersed in his private thoughts far more than he wanted to be. In absolute innocence, Nigel had exposed one of the sore places that Eric thought common sense had healed.

There was no piano in the barn. It was in Marjorie's side of his house. He had taken it there at Gavin's request, and when Marjorie was considering the possibility of renting the half of his house recently vacated by Monica, it had been for her a clinching part of their bargain that he should leave it there for her personal use. Nothing would induce him to remove it in her absence, even if it fell to him to hire and pay for one to be installed for as long as Nigel had need of it.

With that resolved, he went home, and though it was late, rang Benedict's and the Old Rectory, after which Fran talked to Beth, and William to Elyot. All of them went to bed in an optimistic frame of mind.

*

There was no such optimism the next morning at the Old Glebe. Another Saturday, just one week since the Golden Wedding day. George's tide was, if anything, still ebbing, and Molly's was at an all-time low. George was showing his load of misery physically: dragging himself about on leaden feet, stooping as he had never done before in subjection to his painful hip. He was getting very little sleep, finding lying down more painful than sitting, and sitting more painful than standing. He'd never been one to lie awake grieving. He had read somewhere of a Bishop three hundred years or more ago who had said, 'God made man to lie awake and hope, but never to lie awake and grieve,' and had thought it good advice to follow, but it wasn't working now. To lie there hour after hour with nothing but misery to alleviate persistent

347

pain was more than he could endure. He had to be up and moving; but he couldn't stand, unsupported, for many minutes together, and when he sat down in his dear old chair in the kitchen, memories of the past compared with his unhappiness now were too much for him. So he had taken to going out to his new cowshed, and using the cows' feeding trough, to which they were loosely chained when Dan arrived for morning milking, as a support.

That was the hour that gave him most peace and pleasure. He talked to the cows before Dan arrived, telling them things he would not have put into words to Molly who, bless her, had reasons of her own for being so unhappy.

She had given in under the weight of her grief, to which, had he but known, her anxiety and worry about him had added the straw that had broken her. She sat, inert and silent, or stayed in bed so that nobody should see her tears when frequent outbursts of useless, helpless crying overcame her.

Marge bore the brunt of the breakdown of both her parents with indomitable courage, while maintaining her obstinate determination not to go cap in hand to her brother even for their sakes. She had quite enough common sense to know that in the long run it would not be to their advantage to give an inch to Brian, but she had begun to wonder how long one or even both would or could stand up to this present strain. That, until yesterday, had been the burden of sorrow that being able to share with Yorky had eased. It was a blessing to her wearied spirit as well as her tired body and her over-wrought mind.

Pansy's return had been a great boost in its own right and had brought a sudden end to months of sleepless nights and unshed tears. To find Pansy so changed and helpful had been such a surprise that she hadn't yet wholly believed it; but yesterday another Pansy – one of the pair she'd been so proud of while they were children at school – had suddenly emerged, as beautiful and incredible as a dragonfly when it does so from the ugly monster of its 'nymph'.

After all the years of trouble and grief this daughter had given her, the happiness of yesterday morning's miracle had undone Marjorie's stoicism. After Pansy had left again, without seeing

348

either of her grandparents, Marge first had a good cry on Yorky's shoulder and then braced herself to face her parents with the good news. She persuaded her mother to get dressed and come down, while Yorky cooked breakfast for them all.

'Did she say how they are up at Temperance?' Molly asked.

'No. She was far too excited to want to think of anybody but herself, and anxious to get Ginger back before Bri got up. But if we don't hear any more today, we must take it as a good sign, and wait for tomorrow. Do you mind if I leave you in Yorky's care for the rest of the day, and go back to Monastery Farm till bedtime?'

She wanted to be alone. Yorky understood that better than George or Molly did, though they willingly acquiesced. A phone call from Charles soon after breakfast asking if they were all right uplifted them even more. Charles said he had left Charlie at her books, glad of a valid reason to have to stay there. Only Ginger would have tempted her from them – so at present it was a good thing he wasn't around.

Marjorie returned in time for supper, looking relaxed and rested, confessing that she had cried herself out in her own bed and then slept until she'd forced herself to get up to go and do the chores for Eric and Nigel. She hadn't seen either of them to speak to.

She and Yorky had got supper early, and after Molly was put to bed, George sat in his chair again as long as his hip would let him before joining her, so worn out after three consecutive sleepless nights that nature knocked him out almost at once, despite his aching hip. The Glebe's dose of new courage had upheld them all day, but its effect was wearing off now.

Marge, too, had gone off to bed early, and Yorky faced another night in Gran's chair, but with a difference. He was back again in dreamland, and Pansy was his dream. He slept most of the night peacefully, but was awake when dawn broke. He had not had his nightmare, though when he became conscious enough to remember, he began to daydream. Not that he allowed himself to hope for anything; Pansy was as far out of his reach as Charlie. But without dreams there is no hope, and without hope, no dreams. Pansy had restored his belief in the existence of both.

He thought he was still dreaming when he heard the clatter of hoofs coming out of the half-light of the dawn; but they grew nearer and clearer and slowed down exactly as they had done yesterday. He was up on his feet and had thrown the heavy oak door of the house-place wide open by the time Pansy brought Ginger to a standstill in front of it.

'Hello,' she called. 'Be ready to help me up!' She loosed her feet from the stirrups and jumped off, intending to fall and turn a somersault out of the way of her mount's hoofs, as practised many times in the past when in training for show-jumping at some local gymkhana or agricultural show. Ginger, unprepared, reared and more or less threw her off before she was ready. She would have fallen hard if Yorky hadn't been there to catch her. He clasped his arms round her while she hid a scarlet face against him, sudden tears coursing down her cheeks.

'The doctors were right,' she said. 'They told me I'd be lucky if I could ever ride again, never mind being the famous show-jumper my dad thought he could make of me. I'm sorry if I frightened you. I wasn't trying to show off – honestly. I was only finding out for myself what I could still do. It's ages since I have actually been on a horse – till yesterday.'

She was crying in earnest and he held her tight. She didn't seem to want him to let go of her any more than he wanted to, but Ginger was trotting round the yard with his reins dangling, making for the open gate. So Yorky kissed her, and gently disengaged her arms from his neck. 'Go in and wait for me to get you a cup of tea, and then you can tell me as much or as little as you like, but I must catch Ginger before he makes a dash for home. Are you hurt?' She shook her head, and went to lean against the open door to watch him as he caught Ginger and tied him to the cowshed fence. He had never really liked horses, and had no knowledge of how to deal with them. It looked as if he might have to learn.

He disappeared into the kitchen, while she sat drying her face and taking off her riding hat to smooth her ruffled hair; she had known that she had to face up to both past and future sooner or later, but so far nothing had been as she had expected. She made a sudden decision that there was no time like the present, and nobody she would rather begin to explain to than Yorky before she had to tell all to her mum and the others. So when he came back, she began straight away, apologetically embarrassed.

'It was a silly thing to do,' she said. 'I suppose the Pansy I was when I went away is bound to pop up now and then. Charlie always made me feel a complete novice as a rider compared to her, and I always resented it. You see, Poppy and I were sent to a local private boarding-school, where farmers' daughters went to be made into "young ladies" rather than educated, mainly to show that their parents could afford to send them there. The riding-school attached was "extra" and we were both enrolled as "equestrian pupils". I loved it from the start, but Poppy was never very keen.

'Charlie Bellamy was in the very same boat – but with such a difference! I wouldn't have admitted it then, but things have changed since . . .' She didn't finish her sentence.

'Since what?' he prompted.

'Since I went away, and all that. You must know that I am the black sheep of the family?'

'Go on about the riding,' he said. 'There's plenty of time for all the rest if, or when, you want to tell me. But you don't have to tell me anything if you don't want to. I shall still love you for ever, whatever it was.'

He hadn't meant to say anything like that! It was his heart speaking, rushing out to help her over the first fence. She looked up, startled, right into his face, and knew that he meant it. A blush that began somewhere down inside her jumper rose till it suffused her face and made her twice as beautiful as he already thought her. She gulped a couple of times, found her handkerchief, and tried again.

'Well, it's all about nothing, really. The riding business, I mean. I enjoyed it partly because it often got me out of lessons I hated, and partly because it pleased my father when I was always picked for the school's gymkhana team. I went along with Dad because it suited me. I could always get my own way with him if he could

351

have the pleasure of showing what his money had made of me. They say that Poppy takes after Mum, and I take after him. Perhaps I do. I'm not sure – though I hope I don't.

'He was one of those who thought that what he had become from a very humble beginning was the result of his own cleverness and he was the most God-Almighty snob. A social climber with few graces – especially where Mum was concerned. He'd only got where he was on Grandad's money, and he was accepted because of Mum being a Bridgefoot. I played up to him, though I was often ashamed of him – and myself. By the time we left school I'd let myself in for a "horsey" future – he was intent on setting us up with a riding-school. It was, in his eyes, "the thing", the way into the new set of rich country gentlemen, one of whom he hoped would marry me and make him the father of Lady Muck. It never happened because Poppy rebelled, but I had got into that "set" and had landed myself, and him, into a social pigsty. I'd begun to accept it too, by the time he broke his neck.

'I'm not sure I want you to know the rest. I was very ill last year after I had gone away and had to stay away till I was better. I thought I was different, but my silly exhibition just now proves I'm not. I'm still like him.

'In Charlie's case it was her mother doing all the social climbing. She never wanted Charlie, and rejected her from the time she was born – which was Charlie's good luck. She went to one of the very best boarding-schools money could buy. We didn't know her because they lived in the fen; she only came home to her father at Castle Hill after her mother began a divorce suit. She insisted on leaving school then to be with him. That's when Charles met her – they just fell for each other. I still envy her.

'Everybody's being too kind to me, considering what I've put them all through. I don't deserve it. I don't grudge Charlie anything – except Charles. Not that I want him – he's my cousin, anyway – but I do envy what they have between them. I want somebody to love me as much as Charles loves her. I'm sorry, Charlie. It isn't and never was your fault! It's all mine. If only . . .'

The anguish of listening to her pouring out such a jumble of self-accusation was almost more than Yorky could bear, but even those disjointed fragments had given him some idea of what sort of a hell she'd been in. It would come out, one day. This was only a first brief opening of the safety valve. He kept silent, but held her hand while shuddering sobs once more shook her.

'Somebody did love me like that once,' she said. 'He wasn't good enough for Dad's big ideas. So here I am, alone, while Charlie's got Charles and Nick has come back to Poppy.'

He put his arm back round her, and pulled her head on to his shoulder. 'What happened?' he asked. 'Did he throw you over to please your father?'

'No,' she said flatly. '*He died.* Dad kept telling me it had only been a schoolgirl romance, and I'd get over it. I believe Grandad understood, and perhaps Charles did too, because when Charlie ran away to be rid of her mother, Charles made himself ill. Dad tried sending me away but I came back not caring much what happened to me. Plenty did. So here I am, home again – and just look what I've brought with me. Bad luck for them all, except for Charles and Charlie.'

He let her cry, cradling her against his heart, enjoying the bitter-sweetness of the moment while it lasted. After a while she sat up, and went to wash her face. As she came back into the house-place, a car braked noisily in the yard outside.

'Yorky, look! It's Charles! What can have happened now?'

As Molly had often said, Charles Bridgefoot was 'like a bit dropped off his grandad', except that he had inherited his mother's fair, crisp, curly hair. He was as tall as his grandfather, but the astonishing likeness was in their temperaments. Neither lost his temper except on extreme provocation, and both were always more inclined to count their blessings than their grievances. But there was no mistaking that Charles was in no good mood as he scrambled out of his car that morning.

Seeing the door had been unlocked, he walked in, and at the sight of Pansy his face cleared. 'Pansy!' he said, in a very relieved voice. 'Did you bring Ginger up here?'

'Yes. Why? I've been away for so long I need a lot of riding practice, so I chose the early morning to have another gallop.'

'Well, that's a relief. Is there a cup of tea going – 'cos I could certainly do with one.' Yorky went into the kitchen to make it.

As soon as his back was turned, Pansy asked in a whisper, 'Charles, what's the matter?'

'Dad, putting himself out about Ginger. He'd been out that evening when I brought Ginger up for you and put him in the stable. Dad came home in a filthy temper, found him there and rang me up to tell me to fetch him away, there and then. He wasn't going to have anything belonging to Charlie on his premises. I thought he must be drunk – we've had our suspicions that he must be drinking too much, just lately. He said if he found Ginger still there next morning, he'd shoot him. I didn't want to upset Charlie, and decided I'd get him next morning. So I went up there at the crack of dawn yesterday, to see you if I could and to tell you I had to take Ginger home. But Ginger wasn't there, and I was really scared in case Dad had carried out a drunken threat. But when Dad went out after getting up late – about eight o'clock – there was Ginger, back in the stable. So he rang me again, out of his mind with anger till he just suddenly stopped, and hung up. So I rang back at once, and Mum answered, saying she was scared and you were doing your best to cope with Dad. I said I'd be up straight away but she pleaded with me not to go. She said to wait till this morning, for everybody's sake. So I did, after ringing here. I went up again just now to find him gone again! I thought I should have to do what I've always done before – come and consult Grandad – and here Ginger was, safe and sound. What's it all about? Why didn't you ring me, Pansy? You must have known what a state I'd be in?'

'Because your mum begged me not to,' Pansy answered – and then, without warning, burst into a fit of passionate crying again. Charles turned very white and said, anxiously, 'Tell me, Pansy. I must know. We can't go on like this. What's happened?'

But she was out of control. The two men looked helplessly at each other, and then Yorky picked her up, went to Gran's chair, and sat down again with her on his lap, shushing her like a baby. Charles watched in silence; the last thing he wanted was for Grandad to come down in the middle of this. But she pulled herself together and sat up, though making no move to free herself from the safety and comfort of Yorky's arms.

'I'm so sorry, Charles, but I can't cope any longer up at Temperance. He raved like a lunatic that first time he found Ginger there and accused your mum of being in some plot against him. He stood over her and threatened to kill her – I'm sure he had no idea what he was saying or doing. When he rang you, I went back to comfort Aunt Rosy, so I didn't hear what it was about. After he stopped swearing at you and hung up, I crept down to see if he was all right. He was muttering that he'd see to it in the morning, but he'd get his own way with the lot of you. Then he went off into a deep sleep, and I went back to your mum. Everything had been quiet all night, so I left your mum asleep and came out for my first gallop. So of course Ginger was back in his stable by the time your dad got up. He was either asleep or muttering threats all day yesterday, and I'm scared for us all. I can't take any more. They're your parents, Charles, not mine. And your mum's very frightened. What are we going to do?'

'Leave Ginger here and go and get Charles's mum. Leave Brian by himself to calm down. There's plenty of room here for her and we'll all look after her.'

'Thanks, Yorky,' Charles replied, 'but we can't do that without asking Grandad and Aunt Marge and Mum herself, first. And she wouldn't come. She'll only say Dad will get over it and she won't have Grandad upset any more – or let the rest of us down. Listen! I think Grandad's getting up. What shall we tell him?'

'That your dad's put himself into a temper with Pansy, so that she can't cope any more and she won't be going back. We shall have to make different arrangements. I think it would be a good thing all round if Pansy wasn't here – or me – while you hold a family conference. I'll take her out with me and look after her till about tea-time. Come on, my pet. Let's leave Charles to do his best.'

To Charles's utter amazement, Pansy let herself be led outside and put into Yorky's car without a word of protest. It was only then that he remembered what she had been through during the last years.

It was not Grandad coming down but Marjorie, and Charles was glad. He wanted to get himself and his chaotic thoughts in a little more order before he had to worry Grandad. So he told Aunt Marge his tale as briefly as he could, ending with Yorky taking Pansy out of the way.

They heard the rumble of a slow heavy tread in the bedroom above, meaning that Grandad was awake and would soon be down. Charles was going to need all the courage he could muster, and was very glad of his aunt's strong presence beside him.

'Aunt Marge,' he said, 'have you any idea why Dad is behaving like he is? I mean, are you keeping anything from Grandad, or from me, that we ought to know? If he were anybody else's father other than my own, I'd say he was either going round the bend, or had some awful grudge against Grandad. He's never got on with me since I fell in love with Charlie, so I accept that some of his attitude to me is my own fault. But why Mum? Why you? Why, in heaven's name, poor old Grandad?'

She shook her head, being unable to speak. 'I don't know,' she said at last. 'And that's the honest truth. If I give as truthful an answer as I can, it would be that I don't think he knows why either. It's so unlike any Bridgefoot I've ever known or heard of. Right out of character. I can only suppose he's turning some private grudge he has on those he did once – if he doesn't still – love best. Sometimes I think Vic must have left a bit of his soul in Bri's keeping! He got very thick with Vic at one time – I never could understand that – but when Vic was killed he took my part a hundred per cent. I don't know how I could ever have got through without the support I had – from everybody, but especially from your grandad and your mother and Bri. Something's got into him. I can't forgive him for what he said to or about me, and I won't apologize – well, at least not unless he squares himself up a bit first. But we must give him time, Charles. For Grandad's sake, and for your mum's, as well as his own. We must all be patient, and go on making excuses for him till he gets over this bad patch. He isn't all that much worse than he was when you were so ill after Robert died and Nick had been knocked out, and Charlie had run away. He had this thing about doctors even then

– poor Alex got the worst of it that time. Sh! Here's Dad. Let's put as cheerful a face on it as we can, for his sake.'

George came slowly, and with heavy but careful tread, down the staircase and through the hall into the house-place. His face lit up at the sight of Charles, only to be stricken with fear again as he sat down clumsily in his chair and hutched it close to the table.

'I'll soon have you a cup of tea, Dad,' Marjorie said. 'Talk to Charles while the kettle boils.'

'Something's wrong,' said the old man. 'Why are you here so early? Where's Yorky? Gran's waiting for her morning cup of tea. He usually takes it up to her once I'm down. Tell me, my boy. Your mother isn't worse, is she?'

'No, Grandad, no. Don't go getting yourself into a tizz about what hasn't happened. I'm here because of what has!'

He told his tale as lightly as he could, making the bit of 'now you see him, now you don't' about Ginger more or less into a joke. George listened, but drew his own conclusions. He waited until Marge came back, after taking her mother a cup of tea, and sat down with them.

'So where's Ginger now?' George asked.

'I found him tied up to the cowshed fence when I got here,' Charles answered. 'Talk about relief! Pansy had fancied another early morning gallop but I really feared Dad might have carried out his threat. Under the circumstances, I think it would be wise not to try taking Ginger back to Temperance again. Can I use one of the old carthorse stables to put him in till we can work some other plan out?'

George looked him straight in the eye and told the truth. 'You could if I dare give you permission,' he said, 'but you know as well as I do that I don't have any say in anything here now. That ain't my yard, down there by the barn, no longer. I ain't sure as I ought to let your father find him tied to what I still think of as my cowshed fence. Take him home with you to Danesum. Brian don't have any say in what you do down there.'

'Grandad, Ginger was only up at Temperance in the first place because it gave Pansy a way of getting away now and then. It took her too long to walk. Charlie lent her Ginger for exactly that

357

reason. He's no good to her if she's at Temperance and he's at Danesum, is he?'

'He's no good to her here then either, is he? Where is she? What does she say?'

Marjorie took upon herself the difficult task of explaining what sort of treatment Pansy had been receiving at Brian's hands and her resolution that she would not go back again. 'Dad, I'm afraid we're all in a real mess. Pansy still wasn't at all well when she came home for your Golden Wedding: there's a lot we don't know yet about what she's been through. She has only just completed a carer's course, and offered herself for one night to look after Rosemary when Bri insisted on breaking up the party and taking Rosy home. She hasn't complained until this morning, but she has had a week non-stop at Temperance, and this row about Ginger's been the last straw. She won't go back to Temperance, come what may. *And neither will I.* Yorky suggested we could fetch Rosy here and look after her, but he doesn't know Rosy. Wild horses wouldn't drag her away from Bri, however badly he treats her. And somebody has to be here with you and Mam, but I'm at the end of my tether, too. Pansy was in such a state this morning that Yorky suggested he should take her out for the day somewhere – just as she was, in her riding gear. He saw how near to breaking down again she was if she had to face any sort of argument. What she wants is to be "home again", and that means to be with me, in my home, where we can share all there is to share between us – in confidence. It's what I want, too, Dad. I can't keep this up, either. So what are we to do? You and Mam ought to have somebody here at nights, but so must Rosy.'

'That leaves me I suppose,' said Charles. 'And Charlie. It isn't fair on any of us, but we have to do something. Make some arrangement.'

George stood up, and looked down on the two still sitting at the table. 'I'm going out to be by myself a little while among the cows,' he said. 'I'm forbid my pew in church, and my own place in the barn, but the cowshed'll do. It had to stand in for a room in an inn, once.'

*

They watched him go in silence, though in deep sorrow, with their problem unresolved.

'Dad wouldn't have Charlie anywhere near Temperance in his present mood,' Charles said. 'The mention of her is like a red rag to a bull to him. Could we suggest to Yorky that he goes home at nights now, and leaves you and Pansy here together with me on call for any emergency at Temperance? As Pansy pointed out to me none too gently, they are my parents when all's said and done.'

'That's a possibility,' Marge replied, looking slightly relieved, 'as long as it doesn't have to go on for too long. I can't last out much longer, but the same applies to me and my parents as Pansy said to you about Bri and Rosy being yours. I've got nobody to call on for help any more than you have. I can't get Lucy from London, because for one thing she has a job and for another she'd have to bring Georgina. I'm not at all sure that Alex would wear it, either. He makes no bones about saying he had quite enough of Bri when he tried to help once before. But yours is the best suggestion so far. I'll test it out on Pansy when she comes back. Till then, we have to get through today. Wouldn't it be sensible for you to take Ginger home in case Bri should turn up here? Oh God, here he is!'

She had been alerted by the sound of a car outside the door; but when the door was flung open, it was Pansy who came in.

'Good job I had to renew my driving licence as part of my course,' she said. 'We'd barely got as far as the main road when Yorky began to turn pale and sweat and confessed he thought he was in for one of his bad panic attacks. He had to stop the car, saying he wasn't safe, and I told him I could drive if he told me where to go. He said to his flat – it was the only place he felt safe when these attacks came. I got him there, and suggested I should send for his doctor, but of course his doctor is Dr Hardy, on leave just at present. He wouldn't hear of consulting another one who didn't know his case, so he begged me not to leave him. And I shan't. Sorry, Mum. Sorry, Charles. I can imagine what you're all thinking – but don't forget that I'm the one with no reputation to lose. And John needs me as much as I need him. I've left him just long enough to come and get my clothes and borrow some toilet things. Mine are still up at Temperance.'

She ran up the stairs and came down again loaded. 'Don't worry about me, Mum. I'll be back as soon as I can, but not till John is well enough to come back with me. All the tension here has been too much for him – this was bound to come sooner or later. He's in a dreadful state about having to leave you all in the lurch, but I judge that this is the wisest course. If he caught sight of Uncle Bri upsetting any of you again, I think he might flip altogether. Bye for now, and don't worry, Mum. It'll come right for us all in the end.'

Marjorie put her head down and cried. Charles sat uncomfortably watching her, until he could bear it no longer.

'It hasn't changed our problem, Aunt Marge. It's only made it worse, if anything. But I think I must get Ginger out of sight in case Dad does turn up here. Charlie has promised her dad she won't ride him till he says she may so I'll take him myself up to Castle Hill. I'll ring her from there and ask her to pick our car up here and come to fetch me. Can you cope till I get back?'

'Of course I can.'

'Don't hesitate to ring Castle Hill if you have any sort of need,' he said. 'I won't be a moment more than I need be.'

At Castle Hill Charles found Bob in what was obviously a strange mood of excitement.

'You've only just catched me,' he said, 'but I can see what a pickle you're in. It never rains but it pours. I suppose Charlie will have to walk up to Glebe to pick up your car? I can't leave here myself, because I'm expecting William – but if I ring him quick he'd go and get her from Danesum and take her to Glebe. You be settling Ginger into his own old stall here. Fancy her keeping her promise to me like that – and you making sure she did. It's the sort of good omen that always cheers me up. There's an answer to every problem somewhere, my boy. It's just up to us to help each other to find it.'

He made for the nearest telephone, and Charles took Ginger stablewards. Bob never failed to cheer him up.

*   *   *

The feeling of encircling gloom had lifted from Benedict's a good deal since Eric had reappeared on the scene and, as it turned out, acted in such a perceptive and forceful fashion. It did nothing to lessen their worry about the Bridgefoots, but it made them feel less helpless, and more hopeful that once Christmas was over, some solution might have offered itself to put them back on an even keel. Those closely concerned had all agreed to keep their heads down till the holiday season was over. They sat at breakfast that same Saturday morning, discussing what it would be possible to do to keep up the merry-go-round with such of their friends as were still available. The notice now was short.

There were only six more free days before the Fenley school concert, and then one more week to Christmas Day. Fran had given her promise to be present to Greg, Jess, Bob and Jane – and, much more important, to Jonce and Stevie. From that obligation there was to be no running back. William felt frustrated by the prospect of not being able to 'get on with things' for almost three weeks. But Fran had cheered up a lot, and that cheered him. Besides, he was going to see Bob later that day, and he thought he had detected an element of excitement in Bob's voice. Some new idea of where to look for that bit of essential evidence, or news that Effendi's lawyers had found something relevant to the church in the land register search he had set them on?

Fran was planning meals. As a delighted Sophie had remarked, 'enough to feed a rigiment', but she hadn't argued about either the catering or the cooking involved. There was a distinct difference in Sophie's lexicon between 'Holy days' and 'holidays'. Go to work on a sabbath or a Holy day she would not; but if there was anything she dreaded, it was being forced to observe a holiday when she would rather have been at work.

'There ain't neither sense nor reason in what they call "the Christmas 'oliday" nowadays,' she said. 'Christmas is Christmas, and comes but once a year, like any other birthday. I don't grudge them as work in fact'ries and such heving three days over Christmas, but now they throw New Year in with it as well, so as it lasts a good fortnight for 'em to do nothing only sit in pubs a-swallering liquor as they can't afford. I can't abide it, unless I'm got something to do besides setting by myself and wishing I could come to work. So apart from Christmas Day, when me and Dan'el and Aunt Sar'anne hev all been asked to go to Hetty and Joe's for dinner and tea, you can count on me to be 'ere if you want me.'

It was into this hopeful, fresh prospect of the approaching festival that the telephone intruded: Bob asking William if he could come earlier than arranged, and go round by Danesum to pick Charlie up and drop her off at Glebe to pick up the car Charles had left there.

'I've got Charles here now,' he said. 'He's just brought Ginger up for me to look after, and I must say I'm glad. There's a lot going on at Glebe I don't like the sound of, though I knowed it had to come afore long. I hoped Charlie needn't be mixed up in it, but till I've heard all that Charles has to say, I can't tell you more than that. Charlie don't know yet that there is any trouble this morning so don't let on to her if you can help it. From what I gather, it might be better to let Charles tell her hisself.'

William promised, simply told Fran that his meeting with Bob had been put forward, and left Fran and Sophie planning menus to the accompaniment of Olive on her knees on the pantry floor, treading in his footsteps as 'Good King Wensis last looked out.'

Charlie, alerted by Charles, was ready and waiting when William reached Danesum. 'What's it all about?' she asked, but William denied any knowledge except that for some reason Charles had taken Ginger to her father for 'safe-keeping'.

'I can't imagine why,' she said, 'but I know Dad'll be pleased. He's having bad dreams about something happening at Glebe concerning farmyard animals. I know his presentiments are often right, but I honestly believe this one's only a repercussion of his reaction to somebody telling him of my christening Grandad's bull. He said not, and warned me to be careful of Ginger putting his foot into a rabbit-hole when I was riding him bareback. I promised him I wouldn't ride at all till after Christmas and lent Ginger to Pansy. I wonder what's made her send him back?'

By this time they had reached Glebe, and William stopped to let her get out. Charles's car stood in the roadway between the back door of the house and the new cowsheds.

'Drat,' said Charlie. 'Looks as if he was in a hurry. I shall have to back out. I must just go in and see how they all are before I come on, but you can tell Charles I'm on my way. I'm afraid there may be something amiss, so I won't be long.'

William let her go without offering to go in with her. He guessed it was no time for any outsider to intrude.

Charlie went to the back door of the house and listened. It was all so deadly quiet – no sound of voices or clattering breakfast utensils – that she decided against going in. Better get to Charles as quick as she could. She looked at her watch and saw that it was later than she had thought, so Dan must have done the milking and was probably strawing the yards. Perhaps she could glean a bit of information from him.

There was movement in Chum's yard, so she went to look there first. It was only Chum himself, mooching placidly round and round his confined space. He turned to face her, and stood looking at her with his ears alerted and his big, beautiful eyes watching her every movement. She climbed on to the second bar of the iron five-barred gate, leaned over, and gave him a cheery good morning in French. He didn't respond, so she tried English. 'Call yourself a pedigree Jersey, and don't understand French?' she said. 'We'll soon change that, once I'm free from these dratted exams. No time this morning, though. *Adieu, mon ami!*'

He was moving gently towards her, and she waited, keeping still, till he came as close as he dared, as they took stock of each other. 'You're just too beautiful for words,' she said. 'I'll see you again soon.'

Then she turned back to see if Dan was still there strawing the cows' yard. He wasn't, but the cows were there, and so was Grandad. He was in the cowshed, leaning with both his elbows on the manger. His hands were clasped and his drooping head rested on them.

She was far too sensitive not to understand the significance. There was something very wrong! She crept away without breaking into his commune with his Great Adviser, backed the car out as silently as it was possible, and within ten minutes she was greeting Charles at the front gate of Castle Hill Farm.

He led her across the familiar farmyard to what, in days past, had been her own tack-room. Since her marriage to Charles it had been kept by Bob just as she had left it: clean, tidy and immaculate. It had become Bob's own sanctuary, a place of memories that even Jane and the 'littl'uns' did not invade. There she found her father and William, who rose to welcome her, and vacated the haybales covered with one of Ginger's old blankets for her and Charles to sit side by side on.

Charles took her hand and held it while he told them exactly how the situation had stood when he had left Glebe. 'He can't be drunk all the time,' Charles said, 'but what other explanation can there be? He's acting like a madman and as far as I can see I'm the one who has to find some way of coping with him, with the farm, and looking after Mum at Temperance, Grandad and Gran at the Glebe, as well as seeing to our own concerns at Danesum. I think Aunt Marge has just been knocked out by Pansy's desertion to look after Yorky, but in the long run that may turn out all for the best. Once he's better again, he'll come and help as well as Pansy. But neither Aunt Marge nor Pansy will ever go up to keep an eye on Mum again at Temperance, and Mum won't leave Dad. What am I to do?'

'You've left me out of the reckoning,' said Charlie. 'I'd be kicked out of Temperance, but I could work just as well from Glebe as I could from home – except for a bit of time to help Aunt Marge to look after Grandad and Gran. If I stayed there at nights, and you stayed at Danesum with the telephone by your bed to keep you in touch with your mother or me if I happened to need your help, we could perhaps ride over this crucial time. But I do think we need medical help on tap. What do you think, Dad?'

He was a long time answering. 'When you find a rabbit in a snare as has gnawed it's own foot off to get free,' he said, 'you want to take your gun and shoot the chap who set the snare. But it don't do the rabbit no good. I can see, my boy, that that's the way you see it now. I reckon Charlie's suggestion is about the only one for the present time, and she's got too much sense to let it interfere with her plans. And I reckon you've forgot as there's others as'll do their bit to help how and where they can: Fran would be welcome enough at Glebe, and Beth Franks would very like lend Emerald to sit with your Gran an hour or two now and then. I'll take a turn myself whenever I can, but I can't let Jane down till this concert's over. Seems to me, Charles, that you ought to be able to rely on Charlie and friends and neighbours to keep them going at Glebe. Temperance is different. Your dad's the chap who set the snare, and you want to go and shoot him. But did he know what he was doing? Charlie's hit the nail on the head about you needing medical help. Hardy ain't the man I think he is if he won't listen and advise, though he is on official leave with things of his own to see to. Then there's his young locum. He looks to me like a chap who's got all his buttons on. None of 'em would be let in at Temperance, not even to look after your mother. This is the beginning of the end, and it'll be bad for everybody while it lasts.'

'What you're saying is that Dad's going round the bend, and I think you may be right. How can we find out? What's worrying me is what will happen if he is? I couldn't take charge of all the Bridgefoot farms, and my own land, waiting for him to get better, could I? And what about our plans at Danesum? I won't let Charlie down, whatever happens. I'll do my very best for Grandad, but Charlie comes first.'

There was such distress in his voice that both Bob and William were silent, remembering only too well when they had been in similar straits. But Charlie sat up and pulled Charles's head towards her.

'Charles, my darling,' she said. 'I married you, not a veterinary practice. It won't be the end of the world for us if we have to wait to set up our own practice. I could probably find myself a job with another vet somewhere not too far away. If I had to take next year off to help you, no real harm would be done. I can still go on with my training. Heavens above, I'm only twenty-one – barely that, yet! Stop worrying about me. We're in this together.'

'Won't you be dreadfully disappointed?'

'Of course. Nobody gets everything they want. So first things first. We've got all the future to put things right for ourselves. We can wait. The others, like your Mum and Grandad, can't. Look, ought we not to be getting back to them now?'

'Yes,' said Bob, simply. 'And stick to what you've just said. The darkest hour's just before the dawn. I'm here if you want me.' He turned away so as not to show his feelings too much. Charlie flew into his arms and hugged him, while William held out a comforting hand to Charles. 'So are we; me and Fran. But I do think you ought to get back to Glebe now, before anything else happens.'

He was anxious for a word or two alone with Bob, but for once everything else would have to wait. Maybe Fran had been right to listen to young Jehan. The whole idea that Brian might be mentally unbalanced was beginning to seep into too many people's consciousness for complacency. He wanted to get home to consult Fran.

He told Bob exactly how he felt, and why, and what a wonderful girl Charlie was. Bob nodded, his mouth trembling. Then he looked up, and said, 'They'll weather the storm, together.'

'I can't stop much longer, Bob. I'm going to see if I can waylay Terry Hardy; but what was it you wanted to see me about?'

'It can wait,' Bob said. 'I'm been cleaning up in the front of the church as much as I can, and doing a lot of thinking while I was at it. There's a lot of questions as I want to ask you – and if I'm right about what I think, it may lead us to another place to look for that sword.'

'*Sword?*' asked William, astounded. 'Who said it was a sword? I never mentioned such a thing!'

Bob smiled his mischievous smile. 'No, I know as you didn't, a-purpose. But I should ha' thought you'd know by now as I weren't born yist'day. It's like my old Uncle John said once when a stranger as asked 'im the way treated him like the idiot he expected a fenman to be. Uncle John looked after him as he drove off in what Uncle called his "montecarlo" and said to my dad, as happened to be there as well, "I don't know why that chap thinks he's so much cleverer than me. I were born with the same brain as he's got, and I'm never used none of mine up."'

They laughed, and agreed to meet again on Monday.

*

William retailed to Fran over lunch all he had heard at Castle Hill about the worsened and worsening situation at Glebe. It was clear, he said, that it was beginning to dawn on Charles – and perhaps on Charlie – that Brian's behaviour was not that of a normal, reasonable man; that what had been said several times in irritation or anger, that he 'must be going round the bend', or was 'acting like a madman', might have some validity. He told her how Charlie had declared that whatever arrangements they made, for everybody's sake they should have medical help of some kind laid on in case it should be needed.

It had been a bit difficult for him, William said, because none of the other three present this morning were as well aware as he was of Brian's antagonism to doctors, demonstrated so venomously during Charles's illness. It was Charlie's absence that was the cause of that illness; Bob knew of it only by hearsay, though he had been the one to apply the right treatment – to Brian's increased fury; and Charles himself would not cooperate, because all he had wanted to do was to die.

'So although Charles and Bob were agreeing that Brian's present behaviour was very strange indeed, it was Charlie who classed it as being extraordinary enough for them possibly to need medical help on tap. I could do no more than say I thought so too, and offer to try to get some sort of opinion as to what to do next out of Terry. The trouble about that is that he's the last person who'll want to discuss it, especially just now, but, darling, I think it's reached a critical stage. You instinctively paid far more attention to what Chandra said than I did, and if I remember correctly, Terry ignored his colleague's unguarded remark except

367

to make it clear that there was nothing more he could do. But somebody has to do something soon, before it turns into a ghastly tragedy. The question is: what, and how?'

She considered it for a moment, conscious of a feeling of relief that the seriousness of it had at last got through to someone other than herself. 'A straight line is the shortest distance between two points,' she answered. 'We are at one point, and Terry at the other – on leave or not. Let's ring him up, and ask him to come here, where there is no one but us to have any idea why he has come except as a friend who's at a loose end because his wife-to-be is temporarily out of his reach. No subterfuge – but even telephones are dangerous. Get him here by saying we have a problem which we can only tell him when he gets here. He'll come. There must be some way round such cases. If necessary we can call on Alex to back up our statements.'

So William rang and found that their estimate of Terence was correct. He asked no questions, said he would be having supper with Jehan, and would come round immediately afterwards.

Meanwhile, Charles and Charlie had arrived back at the Old Glebe. Marjorie was creeping about with eyes so swollen with crying that she could barely see out of them, making alternate trips between Gran lying inert in bed, and George sitting uncomfortably in his chair, looking ten years older than he had when Charles had talked to him last. He greeted them normally, but it was plain that his morale was at an all-time low. During his lonely sojourn in the cowshed, he had tried to lay all his problems before his unfailing Friend. But hearing his own thoughts so poured out, for the first time he entertained a suspicion that there had to be serious reasons for Brian treating him and Mother and Rosemary as he was doing. One could be that he was ill, and would not admit it; another was that the family was in his bad books for preventing him from carrying out some far-reaching project to modernize the farms. If either or both were the case, it would spoil George's own new-found contentment. But why didn't his son come and discuss it with him, man to man, instead of making them all miserable and worried to the point of being ill, as was the case at present?

He heard, more or less without comment, the proposals that Charles put forward to spread the care of Rosemary, Mother and himself between those still available. To relieve Marjorie, Charles was now taking Charlie home to collect her things, and would then bring her back to stay for as long as it took.

Charles would take some of his things up to Temperance, so as to be able to stay at nights with his mother if she wanted him; he would have to work during the day, so would make Danesum his base, where they could keep in touch with him by telephone if he couldn't get to see them twice every day. They could, and would keep in constant touch with each other.

'Cheer up, Grandad,' Charles said. 'It's the best we can do for the time being. Quite likely Pansy and Yorky will be back by tomorrow. And William said we were not to forget that we have a whole lot of friends to call on as well. Fran will come and sit with Gran, for instance, and if you need him, he'll be here as soon as he can. Charlie's dad will do anything he can to help inside or out, and there's always Dan to look after things. Can you hold the fort here for another hour or so, Aunt Marge, till I bring Charlie back?'

Marge gave them a weak smile. 'Just about,' she said. 'I'm only over-tired. I could sleep pegged on a clothes-line, but I'd got out of the habit of sleeping before all this started. The tireder I get, the less I sleep. It'll be lovely to know that Charlie's here. Don't worry about her – we'll look after each other.' She kissed Charlie, and went hurriedly back upstairs.

'God bless you both, now and for ever more,' said George. 'Them as put their trust in God are hardly ever give more to bear than they can cope with. Whatever happens, we must put up with it in as good heart as we possibly can. After all, we're still Bridgefoots, and we've known trouble afore now. It's all in God's hands, do what we may. Our part is to keep faith with Him and each other, and meet trouble with a brave heart. I wasn't sure as I could, this morning, but you've all made me feel better.'

'Grandad's found his courage again,' Charlie said as they drove away.

Charles had some difficulty in answering her. 'It's what it's doing to you and all our plans that I can't face,' he said. 'And I want you at home with me. I need you more than all the rest of them put together. Whatever should I have done without you?'

*

Fran had persuaded William to take the bull by the horns; that he should tell Terry how matters with regard to the whole Bridgefoot family stood, and ask for his advice on what they could do. They appreciated that he could do no more than to put them on the track of getting other medical help before it was too late to save what the Bridgefoots were, and stood for in the village.

'I'm on leave,' he said. 'I'm not, at this precise moment, anything but a friend with some specialist knowledge which is at your disposal if I can help at all. I've met opposition from people who had good reasons of their own for not wanting to hear what a doctor has to say, and I know that many people fear hospitals and react badly to doctors who, these days, can't cure them with a bottle of medicine handed to them on the spot. Usually the reason for it is financial: fear of being off work when money is tight, and so on. Which doesn't apply at all in this case. Then again, it sometimes results from bad experiences when young: fear of any doctor, in fact. As far as I know, that doesn't apply, either. And as I told you before, he can't be made to have attention he doesn't want unless he is a danger to other people – physically violent or infectious, for example.'

'In this case, it appears to be pathological,' William said. 'And we have had one instance of it before, as I explained to you, when Alex Marland got the worst of it. Would a conference with Alex help us at all?'

Terry was hesitating. 'It isn't that I won't help,' he said, 'but I have to be in London on Wednesday, and I doubt if Dr Marland could set up a time to meet us before then. It would have to be early in the morning. Jehan is driving me up, because he's used to London, and I'm not. And I may be away for some time after that.'

The mention of Jehan prompted Fran, who had so far left it all to William, to ask the question that was bothering her. She reminded Terry of Dr Chandra's off-the-cuff remark that if Brian was going to keep up the sort of behaviour he had exhibited that morning 'as long as he lived', it might not be long.

'I know he didn't mean it flippantly, as that somebody would dot him one in anger,' Fran said. 'It was an incautious, spontaneous diagnosis, and as such I took it, but William wouldn't listen to me. Tell me what you made of it.'

'Like William, I considered it best forgotten, for both men's sake. I didn't blame Jehan; I'd seen him literally kicked out of the house because he was coloured. But I thought it best to warn him that there might be others in and around here who felt the same, even if they didn't act so stupidly. To my surprise he said he had meant it seriously and told me why. But that is something I can't repeat, though if we could meet Dr Marland, Jehan could tell him himself.'

'Alex has let it be known he doesn't want to be involved again,' Fran said. 'It would be different if we could wait till Alex is around at Christmas and had an informal chat. But I'm afraid to try and set up a meeting in London would be out of the question. Forget it, Terry. You've done your best to help. Just keep your fingers crossed for them all while you're away. Will you be away at Christmas – and if you are, will Jehan be standing in for you? We must see that he gets invited out to lunch somewhere on Christmas Day.'

'Too late, Fran dear,' Terry told her. 'He's fixed up already – at the Old Rectory. He took one look at Emerald and fell flat for her. Beth *is* a patient, so he can call as often as he dare without raising comment. She took the hint and told Elyot, who is amused. He seems to have got a new lease of life in the last day or so.

'I wish I could be of more use to you, but it has all happened at a busy time for me, personally.'

Discreetly, they asked no more questions.

*

Charles, in very low spirits, delivered Charlie back to Glebe and then went home again to Danesum to try to come to terms with the new situation. This vacation had been looked forward to for so long – it being the last but one of Charlie's first degree – with all their future depending on making forward plans for it now. In the present circumstances, to plan even a day ahead was impossible; or even for the next hour.

He had done all he could for those at Glebe: lending them, as it were, his greatest treasure. Bless her for being so willing to help, even to suggesting that if need be they could postpone or alter their own plans. He had hated having to leave his wife at Glebe, knowing that he was not going to be able to fetch her back home to sit with him before their glowing log fire, making the most of the present while looking into the future – with ambition backed by courage – before it was time for bed. Together.

Now he sat alone and faced the reality that it was not only this Christmas that was in jeopardy, but their entire future. Without Charlie, he felt terribly alone and helpless.

*   *   *

Next morning, the clock reminded him how time was flying, and that as he had taken upon himself the task of looking after his mother (which meant his father as well), he ought to be heading towards Temperance. It was the inclusion of his father in his obligation that was keeping him sitting where he was, instead of reluctantly getting on with what he had to do.

He was afraid that if his father was at home when he got to Temperance, there was more likely to be a row than a welcome awaiting him. But while Grandad and Gran now had Charlie with them to cheer them up, his mother had nobody – except him, now that his aunt was banned from visiting her. She had backed him against his father when the chips had been down once before; it was his turn now to stand by her.

He was relieved to see that his father's car was not in sight when he arrived at Temperance, and more than surprised to find his mother up and dressed, pathetically pleased to see him.

She was sitting alone at the table in the kitchen/house-place. 'How have you managed to get up?' he asked, suddenly filled with hope. 'Did Dad help you? And get you your breakfast?'

She shook her head, valiantly trying to hold back tears. 'I haven't seen him at all since last night,' she said. 'He went out about seven, saying he was going to fetch us both a take-away supper, and I thought I heard the car come back. But I haven't seen him since. In the end I came downstairs and made myself some bread and milk.

'I'm feeling a lot stronger and it doesn't hurt me half so much to move as it did. So I decided to try to get myself up without help – and here I am. I'm glad you came, though, because I haven't had a cup of tea yet. I was just trying to make myself get up to put the kettle on when I heard your car. I thought it was your dad, so I sat still to see what sort of a mood he was in.

'Charles –' she said, suddenly urgent. 'I'm so glad you've come before he does. *I'm so frightened of him!*'

He set the kettle down and turned back to her, horrified. He sat down beside her, and she clung to him. He wondered if it was she who was having delusions, sending his father into fits of temper by accusing him of having 'another woman'. But past experience told him that was not the case.

He let her cry, and made her a strong cup of tea and some toast, waiting for her to calm down enough to be able to talk rationally with him. He dared not leave it much longer before telling her the latest arrangements, in case his father should appear. His plan, thought up on the spur of the moment, was to persuade her to let him take her back with him to Danesum.

More secure than she had felt for a week or more with this six-foot-something young, strong man beside her, she ate her breakfast hungrily, and pushed her plate aside. Then he began to tell her exactly how matters stood at Glebe, pulling no punches. She had to know.

'Grandad looks ten years older than he did when you last saw him,' he said. 'He's bewildered. Knocked sideways. Gran's just staying in bed and crying, which you know isn't at all like her. I think it's more because she doesn't want to see Grandad in such trouble, or hear Aunt Marge going on about Dad than anything wrong with her. Gran doesn't want to have to blame Dad. She loves him best because he's her first child and her only son. But poor Aunt Marge can't forgive him, and won't, for telling such awful lies about her. And Mum . . . I know she's dreadfully upset again about Pansy going off with Yorky. Apart from everything else, it's robbed Aunt Marge of the two people whom she thought she could rely on to help out. Pansy was doing her best for you up here, and Yorky was relieving her of all the cooking and washing-up and such at Glebe, so that she could get a bit of rest in the afternoons, and I think, have a good cry. Now she's disappointed that Pansy is letting her down again.'

'Don't blame Pansy!' said his mother, in a firmer and more positive voice than so far he had heard this morning. 'She's been an angel of patience and loving care to me, and to your dad as well, when he had awful headaches or fits of crying. She wouldn't have let us down – any of us – if she could have stood it. But she's not well herself yet, nor strong enough to put up with your dad's tantrums. He frightened her off, honestly, being so violent as he was. She probably cleared off because she didn't want to tell Grandad or Aunt Marge the truth. Look how he was towards that nice new young doctor. Mad with temper – unless he was drunk.

'Pansy had sat up with him all night because he was having one of his terrible headaches, but he dropped off to sleep at last, down in his office. She stopped with him till he roused and then asked him if he wanted anything. He told her that all he wanted was for her to get out of his sight and out of our house. He didn't want a trollop like her or her mother over his doorstep again. She stood it one more day before she gave in and rang Charlie. Do you wonder?' And to Charles's dismay, Rosemary put her head down on the table, and began to cry: racking, helpless, despairing sobs such as he had never seen or heard from her before.

'Mum,' he said, 'we have to do something quick now, before he comes in and I lose my temper and lay him out. Can you get some things together, so that I can take you home to Danesum with me? I can look after you better there, and I don't think he'd come and play his tricks with me up there like he does with Grandad at Glebe. Let me get you away safe, while we've still got time.'

He was trying to help her stand up, but she pushed him away. She sat up, dried her eyes, and looked her son in the eye. 'No!' she said. 'I won't agree to that.' He knew she meant it. She went on: 'You'll never understand what I owe him, and all the rest of the Bridgefoots. I married him because I loved him, for better, for worse. He gave me all that I treasure most: my comfortable home, a loving family who took me in as one of them from the very first; and most of all, he gave me you. A fine wife I should be if I left him now, because however much he has changed, and whatever he does, there must be some reason for it that we don't know yet. While he lives I shall never leave him – though I think he may leave me. If he does turn me out, well, we'll cross that bridge when we come to it. You can see how much better I am than I have been, so I can cope by myself for a few days if I have to. This is my home, and he's still my husband. I have no intention of losing either because I can't wait a little longer to find out what's the matter with him.

'I know I've given in to him far too much in the past, for the sake of peace and quietness, but when it comes to the crunch I know right from wrong. If I took his side against you over Charlie, I hope I made it up to you later by holding out for you to have my shares. That's something he'll never forgive me for. I had to be strong when it was a question of your rights against his. I'm like your grandad in things of that sort. We do as we would be done by. He does what he wants. So let me be, Charles, please. I'll cope somehow.'

He knew when he was beaten. He told her he would be up again before dark, and would stay the night if she wanted him to. Then he kissed her again, and left, not having seen his father, for which he knew he had cause to be thankful. He was still too angry for any encounter with him, yet.

He couldn't take his mind off Glebe, so he went back there as soon as he'd seen to things on his own farm that had to be done, and found himself a snack lunch. Charlie was washing up in the kitchen, so he got a cuddle and a word with her before he had to see the others.

It was as plain as a pikestaff that Charlie's presence among them had already been a good tonic. The whole tone of the house was brighter. Gran was having her afternoon snooze, Charlie said, but she had been up and about this morning. Charlie guessed she'd got up to be able to keep one eye on Grandad. Fifty years spent together had made them react to each other's feelings, and Molly couldn't lie in bed till he'd recovered a bit of his ordinary courageous self. She had known, the moment he'd come in from the cowshed, that he'd found that what the Rector had called the 'everlasting arms' were still ready to support him if his load of grief became too heavy for him to carry unaided.

Marge came downstairs looking a great deal less tense than she had been earlier, and made cups of tea for four. They sat round the house-place table to drink it, while Charles unfolded the budget of his visit to his mother. There was a long silence when he had finished. It was George who broke it, his voice resolute again, if tinged with sadness.

'He's been nasty a good many times before, when he couldn't have things all his own way, though to my knowledge he's never showed no violence – least of all to Rosy. She's been behind him at every turn, and backed him a good many times when I wanted to take him down a peg or two. So I think she's right to stick it out now, though if he ever lays hands on her I'll teach him a lesson myself, old as I am. But I needn't tell you how to look after her, my boy. If I were you, though, I'd do my best to keep out of his way. Tempers get frayed in a crisis but sooner or later there's going to be a souser of a thunderstorm to clear the air. It must come soon, and we shall all feel better afterwards.'

'Dad says it's bound to get worse before it's better,' Charlie said.

'I wish I hadn't got so steamed up again about Pansy,' Marjorie confessed. 'It never crossed my mind that she was *frightened* of him, but from what Rosy told Charles, both of them were. And if he ever set for Pansy like he did me, I don't blame her for walking out. Bless her. I'll bet she went off with Yorky because she was afraid she'd break down and pour it all out to us. And I've been so furious with her I felt as if I never wanted to set eyes on her again. Worrying about her's been half my trouble. We never had a chance to make it up properly.'

'She was a brick all the way along,' Charlie said. 'We'll make it up to her, see if we don't.'

'Come and see me off, lambkin,' Charles said.

She needed no second bidding to have him to herself for a few minutes. 'Let me put my coat on,' she said. 'I want to go and see Chum. I've decided that if I only ever speak French to him, he'll get to know me from everybody else who bawls at him in English.' George shifted in his chair to ease his hip, and chuckled. She never failed to have something up her sleeve to amuse him.

He got up and went to the door to watch them as they went, arms round each other, towards Chum's pen. Charlie climbed up a couple of bars of the fence, leaned over, and began to chatter to the bull, who after a bit of hesitation, came closer. 'There, what did I tell you?' she asked triumphantly of Charles, who picked her away into his arms to kiss her. But he left her leaning over the fence again, singing '*La Vie en Rose*' to a puzzled bull.

*

Later the same day, Marjorie asked Charlie if she minded being left alone for a couple of hours with Gran and Grandad, because she wanted to go to see the Rector. It was just possible that Pansy had let him know where she was, since it had been he who had been responsible for bringing her home.

'She *had* changed,' Marjorie said, 'and I can't believe she would let him down. Nothing was fair to her when she came home expecting to be loved and forgiven – and then was put under far too much strain. I don't know what she's doing now.'

Charlie agreed, and rang Charles to tell him that she would be alone; she didn't mind in the least, but if he wasn't going up to his mother for supper, why not come to the Old Glebe instead?

He was sorely tempted, but his mother was his first charge, so he said he'd find out whether she needed him, and let Charlie know. It was only a matter of minutes later that his telephone bell rang.

'Hello, Mum', he said, put immediately on guard by the tone of her voice. 'How are things now? I was just going to ring to find out. Do you want me to come ready to stay the night?'

'No!' she said, keeping her voice almost to a whisper. 'I wanted to get in first to stop you from coming. Your dad was asleep in his chair in the office when you arrived this morning, but awake enough by the time you went to know you had been here. Watched you leave, in fact. Then he came and asked me what you had wanted, so I said only to help if you could. He wasn't in a good mood, and he had a good deal to say about you minding your own business and leaving him alone to mind his. When he asked who had helped to get me up and dressed, and I said I had managed by myself, he was nasty and said in that case there'd be no need for me to have a baby-sitter at night any longer. He was fed up with having folk in his house that he hadn't wanted, and he wasn't putting up with it any longer. He'd been spied on long enough, and the last person he cared to have know his business was Charlie. I'm sorry, my son, but I had wondered whether always having somebody about here was getting to him. And he can't but know how we all feel about the way he's treating Grandad. Perhaps it would be better to humour him. Don't worry about me.'

'But, Mum, you told me yourself this morning that he got into such rages that you and Pansy were *frightened* of him! I can't leave you alone with him like that, can I?'

'I'm asking you to, please, Charles. I can always ring you somehow if I want you. I'm sure it's for the best, and I'm all right, honestly.'

'Where is he now?'

'I don't know. He goes out in his car often without telling me where. But he did say he'd be back before long, and didn't want to find anybody here but me. That's why I'm able to ring you.'

'Well, I'm going up to Glebe in time for supper, but I'll come back here to sleep – and will be ready to come if you want me. And I shall come in any case first thing in the morning.'

He wasn't at all satisfied, but there was nothing else he could do to help her but let her have her way in trying to placate his father. All the same, he wouldn't leave Danesum just yet. He still had a few little jobs to do, but wanted to stay where he could hear the telephone bell. When nothing happened, he banked up the fire, fed the dog and the cats, and reluctantly left the warm room with its flickering firelight. He would have left it for nowhere else other than the place where Charlie flickered even more warmly and brightly for him.

Charlie had persuaded Grandad to put his troubles behind him and play dominoes with her. Molly, watching from her chair, saw how much more at ease he was to have something to keep his mind off his troubles, and she slipped into a nap. She slept there in her chair for a while better than she had done in her bed since the day of their party.

Charlie had begun to think Aunt Marge had been gone longer than she had intended, giving way to the sort of niggle that won't be set aside when trouble is in the air. She 'gave herself a good talking to', and when they had had enough of playing dominoes, looked out of the window to watch for Charles's car lights or, perhaps, Aunt Marge's, coming down the lane. That would be the signal for setting out their supper. Molly roused up at that, and said she'd be glad to see about supper. Marge had decided what they were going to have, anyway. It was a clear, cold night with a moon not yet quite full but risen high enough to flood the world with glimmering light, reflected and thrown back by every shiny surface, and by contrast darkening every shadowed spot its beams did not reach.

'Grandad,' she said, 'do you mind if I put my coat on and go and talk to Chum while I wait for Charles? Do you know, I'm sure he's beginning to recognize me! He looked quite goo-goo-eyed at me when I sang to him this afternoon, turning his head from side to side and now and then making a little low noise as if he'd have loved to join in.'

George laughed. 'I don't disbelieve you,' he said, 'though thousands would! After all, he's male. That's what we bought him for – and I've never yet seen a cow as could hold a candle to you. Perhaps you'd better try singing in French to your Uncle Brian.'

'Italian, I think, for him, but I doubt if it would work. I'm the very last one whose music would have any charms to soothe his savage breast. I do wonder what can be the matter with him.

Now, try not to go back to worrying about anything while I'm gone. Charles will be here soon, so let's try to forget everything else.'

She had put on her outdoor coat, wrapped a long woollen scarf round her neck, and wore a jaunty little cap on the crown of her head.

'You look good enough to eat,' he said. 'Charlie, don't take too many chances with that bull, will you? We haven't had him long enough to be sure of his temper, though Dan's pleased enough with him. But accidents happen and we don't want anything else just now.'

She came back and kissed him. 'I've had to promise Dad I wouldn't ride Ginger and Charles that I'll never go into Chum's yard with him again by myself. I keep my promises, Grandad.'

He didn't answer her, but his eyes filled with tears as he held her hand to his face and kissed it before letting it go. How could he have been so lucky to get her for a granddaughter-in-law? To mother the next generation of Bridgefoots? That's what she had meant when she said she always kept her promises.

He closed his eyes and sent upwards a paean of wordless praise and gratitude. This cloud would pass in the course of time. With so many blessings, he must be prepared for some of them to be taken from him sooner or later. He prayed for strength to meet whatever was in store.

Charlie sat on the top of the fence round Chum's yard, with her back up against the buildings that separated his quarters from that of the cows. They provided a windbreak for her against what little breeze there was, and gave her a view of the moonlit scene, as well as of the gate through which at any moment she expected Charles or Aunt Marge to drive. Though the clean shiny straw of the yard silvered in the moonlight, there was no sign of Chum. He had, she guessed, been loosely tethered inside his own shed by a thick rope through his nose-ring, which she detested, but knew had to be. She could hear him moving about, and from the dark shadow of her sheltered nook began to chat softly to him in French, and was gratified to detect that he was standing still to listen. When, just as softly, she began to sing, she was answered by a soft, gentle sound somewhere between a snort and a moo. Though she hardly believed it herself, he was definitely showing signs of recognizing her voice. And here was Charles – or was it Aunt Marge back? Till she knew, she stayed put where she was.

Across the little yard from where she sat, close by the house, was a smooth patch big enough for two cars to stand side by side, though mostly only occupied by one: Aunt Marge's. Most other casual callers drove right to the door, turned in a space only just big enough, and went again. This must be Charles. He drew into the vacant car-standing space, and was getting out when she called to him. He crossed towards the sound of her with huge strides, looking for her.

'Darling, I'm here,' she called. The moonlight being so bright made her almost invisible in the dark shadow. He climbed up beside her and greeted her as if he hadn't seen her for years.

'Lambkin, you shouldn't scare me like that! I honestly thought for a moment that you were playing tricks with the bull again. Don't ever take silly risks – for my sake.'

She laughed, cuddling up to him. 'I have got some sense, you know,' she said. 'For one thing, I'm old enough to know the facts of life! I'm well aware that if one of the cows comes into season, Grandad and Dan'll be glad they've got him ringed. I said so to Dan the other day, to let him know he needn't worry about me being on too friendly terms with Chum, and do you know what he said? "If that were the way of it, Mis' Charles, it'd be the cow as you'd need to stop away from! Cows are like gals are nowadays, mad after the men. But then – there's a lot o' women like that for no reason at all only wanting to hev everything their own way"!'

'This is nice,' Charles said. 'Let's stop here for a few minutes to be by ourselves, if you're sure Grandad and Gran are all right.' Then he added, rather hesitantly, 'Lambkin, are you sure you're all right? After Mum telling me that she and Pansy were really scared of Dad, I don't like leaving you here by your-self. Like tonight. He's used to coming in and out of this house without knocking any more than I do, just as he likes. While he's in this mad sort of mood the sight of you being here would be like a red rag to him. If he ever lays a finger on you, I'll kill him . . .'

'Ssh!' she said, her lips against his ear. 'I can hear somebody coming up from the barn way. Keep still and be quiet . . . and watch.'

They crouched back into the shadow and sat listening tensely as somewhat furtive footfalls came nearer, but turned towards the house before reaching them. Charles leaned out a little to see better. The moonlight now was full on the old half-timbered house, against which the dark figure of a man showed up clearly.

'It's Dad!' Charles hissed. 'Whatever's he up to?'

There was no doubt at all what he was up to. He went to the window of the house-place and listened. (Of course, as Charlie worked out for herself afterwards, he didn't know that Marjorie wasn't there. He'd taken it for granted that Charles's car was Marjorie's.) After a very long-seeming five minutes or so for the silent watchers, he listened at the door, and then made straight towards them – but to their relief went to the fence on the cows' side. They heard him fiddling with the gate's bolts, open it, close it again, and then stride off towards the barn.

Charles was livid with impotent rage. 'So that's how he's been getting the low-down on everything!' he exploded. 'Casing the joint like a burglar, to make sure he keeps one step ahead of Grandad. And poor old Mum grieving her heart out thinking he was seeing another woman! The craftiness of coming in the back way and leaving his car down by the barn, so that he could keep watch on us without us seeing him! Lambkin, do you honestly think he can be in his right mind? I do begin to wonder, and I'm afraid for Mum, and for you, and for Aunt Marge. She's late, isn't she? Where's she gone?'

'To see the Rector, because she thinks he may have heard from Pansy.'

'Well, I'm not leaving here until she gets home. But I'm jolly hungry. What's for supper?' He swung her from her perch on the rail and carried her triumphantly into the house where, to their surprise, Molly had got ham and cold beef and potatoes in their jackets and pickles ready on the table. 'And a roly-poly jam roll still cooking,' she said. 'Marge got it all ready for me to finish before she went, while Charlie was cheering Grandad up.'

They said nothing about having seen Brian; and when Charles finally left, though Marge had still not returned, George went to wind up the old grandfather clock. Charlie went with him. 'Can I learn how to do that, Grandad?' she asked.

'No, my pretty,' he said. 'Nobody else but me may do it till I have to pass it on. Country folks are superstitious about clocks, you know – like stopping every timepiece in the house when anybody's a-dying, and taking it as a sign of death if one as has been properly wound up stops for no reason.'

He opened the door of the clock, showing Charlie its huge, misshapen lead weight, and the thick spliced ropes by which he was raising it.

'There's a bit of that rope getting rather worn, Grandad,' Charlie said. 'Had you noticed? What do you do when it wears through?'

'I don't let it wear through,' he said. 'I get a new length o' rope to splice, and replace it afore it breaks. I'm glad you reminded me. All this other business has took it out of my mind. I must see to it soon.' He closed the door and fastened it with a bent hairpin that had been there since he was a child. Then he patted the clock's face, and said, 'Goodnight, old friend. Ah! Here's Marge home, safe sound. We'll hear all her tale in the morning' – a suggestion that Marjorie was very glad to agree to.

*　　*　　*

Marjorie said next morning that she had found Nigel at home when she reached Church Cottage, absolutely worn out with hard physical work and hunger. There had not been a moment to spare since Saturday, when he had been with Eric to inspect the barn at Monastery Farm, and pronounced it almost too good to be true; they had begun there and then to plan for such popular events as a carol service before Christmas and a watch-night service on New Year's Eve. Eric felt better for knowing that he would not have to let any of his special Christmas clientele down, and indeed might – by using both the other ancient church and this barn, updated as it was with new technology – perhaps be offering them something different, that in future years they would enjoy as well as the traditional events.

But they had been faced with difficulties that two men couldn't deal with themselves, especially as one was old and had many other duties to attend to, and the other out of his depth with the top-class recording and synthesizing equipment that Gavin, his son, had left ready for use when or if ever he came back. He was shocked to find how grubby and dusty the barn was after being neglected for so long. And there was no piano.

Eric, at first a bit appalled by what there was to arrange, had a brainwave. He rang young Nick Hadley-Gordon in Cambridge, told him the position and asked if he knew anybody, from professional expert to keen amateur, in the hi-fi business. Yes, Nick did know such a person whom he thought would be too intrigued by it all to want to be left out. Nick rang later to say his friend would be out on Monday. Boosted by one success, Eric next rang the biggest music shop in Cambridge, and succeeded, with very little fuss, in arranging for the hire of a grand piano to be *in situ* in the barn by the end of the following week. It was very short notice, the manager of the shop said, so there would have to be a bit of extra cost. Extra cost? Who cared? Forget it. Whatever it cost, he himself would be responsible for paying it. He was more than busy again, and consequently happy.

On Sunday, they had looked around them again at the dust and muck in the barn, and remembered all the chairs that would have to be hired and set up. And there was the question of insurance . . . A day in Cambridge, they decided, would cover all outstanding problems except the dust and muddle. The two men set to work, but soon Nigel was exhausted.

It was Nigel's turn for a brainwave. Surely regular members of the church would do what they could to help? He rang up Fran Burbage to ask if she thought Sophie and Daniel Bates could be persuaded to wield brooms and dusters? Yes, said Fran, she was sure they would, and she'd tackle Sophie; but so would Ned, who'd probably round up some of the other bell-ringers to help as well. She had no doubt that Greg and Beth would take turns at the piano, and might even be able to find other volunteers.

It was, said Nigel to Eric, one of those occasions when God was showing the truth of the adage that he helped them who showed willing to help themselves. But alas, it was by now getting late, and he was very tired as well as hungry. He'd had nothing to eat since breakfast. He was afraid that if he didn't soon go home and take a rest, his bad leg would give out on him, and disrupt all their plans.

So Eric had hastily sent him home, where he put his aching leg up on a settee and decided he was too tired to get himself anything other than a good strong drink.

There Marjorie found him, and was immediately covered with guilt and shame. It was her job to look after him, as he had looked after her – and Pansy. She had let him down during this last week, but at least she was there now, and could make him his supper! Which task she proceeded to do with goodwill and expertise, tidying her way round the cottage as she cooked.

It was only after he had eaten and rested a little, while she was washing the pile of accumulated dishes in the sink, that he called her to come and talk to him.

'Thank you,' he said. 'That was really delicious. But I must apologize for being so selfish! You didn't come up so late in the day just to cook my supper. You must have needed to see me about some other matter. Am I right?'

She nodded. 'Pansy again, I'm afraid. But I ought not to have expected you to have time to give me, when you have such a load on your plate, and have already done so much for her – and me. Please don't bother about it now.'

'But you've done more for me in this last hour than I for any of you today. I've missed your help, but with one thing and another I haven't found time even to get to see your father in his distress. Eric told me that he feared it was all boiling up to a crisis with your brother, but apart from keeping your father in as good spirits as possible, there's very little more anybody can do. Except to pray that the troublemaker, whoever he may be, recovers his senses and lets us all return to normal. So, please tell me what you came for. I shall sleep better, you know, if I know what I haven't done, rather than lying awake worrying what it could have been.'

She gave in to his skilled manner of probing anxious hearts and handling broken hopes. She told him all.

'O, that!' he said, when she had done, in such a tone of relief that it made her laugh.

'What on earth were you expecting?' she asked. 'And why are you treating it as only a pinprick to set beside everything else that girl has done? She owed us better than that – let alone you. Not that it was her fault, but she might have thought of Dad and Mum and – and me. She'd only been back a week when off she goes again into the unknown, as if we meant nothing at all to her, and her nothing at all to us. I came here because I hoped she might have had the decency to ring you and thank you, if nothing else.'

'My dear Marjorie, you know she's with Yorky at the junction of Lane's End Estate and Hen Street. I'd hardly call that "the unknown"! She has rung me, but I understood from her that she did tell you where she was going and why. She has been giving all her caring skills to Yorky, and from what I gathered when I visited them "caring" is the operative word. I have great admiration for her. She didn't ask me to tell you or not to tell you. I think she had her hands so full that she took it for granted I would. But this has been no normal week for any of us and I'm afraid she came rather a long way down my list of priorities. I honestly believed you'd know how the matter stands now.'

'Yes, I do understand that she had to stop till his fit of panic was over. But I can't see how that excuses her for leaving us flat when we were so much in need of her help with all her family. To take Yorky home and put him to bed and send for his doctor was one thing, but she just went and didn't come back. She walked out on us, just like that. It was as if she had deliberately chosen to slap my face, and let us know what a lot of suckers we were to take her back without asking any questions, or being given any explanation, and without a single word or sign of repentance for all the misery she's caused us since her father was killed.'

'Are you sure that's right, Marjorie? Wouldn't it be truer to say "Since the death of her first love"? She was lost without him, and from what my old friends who took over her rehabilitation gathered when she was so ill, she didn't want to live. She had tried to kill her pain by using drugs other than those the doctors offer and by "living it up" with alcohol and smoking and promiscuous sex – the sort of things that people with money think will make them happy. She found out the hard way that nothing but Love can cure Love's wounds. That's what my wonderful friends were able to teach her and give to her. Through them she had also begun to regain her self-respect. Perhaps it was my fault that she came home before she was quite ready to face the ordeal. I knew she would be enfolded by Love at home, and no recriminations made, or I wouldn't have risked bringing her.'

'But she did have all that, from all of us except Brian,' protested Marjorie, 'even under the unhappy circumstances we were in. I agree it was very sad that we had no option but to accept her offer to go and look after Rosemary. It wasn't my fault, or anybody else's but Brian's, perhaps, that she cleared off again. Why did she do that to us? Kick us when we were already down? Was it to get her own back on us for all she had suffered? If so, her so-called "cure" is nothing but a sham.'

As he had been expecting she would, she had begun to cry. He got up, mixed her a stiff brandy and soda, and sat down beside her.

'Drink that,' he said, 'and then listen. She had to make a choice yesterday, and it wasn't an easy one for her. It was a case of there and then, without a chance to think or talk it over with anyone, not even with her own heart or conscience. Have you ever heard the story of Sir Philip Sidney at the battle of Zutphen? You've all been through such a battle as that and have all been wounded, Pansy as much as anybody. Sir Philip was wounded, and dying. So were many common soldiers lying round him. He called for water and, because he was a nobleman and an officer, it was brought to him; but nobody heeded the tortured cries for water of a common soldier lying close by – except Sir Philip himself. "Give it to him," he is supposed to have said. "His need is greater than mine."

'I think it was just that sort of decision Pansy had to make yesterday. She had to judge who had the greatest need of her – not just of her care, but of her love. Yorky was *in extremis* because of lost love and she had filled the empty place in his heart. His panic was caused by his belief that he had nothing at all to entice her to stay near him, not just for that day, but for always. Nothing but Love.

'What he didn't know was that his love and need of her was the one thing that would and could cure the still open wound the death of her first sweetheart had caused. Like that boy who died, Yorky loved her for no other reason than that he did. And she loved him, as she had loved the boy, only for the same reason – that she did.

'Try to understand, Marjorie. She made her decision to stay with him *for always* – a tremendous decision in a moment of great crisis. Sir Philip, and the man he tried to help, both died. If the rest of you now accept Pansy's choice, both of that couple will live. And if I may be permitted a hackneyed cliché, it is that I think you will not have lost your daughter this time. You will have gained a son.'

*　　*　　*

William could hardly wait to get to Castle Hill and Bob again. He dared not hope for much, but there had been a lift in Bob's voice that weighed against the overall pessimism related to the Bridgefoots. Though he tried to be as objective as he could about it, and as rational as his long training in academic research bade him, his faith in Bob's fey sort of magic, backed as it always was with high intelligence and keen practical observation, grew stronger all the time.

It was Monday. Fran and Sophie, having decided that they must prepare against whatever Christmas brought, were enjoying themselves making lists for catering and cooking, consulting well-worn, handwritten cook-books that had originated with Sophie's mother, because Sophie had refused from the beginning to have any truck with 'them there French grams and "lighters", nor yet them silly American "cups". What's a cup?' she asked scornfully. 'That ain't no measure for nothing only laziness, far as I can see. Cups come in all sizes. There's neither sense nor reason in these new-fangled measures. We'll stick to our own old wayses, and receipts as are been tried and can be trusted to turn out right.'

'I'll soon be out of your way,' William told them, though to tell the truth, when he had nothing else particularly on his mind, he enjoyed listening – but when Olive, too near to him for her voice to be ignored, suddenly lifted it to declare loudly and very much off key that she loved Rose-Marie, and that of all the queens that ever reigned she choosed to be ruled by her, he kissed Fran and beat a hasty retreat.

It was another fine December morning, if not a bright one. William made direct for Castle Hill, still endeavouring to subdue his quite unwarranted feeling of excitement by admitting to himself that if what he was feeling was false hope, he would have to agree to the matter being shelved till Christmas was over. Whatever it was that Bob had up his sleeve, it would, like Sophie's 'receipts' have to be tried before it could be trusted, and there was so little time left. He would have to be patient. As he went up the rise towards the little church, he smiled to himself, remembering the autograph-book rhyme of his schooldays which went:

> Patience is a virtue
> Possess it if you can.
> Seldom found in woman
> And *never in a man*.

How many aids to their social understanding of everyday life the young of yesterday had had compared to the never-ending stream of 'expert' advice available to them from social workers and the like nowadays.

As he expected, Bob was already waiting at the church door, equipped with a scythe, a rake, a pair of long-handled secateurs and a chisel-ended crowbar, as well as a twinkly-eyed, cheery greeting.

'Let's leave all this tackle here and go in while I tell you why I wanted to see you,' Bob said. So they went in, sat side by side in their usual seat, and William waited for Bob to begin. Bob was never to be rushed. Like Ol' Man River, William thought, he never seemed to hurry, but he got there just the same.

'Nothing much from the lawyers yet,' Bob said at last, 'only that them fields as you thought might be glebe lands weren't named as such in the agreement between the college and the War Ag., when they took it over. The chap as left it to the college in his will never mentioned 'em as such, either. He seems to have took it for granted that he owned 'em, and could do as he liked with 'em, same as he had done with the church. He appears to have been a real old eccentric with more money than taste – if my house is anything to go by. Name of du Gamboisson, but that's such a mouthful I call him "Old Gamby" for short. Effendi reckons that so far we can go on poking about as we like – at least, he thinks, till the spring. But who knows, we may have years and years yet afore any lawyer will let it be settled. Still, it would pay us to make hay while the sun shines.

'I were sitting here one day last week, just wisening to myself, when I thought as we'd never give much thought to why a little church like this should have a porch on both sides. It alters the shape of the line of the roof on the north, and makes it different from the south side. There has to be a reason for it being like that.'

'There is,' William said.

Bob eyed him with an inquisitive twinkle. 'Ha, I thought so. You read it in the old book as I found, but it's one o' the secrets you're still keeping from me. You're the detective, but I'm only the bobby out on the beat, keeping his ears open.'

'So what have you heard, and from whom?'

'Old Ben Peters as used to work here. I come across him when I took over Jane's turn to get the kids to Fenley, and stopped to have a word with him. He were the one as told me when I first come that I should never have no luck farming here, 'cos nobody ever did. It were 'cos some old monk from Ramsey Abbey had put a curse on it when they were turned out and some o' the Crum'ell family took it over. He's all'us good for a few tales like that, and I like to hear 'em 'cos it seems to me there must ha' been a grain or two of truth in 'em once. So I asked him if he knowed anything about that porch on the north side – and he did. I invited him to get in the car with me, and tell me what he knowed. First he said that it didn't get used a lot, only when they had to bury the vicar or a churchwarden, 'cos in days gone by there were a bit o' the graveyard reserved for them, the bit as lays alongside of the church wall, between the porch and a path as used to be there once. The only other time as it were used were on New Year's Eve, in olden days, when them as dared went and set there till midnight, when the ghosts of all as were doomed to die in the coming year come one after the other through the porch and into the church. Ben said people about here still believe it were so, 'cos it had come down in their families as folks setting there very often see their own self go by as a spectre – and sure enough, they died afore the year were out.' Bob grinned. 'No wonder! Died o' fright, more than likely.

'Anyway, talking about it to Ben sent me round there to have a look for myself. Talk about a wilderness! All that bit as Ben said used to be kept for burying priests and such in can't have been cleared up since Old Gamby died. I were interested straight away 'cos it's growed up just like fenland does as is left to itself, with long grass growing there every summer and rotting down every winter till, thousands o' years later, it's turned into peat – though this were more like a patch of carr round the boggy outside of a mere. It's completely growed over. Apart from the grass and weeds like twitch and such, there's ivy with stems so thick they must ha' been a hundred year a-growing, and creepers self-sowed among it, and young bushes of buckthorn and alder, and as for the brambles – I never have seen such thick and vicious old things as they are, growed away from the wall towards the light so they make a sort of canopy over all the rest like as if they was guarding it from intruders. I couldn't help thinking so, 'cos they're still got a lot of leaves on them, like red flags warning you to keep out.

'Well, I come in and set down, and did a lot o' wisening. In the first place, I know of other churches where the bit close to the porch is kept for burying parsons. Sort of place of honour. But there ain't been no parsons nor churchwardens to bury here for as long as anybody knows of, so that accounts for it being let alone to go back to nature. And then I took in where that porch is outside in relation to where the altar is inside. It's away out towards where all them old graves are as we looked at when you were trying to find a clue to the key to the code as all the last part of the old book's writ in. I wouldn't be surprised as there's a lot out there yet for us to find. But I kept sitting here and thinking about Old Gamby. He were set on making the inside over as much like a Victorian church as he could, and hired local stone-masons, likely, to do whatever he told 'em to. One thing was to put a new top on the altar: a beautiful bit of mahogany cut exactly to fit as we know, 'cos when you thought as whatever it is you're looking for might be still inside the altar, we lifted it up and took a decko for ourselves. There weren't nothing there. But that set my imagination at work. It weren't very likely as Gamby stood over 'em while they worked; he might even be gone on a visit somewhere. Suppose when they'd took that other old oak door off, they did find it full o' rubbish as they didn't know what to do with? He'd left 'em orders to clear it out and clean it up. The easiest thing to do was to take it out by going through the porch and chucking it on to the wild patch. It could ha' got left there. It was worth a bit of trouble to see if there was anything left as could prove it. So I went and investigated – and I'm found something as I think you'll be interested in, though I don't hold out any hopes as it'll be the sword you want to find.' Bob twinkled at him again. 'I notice you don't deny as it is a sword as you called "the murder weapon"?'

William didn't answer. He was experiencing such a mixture of hope and doubt that he was almost incapable of speech, but he followed Bob back to where they had left the tools, then round the east end of the church to the patch of wildness beyond. Bob had been very careful to disguise the fact that he'd cut himself a path through the young carr towards the corner where the porch wall and the church wall met. Pulling the covering bushes away, and cutting cruel clinging brambles with the secateurs, he cleared a path for William to tread, and together they began to pull away the growth of many years from what was still standing there. There could be no doubt in William's mind what it was: a muniment chest, almost a twin to the one in which Bob had discovered the manuscript, though of larger proportions. In spite of his exertions, William, on his knees in the mud, was now very pale, and trying to still the queer feeling across his diaphragm. He looked up helplessly at Bob as he realized that the heavy chest was buried almost a foot into the matted grass and mud-soaked compost all round it.

'It'll fall to pieces if we try to lift it,' he said. 'And we mustn't expect to find anything in it worth finding. Everything made of metal will have rusted away, and any paper or textile rotted by a hundred years of damp.'

'I wouldn't be too sure about that till I'd looked,' Bob, unhurried, countered, leaning on the rake he had been using. He was a bit concerned at the effect it was having on William. 'I took as good a look at it the other day as I could. It's all solid oak, with every joint mortised. Less likely to fall to bits for being damp than if it had been too dry. That's why they use oak for coffins, ain't it? Apart from elm, it's the best wood for keeping damp out as there is.'

'Can't we get it open where it is? Good God – it's padlocked! And we haven't got a key!'

'Fat lot o' good it would be if we had,' said Bob the determinedly imperturbable. 'If whoever it was put anything he cared about inside that and then left the key with it, he'd be a bigger numbskull than you are to suggest such a thing. Besides, if by any lucky chance we could find a key to fit, it wouldn't turn them rusty old locks. I think our best plan is to let me use the crowbar as a hammer, and see if I can break 'em off. Do you want me to try?'

William, beyond speech once more, nodded. Bob helped him up from his knees and gave him the rake to lean on. 'Come far enough out o' the way then,' he said, 'and stand clear.' William obeyed, like a man in a trance. He shut his eyes as Bob raised the crowbar and brought it down smartly on the nearest padlock, which gave way under the blow, and fell to the ground. A second blow broke the other into rusty pieces. William pulled himself together.

'Now for the moment of truth,' he said, steeling himself against disappointment. 'Open it.'

'No, you come and open it yourself,' Bob said. 'Remember as I'm only the bobby on the beat.'

'Let's do it together, one at each side. Without you, I'd have never got anywhere.'

Bob didn't argue. The sooner they got this tension over, the better for William. They knelt in the mud and muck side by side, and tried to lift the freed lid. It wouldn't budge.

'I'll use the crowbar to prise it up,' Bob said, reaching for the tool but keeping one wary eye on his ashen friend. He applied the chisel end to the place where lid and side met, and heaved gently till it began to move. Then he knelt down again, and slowly they raised the lid till it fell back. Both recoiled from the smell of mould that wafted out to them, but after a moment they leaned over the chest again. It was as William had expected, full to the brim with mildewed and mouldy old vestments; cassocks and surplices, as well as bell-ropes and sallies and other oddments, all in a state of decay. But William kept on throwing them out till the chest was three parts empty, and Bob, watching him, saw the shudder that passed through him as his hand encountered something hard. He lifted it out with great care: a bundle wrapped round and round in a mildewed old black cassock, and secured by a thin rotting rope at each end. One end was knob-like, the other thinly tapered. There was no mistaking what it was. Bob caught him as he fell forward, and set him on his feet again, the long bundle still clasped in his hands.

Bob led William, unprotesting, back through the porch to 'their' pew. 'Sit down before you fall down again,' he said, 'and don't try to do anything till I come back. I'm going to put all the other stuff back in the chest, then shut the lid and cover it up as well as I can with ivy and brambles and stuff. We don't want nobody else noticing what we've been up to. In the ordinary way, nobody would be likely to come here from one year's end to the other, but seeing as it's going to be used come Christmas, we may get a lot of nosy visitors. I won't be no longer than I can help. Just get your breath back.'

He left William sitting, still looking dazed, with the long bundle across his knees, and ran as fast as he could up to the farmhouse, returning in ten minutes or so with a bottle of brandy and two glasses.

'I'll clear up the mess outside later on,' Bob said. 'I thought you were going to faint. Do you feel well enough now to undo it? See what sort of a state it's in?'

To Bob's great surprise William shook his head. 'It doesn't matter all that much,' he answered. 'It's the fact that it's here at all that does. It proves, beyond all reasonable doubt, that the manuscript is genuine. That's what matters most to me. And if you don't mind, I'd rather leave it till we can take it somewhere more suitable before we try to unwrap it. We might damage it – specially in the state I'm in now. May I leave it with you till tomorrow?'

'Let's put it where it was meant to be found – back inside the altar,' Bob said.

They lifted the oak altar top, made a support for the bundle out of three very worn hassocks, and laid it gently across them. Then they replaced the oak top, by which time William had regained his composure.

'Tomorrow at eleven? If you can spare the time?'

Bob nodded, and watched him away.

*

William arrived back at Benedict's feeling, as Sophie would have said, 'as if he had been put through a mangle'. Like a sheet in the days before everybody had washing machines: dunked, thumped, 'dollied', twisted, rinsed, wrung out, exposed to every emotional element there was to be exposed to, and finally folded neatly up and squeezed between the wooden rollers of a mangle to make him ready again for what lay ahead.

He could not be bothered to put the car away; as he drove up to the front door, he hoped fervently that Sophie – and Olive – had gone home. The last thing he could put up with just at present was more talk of Christmas, especially of 'puddings and pies and all things nice'.

All he did want was time to sit quietly with Fran in view, and take in the enormous significance of this morning's revelations. What a tower of strength Bob had been! Though deliberately kept in the dark of all it meant to William, he had detected the rising tension, and though assured himself that all would turn out well, had put his own excitement aside, and looked to the very practical matter of what it was doing and yet might do to William.

William sat a moment at the wheel of his car, concentrating on his gratitude to whatever god it was who had given him a friend like Bob. Resolve accompanied the thought: Bob must now be part of whatever was left to be done before he could settle down to write. That was the best way he could ever hope to repay him.

And in his present state of euphoric bewilderment and confusion, he must still keep a strict guard on his own tongue, even to Bob and Fran. The 'secrets' of the manuscript were his alone, till he could lay the printed book at Fran's feet, and sign a specially bound copy, suitably inscribed, for Bob. For the first time, it seemed that the daydream might and could come true.

Fran was sitting at the kitchen table where he had left her – praise be to the gods, alone. She had heard the wheels of the car on the gravel, and waited, gathering strength to comfort him if her fears should be realized, and gearing herself to share his joy if hope was still alive and well. '*If hopes are dupes, fears may be liars.*' That was her motto for the moment, and might have to be yet for quite a time. Fears were uppermost as she heard him take off his overcoat and hang it in the cupboard under the stairs. The first glimpse of his face told her that they had been liars. She was up and in his outspread arms before there was need for a single word.

'Come and have your lunch,' she said, 'and then tell me.'

'I can't eat,' he replied. 'I'm too full of all that's happened to face food.'

She looked anxiously at him, and said firmly, 'Now, my darling, don't be silly. Stressed and worried as you have been and excited as I can see you are now, you need food all the more. I'm not going to listen, desperate as I am to know, till you please me by eating something. Now, what are you going to have?'

To please her he gave in, and found that he was quite hungry. As he relaxed, he watched her relax as well. Laying down his knife and fork, he looked across the table and raised one eyebrow at her. 'That was delicious,' he said. 'And you were quite right, I did need it. How did you know?'

'I haven't forgotten the scare you gave me when you let stress get on top of you once before, and you blacked out at Eric and Nigel's feet. Nor do I need telling what stress you've been under all this time about Bob's book. I guessed that if I didn't take charge we should have a repetition, remembering what Terry said on that occasion: that the crunch comes when the pressure is suddenly taken off. Rice pudding?'

To his own surprise, he began to laugh. 'That,' he said, 'is as good an example of bathos as I can recall. But as always, my sweetheart, you're right. I should love some rice pudding, as long as you'll sit there and watch me eat it. Then I'll tell you as much as I can.'

He marvelled at her intuition, as he had marvelled at Bob's. It wasn't the food that was making him feel so much better; it was the time she had given him to get his bearings again, and to edit in his mind what he dared tell her, and still keep to himself alone the great secrets revealed in the manuscript.

He was no longer disoriented. The world was the same as it had been at breakfast-time – but full of hope instead of problems. She knew that he had wanted to find something that would disprove his fears of Bob's book being a false, modern fake. She had not known what it was he had hoped to find. So he told her that it had been a sword that was part of the story told in the manuscript, and how, helped by Bob, they had this morning found one.

'Don't get too excited about it, darling,' he said. 'We're not quite out of the wood yet. What we actually have now in our possession is a bundle that by the shape and size of it must be a sword, I think; but it has been out in the weather – though inside a chest – for a hundred years, and wrapped in its mouldy old wrappings for three hundred – if it is the one mentioned in the story. I'd had it by the time it came to light. Bob saw how near I was to passing out, and poured brandy down me, and agreed with me that the less we handled it, the better. So we hid it again, until we can unwrap it tomorrow, when it may have dried out enough to stand a bit of handling. The real test will be if there's enough left of it for an expert to date. Till then, my sweetheart, the whole affair must be kept *sub rosa* to everybody but you, Bob and me. Another bloody secret for you to keep! But once I know it's of the right period, my last obstacle will have been cleared. My New Year's resolution shall be to begin to write. Let's leave the dishes, and take our coffee into the sitting-room. I just want to sit, and let it all wash over me.'

He saw the frown that crossed her face, and asked, 'Can't we? Why not?'

'Because we're going to get a visit from Terry at any minute now. From his hurried and rather garbled phone call, I gathered that he's about to mix a bit of serious business with what was to have been a pleasure trip to London on Wednesday, which he said he had warned you about; but since then he's had reason to think you may be the right person to help him. He needs to talk to you urgently. Sophie and Olive were here when he rang, so we both had to be circumspect in what we said, but I think it's another chapter of the Bridgefoot saga. I told him you would be home this afternoon, and he said in that case he *must* make an effort to find time to come and see you. And here he is!'

Disappointed though he was, William could not in all conscience put his own concerns above any new emergency at the Glebe. As he got up to go and open the door to Terry, he was almost staggered by an idea. If Terry was going to London on Wednesday, and there was need for him to get involved, he could take the sword with him, and show it to Colin Brand, the only person in that line he knew well enough to ask for a consultation at such short notice: one of London's top authorities on armour and weapons. Why on earth hadn't he thought of Colin before? He supposed because there had been no need till today.

Apart from any help Colin might be able to give him, it would be nice to meet his obstinate student again, who had the courage of his own conviction, and had insisted on throwing up a promising degree course to follow his passion for the actual hardware of the wars that until recent years had dominated history. William himself had always been interested in this aspect of the medieval history he was responsible for, but his knowledge of arms and armour stopped at the end of his period. Colin had since embraced the whole field, and was now the proprietor of a very exclusive shop where arms and armour fanatics could go for expert advice and good, honest deals if, for any reason, they wanted to part with treasured antique militaria.

All this had shot through his mind in the time it took him to get up from the kitchen table, go through the hall, and pull open the heavy front door. Yet only an hour ago he had thought himself worn out! Fran had made coffee for three, and brought it into the sitting-room. Terry, apologizing for his own lack of time, launched at once into his reason for bothering them.

'I had a phone call late last night from Charles Bridgefoot,' he said. 'He was very apologetic for insisting on speaking to me, because of course he knows that I'm not on duty; but he was in distress, and in his predicament Jehan was out of the question and as an unknown doctor no good. What it amounts to is that Charles is convinced that his father has reached the stage of becoming a danger to others – the one condition on which he could be forced to take medical advice. Charles told me bluntly that his mother and Pansy had both confessed to being afraid of him. He's becoming physically aggressive when in a temper. Pansy has vamoosed again – most probably with Yorky. So he and Charlie have been left in the cart.'

William interrupted him to remind him they were aware of that – he had been at Castle Hill when Charles and Charlie had discussed it with Bob. 'It was agreed that Charles ought to take the responsibility for keeping his eye on Temperance, while Charlie moved in to the Glebe to do all she could to help Marjorie. Losing Pansy again has been a very bitter blow to her.'

Terry nodded. 'That's exactly the background against which Charles told me what he and Charlie saw for themselves last night. I think he has a point – he did confess to being worried stiff at the thought of Charlie ever being the target of one of Brian's fits of violence. The very sight of her is, apparently, enough to throw his father off balance. Poor boy, he was torn last night between having to leave his mother without protection, or his wife at the mercy of a furtive peeping Tom acting in a way that can only suggest mental derangement, whatever the initial cause of it may be. I heard at first hand the extent of the problem with Brian. Charles was in great distress and, on leave or not, I had to listen to him. Jehan was there and agreed that something should be done at once.

'What he was demanding was that I held a conference with his uncle, Alex Marland – immediately. I told Charles that if it could possibly be fitted in, I would do what I could; but there were several things that didn't make it easy. It could hardly be at a more difficult time for me; and I don't know Alex Marland personally. On that ground I said that Charles himself must ring his uncle and see if it would be at all possible for us to meet while I am in London on Wednesday – any time before midday. Lastly, there's the question of professional ethics. I don't know where I would stand with regard to that, were Brian to want to make trouble for me. I am no longer his doctor, but on the other hand, for the safety of the public, somebody should blow the whistle – and who could that be but me? I was the one who was attending his wife when this all blew up.

'Charles said that his Uncle Alex would probably be much more likely to agree to take part if you, William, would be there as well. He didn't remember much about anything when Marland had to be involved before, except wanting to die as quick as they would let him, but Charlie's father had told him that it was you, William, who had given Alex support in facing Brian down, and had then been instrumental in helping to get Charlie back.

'On those conditions, I gave in, and Charles rang me early today to say his uncle had agreed. So if you could possibly be there as well, William, I'm afraid we're committed to it.'

'As it happens, there is another appointment that I'd like to make in London, and Wednesday would suit me fine, but it's a lot to get through in one day. At this time of the year we can't trust the weather, and the days are very short now. Have you been told what time and where the conference with Alex will take place?'

'Yes. He'll snatch half an hour from a very busy morning to meet us at the Combined Universities' Club, which is close to his surgery.'

'Couldn't be better,' William said. 'That's only about five minutes' walk from where I hope to set up my other appointment. I'd like Bob to go with me to that, but what could he do while we see Alex?'

'Bring him along as well,' Terry said. 'Doesn't he have a right to be there? According to her husband, his daughter is the one in greatest danger of being the victim if her father-in-law actually flips altogether. And she's trapped at the Old Glebe where, according to Charles, he just goes in and out as he pleases at any time of the day or night. It was, after all, his home for many years, and is still the home of his parents and the headquarters of the firm he's now head of.'

'I agree,' said William. 'And if there is a man who can see through a brick wall better than most, and judge fairly and without bias, it's Bob. Besides, if Terry's worried about any repercussions on the grounds of it not being ethical, who's to know anything about it? I'm not a doctor, and neither is Bob. Can't a group of old friends meet for a drink and a sandwich in a London club without raising any suspicion? After all, Bob and I have business to do together that day.'

'So have I,' said Terry. 'Jehan is being my chauffeur because he knows his way about London better than I do, and is, as it happens, a member of the same club.'

'Come to that, so am I,' said William, 'though I haven't been in it for donkey's years. I avoid London like the plague whenever

I can. But it does seem that this has been arranged for us. My only worry is that we shan't be able to find two vacant parking meters.'

'Leave such details to the gods,' Fran said softly. 'It usually pays.'

'Right,' said Terry briskly. 'Eleven a.m. at the Universities' Club on Wednesday.'

'Which means a start no later than seven for me and Bob, always supposing I can set up my other appointment for ten or so. Pray for a morning without fog or black ice on the roads.'

Terry left, and William was at last able to sit at Fran's feet close to the roaring log fire.

'I hate the very thought of it,' he said. 'When I'm old I shall be one of those crusty old curmudgeons who won't put his nose outside his own front door. "East, West. Home's best."'

*　　*　　*

William spent a restless night, half gloating, half fearing the unwrapping of the sword the next morning, thinking that he had perhaps been too sanguine in believing it could be the particular one he wanted it to be, or that it could have survived in a good enough state to be datable with any accuracy. There were hundreds lying bent and rusty in museum basements, just lengths of old iron. On the other hand, there were many stories of them being taken out of graves – in the Icelandic sagas, for example – to be used again after two hundred or more years. The sword had been the soldier's weapon from the Bronze Age to the early twentieth century; and had been very much so in the seventeenth. It was only quite recently that history and archaeology had become partners in the study of such matters.

The next time he roused, he was worrying about having to be part of the meeting with Alex, besides being in a chicken-and-egg situation with regard to ringing Colin Brand. If he rang him early, before he and Bob investigated their find, he wouldn't know whether or not he would need Colin Brand's time, but if he delayed until he knew what was in the bundle in the altar at St Saviour's, it would be too late to ask a busy man like Colin to see him at such short notice.

Fran slept on untroubled beside him; that seemed a good omen: she was the one who usually did the early morning 'whittling'. One thing was certain, Bob would be up and about already. He could at least ring Bob and make their meeting early, and invite him to go with him to London tomorrow and hear for himself what was said about the sword. It was still only six o'clock and a dark December morning, but he crept out of bed without waking Fran, and by seven had fixed with Bob that he would be at Castle Hill by eight. That would give him the opportunity of ringing Brand by nine, by which time he would be at the shop. So far, all reasonably promising.

Bob was cool and calm, expecting William not to be, and putting his practical, rather than his fey romantic, foot foremost. 'It'll be too dark to see anything properly in the church,' he said, 'and we need a flat surface. Jane and the children'll be in the kitchen, so I think Charlie's tack-room is about the best bet. I've swept a bit of the floor, and spread some sacks down. There's plenty of electric light there, because Charlie used it as her den when she was at home.'

'Let's take it up straight away.'

Bob lifted the altar-table clear enough for William's long arms to retrieve the black bundle. 'Don't bother about the hassocks,' Bob said. 'I'll put things to rights later.' His pragmatic manner didn't deceive William. Bob was as excited as he was – but wary of him reacting too much, as he had done yesterday. William was astonished afresh by the rapport between them, two men of such diverse backgrounds as they were; it was such that William had already picked up from Bob a feeling of confidence, dredged up, he guessed, from the deep well of Bob's sixth sense.

They set off for the tack-room, which to William that morning seemed as far away as the moon. It had already been prepared. Bob must have been up and at it well before dawn. He laid the bundle on the clean sacking on the floor, inviting William to make the first move by kneeling beside it and offering him his pocket-knife to cut the rotting cords. The mildewed cassock fell away; beneath it the object was still wrapped in another, which together they unwound and put aside with very gentle touch. And there, before their eyes, lay the sword.

Bob took charge, deliberately being practical. 'Handle it careful,' he said. 'The scabbard's rotted; you can see the blade through it here and there. It's been waxed, I reckon, to keep it from rusting. Beeswax, ten to one.' William had seen, and been sent into a daze by what he saw. Bob took note, and after a minute or two, said, 'So what shall we do now? If we try to take the sword out of the scabbard, the leather will just fall to bits.'

William nodded, coming back to reality. 'We mustn't touch it till the chap who knows how to handle such things and what to look for has seen it just as we found it.'

'You'll be able to come to London with me tomorrow, I hope?' William continued. 'I took it for granted that you would but never thought to ask you! Will you be able to spare the time? Can you manage it?'

'I'm coming if only to make sure you get back safe,' Bob said, looking up with his habitual twinkle. 'I somehow didn't think you'd cut me out when we'd got as far as this. But what I meant was, what shall we do with it now at this minute?'

William faced a new dilemma. If he took it home, Fran would ask to see it, which he didn't want her to until he had an expert's opinion on it. He decided quickly.

'We'll wrap it up again as well as we can, leave it here ready for you to bring with you tomorrow morning,' he said. 'My excuse for not showing it to Fran will be that it's too old and may be too fragile to be handled by anybody but an expert. Seven o'clock start? We'll swap it from your car to mine and I'll drive.'

They discarded the outer mildewed cassock. Then they wrapped the sword again in its inner cassock, which had absorbed some of the damp, padded it with sacking, and finally enclosed it all in another clean piece of sacking, tying it in three places with binder-twine, string still to be found on all farms though binders had not been seen there since the war. Nobody could have suspected what hopes and fears, what trepidation or promise, what ambition or defeat lay in that innocent-looking bundle.

William was back at Benedict's just after nine, and he could hear that both Sophie and Olive were in conversation with Fran, so he slipped into his study and rang Colin Brand's number. After mutual exchanges of the pleasure of being in touch with each other after so long, William, very carefully choosing his words, said that he had been instrumental in helping to find an old sword that was alleged to have been hidden in a ruined church soon to be bulldozed down. A few interested in it for reasons of their own were trying to save the church from demolition, and were anxious to know if it could possibly be positive proof of a local folktale.

As he had another appointment in London next day, Wednesday, was there any hope that he could bring it with him for Colin to run his expert's eye over it?

Colin told him that he was in luck because he had elected to mind the shop tomorrow while his assistant, Geoff, went to an auction.

'Nine to half-past, if we can make it that early?' asked William.

'The earlier the better if you want to find a parking meter anywhere near,' Colin answered.

'Depends on the weather, and on the friend I shall have with me. He's a farmer and has a lot to do before he can get away. We'll do our best. See you tomorrow.'

All too easy, feared William. But he must tell Fran.

She was, it appeared, more or less holding court, with Sophie and Olive sitting across the kitchen table from her and Ned at her side. He gathered from the rather sharp tone of the women's voices that Fran was facing opposition from Sophie, and Olive was tipping the balance either way whenever she could get her word in.

'You know as I don't mind giving nobody a hand to 'elp,' Sophie was declaring primly, 'but I don't see no reason for the Rector to get such as me and Ida Barker to clean the place up by pretending it's for the church. More like it's to 'elp 'is friend Choppen. If the church had been fit to goo to a-Christmas

Morning, there might ha' been as many as twenty to thirty folk there, counting them from the 'otel. I doubt if there'll be more'n ten who'll trudge all the way up to Castle 'Ill. So why does 'e want Ned to get some o' the other ringers to 'elp to put nigh on a hundred chairs in rows like a Picture Palace in that there poshed-up barn of Choppen's? That ain't got nothing to do with the church – not like George Bridgefoot's has. That's been there for hundreds o' years, and 'as often 'ad church do's in it. Serves the Rector right as 'e ain't got nowhere to 'old services – he shouldn't ha' been in such an 'urry to get rid of the old school. That belonged to the church, that did.'

'It said so on the front o' the girls' porch,' Olive interrupted. 'They used to make me read it 'cos some o' the big gals used to say I hadn't no right to be there, seeing's 'ow my father come out o' the fens where most o' the people were chapel – same as Oliver Crum'ell were, who 'ated anything to do wi' the church. They do say as it were 'im as turned the monks out o' Ely and pulled their old what-do-yer-call-it down, the – it had something to do with butchers, I'm sure . . . their Abbotoir, that's what it were – anyway, Oliver Crum'ell pulled it down and built Ely Cathedral in its place so it would out-do all the other churches round about. Though I am 'eard tell as when it were all finished, he locked it up and kep' the key in 'is pocket so's nobody couldn't get in it for 'leven year!'

William, listening at the door, could see that for once Fran was in no mood to appreciate Olive. She was, in fact, looking quite grim. 'And what's your objection, Ned?' she asked.

'I dunno as I'm got no objection,' he said. 'I don't mind putting the chairs up for a chance to have a good old sing. All I said to Soph' was why call on the ringers to do it when there wouldn't be no bells to ring. Nor yet at Castle Hill on Christmas Morning. Christmas without bells don't seem right, somehow . . .'

Fran looked gratefully at Ned, and then spoke firmly and coldly to the women. 'I will tell the Rector what you say, Sophie,' she said. 'It is, after all, very little to do with me. As for you, Mrs Hopkins, there is no reason why you should waste any more of your time. The Rector made no mention of your being asked to help. But I don't understand your attitude, Sophie. Let me put you right about one or two things.

'In the first place, the whole idea is to attract more of the people who have found an interest in the church to which you are so devoted – people whose contributions in the last couple of years have helped considerably towards the restoration fund. From what you say, you would have helped willingly if the carol service or any other could have been held either in the Glebe barn or the old school, because they have had connections with the church in the past. You object to Mr Choppen's barn for some reason. Because it isn't as old as George's? Don't you remember it as it was when it was Thackerays' barn before Mr Choppen came? I remember you making a great to-do because he had called his firm "Manor Farms Ltd" – as you said, that place never had been the Manor. It still goes by that name as a business, but what do you call the house where Mr Choppen and Marjorie Bridgefoot live? *Monastery Farm*. Because it belonged to a monastery, before they were all closed. Of the two barns, my guess would be that they are about the same age and were used in the first instance for the same purposes. Both have been restored: George's for traditional farming use, till now; and Mr Choppen's filled with modern technology which he is offering to the church to make whatever use of they can.

'Ned, may the Rector rely on you to find two or three more men to put the hired seating in? Thank you. I'll pass that on to the Rector. Mrs Hopkins, I suggest that as you already know what you are expected to do this morning, you go and get on with it. I won't keep Sophie long.'

William was astounded at this Fran who was angry enough to speak that way to Olive, or to be hard on Sophie – but the inference was clear. She wanted to isolate Sophie, and tell her what for – for once! He had forgotten his own business in watching this new bit of drama develop.

When Ned had gone whistling back to the garden-shed, and Olive had retired, talking to herself, to the utility-room, Fran remained seated, cool and collected, on one side of the table, while a very red-faced Sophie – reminding William so much of their late gander, Oscar, with his neck forward and his head down ready for battle, that he almost lost his own poise – sat the other. He fervently hoped Fran would not look up and catch his eye. She didn't, because she had no idea he was there, and she was truly both angry with and disappointed in Sophie.

'Now, Sophie,' she said. 'This is so unlike you in your support for anything to do with the church that I think – whether you know it or not – for once you aren't telling the truth. I'm afraid I believe your reasons for not being willing to help are purely selfish ones: your old grudge towards Mr Choppen, whom you have never forgiven for trying to buy your cottage, and secondly, the association in your mind between that barn and what you still think of as the "disgrace" of your Wendy becoming a pop-star and leaving you to go to live in America. It was in that barn that Mr Choppen's son discovered what a wonderful voice she has, and he who gave her the chance to use it as she has. The Choppens, both father and son, protected her from people like Jack Bartrum, who were prepared to think she was what her illegitimate child had labelled her. All you are doing in objecting to a bit of anything new is proving to everybody that you can neither forget nor forgive.

'So stop behaving like Thirzah would have done. Perhaps you should go home now, and have a word with Jelly about it. Then, if you change your mind, I won't mention anything of this to the Rector.'

'I don't need to goo 'ome to be able to listen to my Jelly,' Sophie said. She was still as red-necked as a turkey-cock, but one that expected to have its neck wrung at any minute. 'Anywhere as I can be by myself on my knees a-praying'll do.'

'Try our bedroom,' Fran suggested. 'Wasn't it in there, kneeling by our bed, that you first heard Jelly's voice giving you good advice?' Her tone was softer now, and Sophie was beginning to wilt. But she wasn't yet quite ready to admit her own fault, though she knew Fran to be right. She made one more attempt to justify herself.

'I thought as Marge Bridgefoot didn't live there no more,' she said. 'I don't know whether 'e throwed 'er out, or whether it don't suit 'er no longer. She ain't been near to look after Choppen nor yet the Rector like she used to, nor she ain't slept there. And Pansy's gone off again somewhere as nobody knows, and that chap from Yorkshire as they made so much fuss on's gone an' all. Sich goings on as I'd never ha' believed if anybody else 'ad told me.'

Fran pounced. 'Anybody else but who?' she asked. 'I could bet my boots that that silly tale didn't come from Dan, did it?'

Sophie shook her head, and tears began to fall. 'No,' she said, 'and I never ought to ha' said nothing of 'ow I felt to nobody, 'specially you! I'm ashamed of myself, that I am. Olive told me, as we were coming up to work together. Can I goo away and pray aside o' your bed, like you said? And will you tell the Rector as I'll do anything 'e asks to get the place cleaned up! I just don't know what ever comed over me.'

Fran went round the table and put her arms round Sophie, who for once didn't resist, but clung to her as a child might have done.

'Dear Sophie,' Fran said, smoothing the neat, greying hair. 'It's only that this evil virus that we're all suffering from has got at you as well. So cheer up. Things are getting better everywhere except up at Glebe. Nobody knows yet what the end of that will be, but I can tell you something that the Rector told me – in confidence. Pansy isn't far away. She's gone where she can look after Yorky and when he's better, she's going to marry him. There, nobody knows that but the family at Glebe and the Rector, and now us.

'Marge went up, the night before last, to see the Rector – and found him too tired to get himself anything to eat. So she got it for him, and then they talked, and he said how good it was for both of them. If he thinks it's right for Pansy to marry John – Yorky – I think we may rest assured that it is, can't we?'

'God works in a mysterious way 'Is wonders to perform,' Sophie said. 'I'm never been one to question what 'Im Above chooses to do 'til now, and I ought to 'ave 'ad more sense than to believe Olive. But she can't 'elp it. I'll now goo and talk to 'Im and my Jelly for a little while, if that's all right with you.'

409

Fran kissed her, and watched the droop of her shoulders as she went to make her peace with her God, and to listen to the healing voice of her dead sweetheart. Poor old Sophie – what right had she to bring any sort of charge against her? It was she who was now ashamed and wanting comfort. She didn't have to rely on hearing William's ghostly voice from the grave – he was there, at her side, with his arms round her, wiping the tears from her face with his handkerchief and kisses.

From the nether regions rose the raucous tones of Olive, trying to cheer herself up. 'Ra-ma-hoan-a,' she was wailing, blessing the day the lady had been wearing rambling roses in her hair. They could hardly have rambled as much as the singer's voice did from key to key.

Fran and William somehow found themselves laughing.

'Come into the study,' he said, 'and shut the door. I've got a lot to tell you.'

*

He told her, in fact, only what it was necessary to know. Colin Brand had agreed to see the sword between nine and ten the next morning, which was going to mean a very early start. To avoid handling the sword more than they could help, he'd left it with Bob, who'd bring it with him, giving it a few more hours to dry out before they started.

'I'm washed out,' he said. 'Can we leave it there till I get back tomorrow? I need to have my wits about me, for both the consultations – but thank the gods for Bob! I shall drive there, and it depends what happens whether I'll be in any state to drive back. If I can manage to get us out of central London, I can hand the driving over to Bob. Tomorrow's going to be quite a day.

'We shall have to go early, whatever the weather, but if there's any sign of fog I'll see to it that we do most of the return journey by daylight. Now you tell me what all that was about when I came in? I can hear where Olive is – but no Sophie? I hope she hasn't given in her notice, having heard that I have been seen going down to Danesum to see Charlie when Charles wasn't there?'

Her reply almost reduced him to hysterics. 'She's kneeling by the side of our bed, talking to Jelly's ghost,' she said, and proceeded to relate what had happened while he was away. 'She's seen the error of her "wayses" after I'd told her a few home truths. I really was hard on her.' Fran sounded as remorseful as she felt. 'But I think I may have done good. We shall see.'

The noise from the utility-room ceased, and they were startled by Olive bursting in on them, as usual drying her hands endlessly on the coarse hessian apron that on Sophie's orders she wore for scrubbing. 'Seeing as 'ow Sophie's been took, like, and 'as shut 'erself up in your bedroom, I thought as 'ow it'd fall to me to make your 'levenses. I don't know whyever she was making such a hormpolodge about 'elping to sweep that barn out, that I don't. I do 'ope as she'll let me 'elp when it comes to it, but do she don't I shall go to all the do's anyway. It'd be like old times, and them Christmas concerts at school with Miss Budd. We sung carols and things and done plays as 'ad a part for everybody so's nobody should be left out, like, not even me as could never remember the words. But I do, after all these year, whatever Soph' say. 'Cos one year, I were a little fairy called Snowdrop, and me and another gel as were called Hackonite or some such 'ad to go on the stage first, to tell the folks who we was meant to be, like. We 'ad to meet in the middle a-singing and a-dancing, like this 'ere.' She picked up the corners of her hessian apron with her work-worn, roughened fingers, catching the thin skirt below it as well, so that they were treated to the sight of more of Olive's skinny legs than had been vouchsafed to them before. Then she danced trippingly towards William, singing coyly:

> 'I'm a little fairy. Who are you?
> Are you a little fairy, too?'

William's last reserves of strength gave way. He looked appealingly at Fran, and disappeared. Fran clasped her hands together, and said in a tight little voice, 'If Sophie doesn't come down, please bring us coffee in the sitting-room.' Then she hastily followed William. She found him sitting in his chair with his handkerchief stuffed into his mouth to stop his guffaws and giggles from reaching 'Snowdrop's' ears.

'This *is* a madhouse,' he said. 'We're all mad. Must be.'

'Yes,' she said, quite willing to be pulled on to his knee. 'But even little mad fairies have their uses. I think little fairy Snowdrop has given me what may turn out to be a good idea. I'll put it to Beth while I wait for you tomorrow.'

*

Charlie had begun to feel trapped. She hadn't been worried at all, until the Sunday night when they had seen Brian snooping around, and Charles, after leaving Glebe, had called to say he wanted to ring Dr Hardy. He'd poured out to her his misgivings that it was her own presence at Glebe that was sending his father right round the bend, and that he was frightened for her safety.

She'd said she had no fear of his father physically; but if it was going to put him in this sort of a tizz, then she would be worried. She could see that he was truly very fearful for her and about her, so for his sake, not her own, agreed for him to ring Terry and, after hearing what Terry had said, his Uncle Alex.

'I wish we could be together again, even for an afternoon,' she said wistfully. 'If anything is bothering me, other than poor old Grandad and Gran, it's what this is doing to you. We shall have to rethink all our plans for the future. Suppose your dad is really ill, mentally or physically, who's going to run Bridgefoot Farms Ltd? There isn't anybody but you! That means goodbye for ever to my hopes – though, as I said, they could be postponed for a while. But not too long, or I couldn't catch up. And what if this trouble kills Grandad?

'He's feeling it more and more, though of course he doesn't yet know the worst. I try to do my revision, but when I can see Grandad trying so hard to come to terms with all this, I just can't bear to think it's getting worse and he doesn't know. Then I can't keep my mind on what I'm doing, and begin to wonder what it's all for, anyway. I want to have more time with you, and look at what is still possible, not be here without you, mourning for lost dreams. I stop working, and go to see Chum, but I'd rather come home to see you.

'Chum's about the best substitute for you I've got! He's an absolute darling – like you – and so intelligent! He knows my voice now, and loves me to sing to him in French. Can you find time to come up and talk to me? If not, I shall desert and come home to you. No, my darling, you are not to worry about *me*. "*Us*" and our long-term future is quite a different matter.'

She made him think. After his success in getting Uncle Alex to agree to see Terry while he was in London on Wednesday, he'd felt better, and more able to carry the next task through. So as soon as he could on Tuesday, he went up to Glebe, mostly to see his wife, but to set Grandad up to date with the matter as it now stood.

He reflected that neither Grandad nor Gran were weaklings. It would be better to warn them of what was afoot, and ask Grandad to tell him what answers there could be to the problems that might face them at any minute. Crushed in spirit Grandad might be, but he was no fool; and Gran would rather be prepared for the worst than live in false hope.

He found no one in the house but Aunt Marge, who said Grandad was in the cowshed, and Gran was having her afternoon nap. She was, Marge thought, getting her old courage back, saying that, 'What can't be cured must be endured' and that it wasn't by any means the first time they'd had to 'set a hard heart against hard sorrow'.

'Where's Charlie? Where do you think! Making love to the bull. Honestly, when she sings to him, he acts for all the world like boys used to once when they got a crush on a girl – goes all shy and goo-goo-eyed, and tries to get as close to her as he can. It would make a cat laugh to see the way he puts his head down and slabbers, if the cat was in the mood for it. We aren't, and we worry about her instead. She doesn't go over the fence, so you needn't look like that – and, in any case, to make sure she's safe Dan keeps him on a very loose tether when he's in the yard. That's where you'll find her.'

'I want to see Grandad first,' he said.

'In the cowshed,' Marge said. 'I'll tell Charlie you're here.'

George was, as usual, leaning on his elbows on the cows' manger, though this time with his back to it. His face lit up at the sight of Charles.

'Grandad,' Charles said, wanting to get it over as soon as he could, 'are you well enough to come into the house for a chat? I'm afraid it isn't very good news I have for you, but there are things you ought to know. And I want to hear your views on what steps I've taken without consulting you. Just you and me, if you like, or we can include Gran and Charlie and Aunt Marge if you think we ought.'

'You and me, first,' George answered. 'We can tell the others what we decide, afterwards – if we can decide anything. But it's what I've been hoping for, these last few days. We've all got to know where we stand, and do something about it. Go and see Charlie before we begin, but don't be too long about it. Then we can have the house-place to ourselves for a little while.'

Ten minutes with Charlie put Charles's wilting courage back in place. She elected to stay where she was till she was called.

So grandfather and grandson sat, facing each other, while Charles brought George up to date, and told him of the meeting in London tomorrow. Each felt a stiffening of morale in the other. 'It had to come to it,' George said. 'We must be prepared for the worst.'

*

Brian was lying low, which made Charles more anxious than ever. He kept in touch with his mother, but was constantly warned not to go near Temperance.

'He's no better, really, though quieter. He just sits and thinks, or sleeps till some little thing wakes him and he flies into a rage and swears as I never knew he could. Sometimes he's really quite nice to me, but I can't trust him. Other times he goes down to his office and cries for long spells at a time. But Charles, be wary. There's a gleam in his eye I don't like at all. I think he's plotting something – though God knows what!'

He decided not to tell her anything more. It was going to feel a long time, till he could ring Uncle Alex tomorrow night and hear the result of the meeting. Then he asked if Charlie could possibly be spared to come home to Danesum till bedtime. She didn't need asking twice.

The afternoon was a bit raw and cold, but their bed was warm. They made the most of it, and then lay talking.

He told her that Grandad had already faced the fact that Brian might never be well enough again to run the firm. 'I said that meant that I should have to take over, but didn't know if I could manage it all. He said that while he was alive I shouldn't be making decisions alone, and if it was all too much for me to cope with, the answer to that would be to employ an experienced farm manager, until Dad was well enough again to take the reins back in his hands. He can't yet quite face the possibility that he never will be. I didn't press him about that, yet. We may know more by tomorrow night.

'He was more concerned about you than about me,' he said. 'I grew up knowing that one day I should have to be "the" Bridgefoot of Old Swithinford, so it's only a return to what I'd expected for me, without the dreams we've had together, and worked so hard for. But I can't bear for you to have to give them up! It isn't fair.'

She cradled him in her arms, and began to tell him her own view of the situation. 'I don't want to kill any hopes that your dad will ever be well enough to take over again,' she said. 'But I'm afraid they would be false hopes. So let's face it, my darling. You do what you must, which is to take over; I'll try to find myself an apprenticeship with a fully qualified vet, working out in the field with him, instead of being assistant to the main vet in a partnership based here. But there's an obstacle to that easy solution. Suppose your Dad is ill enough to die? We have to face the possibility. You would be the only Bridgefoot Grandad could hope to pass the line down to. To wind the old clock up when he's gone. One more generation and finis! So I think it's up to us. I give up every other consideration to have a baby for Grandad to look forward to, before we know what's likely to happen to your dad. To ease Grandad's fear that the line will come to an end.'

He was overwhelmed. It was too much to ask, too much to hope for, too much of a risk – even for Grandad's sake.

When he gained control of himself again, he said, 'But, my lambkin, if I agree and do my best, how can we be sure it would be a boy? A girl would have wasted your precious time for nothing. We've got girls enough now, if it comes to that. The line has hung on for years with only one boy. It was bound to break some time.'

'Charles,' she said, very seriously. 'Do you think I would have taken such a decision without consulting my dad? I've inherited a bit of his fenland magic, but not enough to trust myself altogether on important matters like this. He says I needn't worry – he knows the first I have will be a boy. His first grandson, too. What shall we call him?' She was partly joking now, as he knew; but he was also aware that she was throwing down a gage to Fate, and went along with her.

'George?' she said. He nodded, having to swallow before he could speak. 'Then Robert?' He nodded again. 'Then Charles?'

It was too much. The tears would come.

'I shall go like a good wife to make my husband a cup of tea,' she said. 'And we'll toast George Robert Charles Bridgefoot with it. By next Christmas. Believe in Father Christmas, and he'll bring you what you want most.'

'I shall never want anything more than I've got,' he said. 'But that won't stop me from wishing . . .'

*   *   *

Wednesday morning was inclined to be damp, but there was no fog. William and Bob beat the worst of the rush hour, and found a parking meter only five minutes' walk from Colin Brand's shop. He had only just arrived there himself, and ushered them in at once. Colin's secretary having produced the inevitable cup of coffee, Colin led them down a flight of stairs to the 'work-room', where bits of military hardware lay around waiting their turn for attention. Colin cleared a table, and took the bundle from Bob. William was holding his breath, trying to tell himself that whatever significance this had for him, to Colin it was a normal routine. What a difference it makes, from which point of view any tiny action is seen!

The wrappings cast aside, Colin bent forward and looked the sword over. 'What is it you want to know, Professor?'

'For heaven's sake, man, don't call me that!' he said. 'You're not my student now, I'm yours! What I need most is an approximate date for it, and after that, any observations you care to make about it.'

'Well, I can tell you at first glance that it's what museum curators and dealers insist on calling a "mortuary sword", the silly name given by the Victorians to any sword with a likeness of Charles the First on it. Utterly misleading, but we're stuck with it. Victorians liked to believe that any such sword must be a memorial to the King who'd lost his head: Charles the Martyr. A ridiculous concept, whichever way you look at it. Very few people during the interregnum would have wanted to be seen wearing such outward signs of where their sympathy lay, and what good's a sword that can't be worn ready for use? The truth is, of course, that such swords were a declaration of the loyalty of the Royalists to the living King for whom they risked everything.' He gave his attention back to the sword lying on the table.

'Mmm. Scabbard gone completely,' he said, half talking to himself. Then he looked up at William. 'It is, I think, a very fine specimen of its kind, by the look of the hilt; but the important part of any sword's the blade. The only thing the scabbard can tell us is that when it was new it must have belonged to someone who knew what he liked, and could afford to pay for it. The chape and the locket are made of solid silver. The leather's gone too far for there to be any hope of saving it. So here goes . . .'

With practised hands he drew the blade from the scabbard and laid it on the table. They craned their necks to see, as Colin produced a magnifying glass and proceeded to go over it, talking as he did so.

'Good blade, but quite a bit older than the hilt. Somewhere around 1550, I'd say, but that's only a first guess till I can examine the marks on it more thoroughly. That's typical; when the nobility of the time went to war, they usually had plenty of swords to choose from, but if there happened to be one with an extra good blade – the operative part, as far as they were concerned – they

417

would have the better blade rehilted in the prevailing fashion, and decorated as they wished. The chap who owned this was obviously a Royalist. Take a closer look at it, William. What's that on the underside of the knuckle-guard?'

'Heads? Good God – a portrait of Charles the First! An extraordinary likeness, too! And other Cavaliers, possibly recognizable as the owner's friends, if one could but know.'

'And a cavalryman on his horse, in armour,' said Bob. 'The chap who put a new hilt on this must have been a top-class craftsman, I reckon, to chisel a work of art like that out of steel. Just look at the legs of that horse!' His voice had a tone of awe in it, and Colin looked up appreciatively at him.

'You wait till it's been cleaned,' he said. 'Actually though, it isn't steel. It's iron – softer to work. He was most likely to have been one of the few master-craftsmen working in Wales or on the borders – somewhere in the West Country, anyway. See these other rather grotesque heads on the flattened parts of the loop-guards? They're not meant to be likenesses of anybody, they're just Celtic designs. We call them "Celtic heads". And the pommel? Didn't have to be very big, because the weight of the guards helped to counterbalance the blade. But small as it is, it has four perfect heads on it. Not just "Celtic heads" though. More like somebody having a joke, I'd say, alternating a handsome cavalier with a fat-faced, lazy churchman. But I'm only guessing again. I'm always surprised at the number of people who ought to know better who have forgotten what a personal thing a sword was to its owner.

'Grip's come loose, but it's a beautiful grip, all the same: twisted copper-wire alternating with plain, with turks-heads at top and bottom. Pity the scabbard's lost.'

'Could you get a new scabbard made for it?' William asked.

'Yes, of course. It would certainly be worth it. The leather's no problem, and the original chape and locket could go back. Do you want to sell it? You'd get a better price if it had a scabbard made exactly like the old one.'

'Good heavens, no! In the first place, it isn't mine to sell, and I don't know who the owner is yet. But it does have an enormous lot of interest for me, and I'll willingly foot the bill to have it cleaned and restored.'

'Whoever put it away knew about swords,' Colin said, becoming more interested every minute. 'He used beeswax, which we still use on them once we've cleaned them as much as we dare without spoiling them – as so many sword-collectors do. If you mean what you say about the new scabbard and a clean-up and replacing the grip, you'll have to leave it with me, and wait for it because I'm up to my neck in work at the moment. But if you have any reason to want information about it quick, I'll make a proper examination of it, and send you a report and an estimate. Will that do?'

William had glanced at his watch, and knew that if they were to make their other appointment at the Combined Universities' Club, they had to leave at once. He was glad to have been forced to a swift decision. He glanced up at Bob, saw agreement in his face, and said that that would suit him fine. In fact, it was an unexpected blessing. The longer he could legitimately keep it from Fran's sight, the fewer questions he would have to answer with half-truths. They bade Colin a hasty farewell and walked swiftly to the next, very different consultation.

*

It was already in session when they arrived a few minutes late. Bob was the only one not known to all the rest, because he had never met Dr Marland, or Dr Chandra, though those two did have a slight previous acquaintance with each other. So Bob sat himself down slightly apart, where he could hear all that was said, but not be required to take part. Alex had already said they must get down to their discussion as soon as possible, because of his tight schedule, so he outlined the situation, from his point of view, as he had heard the details from Charles.

'Of course,' he added, 'this is very difficult for me, because I'm one of the family and fond of them all, except my brother-in-law. But in itself the case interests me. I think the first question to be asked is the important one: is this a clinical case, or not? If it is a clinical matter, has it progressed to the point Charles thinks it has, that his father may now be a danger to others?'

Terry gave his opinion that no man who was not sick in body or mind could act as Brian had been doing recently. William corroborated Alex on the details of Brian's strange behaviour in the past.

'But perhaps,' he said, 'Alex can tell us a bit more about genuine phobias, from a psychologist's standpoint. They can make life hell for the sufferers, who have no defence against them. I happen to know two very sensible and level-headed women, one of whom goes haywire at the sight of a child's balloon, and the other who comes out in goose-pimples and shrieks if she hears the sound of paper rustling or being screwed up to be thrown away. There seems to us laymen no logical reason, but I can't see how they are to be blamed for having such a handicap.

'Brian appears to have doctor phobia. Narrowed down, this means that if any of the medical men here believe that he has any physical or mental disorder needing treatment, they also know that he will neither seek advice himself, nor accept any help offered. Now, do any of you medical men have any reason to suspect that he is ill, physically or mentally?'

Alex replied with another question. 'You see him, or have in the past seen him, more frequently than any of us. At close quarters. Have you noticed any change in him?'

'Nothing but his inclination to avoid any social occasion if he can, and his surly manner if he has been forced to attend such an event. You see him less frequently. Did you detect anything at the Golden Wedding that alerted you to any difference in him?'

Alex was hesitating, but in the end he replied. 'Yes, I'm afraid I did. I thought how much thinner he'd got since I'd last seen him, and noticed how very little he ate. But I didn't pay much attention to him, because he'd offended me by being insufferably rude about our little girl being one of the party. My wife was upset, but for the sake of her sister – who looked as tense as if she were walking a tight-rope – she said nothing. I put it all down to him being "out of sorts", and may have eaten something that had disagreed with him, so that he was in no mood for a family party.

'And you, Dr Hardy?' Alex added. Terence was guarded in

what he said, because his position was the most difficult. He gave them a very brief outline of his problems in getting Brian to agree to any treatment for Rosemary – till he had been forced to conclude that it was her husband's attitude holding back her recovery.

'He was very free with his language, and before he dismissed me from the case, I'd begun to suspect some sort of sexual hang-up. He certainly appeared to be obsessed by sex. I haven't seen him since he attacked Dr Chandra and quite literally threw him out. There are those who have put two and two together, and think he is the author as well as the purveyor of all the scurrilous rumours of his sister's sexual indiscretions – as well as my own. One of our most perspicacious friends believes his aberration to be connected with business matters and his desire to be free to sell land for development scheduled by Local Government. Jehan here has nothing to go by but his own observation. Ask him what his first impressions were.'

Jehan spoke with great dignity. 'You must remember that I was new in the village, and had no idea, really, of what to expect. Dr Hardy took me to introduce me, but sat in the car on the road while I went to the door. Mr Bridgefoot opened the door to me himself, and in that second, before he attacked me and kicked me off his premises, I saw a man sick in both body and mind. No more than my fleeting first impression.'

'I'm afraid I can't stay much longer,' Alex said, 'but think we'd all better go away and think about it, and meet again when I come down to Old Swithinford for Christmas. Such a mass of disparate speculation can't all be right. To make any rational judgement, I need time to sift the evidence, and I can do that at first hand during Christmas. May I suggest that we adjourn till then?'

From his corner, the voice of Bob made itself heard for the first time. 'It's none of my business, except that my daughter is Charles's wife, and the one most likely to suffer the consequences of his breakdown if that's what it is; but as the outsider who sees most of the game, I can't agree with what Dr Marland has just said. I know nothing about doctoring, but I do know how things just happen. He says that all the ideas of what it might be wrong with Charles's father can't be right. But they may. One thing can bring up another till you can't tell where or how it all started. The sky on a bright morning may have hardly a cloud in it, till you notice first a little one, and then others dotted about. Next time you look up, they've collected into one big one that gradually thickens and overcasts the whole sky till everything is dark. That's how I see the Bridgefoots now. A cloud so thick and dark won't just drift away again. There'll be a downpour or a cloudburst. It can't get better till it's been worse – that happens because life ain't all sunshine. This talk of illness and doctoring's only a part of something bigger.' They were all staring at him in a rather astonished way, when Terry glanced at his watch.

'*Help!*' he said. 'Where's the time gone? I *mustn't* be late!'

'What for – and do you mean you really do need help? Because Bob and I are free now. We intended to go straight homewards and find lunch on the way, but if you need help, we're here. What can we do for you, Terry?'

Terry stood up, and they noticed then for the first time how point-device he was from head to toe. He gave them an anxious grin, and said, ' "For God's sake, get me to the church on time" – only I mean Caxton Hall Register Office, and come and stand by me! I've never been there before – the place, I mean – not the ceremony. We've said no word to anybody! Does anybody know the way, or the procedure? I daren't take any chances.'

'I know the way,' said Jehan. 'Dr Burbage can follow me.'

'And I know how to go on, once we get there. I were married there myself, not so long ago,' said Bob.

'And we haven't even time to drink a toast to you,' said Alex. 'We'll make up for it at Christmas. Good luck.'

*

They were later starting home than they had intended, having been given lunch and been sworn to secrecy till after the weekend, when Dr and Mrs Hardy would be back in Old Swithinford to take up residence in Heartsease before Christmas. Secrecy, that is, to all but their wives. Jehan was left to escort the couple.

It had not seemed a very long day to Fran, because she had spent the middle of it, and had lunch, with Beth. Elyot was his old self again, and Fran remarked to Beth that she had never before seen Emerald so sparklingly beautiful. Beth smiled, a long, deep, understanding smile.

'She's in love,' she said. 'With Jehan Chandra. I must be the most well-cared-for expectant mother in the kingdom. Any excuse is better than none for him to call. So in spite of all the unhappiness about the Bridgefoots, "Love is in the air again". It makes a lot of difference.'

To Beth's surprise, Fran's instant reaction was to shed tears. 'I can't help hoping that somehow, somewhere, John Petrie knows!' she said. 'Nothing would have pleased him better than to know she had found happiness with a doctor! He was so nearly one himself – and one who cared almost too much that whatever else they didn't have, his children got enough love. Oh, Beth, may it last! Does Elyot approve?'

'It hasn't come to that, yet, and we mustn't take anything for granted. Jehan's only here, at present, as a locum. But we can always hope.'

'Anyway,' said Fran. 'It's a lovely thought, and something to counteract the sadness down at the Glebe.' They began to discuss the imminent Christmas with all its difficulties, and Fran propounded to Beth the idea that Snowdrop had given her.

'It seems to me,' she said, 'that the best way to help the Bridgefoots is to keep ourselves from being too depressed. Above all, to keep tradition going all round them, though they may not feel like taking part in anything. It's up to all the rest of us to hold the village together so that when these troubled times are behind them, they have something to come back to. So give my idea a bit of thought, Beth, and let me know by tomorrow whether or not you think it makes any kind of sense.

'If it is feasible, I'll put it to Eric and Nigel tomorrow as ever is. We must make sure that everybody who possibly can turns up at Fenley on Friday evening.' She left Beth's feeling very cheerful, and reached Benedict's in good time to welcome William back.

He had plenty to tell her, and in fact gave her an almost word-for-word account of the meeting with Alex – including what Bob had said about there being many reasons rolled into one to account for Brian's present collapse of morale. Next he told her the news he knew would please her most, that he had actually been present at the marriage of Terry and Anthea, and added his name as a witness. 'They asked me to give you their special love, and thanks,' he said. 'And so they should!'

Then, lastly, he told her about the sword, and why he hadn't been able to bring it back with him. 'But there's no doubt at all that it is exactly of the right period,' he said. 'The blade's a hundred years older than the hilt, so it's the hilt's date that matters most to me. I asked Colin to date it as near as he could after such a brief examination. He said between 1635 and 1645. Spot on. So I have no excuse left at all for putting it off any longer. The manuscript is genuine.

'I feel as if I've changed gear today, and actually want to go and start on it this minute, except that I've been away from you too long already – but now there's a long-drawn-out Christmas to endure before I can begin. Not a very happy one, perhaps, for any of us, but as Bob said, the cloud must either pass over or there'll be a cloudburst soon. Funny how telling his simple philosophy can be and how his skill with words can make it clear.

'I was thinking so, the other day, when something reminded me of how much the young people of yesterday learned about life from each other – as Bob must have done. They soaked bits of potted wisdom, so different from knowledge, from the experience of others, with proverbs and aphorisms and rhymes passed down from generation to generation. As in the craze for autograph books that was in vogue when we were growing up. Everybody had one, but it wasn't to collect the autographs of pop-stars or footballers. It was for your friends to write some verse in, or draw a picture, and then sign it. They became cheapened to collections of pathetic attempts at wit, but now and then they still had little gems of wisdom enshrined in them. I remember that Grandfather was the first to write in one of mine, and what he wrote over his signature was "Pray to God in a storm but keep on rowing". Confucius? Doesn't matter. It's stuck with me ever since. Bob had one to fit the situation today:

In this world of toil and trouble,
Two things stand like stone.
Sorrow in another's trouble;
Courage in your own.

'That's common sense. We shan't do them any good by being too miserable about them ourselves to help if there's a chance.'

'That was exactly what Beth and I decided,' she said. 'We shall probably enjoy a lot of it, and there may be happy surprises as well as sad ones at Glebe. What do you propose to do tomorrow? Because I may be very busy on my own account.'

'Rest and prepare myself for the ordeal of Friday evening at Fenley School. It isn't much in my line, but I wouldn't let Greg or the children down – or if it comes to that, John Petrie. As you say, I think he would have been overjoyed for Emerald's sake that a young man like Jehan should cross her path when she was ripe for a bit of romance. Think what her life might have been by now if her mother hadn't abandoned them!'

She threw back her head and laughed, the first real hearty laugh he'd heard from her for what seemed a very long time. 'You sound like Don Marquis's "Archie the Cockroach",' she said, 'who was as full of helpful maxims as any autograph book. He must have been feeling a bit like we have lately when he wrote:

> ' "*for you would not*
> *think that a cockroach*
> *had much ground*
> *for optimism*
> *but as the fishing season*
> *opens up i grow*
> *more and more*
> *cheerful at the thought*
> *that nobody ever got*
> *the notion of using*
> *cockroaches for bait*" '

'You win,' he said, and joined in her laughter.

*   *   *

Next morning, Fran talked with Beth on the phone, who agreed that if her idea was practical enough to be dealt with at this late stage, she should go ahead to suggest it at any rate: which meant finding both Nigel and Eric, wherever they happened to be.

William was engrossed with his own concerns, as she could see, so she told him she was off on a project of her own, and left him to them.

As so often happened, they were on the same wavelength, and almost following each other's thoughts as she set out on her search. They centred on the fact that though the main problem was no nearer being solved, in general the pessimistic attitude towards it was lifting. There was a different spirit abroad.

Both had accounted for it in the same way. However bad the grief and trouble, human nature is geared to accepting it and facing up to it sooner or later. And to be doing something practical was about the best way of adjusting to it. As she told herself, even the death of a loved one – as had been the case with Eric – had in time to be reallocated into the stream of life still going on.

The fact that they had decided to make Christmas a proper Christmas in spite of everything held a lot of promise that they would get to the other end of the holiday season much more adjusted to what was, and what must be, than they had been till now. The best plan was for everybody not closely concerned to keep busy.

She caught up with Nigel, together with Eric, in the barn at Monastery Farm, and told them of her talk with Sophie and Ned, and the hopeful results.

Then she put her idea to them – and they listened.

'If you think it can't be done, forget it,' she said. 'If you think there's a chance at all for it, we must wait till after the concert at Fenley tomorrow night. It just seemed to me that it was such a shame to do all this to the barn, including hiring chairs and a piano, just for one occasion. But we honestly can't know whether it makes sense or not till after tomorrow evening.'

She fixed them both with steady eye, though it was intended mostly for Eric.

'Nigel, you will obviously have to attend *ab officio*; William will do his duty, and so will Elyot. What it needs is for all of us – except the Bridgefoots who obviously can't – to be there *en masse*. And that includes you, Eric. Bob will go because he'll love it anyway, and Effendi because Jane has been so involved. You are the key, Eric. Promise me you won't let me or Greg down. United we stand, even if it is only a school concert. My other idea is an appendage to what happens at Fenley tomorrow evening. Be a man! It won't last more than an hour or so.'

'All right then,' said Eric reluctantly. 'Unless there is anything nobody else can deal with up at the hotel, I'll be there. I shall need people who don't want to take part in politics to support me if I do have to involve myself – the least I can do is to show willing to do as I would be done by.'

Fran felt she had scored a tremendous victory, and went home to think the next moves out.

She was greeted by Sophie, looking somewhat abashed, with Olive at her side. Could they have a word or two with her?

'As many as you like,' she said, addressing herself to Sophie, 'as long as you are not so upset as you were yesterday. I'm trying to make everybody see that we shan't help George and Molly or any of the rest of them by making ourselves miserable. So let me hear what you've got to say quick.'

'Well, it's only to say that I got a real good talking to from Jelly yist'day, and another from Joe last night. I don't know what come over me, but I hev to say as you was right, and I am ashamed of myself for saying what I did. Do, I shall be 'appy to give the Rector and them as much o' my time as they want. But Joe said last night as 'e thinks I should be better without such as Ida Barker and them getting in the way. 'Adn't 'im and Dan'el showed what they could do with a broom at your wedding party? One more woman and them two would be a lot better than a gang as kept stopping to tell each other the latest bit o' gossip, Joe said. So if you can put that right with the Rector, it can be left to Joe and Dan and me and Olive. Will that suit, do'yer think?'

Fran could have crowed with pleasure at the sight of Olive's face. It took so little to give so much innocent pleasure!

'And there's one more thing,' Sophie said. 'Joe told me as Steve is going to be in the concert tomorrow night, and 'e'll be a-looking for us all to be there to see 'im. But Joe won't hev room in 'is van for me as well as Het and Steve and Dan, as 'e's promised a'ready to take. And Olive wants to goo, an'all, but we can't get there. I just wondered if there'd be room for us in your car?'

'Of course. The more the merrier. And I mean that. If you know of anybody else who wants a lift, let me know soon. I rather think it'll be up to me to arrange who takes who.'

There was a gleam of satisfaction on Sophie's face that let Fran know Sophie had got her own way. 'There's a lot o' them old'uns down Mary Budd Cluss as thinks they ought to goo, 'cos when she 'ad 'er Christmas concerts they'd all'us enj'yed 'em – besides them feeling some'ow as they'd be doing it for 'er.'

'Let me know by lunch-time how many,' said Fran bravely, a bit apprehensive of what she had so unwittingly let herself in for.

When she told William, he could only laugh, and remind her of another occasion when they had had to 'go out into the highways and hedges, and compel them to come in'. But had she considered how many people could be got into Fenley School?

'I'll cross that bridge when I come to it,' she said. 'By the looks of it, Old Swithinford will be deserted tomorrow night, except for the Bridgefoot family.'

It was a prophetic utterance – on both counts.

*   *   *

William was as relaxed as Fran had ever known him. Once the sword had been found, and the date of it confirmed as near as it could ever be, his path was at last clear. He was in a mood just to sit and contemplate the project as it lay spread before him once Christmas was over. He was prepared now to accept that his 'duty' for the next three weeks was as much to the present as to the past, and to the community as well as to history.

Fran, on the other hand, found she had bitten off quite as much as she could chew. According to Sophie, all Old Swithinford wanted to be at Fenley on Friday evening, and it was up to her to see that they got there! She made lists galore, trying to utilize every available car, and fix routes so as not to waste time or petrol. It was no easy task, and the mix of passengers in each car often stopped her in her tracks to laugh at the prospect. But she had asked for it herself, and now had no option but to carry it through.

The list of phone calls – interrupted by Sophie time and time again to say so-and-so wanted to go if there was room – was very long, and failure to connect sent her out before lunch to make a round of visits to those friends she was turning into taxi-drivers. It was really all very amusing, except for the sad thought that no Bridgefoots would share the fun. She did, however, come by one piece of news from Eric. He had heard that Alex and Lucy Marland, and their little girl's nanny, already booked in for the Christmas period, were arriving early. Tomorrow, Friday, in fact, though late in the evening. The knowledge gave Fran comfort. She went back to her task until she had completed it, and then joined William in his relaxation.

So Friday evening arrived and, barring small children, for whom Beth had set up a crèche in the charge of Emerald and Amethyst at the Old Rectory, the phalanx of supporters from Old Swithinford filed into the very small school at Fenley.

The twinge of guilt that assailed Fran as she saw how much of the seating arrangements in 'the big room' they took up was only equalled by the transformation wrought in the room by Greg and Mrs Tyrrell and their willing aids. The drab old Victorian classroom had been cleverly and magically set up with a stage (made of children's tables), a pair of huge curtains on a drawstring, leaving a tiny proscenium in front and special spotlights. The school's upright piano was on the floor to one side of this, and a pair of steps on the other side gave access to it from 'the little room'. From end to end the school walls were decorated by children's exuberant symbols of Christmas. Fran, making herself as small as she could, thought that at least she should have had enough sense to consult Mrs Tyrrell and warn her!

And still they came crowding, and somehow they got in, and still Mrs Tyrrell and Greg, wearing his most flamboyant gear to match his mood, gave them welcome and found them room to breathe. At the last minute, when the door could hardly be opened because of the pressure of people inside, and Eric had started to worry in case there should be a fire, and whether the school were insured, William and Elyot and Bob and a few more of the tallest of the Old Swithinford contingent were requested to stand at the back, so as not to obscure the view of the stage from those behind them. Then Greg sat down at the piano and struck a chord.

The door from 'the little room' opened, and the entire school of thirty-odd children filed in, the older ones up the steps to the back of what stage there was, and so on in rows to the 'babies', who perched themselves, scrubbed knees and legs dangling, on the front of it. Last to come from 'the green room' were Jess and Jane and 'Miss Amanda' who, by dint of flattening themselves against the wall each side of the door, managed to squeeze in.

Another chord, and Greg stood with raised baton. The busy chatter stilled, and goose-pimples rose on Fran's neck as down the baton came:

We wish you a Merry Christmas,
We wish you a Merry Christmas,
We wish you a Merry Christmas
And a Happy New Year.
Good tidings we bring, to you and your kin,
We wish you a Merry Christmas,
And a Happy New Year.

A slight scuffle, and the youngest were now standing in front of the stage. Their voices alone filled the room.

'Now bring us some figgy pudding', till the chorus was reached and the rest joined in. Then there was one little voice alone, clear as a bell and perfectly in tune:

For we all like figgy pudding
So bring some out here.

The chorus hid Sophie's audible sobs as Fran turned to look at the row of Sophie, Joe and Het, and Daniel. The little soloist was Stevie. Greg turned to the audience. 'Now your turn,' he said, and Fran would have sworn that everybody obeyed the authority of his baton till he sat down and accompanied the last chorus with his own particular brand of musical panache.

Magic was at work. It was as if they had all been returned to their childhood. What followed was almost unbelievable in its variety and expertise. Behind those curtains a puppet theatre had been set up, to cater for every kind of puppet from 'stick puppets' to marionettes made and manipulated with extraordinary skill, so that every child's effort at making his own was displayed at its best. There were musical items, including recorders and percussion, choral speaking and poems turned into little dramas, fitted in between the hilarious bits of puppetry, 'live items' in which every child had a part, using whatever skill he or she happened to possess. One turn almost brought the concert to a standstill, when Greg vacated the music stool in favour of Jonce, and Stevie alone occupied the stage. With complete aplomb, they rendered 'Twinkle, twinkle, little star' as nobody there had ever heard it before.

It was over all too soon, and the speeches of thanks made. It was then that Fran learned that Greg and Mrs Tyrrell had been warned of her idea: that as many items as it was possible to use in a new location should be repeated as the first half of an evening's entertainment in the barn at Old Swithinford, as it was now set up, in the gap between Christmas and the New Year. Mrs Tyrrell said she'd have to consult every parent, but she saw no difficulties. She would let the Rector know as soon as she possibly could.

It was then that Eric added his contribution. 'If the parents agree,' he said, 'I'll make sure that the children are transported both ways, insured for the whole evening, and fed in the interval between the concert and the adult-only part of the evening – whatever such a gathering is called. I know but I've forgotten.' He turned inquiringly to Fran.

'Eric!' she said, delightedly. 'A "horkey"! It's exactly what Old Swithinford needs this year.'

Eric held Mrs Tyrrell's hands and thanked her, and through her, the children, for showing 'what education could and should be'.

'And there,' said Fran to William, 'speaks the candidate for our ward of the District Council. Whoever would have believed it!'

*　　*　　*

Even at Glebe, the atmosphere had become a little less doom-laden. That Charles, so young and already with so much responsibility on his own and Charlie's account, should care enough to maintain what to George was so very important – the honour and integrity of the Bridgefoot name within the community – was in itself enough to send the old man's spirits up a notch; that he should have seen for himself what Brian's defection from the Bridgefoot tradition, whatever the cause, would mean in practical terms was a comfort George hadn't expected. He had dreaded having to admit to Charles that if Brian did defect, whatever his

432

reason for doing so, there was no way he could handle the firm alone, especially if he had to fight his own son every inch of the way. He hoped and believed that Charles would want to save his heritage, but it wasn't fair to make him choose between that and his and Charlie's own ambitious plans. She had given Charles his very life back when he had been in danger of losing it; and George was realistic enough to appreciate the new blood she had brought into the family, to strengthen a weakening strain.

He felt a bit of guilt towards Brian for his partisanship of the girl against his son's wishes; he wondered if part of what appeared to be Brian's deliberate attempt to hurt him was based on resentment about that; but he was too honest with himself to accept all the blame. Brian's rejection of Charlie had been on the very same grounds as George's delighted acceptance of her had been. Brian had hoped to use his handsome, well-off son as a bait to catch a bigger fish for his own prestige; he had hoped for a rich heiress who would put her father-in-law into the landowner, rather than the farmer, bracket. He had not forgiven Charles or Charlie for both wanting to keep their feet on farmland, even if Charlie's ambition ran to a different branch of the rural economy.

He had suffered in mind and body after the first shock of Brian's intentions. The wounds to his heart were the cruellest and deepest, wounds he thought he would never recover from and which he had done his best to hide, especially from Molly. He had done his best to come to terms with the fact that it was old fashioned to think that things would or should go on as they had done for so many generations. He had given in, and let Brian have more or less his own way, but he had not expected to be repaid like this. He should have known that if Love cannot earn love, there is no way of buying it. His mind had been a writhing mass of self-recrimination and despair that in doing what he could for his son, he had robbed his grandson – and Charlie. He could see no way out, and lost hope. He had sometimes looked towards the churchyard, where his Bridgefoot ancestors lay at peace, and thanked God that He had seen fit to decree that death should close all suffering.

And then, without warning, he had found that he was not

alone. Charles had come to him, and by doing so lifted the weight from George's old shoulders to his own young ones. He had not only understood, and grieved, he had taken it upon himself to do the only thing that seemed to offer any hope – for Brian himself, and all who still loved him, however much he had hurt them. He had acted, in George's opinion, not a minute too soon. Alex would be rather hesitant about telling him the majority view of the medical men on the evidence they had, but he was glad he would now have to face up to whatever it was.

Then had come the phone call from Lucy, his youngest daughter and Alex's wife, that they would be arriving earlier than expected to be home for Christmas. Alex had told her all, and she was worried about him and Mum. They would be too late to get to Glebe on Friday evening, but would be up straight after breakfast on Saturday; and he was not to worry, because the doctors had agreed at the last minute that the sensible thing to do was for all of them who could to observe Brian in the flesh, sift the evidence, and leave any decision till after Christmas.

He didn't know whether that was sensible or not, but it did mean that he no longer had to carry all the worry himself. He went straight to Molly, to tell her of Lucy's impending arrival, and saw her face light up. She, too, had come to accept that what would be would be. They still had each other. And Rosemary, who was suffering quite as much as they were. And Marge and the twins – they had been assured by Nigel that Pansy would be back to help as soon as ever Yorky was well enough to come and do his bit with her. And above all, there was Charles and that beautiful girl over there on the fence singing French love-songs to Chum. For the first time in days, George laughed aloud, and called to Molly to come and look.

Charlie rang Charles to tell him that Aunt Lucy was coming. He said he was standing by in case his mother wanted him – she was a bit down because she daren't leave home without telling Brian that she had only gone to a school concert at Fenley with Fran and William Burbage. But he hadn't been seen since breakfast time, so she had rung Fran to call it off.

'So I can't leave till I know he's home,' Charles said. 'But if they are all OK at Glebe, why don't you come home for an hour or two?'

'Will do,' she said. 'But I must be back in time for supper. I have a feeling that neither of us ought to leave our lookout posts until we know he's safely home again at Temperance. Something's niggling at me, telling me we may be needed.'

'I see. If you say so, my lambkin. I know you. Faithful unto death.'

'Heavens, darling! I hope it hasn't come to that! I said nothing of the sort! The truth is that I can't bear to leave my new sweetheart for too long without his lullaby. Even Dan is deserting him tonight to go to that concert.'

*

The evening dragged slowly on. Charlie was restless and wanted Charles to go back with her to Glebe; but he rang his mother, who said his father had still not come home, and she was getting very worried. 'Where can he have been all day?' she said.

He tried to soothe her. 'Don't get too upset,' he told her. 'It won't be long now before Uncle Alex arrives at the hotel, and if Dad still hasn't come in I'll get Uncle Alex to help me set up a search for him.'

'I think I must stay here,' he said to Charlie. 'But I agree that you'd better be getting back to stand by Grandad and Gran – to be there if we do have to set up a search. I'm central here to both of you. And for another hour or so we shall be a bit short of help – till Alex arrives and all the others get home from Fenley. Promise me that you'll go straight indoors when I get you back to Glebe. I don't like the thought that he may be hiding there somewhere till it gets dark.'

'I promise,' she said. 'Oh dear, I do so want all this to be over, so that I can come home to you again.'

She kissed him, and they left hurriedly. She didn't like the insistent thought that she ought not to be away from Glebe. It was too much like her father's premonitions.

However, when Charles delivered her back to Glebe and she went in, all was quiet, with an air of peace about that she hadn't felt before since she'd been staying there.

Aunt Marjorie sat at the table writing, and at the opening of the door, looked up and smiled at Charlie, putting a finger to her lips and gesturing gently towards Grandad and Gran. Gran had slipped off to sleep in her chair, breathing deeply and regularly. She hadn't had much real rest lately, though she had spent more time in bed than ever in her life before. And Grandad, too, was asleep in his chair, sitting almost upright because it was drawn up to the table. His spectacles were pushed up on his forehead, and on the table at his side lay a coil of new rope, scissors, and two or three other tools. One hand was resting on the arm of his old Windsor chair, still lightly clasping an awl. Charlie took it all in at a glance, and put her thumbs up to her aunt.

Charles had forced the issue of facing up to Brian's problems that both the old people had been dreading, knowing, as both George and Bob had said more than once, that sooner or later it must come. Alex was on his way now to tell them about the meeting and they were glad. Molly had grieved till she could grieve no more, and was letting kind Nature take its healing course.

Grandad's reaction had been different. He neither hoped nor feared now; it was in the hands of God. But he was still a healthy and hearty old man who had had a good life in which there had been more blessings than tragedies. Whatever happened now, he had to go on. That made him remember that he had not yet spliced the new rope for the clock. He had fallen asleep in the very act of starting on the job – as a sort of earnest that he would take what was still to come without rage or whimper. The words that flashed through Charlie's head were that they had crossed their Rubicon.

She sat down by Marjorie and they began a whispered conversation. Reinforcements were on the way. Alex and Lucy were coming early *because they cared*. That in itself had been enough for Molly. Then Pansy and Yorky had made a brief appearance, and laid their cards on the table. They needed each other: not just for now, but for always.

Marjorie wiped away a tear that insisted on escaping down her face. 'I didn't know!' she said. 'I didn't know half she'd been through.'

Yorky had made it clear that he had had no thought of such a thing till it had happened. He had nothing whatsoever to offer Pansy but his love. He had not been afraid to use the old-fashioned word – so Grandad had intervened to say that that, as far as he was concerned, was the only thing that mattered.

'That's just what the Rector said,' Pansy told him. 'He came to find me – and probably to "save" me again – but he left well alone. All he asked was that in time, when we could face it, we would let him marry us.

'I took courage from his being there to tell Yorky all the grisly details about myself that he didn't know,' Pansy had confessed. 'I think the Rector knew most of it – but Yorky didn't. Worst of all was having to admit that however married we might be, there could never be any children.'

'I ought to have guessed,' Marjorie said. 'I'll do my best to make it up to her when I can.'

'Sh!' said Charlie. 'We'll all do our best to give her a fresh start. One thing at a time. It's had a bracing effect on Grandad and Gran, anyway. Or at least, something has. Let them sleep while they can.'

She had hardly got the words out before a bang from outside made them stop and listen apprehensively.

'What was that?' Marge whispered.

'Somebody playing tricks out in the yard,' Charlie answered. 'Sounded like a firework, but it can't be, surely? Stop here in case they wake up – I'll go and take a peep outside.'

She knew before she opened the door who it was she would find out there, but guessed he was just snooping again. She froze with horror as the truth dawned on her. She could smell smoke – and the next moment there came such a hullabaloo from the cowshed that she was galvanized into action. She put her head back round the door and yelled at Marge to ring Charles, and tell him to send for the Fire Brigade. 'You look after Grandad and Gran – I'll go and do what I can till Charles gets here!'

There was no light but the moon, now in its third quarter, but to her dismay, she realized a dozen or so tiny fires were burning in the straw of the cowyard, where Brian was setting fireworks alight as he moved furtively like a dark shadow among the bellowing cows. Charlie's mind was, by this time, as knife-sharp as it had ever been. She stood quite still so that he should not be aware that he was being watched.

That he was as near to being insane as made no difference became clear to her. He must have planned to burn those buildings down without giving any thought to small details. He had hoped to have the whole mass well alight before anybody was alerted – and had been clever enough to think the fireworks just the thing to serve his purpose. The detail he had forgotten was that some fireworks make a lot of noise and that terrified cattle would panic at the first sight of flame or smell of a wisp of smoke.

She could not tackle him alone – but she must save the cows! Could she slip across and open their gate without being seen? While she hesitated, sounds from the inside of the house told her that the cows had roused George and Molly and that Marge was doing her best to keep them from rushing out. They mustn't see! They mustn't!

'Oh come on, Charles. Come on,' she kept repeating to herself, knowing perfectly well that he could not reach her for at least another ten minutes. She shrank into shadow, watching Brian standing dazedly among the plunging cows, still attempting to light more fireworks in straw that was too damp with the evening dew to flare up readily from such weak sparks as old fireworks provided.

A cow bumped into him, and he became aware of his own danger of being knocked over in the smouldering straw. He made for the gate, and threw it open. The cows, thank goodness, had been left free till Dan came to see that all was well and shut them up for the night when he got home from Fenley.

Marge was blocking her father's attempts to get out of the door which meant that Charlie couldn't get in; she had enough sense to realize that if she stood still, she was in no real danger from the cows, who would probably make for the road as their nearest escape from the fire. The danger she saw ahead was that Charles in his haste would come upon them and, if nothing worse, lose time by trying to round them up. As it happened, once out of the gate they turned the other way.

The worst thing would be if in this mad mood Brian should see her. There was nothing she could do but keep herself under control and not lose sight of him. He had left the cows' yard after the last cow had blundered out, and was fumbling at the gate of Chum's yard. She could hear Chum's bellowings as he reacted to the flight of the cows, and with awful, sinking heart realized that Dan, after restrawing his yard this afternoon, had tethered him in his stall. Brian went boldly into his yard, and closed the gate behind himself. Charlie, almost paralysed with horror, saw his face for a moment in the light of a flaring match as he struck it to ignite another batch of fireworks. It was demonic – and told her plainly what was his main objective. He was going to burn Chum to death!

She left the safety of the dark shadow, and rushed, screaming at him, across the yard to climb on to the fence. Brian turned to face her – and everything happened at once. Charles drove into the yard, his headlights illuminating the scene. His first thought was to catch her as she climbed the fence, which he did, though it was too late. Brian had reckoned wrong again. Chum had been shut in his stall, but not tethered. Finding himself trapped and smelling fire, as well as being excited by the bellowing of the cows, he had used his massive strength and broken down the door that shut him in. There, in the middle of his yard, stood a puny man with fire in his hand. Chum lowered his magnificent head, and charged. Brian was sent staggering across the width of the straw. He hit the buildings on the opposite side, and fell. Chum lowered his head and followed – but his quarry lay limp and still in the straw, which was alight in only one or two places. Charles had plucked Charlie off the fence, and prepared to go over to his father's rescue himself. Charlie beat him furiously with both fists as he dragged her away, screaming at him to have more sense.

'He's only holding back because your dad's not moving,' she yelled. 'He'll turn on you if you move – and kill you with his next charge. Get yourself Dan's hayfork from the cowshed.'

Charles obeyed her. All he really cared about now was that he had got there in time, and that she was safe, both from a madman and a mad bull. He had no idea what to do next – except to remind himself that if a fire engine turned up it would probably only madden Chum more.

'Tell Aunt Marge to ring for an ambulance,' he yelled as he went to get himself a weapon. The fire engine had found the road obstructed by cows and had had to extricate itself before coming on. There was no major fire to put out, but their lights, and those of Charles's car, showed them that it was not so easy a case as they had supposed. The bull, with head lowered and fore hoofs pawing the ground, was poised to attack the supine figure of a man lying between him and a wall. There was no doubting that the bull was in a very dangerous mood and would attack the first person to go over the fence. Marge had had to let George out while she went to the phone, and then she'd had to give all her attention to Molly. The sight of Grandad standing helpless by the door was more than Charlie could bear. She went towards him, and they clung to each other, but to her surprise he was very calm and inclined to be fatalistic.

'If only Dan was here,' was all he said. 'He knows Dan. They'll never get Brian out alive if they rush it. Don't let Charles in with that fork,' he added, raising his voice and pushing her towards where Charles was preparing to climb the fence.

'Don't be daft,' she screamed at Charles – and he stopped.

The firemen and the ambulance crew were used to dangerous situations, and were trained to deal with them; but this was something they had never met before, and they had neither experience nor rules laid down to help them deal with it.

The chief fireman took charge. 'He may be dead already for all we know,' he said. 'It's no use you fellows' – he glanced at the ambulance team – 'or anybody else risking another life to find out. Bravery's one thing, but this is a case for clear thinking and strategy rather than heroics.'

A girl's clear voice rose above his. 'I'm sorry, Charles, but whatever you say, I'm going to try. Come with me if you must, but tell everybody else to stay in Chum's sight, ready to rush in and pick Brian up if I succeed in taking Chum's attention for a moment. I shan't go in the yard to him unless I have to. I do have some sense. Just you keep out of sight and let me draw his attention.'

The group ranged along the red iron fence on the house side were almost mesmerized into obeying her orders to stand in view but keep still. The doors of the ambulance stood open, and every man prepared for quick action. They had no idea what it was all about, or why this slip of a girl was giving the orders.

She came into their sight behind the fence on the other side of the yard, calling to the bull by name, and as they realized, chattering to him in a foreign language. He took no notice of her.

'Chum!' she said in English. 'You're not listening. All right, I'll come and sit on the fence. Come and talk to me.'

She climbed without haste or fuss to sit on the top rail, though, as they could see, in such a position that with one movement she could propel herself backward if she had to. Charles was hiding in shadow to rescue her if he had to. She leaned towards the bull, raised her voice and spoke to Chum, this time in French again. *'Quoi faire, Chum? Tout va bien, mon ami.'*

The waiting men could not believe they were seeing straight when Chum raised his head and looked towards her. The pawing hoof stopped as he gave the girl more of his attention, and the firemen made their plans as to which should venture to pick the victim up while others prepared to protect them as much as possible. Charlie read their intention and without stopping her chat, signalled to them to wait. Then, to their utter astonishment, she began to sing. In the dead silence, her voice rang out as clear as a bell, as she racked her tired mind for the words of songs in French. *'C'est si bon'*. *'Sous les toits de Paris'*. *'La mer'*. *'Plaisir d'amour'*. Keep it up, she told herself. It may work.

She was keeping one song back in case he turned his head wholly towards her. When, at last, he did, she dropped her voice to an intimate, loving tone that Charles would have termed 'croodling', and began to sing the song he was most familiar with: *'La vie en rose'*.

It was working. He went towards the sound, sidling alongside the fence to get as close to her as he could, lifting his head for her usual caress between his ears. She went on singing as she stroked his muzzle, and ran her fingers against the ring in his nose. Still keeping the tune going, she sang louder, fitting new words in English to the tune: a string of orders to the tense, waiting men, though mostly to Charles.

'Go – and get his rope – and bring it here, while I still hold him,' she sang. 'I – can slip it through – before he knows – what I am doing. Then – we'll tie him to the fence – till someone else – gets here to hold him. So be quick, my darling, he may change his mind – it's all right, my Chummy, no one's going to hurt you . . .'

Charles was back with the rope and a couple of hefty firemen. The trained paramedics had Brian on a stretcher and through the open gate on the other side, before Chum had even tried to back away.

'Shut that gate and make it fast,' yelled Charles. As soon as the bolt went home they let the rope slide out of the ring and Chum was free again. Charlie turned to her bemused husband. 'Help me down,' she said. 'I'm going to be sick.'

*

The ambulance team went off at once, asking Charles to see that someone followed them to the hospital at Cambridge. RAF Ely was nearer, but in their judgement they might as well get their patient to Addenbrookes first as last.

The family's problem was who to send to break the news to Rosemary.

'I'll go,' Marjorie said. 'There's no reason why I shouldn't if Brian's not there.'

Gran suddenly perked up and asked if the cows were still out. Nobody had given them a thought! Grandad, displaying far too much fatalistic calm for their liking, said Dan would be back as promised to shut Chum up. They could rely on him to go and look for the cows. What was the time?

Just past eight o'clock. Charlie, having recovered but still rather wan for her, said Uncle Alex should be at the hotel by now – wasn't he the help they needed? He'd know what to do next better than any of them. Why not ring and find out?

No sooner said than done. Alex had booked in, and had

dinner. He'd be round to Glebe in a couple of shakes. He was there within ten minutes, and took charge of the very disoriented family. His unhurried professionalism made them all feel better.

'It sounds as if your diagnosis was the right one,' he said to Charles. 'If somebody must go to the hospital, I think it should be me. I'm not only one of the family, in a sense he has been my patient. It's also possible that they'd tell me more than anybody else. I understand that we don't really know what happened. Will somebody put me wise before I go? He may regain consciousness at any minute – and under all the circumstances, I'd like to be there when he does, if they'll let me.

'There's a lot to think about. If they want to send him home, will it be safe to let him go to Temperance? Who's free to be with Rosemary? No, Charles, not you! For a dozen reasons. We have to be prepared for anything – for example that he may never come round. Marjorie, if Rosemary shows signs of great distress, tell her that Brian is being kept in for observation – which is my guess of what will happen. Wouldn't it help if she could come here? Don't involve Charles if you can help it, I may need him at my side if the worst should come to the worst. Did any of you actually see what happened when the bull charged him?'

Charlie said, 'Only me, I think. I'd got shut out by Aunt Marge who was trying to stop Grandad from leaving the house while Uncle Brian was trying to set fire to the place, so I hid in the shadow because I was a bit scared of him – of Uncle Brian. Only a man as mad as a hatter would have been doing what he was doing! Besides, I was expecting Charles, and I wanted to be there to warn him. Uncle Brian was lighting silly little fireworks, and the straw in Chum's yard was fresh enough to catch here and there.

'Then Chum knocked his door down and came out charging – and Uncle Brian was there – but I didn't really see.'

'I must go – quick. Charles, we may all be in for a long and anxious night. My advice to you – all of you, in fact – is to get some rest while you can. I'll be in touch the moment I have anything to report. Go to bed, Gran, and persuade Grandad to go with you. You as well, Charlie. It's been a pretty stressful time for you. Charles, I suggest you get what rest you can in Gran's chair. I may need you.'

George looked up at his son-in-law with the respect he had always been accustomed to accord to doctors, but with a very stubborn expression. 'You're overstepping the mark, Alex, giving me orders in my own house. Your patient is *my son*, as well as Charles's father. I shall sit up and wait for news if it takes all night.'

'Let me put you to bed, Mum, before I go,' said Marjorie.

'I'll go, if it will please Alex,' Molly said. 'But I haven't lived to be seventy-odd without learning how to cope with times like this – or how to put myself to bed. Get you off to Rosemary, Marge. I shall be all right. I don't promise as I shall sleep much, till I know how my son is. But I'm going to say what I mean to you all before I go. We've all seen this coming. If it's a question of my son dying, or living shut up in a lunatic asylum till he does, I shall be praying for him to die now.'

Leaving them all a bit stunned, she made for the stairs as if she were seventeen instead of seventy, and didn't turn her head to look back.

'All right, Grandad. You try to sleep where you are, if you can. I'll stop with you and Charles until he has to go,' said Charlie.

Charles was ready to succumb to the dreadful weariness that suddenly came over him. Charlie made him comfortable, gave him a lingering kiss, and went to sit at George's feet, with her head against his knee. Marjorie and Alex went out together. George sat staring into the distance, absent-mindedly stroking Charlie's hair. 'As long as you didn't get hurt, my pretty,' he said, 'I can put up with whatever else we have to face.'

*

The evening was long. They heard nothing from Alex or Marjorie. Charles slept, exhausted by the emotion of the last two days. Only Charlie remained wide awake; Grandad, though not asleep, shut his eyes and kept silent vigil with his thoughts. Charlie heard Dan outside, and crept out to tell him what had happened. He had met the cows and brought them home. She said they were now waiting for news from the hospital, so he took the hint and went. Next moment, the telephone bell jerked Charles to instant wakefulness. He reached for the receiver before Charlie had shut the door.

'Uncle Alex,' he told her tersely. 'I'm to go at once. Doesn't sound like good news to me. Look after yourself, my darling, and do what you can for Grandad.' Then he was gone, and only George and Charlie were left to sit out the strain of waiting. 'It's in God's hands,' George said. 'All we can do is wait, and hope.'

It wasn't like him to speak such platitudes, and she began to question what this was doing to his courageous, trusting old heart. There was hope, because at any rate tonight's crisis had landed Brian in the hands of skilled medical men whether he wanted them or not. Yet Grandad's voice had told her that he had more or less given up hope. She began to be worried about him.

He needed to get up and move his aching hip, so he stood up, stretched, and went to wind up the clock. He stood a moment facing it, tall and straight and refusing to let his shoulders sag. Charlie gazed up at him, understanding what courage it took to face this particular tomorrow. She watched him, aching with love for him, as he opened the door of the clock, and without looking inside, felt for the ropes to raise the weight. He didn't need to see what he was doing, he had done it so many times that he could have done it in his sleep. Winding it up meant much more to him than keeping it telling the right time. It was more than any family Bible or Victorian photograph album. The ritual was a nightly communion with his roots and all the other Bridgefoots who, for centuries, had performed the very same task.

Charlie had locked on to his wavelength, and could almost read his thoughts.

The old ropes made a slight groaning noise as the worn part reached the wheel of the pulley, and George, as he always did, stopped pulling downwards gently with his right hand while he helped lift the heavy weight with his left. But he had not been paying enough attention to his task tonight, and his instinctive caution was too late. With a heavy rumble and a resounding thump, the misshapen lead weight fell from his hand and landed with a crash into the bottom of the case.

445

He stood staring at the pendulum until it stopped swinging, and the clock stopped ticking.

Charlie didn't move or speak because she couldn't. She wondered if he had known what would happen, and had used the clock as a sign. She noticed how the old lion's shoulders were squared, and the grey leonine head held high on stiffened sinews, as tears began to glissade down his paling face. When the clock was dead, he put his hand up to its face, but tonight uttered no words.

He turned away, lifted his hand in blessing over her as he passed, made his way with slow dignity to the staircase in the hall, and began to climb. His need was to be near Molly, to lie beside her, to touch her, to share with her the age-old omen of death. As he had shared with her all their son's life, they would share this portent of his death. Christian to the marrow as he was, all his faith could do for him now was to give him strength to bear their loss.

Charlie sat on alone till the heavy footsteps overhead were silenced – and she was suddenly filled with anger. She was as pagan as her father was at heart, but why did sensible folk like Grandad extend the period of their suffering by watching for such signs of doom? To prepare themselves for it, of course, but even death could be staved off nowadays by the progress of medical science. Such warnings could be self-fulfilling if you gave in to them too much or too soon.

She would defy this omen to mean the end of the Bridgefoot line. For one thing, Uncle Brian wasn't dead yet, and as to the continuance of the Bridgefoot name, she hadn't been given a long enough warning to be able to reassure Grandad about that by putting another Bridgefoot boy into his arms. But she wasn't going to give in to folklore omens till she'd done everything she could to give Grandad some hope to cling to. Tired as she was by now, her mind started to work at top speed.

If only she could 'magic' the clock into life again by the time Grandad faced tomorrow, it would do the trick. But there was no way she could manage that. The ropes were broken, and knots wouldn't let it work. The rope that Grandad had meant to splice still lay in a coil on the table, with his tools. Who was likely to know how to splice a rope? A yachtsman? A sailor? Elyot Franks?

Elyot had been in training for seamanship since he was thirteen; he must have learned how to splice rope in those days. Intuition told her that it was like swimming or riding a bike: once learned, never forgotten. But she couldn't leave her post in case Charles rang from the hospital, or Aunt Marge couldn't manage Rosemary by herself. On the other hand, *she must catch the Commander before he went to bed*. That was what *she* had to do. It was a chance in a million that she had to take; she knew what her father would say about a feeling as strong as that. Whom could she ask to come to her help? Charles said he always turned to Benedict's when at his wits' end, so why not she?

'Of course,' said Fran. She'd be there within five minutes; William had not yet put the car away. Charlie had not told them anything but that she had to leave for an indefinite time and needed somebody to man the telephone. Not to worry, Fran said. That's what good neighbours are for. So Charlie was ready to set out the moment they drove into the yard. She barely stopped to greet them, but called, 'I've left you a note,' and began to run.

It was no distance; she was being driven by something stronger than her desire to stop before she collapsed. She lost track of everything but the feeling that she must get there at the very first minute possible.

Thank heaven, the outside lights of the Old Rectory were still on! For the wink of an eye, reality returned to her long enough for her to remember that a lot of children too young to go to the concert had been left there in Emerald's care.

She was gasping for breath and unable to speak, partly from lack of breath and partly from surprise, when the door was opened to her by young Dr Jehan.

'The Commander – is he in? Oh, please, please, may I speak to him?'

Elyot, who had done a lot of chauffeuring of neighbours that evening, had not yet had time to get his coat off, and was still in the hall; seeing who it was and wondering what could be the cause of the state she was in, he went to help her.

447

In desperation at her own inability to make it clear what she wanted of him, she opened the bag she was carrying and pushed the rope into his hands. He said afterwards that the feel of the rope was more explanatory of what she wanted than all her garbled, breathless attempts to tell him. All he gathered from her were single words like 'Clock', 'Weight' and over and over again, 'Can you splice it?' He simply nodded and said, 'Come and sit down. Jehan! You're needed here.'

She never did remember the next few minutes. She returned to her senses to find Jehan and Beth beside her, one holding her and stroking her while the other was busy with his stethoscope.

Then she began to cry, as if she would never stop.

*

When at last she was capable of speech, she sobbed the whole story out to them, from the night that she and Charles had decided they had to get medical help for his father, to the point where Grandad had taken himself off to bed and she had done the only thing that she could think of.

'I'm so sorry!' she kept repeating. 'I ought not to have bothered you!'

Jehan was thinking that it was no wonder she had given out, and perhaps a good thing too. He suggested to Emerald a cup of hot, strong, sweet tea. Charlie took it at his orders without arguing, giving him a tremulous smile that made her look much more like herself. She had feared that they might think her mad, but she had suddenly remembered that this young doctor was the one whom Brian had actually thrown out of his house, and had also been at the meeting with Uncle Alex in London. She felt on firmer ground again, and looked around for Elyot, but of him there was no sign.

When she was calm again, and still apologizing profusely, Jehan went to the workshop to find him.

Elyot said, 'The piece of rope and what I had managed to gather from you leads me to believe that you wanted me to splice a new piece of rope for the Bridgefoot family long-case clock. I've been practising in the last half-hour, and think I'm capable of doing what you want – except, of course, that you didn't bring

448

the old rope to go by for length – I took the liberty of looking in your bag – and clocks of that age are by no means all the same. But if it means so much to you as it appears, I'll take you back to Glebe, and do it there. Will that do?'

'Gosh!' she said. 'Will you really? I was in such a dreadful tizzy that I couldn't think. I was afraid you would think I was mad, as well as Charles's dad. But Grandad is so knocked out by it all that he's in danger of giving up, because a clock stopping when there's illness in the house is a sure omen of death. He's lost hope that anything can be done for his son – and I just couldn't bear it. It was as if I was being pushed to get that clock going again before morning to show him that it didn't always come true. I expect you must think I'm the daftest young woman in the world, to take any notice of him and his superstition! But all country folk are superstitious. My dad is, after his own fashion. But now I can only feel ashamed of myself for being so silly. All the same, if it isn't going to take you all night, I'll still be most awfully grateful.'

He stood over her, and then, leaning down, kissed the top of her head. 'You came to the right shop,' he said. 'If there is a race of people more superstitious than country folk, it's sailors. Are you OK now? Then let's get off. It may take me a long time, Beth my love. If you need me, ring me at Glebe. Take care of them, Emerald. I'll be back as soon as I can.'

*

Elyot and Charlie returned to the Old Glebe where William and Fran were waiting. When all had been explained, Elyot got down to work on the clock with his own superior tools, with great satisfaction to himself, and much interest from the others. It all seemed most unreal, to be sitting and talking and working in somebody else's house, with the owners upstairs not knowing they were there. When the pendulum of the old clock once again started to swing, Elyot set the hands to the right time and the striker to sound the next hour, but Charlie intervened. 'Grandad might hear it strike midnight,' she said, 'and he'll take it as another supernatural omen. Set it for seven o'clock, and stop it now. I'll promise to see that it's started again in the morning.'

449

They celebrated with a cup of coffee, but none of the other three felt that Charlie ought to be left alone. It was past midnight when the door opened, and Alex and Charles came in.

'Well?' said Charlie, reading in Charles's face that all was not well, but that there was a measure of compensation for him somewhere. Alex expressed his appreciation at finding William there. The reasons for the gathering were explained yet again.

'Tell us,' Charlie pleaded. Charles seemed to be numbed. All he wanted was to hold Charlie's hand, and let Alex do the talking.

Brian had not yet regained consciousness, and there was a possibility that he never would. All sorts of tests had been arranged to make his physical condition clearer – but Alex had already reached conclusions of his own.

'I think Bob Bellamy hit the nail on the head,' he said, 'in drawing our attention to the fact that all our theories could be right, and that what we could be facing was the sum total of many things. It begins with his personality being so different from the rest of his family; and his scorn at the traditions that are part and parcel of them, plus his desire to be in the forefront of the new rural society. All a matter of genetics, which we didn't take into account till now. Then the first signs of his doctor-phobia. It began while he was having to come to terms with the rudimentary fact that his new wealth couldn't buy him Charles's life, however famous the specialist of his choice and however big the fees. I'd got as far as that while we were waiting to talk to the consultant who'd been sent for at my request.

'He asked me if I knew that Brian had been having prostate trouble – for at least two years, he guessed. No, none of us had had even a hint. But Charles was on to that like a shot. It accounted for so many things – Brian's using the office that had been Aunt Esther's flat so much – stopping there at nights as well as spending so much time there by himself any time of day. The loo made specially for Aunt Esther was only a step or two away.'

'And poor old Mum was thinking all the time that he wouldn't sleep with her because he had another woman!' Charles said.

Alex paused, as if to give them a chance to take in the next bit. 'It could have been dealt with then, but this is where the next bit fits together. He and Vic Gifford were on the point of investing a lot of Bridgefoot money with Bailey and Co., in Brian's case with a secondary objective of saving Charles from the mistake of marrying Charlie by turning her father out of his farm. My guess is that a lot of his nastiness just at that time was due to him finding blood in the lavatory pan. Almost any fool knows what that *may* mean, but he wouldn't seek advice because as well as his fear of what he might learn, it was the very wrong time for him to have to take time off for treatment. It's just been growing – and he was too frightened to let any doctor near him.' Nobody needed telling what 'it' was.

'Cancer?' asked Fran, horrified.

Alex nodded. 'Young Jehan diagnosed it the moment he set eyes on him. It went first to his bladder, and then into his groin, the lymph glands. Remember, I'm only telling you what I think. It isn't official – but I'm very much afraid it soon will be. What they did say tonight was that they feared a tumour on the brain. If it's a malignant one, there truly isn't much hope for him. And he'll have to be hospitalized for a very long time.'

'Who's going to tell Grandad and Gran?' asked Charlie, awed.

'I am,' said Charles. 'In the morning. If Uncle Alex is right, and I think he is, there is much more to it than Dad's condition. We shall have to make new arrangements for the firm, and for all the rest of us, as well as for him.'

Charlie whispered, her voice tense, '*Is* there any hope for him, Uncle Alex?'

'I think it depends on whether or not it is operable.'

'Then how long would you say he might live?'

He wondered at her persistence. 'Possibly no more than a month; possibly as much as a year.'

'Nine months would be enough,' she said. 'That's what we must hope for. That's why the clock had to be going when Grandad hears what we've just heard. No, there's nothing to tell him yet, but that will give him enough hope to keep him going. Charles and I have already agreed that that is the least we can do for him. Our own plans can wait.'

She left Charles's side, and went to Elyot. 'I shall never be

451

able to thank you enough,' she said. 'How can I possibly repay you?'

'Just kiss me,' he said, enfolding her in his arms. 'I shall hope that my daughter turns out to be as wonderful a woman as you are.'

*   *   *

It is one of the mysteries of rural life how news escapes and runs from mouth to mouth, and as everyone knows 'Bad news travels fast'. But there was no mystery about how the stunned village came to know about what had befallen the Bridgefoots.

George himself told Dan, and Dan had told Sophie. There were no restrictions on her tongue about the truth of this; nor was there a breath of scandal in it. Such universal sorrow was not the stuff of which gossip is made. It was the will of God, and as such must be accepted. She was free to discuss it as and where she would, but this time she did not choose to.

A cloak of dignified, discreet silence covered the whole village. While the Bridgefoot family drew ever closer together in its grief, its neighbours, united in their sorrow, formed a circle of sympathy round it like a stockade fence, both defensive and protective.

It was the only way they could show their true feelings: keeping silent and getting on with their own business. There was no actual death to mourn, no funeral at which they could outwardly display the respect they had for the entire family.

Plans for Christmas and the New Year had been made; they must be carried through. That would be their tribute to the grieving family who would not have had it otherwise. The Bridgefoots themselves, having been given both diagnosis and prognosis very much as Alex had predicted, dealt with the grief with typical courage and solidarity. The most urgent need was to look into the future. They discussed it in small groups when all collected together in the shadow of George and Molly's wings. 'All' consisted of George and Molly, Marjorie, Rosemary, Lucy and Alex, Charles and Charlie. George and Charles stood together at the centre, and it was with them that the process of reconstruction began. Till they became concrete, practicable proposals and ideas for readjustment remained only ideas.

When the time was ripe, it just happened. George suggested they should meet again on Monday and 'talk it out'.

'Grandad,' Charles said, 'don't you think we should invite Pansy and Yorky? The more I think about it, the more I believe they might solve some of our worst problems.'

'In times like this,' George replied, 'you find out whether a family is a family. It's a case of "forgive and forget".'

And so it was that they, too, were part of the discussion. It was taken for granted that Rosemary would represent her husband, which meant all shareholders were present, as well as some who were not. Lucy was to inherit Molly's shares, Marjorie's covered any interests her twins might claim.

George said that they must make no arrangement too binding, 'in case'. They did not yet know whether Brian would recover; till then it was obviously Charles who would have to bear the load. So what should they do?

Charles showed himself to be both a farmer with a business head on him, and a Bridgefoot through and through.

'If everybody agrees,' he said, 'I think we should carry on as much like we were before Dad took over from Grandad as is sensible, but go some of the way along with Dad in keeping up with the times. I can't take on the amount of work that Grandad, Dad and me all helped with then. Grandad and I can make all the decisions – we shan't argue – but it wouldn't be possible for me to do all the work, and Grandad can't do any more than he does now to please himself. This has forced me and Charlie to put our plans aside for the time being – they're only postponed. What that does mean, though, is that the empty side of our house could be offered as accommodation for a farm manager, instead of the vet we'd planned would use it. That's part of the new pattern of farming, anyway. With the sort of implements Dad bought, a farm manager can work a big farm all by himself. Agricultural colleges turn them out with careers in farm management in mind.

'Mum, I hope you won't be too upset if I don't run the business from Temperance. If you all agree, I shall move the office to our granary, which was to have been the small animals' surgery. That way, both the manager and I can be close to it, and to each other. But it would leave you absolutely alone, and we can't let that happen. Do you want us to move you out of Temperance?'

Rosemary shook her head. She had not yet fully absorbed all the effect that Brian's illness and eventual death would have on her.

'Then you must have somebody to live in, to look after you, and keep you company. That's why I asked if Pansy and Yorky could be here. I'm sure you all know that they intend to get married, so Yorky will be as much a part of our family as Uncle Alex, or Charlie. We could all do with the help of a master-of-all-trades like John – I'd rather think of him as John than Yorky if he's going to become my cousin. There's a lovely little self-contained flat at Temperance with all mod cons, made to house Mum's awkward old Aunt Esther only a few years ago. You could move straight into that, and John could start decorating it just as you want it. Pansy, are you interested? Mum? Would that suit you?'

'I can't think of anything better, if it would do for John and Pansy. Next best thing to having you and Charlie.'

'It isn't furnished, is it?' asked Marge. 'Bri was so glad to get rid of her when she died he threw it all out. They could soon get whatever they wanted.'

'Think on, lass,' said Yorky, breaking in. 'What with? I told tha that I had nowt to offer Pansy but me'sen – not much good either, as I am now. Ah've got nowt. The flat Ah've got now is furnished, after a fashion, but it's not fit for a girl like Pansy. Tha mustn't tek too much for granted, though Ah'll do my best – O-God-aye I will – but I'm not a Bridgefoot. I'm still only John Postlethwaite.'

They were all looking at him with some bewilderment. It was Marjorie for whom the penny dropped: that in this comfortably-off circle with regard to means, he was the odd one out. He was making it clear, as politely as he could, that he was not prepared to accept any form of charity.

'If you mean you couldn't furnish the flat, stop worrying,' Marjorie said. 'Rosy and I are dab hands at picking up bargains at auctions.'

'Even second-hand bargains need cash to pay for 'em,' he said stubbornly.

Pansy looked appealingly at Charles, who got the message.

'Now you hold on, John, before you jump to conclusions. You don't imagine we're trying to set you up with a job and a home out of the goodness of our hearts, do you? Haven't I made it clear that you are just the sort of man we need? We shall pay both of you, of course, at the going rate. The flat would be rent free as part of the bargain. This is business. It'll be up to you, and you alone, what you put into an empty flat. You'll have to have a reliable car as well – the firm will provide that. So before you get too far on your high horse, give Pansy a thought or two. Ask her how she feels. We're asking you to let her come back to us, and bring yourself with her. We've got our pride, too – and a good name for being fair. Don't throw it all away because of a bit of Yorkshire pride. We've got our own sort!'

His mother was looking at him with amazement. This was her son, the one she had nearly lost because a sick husband hadn't confided in her or anybody else. Brian must have suffered terribly, but he'd made them all suffer as well: Charles, perhaps, most of all, unless it was his poor old father. She looked across at George, and watched the same trend of thought crossing his face. While Charles lived, so did the Bridgefoots. He held up his hand, as if to demand their silence while he had his say.

'Pansy, my girl, there's something as you all seem to have forgot except me. I owe you a cheque for ten thousand, as you never got when you were twenty-one. Marge, will you find me my cheque book? Call it your joint Christmas present, if you like.'

Pansy was crying quietly, seeking Yorky's hand. Would he accept that this was not charity? Like George, he was finding strength in accepting whatever life had sent him: good and bad, and making one balance the other. He was beyond bothering about his working-class pride by now.

Marjorie was showing her relief. Even the loss of a beloved brother, son, husband, father, had to be seen as a counterweight to all the good fortune of the past. And hope was not dead yet.

'Christmas presents?' she said. 'I haven't been able to give them a thought! If you're going to be living at Temperance, Pansy, what about a horse?'

If anybody heard Charlie's sigh for what might have been, it was Charles. He reached for her hand, and held it tight. Their long-planned hopes had gone down the drain, but there was plenty of time ahead for them yet. They had a new hope, now, and though the thought of it was a bit premature, perhaps, as the old women of the village always said of a very small, premature baby: 'it had all the world to grow in'.

*   *   *

That very Monday morning, with Christmas now only three days away, the trio sitting round the breakfast table at Benedict's was subdued but resolute. Life had to go on. Sophie shed a few silent tears, Fran philosophized in her own way, and William wished more than anything else for time to pass quickly so that all could return to something approaching normality.

He was wanting now to get down to starting on his book, but two things were preventing him. He hadn't yet heard from Colin Brand and he was very well aware how undiplomatic it would be for him to absent himself from any of the efforts Fran was so courageously making to keep everybody else's spirits up till this long Christmas 'holiday' was over and the dark cloud over them all dispersed a bit to let the sun through again.

From somewhere in the house, Olive's voice rose, serenading Rose-Marie in a louder, more varied version than usual. William was reaching the point of no return with regard to both the singer and the song. In his present strung-up mood, he felt he really could not take much more of it.

'What puzzles me,' he said, 'is why she never sings anything else. She must have learned the three or four songs she does sing – if you can call it singing – in her early childhood. I doubt if they were Mary Budd's choice to teach in school.'

'That they wasn't,' Sophie said, rearing up to defend her idol from such calumny. 'She taught us songs like "The Hash Grove" and "Bonny Mary of Our Guile", "The Minstrel Boy to the War has Gone" and "God Bless the Prince of Wales" so as on Empire Day we could look at the map and sing a song for England, Ireland, Scotland and Wales. Then we went outside and danced round the maypole. But I do know 'ow it come about as Olive learned such songs as them. One of 'er Job's brothers died, down in the fen – and you know 'ow it is then in any family. Everybody's frit that they won't get as much as the others. Seems this one as 'ad died were the only one o' the fam'ly as could talk real proper, and he liked to sing. So 'e'd bought hisself one o' them wind-up gramophones at a sale – and that were all as Job got, with a few records. When the time come as 'e were struck dumb, she started to play them records over and over again to stop 'erself from going mad. Poor woman – can you wonder?'

William felt ashamed. He'd better buy himself some ear-plugs.

'Here's Eric,' said Fran, surprised. 'I hope nothing's gone wrong with his plans for Christmas. We're expecting him to spend it with us. Let him in, Sophie,' but she was too late. He had let himself in, and they saw at once that if he was suffering from any emotion, it was satisfaction.

'Happy Christmas, everybody. Has your morning mail arrived yet? Oh, well, I shan't tell you anything till it has.'

The clank of their old brass letter-box informed William that it had just arrived. He beat Sophie to the door, which gave him a chance to look for the letter he was hoping for among the mass of Christmas cards. There it was, at last. He slipped it out of the bundle, and left it lying on his desk till he could give all his attention to it. Then he put the others down in front of Fran.

'Never mind all the rest,' Eric ordered. 'Look for the one with a Cornish postmark.' He produced one from his own pocket, and sure enough there was a duplicate of it among Fran's pile. 'Open it and see who it's from.'

Catching Eric's excitement, she tore it open. A large card, with stiff covers, and a letter tucked into the middle of it. 'We hope this will give you a very happy Christmas,' she read in Roland's writing. And there was the photograph that told the story, before she needed to read the inscription, signed 'From Roland and Monica and the twins – *all* legitimately Wagstaffes now.'

She laid it down beside Eric's, which was exactly the same except that it was in Monica's writing. And the photograph, of course, was of a wedding.

William stood aside and watched as Fran and Eric hugged each other.

'The letter explains everything,' Eric said, 'so I'll get off and let you read it. I just couldn't bear not to share it first with you two, apart from our personal feelings about it, it gives me a wonderful boost. I can't be called a "furriner" altogether if I am the grandfather of two legitimized Wagstaffes, can I?'

He held out his hand to William, and hugged Fran again, and was gone.

William sat down to listen to her reading Roland's letter. Sue, Roland's wife, had died. Her mother said she had been absolutely worn out physically by the amount of caring for the poor and sick the Sisters took on. She had picked up cholera among them, and succumbed to it.

William listened with rather mixed feelings. Of course he was as delighted as Eric and Fran, but he could not help a tinge of jealousy of Eric. Nothing could ever 'legitimize' him as the grandfather of the twins, could it? He held Fran and kissed the tears away from her face, and told himself he was an ungrateful so-and-so. Then he left Fran to spill the good news to Sophie. He was glad he had something of his own to interest him before he let himself become maudlin.

He opened Colin's letter and began to read. It was a detailed description of the sword, giving the reasons for being able to date it, as well as anything but intrusive methods of scientific research which might devalue the sword could prove, to a period as what he had guessed: between 1635 and 1645.

He himself was looking forward to restoring such a splendid example of a 'mortuary' sword as this, and was sorry he had to leave it now till after Christmas. 'But I couldn't resist dismounting that loose grip,' he wrote.

I thought that in view of the state of preservation of the rest of the sword, that grip must have been redone in something of a hurry. It would have to come off in any case. Grips come loose because the wooden core shrinks, and the only way to tighten them is to dismount them, push the pommel a bit further down to hold the two halves of the wood closer together, and then rivet it over again. When it's necessary to do as much as that, it's a chance to look for any information there may be on the tang. And you never know what else you may find between the tang and the wood. It was a favourite hiding place for a prayer, a good-luck charm, or any other sort of talisman: a relic of a saint's supposed robe; or a few strands of a wife's, or more likely a mistress's, hair. So I wasn't exactly surprised, when I took the wood off, to find the enclosed wrapped round the tang. I have found several before: slips of paper with a row of letters signifying well known Biblical texts, or in one case a thin slip of paper bearing the words 'Ah mihi Beate Martine', which, as you probably know already, is supposedly the origin of 'All my eye and Betty Martin'. Trust an English soldier never to sully his tongue with a foreign word if he can help it! Which brings me back to what I found wrapped round the tang of your sword, and which I have sealed safely in the smaller envelope. I was intrigued from the moment my fingers encountered it, because as you'll see, it is not paper, but high-class parchment that must have caused whoever put it there a hell of a task to get it small enough to insert it. In fact, he didn't — he had to hollow out the middle of the two bits of wood slightly to accommodate its thickness. I opened it, but it's in Latin, and might as well have been in Chinese as far as I'm concerned. If I remember correctly, it will be as easy as 'abc' to you. I hope you'll find it of some interest. I shall repack the wood before binding the grip, so you can keep it if it is. On the other hand, if you want to leave the sword as I found it, let me have it back as soon as Christmas is over.

William's hands trembled as he reached for his ivory paper-knife to slit the smaller envelope. The piece of parchment, rolled as tightly as it had been for so long was difficult enough to read, even if it had not swum before his eyes. Interesting to him? It was beyond all belief! His first instinct was to rush out to show it to Fran – but the voice of Olive stopped him in his tracks, and he sat down before his legs gave way under him.

This was the answer to one of the manuscript's most puzzling secrets. He had never hoped to find out the truth behind it. He battled with his desire to share it with somebody – who but Fran? But he had made his bargain with himself that she should know nothing more till he could lay the printed book at her feet. He had promised her the best birthday present she had ever received from him for her next birthday – or the one after that – meaning his completed novel in print. He would have to get on with it now! He wasn't at all optimistic that it would appeal to his erudite English academic publisher.

There was an aching void in his middle, and his head was spinning. Shock and delight were at war in him, but he simply had to control himself, or he would faint and give the whole game away. He reached for the bottle of brandy, kept with other bottles to offer his visitors a drink in his study, and took a large swig. He still felt very queer, not ill, but definitely 'not with it'.

'Hang on, Galahad. You can't faint now,' he said to himself. How utterly daft that Fran had ever called him Galahad! She, above anybody else he knew, should have known better. She knew perfectly well that Galahad had 'never felt the kiss of love, nor maiden's hand in his'. And that he most certainly had, for if ever a man was in thrall to a woman, he was to her. He'd have to go and tell her so. No, he wouldn't, or he'd blurt everything out to her. He didn't know what he was thinking, saying or doing.

His head was clearing a bit. She must have called him Galahad for some other quality she saw in him. 'O just and faithful knight?' Yes, that must have been it. The one whom she could trust to keep his word, even if, as at the time she had first so named him, it worked against him, against her, against them. Now he had to prove her faith in him to keep his word to himself justified. He would keep the bit of proof till the right moment came.

The best thing to do would be to get it into a bank's strong-box at the very first opportunity. Till then, he would secrete it with his father's Military Cross.

Once it was locked out of sight again, he felt better. If he didn't soon go to her, she'd come looking for him, and would want to read Colin Brand's letter. That wouldn't do, either. She'd ask him what 'the enclosed' was. He locked the letter away too – just in time.

'What's the matter, darling? You do look pale,' she said.

'Just excitement, sweetheart – Colin has dated the sword *exactly* to the decade that it had to be to make sense of the book.'

'Come and have a cup of strong coffee,' she said, kissing him. 'Ugh! You've been drinking brandy! "*Alone and palely loitering.*" Shame on you.'

He followed her out into the kitchen, glad to sit down and take another stimulant. He wasn't quite right in his head, yet.

He now had everything he had ever dreamed of – the key to his own ancestry. Not only a Burbage going back to the days of the building of the first Globe theatre, but more, much more. He knew the origin of the other side of his family too. He made a terrific effort to appear normal. It really was too much to believe, but he now had the absolute proof.

'Sweetheart,' he said. 'Now that I know the manuscript to be authentic, must I wait till after Christmas before I begin on my book? All I want at this moment is to be in my study, at least thinking and planning it. Do you really need me here? Because you know quite well that if you say you do, I shall stay here.'

'No, not really – but after all this never-ending time of putting it off, why choose today, when I wanted to talk to you about Roland and Monica?'

He had no excuse that he could disclose to her, and resigned himself to a session with her, to please her – as she had so often resigned herself to his seemingly endless procrastination. From the pantry close at hand rose Olive's voice again.

'I am calling you— hoo-hoo-hoo-hoo-hoo-HOO.'

'There's your answer, my darling! I am being called away from you.' And he started to laugh, and laugh, and laugh. She joined in, though she had no idea why, and clinging together they laughed themselves breathless.

'I mean it,' he said. 'I simply cannot endure those off-key variations a moment longer. I'm off to shut myself in my study, with cotton wool plugged in my ears, till she has departed from us at lunch-time.'

He went, and she continued to laugh. Where she had failed absolutely to drive, persuade or cajole him into his study, Olive had succeeded!

*   *   *

Over Glebe, the lowering storm that had hung over their heads so long had burst. They had all been aware that it was gathering, but had gone on hoping that it might pass without too much damage. Each one had made his or her own excuses for Brian – because he was one of their tightly knit family – and they loved him. They had never really envisaged any sort of fulmination that they could not cope with while it lasted – until the last month or so, since when each had kept his growing apprehension to himself, and gone on hoping that the cloud would pass. It hadn't passed. It had broken, and only begun to clear after a dramatic storm, which had left a lot of debris to be cleared away.

After the storm, the calm. George, heart-broken as he was about his only son, had accepted it – and, more surprisingly, so had Molly. Charles had been through the whole gamut of emotion, from filial grief for his father, and aching love for his mother and his grandparents, to a realization that he and Charlie were in the end going to be those who would suffer most, go through the roughest times. But they were young and resilient, and had each other.

Alex, willy-nilly, had been forced to take part in the drama again; as a member of the family and a professional who knew the odds. His part was to play the chorus that kept the other members of the cast *au fait* with the overview of the play. Lucy felt guilty that she had not seen more of her parents or her siblings, and could not do enough for them now she was there in their midst.

It was Marjorie who had undergone more than her share of real suffering. Like many another 'unattached' daughter, it had unconsciously been accepted that she was 'free' to be the mainstay of her ageing parents. Lovingly and willingly she too had accepted her role in the cast.

What she was inclined to resent, when she had time to think about it, was that the others seemed to ignore the sadness of her past life with her husband, and her more recent troubles with Pansy. What Brian had been to his parents, Pansy had been to her; she had had a double load to carry, and had carried it largely alone. The support she had relied on most was her brother. When he failed her, she had thought that she could not take any more; but for a brief day or two, Pansy had come back to her – only to leave again when the crisis was about to reach boiling point. Pansy had taken from her the last strand of hope that she could ever be really happy again.

And then, as nature usually decrees, the worst was over and they had all found new strength and courage from somewhere. All of them had new roles to play from now on.

Rosemary, more like a real daughter than an in-law, refused adamantly to leave Temperance, on the grounds that if Brian did recover at all and was sent home between spells in hospital, it would be best for him – and her – to be in familiar surroundings. For the time being and until after Christmas, she would go to Glebe.

That would give Pansy and Yorky a chance to keep an eye on Temperance, pack up Brian's office stuff ready for it to be moved to Danesum, and prepare the flat for themselves. How could any of them but feel better that that was all settled so amicably?

For the first time in ages, Marjorie had time to think about

463

herself. She was, for the moment, more or less redundant at Glebe, because Lucy was putting in a lot of attendance on her mother. Rosemary, acknowledging that she had no need now to be afraid of Brian, made a rapid recovery in what she could do for herself, and was a blessing to Molly now they could sit down together and talk out their grief for Brian, born of their mutual love for him. Their grief and anger turned gradually to pity and forgiveness, with a bit of stoic country philosophy added: that what could not be cured must be endured. It was quite surprising that by the morning of Christmas Eve, there was relief, and some measure of optimism in the air.

It was just after lunch that Marjorie went in to where Molly, Rosemary and Lucy sat chatting.

'Are you three all right?' she asked, 'because if you don't need me here, I'd love to go and tidy my own house before tomorrow, and be quiet by myself there till bedtime. Would you mind?'

'You do whatever you want to, pet,' said Molly. 'You've been an angel, doing all you could for us for so long. It's only fair that you have a bit of time for yourself.'

Marjorie was tired, but it was a physical tiredness that would evaporate quickly with the easing of emotional strain. By the time she let herself in to Monastery Farm, picked up four days' mail from the table where Eric had left it, made herself a cup of tea, and had drunk it in the peace and quiet of her own kitchen, the last week or two began to fade into the background like a bad dream only half remembered.

If her own, unoccupied side of the house looked as dusty and unwelcoming as it did to her after only a few days of neglect, she could imagine what Eric's sitting-room looked like. Discarded newspapers everywhere, ashtrays full of stale dottles from his pipe, bottles and glasses making rings on tables that in the ordinary way she took pride in polishing. Before running a duster round her own sitting-room, she'd go and make his side welcoming to him when he came in tomorrow after spending the day at Benedict's.

It was exactly as she had thought it would be, only worse. Yet somehow it reeked of his presence, and she regretted having to exchange the aura of him that was left there for the smell of wax polish.

Then she went back, and tackled her own part of the house. By this time the dusk had fallen, so she left her sitting-room until last, and sat there with another cup of tea in the twilight. It was so good to be in a home of her own again! She had had no idea how much she had been missing it.

She went languidly to the bathroom to wash her face and brush her abundant glossy hair, grey though it was, and made up her face to give herself a bit more colour. She was filled with an extraordinary conviction that in doing so she had washed off a lot of the unhappiness that had darkened the year's ending, and prepared herself to greet the new year afresh. Both her daughters were now safely within reach, and would be, she hoped, for as far into the future as she dared look. It would be silly at this stage to hope for more.

She must not be too late getting back to Glebe, because Lucy would leave to go to see Georgina put to bed and Rosy mustn't be allowed to overtire herself. Charlie had taken the opportunity of going home to Charles for the night. It would be asking for trouble for her to leave her father and mother to rake over their grief alone. But she was reluctant to return; there was something very comforting about being in her own home again.

She must dust her sitting-room before she left. As she went round with the duster, the familiarity and comfort of it tugged at her frayed heart-strings. Everything here was dear to her, because it was where she had found freedom from the shadow of her life with Vic Gifford. Every bit of furniture was of her choice, not his.

Except, of course, the piano. It was a lovely piano, and she dusted it with special care, remembering with nostalgia the dear little cottage piano on which she'd learned to play, and which had gone with her to her new home with Vic. When he had become such a tyrant in the days after he'd made money, he had thrown it out to make way for that awful, ostentatious new three-piece

465

suite. How she had hated that, and how she had grieved for her piano!

She opened the grand piano in front of her, and began softly to play by ear. She was not a brilliant pianist, but she was a reasonably competent one. Nothing could have soothed her bruised heart more than to sit there in the twilight and play softly to herself melodies that, like the scent of roses or lavender, recreated for her scenes from the past.

She slipped from one to another, her memory filled with brief glimpses of herself in the past. The strains of '*Salut d'amour*' satisfied something she did not recognize, so she repeated it. She heard the door open, but in her state of half dazed pleasure she played on. A well-known voice at her side whispered, 'Don't stop, Marjorie. Please don't stop.'

She finished the piece, and looked up in the dim light to find Eric by her side, and remembered guiltily that when she had first played his piano he had asked her never to play that particular piece when he was within hearing. It hurt him too much, because of the times when his late wife used to play it at his request.

'I'm so sorry, Eric,' she said. 'I didn't hear you come in.'

'I made sure you didn't,' he said. 'Have you come home for good?'

She shook her head, sighing. 'I wish I had. I don't want to leave here again.'

'I don't want you ever to leave here again,' he said. 'I should never have believed how much I've missed you. I want you back. Not just as a tenant or a housekeeper, though, so please think before you answer. Is it possible that you may have changed your mind as much as I've changed mine? Come back as my wife, Marjorie. I can't bear this house without you in it. Will you marry me?'

She sat down hard on the piano stool again, and hid her face in her hands. So that was what had been the matter with her? She hadn't been able to be so nearly a wife to him without growing to love everything he stood for. She knew now what had been the matter with him, too. How stupid they had been not to know that their silly bargain would not stand up for ever to such familiarity and propinquity!

He had come round to sit beside her on the piano stool. The silence grew long, and the twilight deepened. At last he said, gently, 'Well, Marjorie?'

She took her hands from a glowing face in which he could only see the brightness of her eyes. '*Very* well, Eric, if you're sure you mean it.'

He put up his hand and drew her head closer to his own. Such peace. Such tranquillity. Such safety. Such hope.

They sat wrapped in the comfort of having each other so near, neither asking for more, till he said, 'So what now, my dear one?'

'Can you be patient with me as only your tenant just a little longer? I can't really expect the others at Glebe to be overjoyed till they have got over the last shock, can I? Can we leave it till Valentine's Day?'

'As long as you don't go back on your word to me. I've been so miserable, so jealous in case that Yorkshireman stole you from me from under my very nose.'

'Oh, Eric!' she said. 'You darling idiot,' and she began to laugh, but it turned into a sob, and she hid her face against his shoulder.

'I wish women didn't always cry when I have them in my arms,' he said. 'Do you mean that we should stay exactly as we are till we can announce a wedding?'

'Please,' she said. 'You see, I know how delighted Dad will be, and he'll want to make a proper family wedding of it; celebrate it as he has always done for a family wedding, with a party in the barn. If anything can make him understand that his word counts again, that will be it. Bridgefoots always get married with a party in the barn.'

'Wait till I tell Elyot,' he said, suddenly gloating. 'Think – once I have married you, I shall have one foot in the Wagstaffe camp and the other in the Bridgefoot's. Nobody can possibly call me a "furriner" again!'

She was serious when she replied. 'Dad will say it was all meant to be,' she said.

'I think so, too. So am I now to say goodnight to my tenant, or to my future wife?'

'Both, please,' she said.